KU-034-677

Praise for Sophie White's novels

'A sharp, funny story of female friendship at its best,
with characters you'll fall in love with'
Beth O'Leary

'One of the best flawed heroines in Irish commercial fiction
since Rachel Walsh in Marian Keyes' ground-breaking
Rachel's Holiday'
Sunday Times

'A modern, witty, razor-sharp page-turner'
Emer McLysaght'

'Written with heart and humour, *Filter This* peels back the
social media mask so many wear as a disguise and reveals the
real people beneath' Cecelia Ahern

'Fresh, current and thoroughly enjoyable' Eithne Shortall

'Witty and wonderful – I devoured this in a single sitting'
Image

'Shades of Marian Keyes in this highly entertaining satire'
Sunday Independent

'White's sharp-eyed take on modern life couldn't be more on target'
Irish Independent

'Unsettling, sharp . . . strikingly witty'
Irish Examiner

Sophie White lives in Dublin with her husband and three sons. She writes regularly for many Irish publications, including her weekly 'Nobody Tells You' column for the *Sunday Independent LIFE* magazine and also co-hosts two podcasts, *Mother of Pod* and *The Creep Dive*.

ALSO BY SOPHIE WHITE

Fiction

Filter This

Unfiltered

Where I End

Non-Fiction

Corpsing

Recipes for a Nervous Breakdown

The Snag List

Sophie White

HACHETTE
BOOKS
IRELAND

Copyright © 2022 Sophie White

The right of Sophie White to be identified as the Author of
the Work has been asserted by her in accordance with the
Copyright, Designs and Patents Act 1988.

First published in Ireland in 2022 by HACHETTE BOOKS IRELAND

First published in paperback in 2023

1

All rights reserved. No part of this publication may be reproduced, stored in
a retrieval system, or transmitted, in any form or by any means without the
prior written permission of the publisher, nor be otherwise circulated in any
form of binding or cover other than that in which it is published and without
a similar condition being imposed on the subsequent purchaser.

All characters in this publication are fictitious and any resemblance to
real persons, living or dead, is purely coincidental.

Cataloguing in Publication Data is available from the British Library

ISBN 9781529352733

Typeset in Arno Pro by Bookends Publishing Services, Dublin

Printed and bound in Great Britain by Clays Ltd, Elcograf S.p.A.

Hachette Books Ireland policy is to use papers that are natural, renewable
and recyclable products and made from wood grown in sustainable forests.
The logging and manufacturing processes are expected to conform to
the environmental regulations of the country of origin.

Hachette Books Ireland
8 Castlecourt Centre
Castleknock
Dublin 15, Ireland

A division of Hachette UK Ltd
Carmelite House, 50 Victoria Embankment, London EC4Y 0DZ

www.hachettebooksireland.ie

For Seb

Prologue

'MS REID, CAN YOU TELL US HOW YOU CAME TO BE in possession of the video clip featuring your husband and former business partner, Adam Zelner? The contents of which, I should add, were intended to remain private.' Adrian, the craggy sixty-something acting as Adam's representative, paced before her.

Lindy sensed she needed to rearrange her facial expression if she was going to retain the sympathy of the judge – a neat man in his fifties over to the right, looking at her through tortoiseshell glasses. Bald disdain was not a great look when trying to convince people you weren't a treacherous bitch out for revenge.

In a way, though, an unanticipated boon of her job was that she was actually perfectly prepped to stand up and be judged. In the last few years, everyone had an opinion. On the fact that she put her kid on the internet. On her family. But most especially on her. It was negligent; it was selling your child's childhood. It was tantamount to abuse.

Luckily, it wasn't illegal. Yet. And the wood-panelled room of judgement she was standing in was a commercial court and not a criminal one. Sued by her former business partner and current husband. Ooof.

As one internet commenter had put it: 'Corporate litigation between husband and wife? Now that's a shitshow.'

'Who starts a business with literally NO contingency in place for how to dissolve it? Especially when there's a child involved?' another had added.

'Do you need me to repeat the question, Ms Reid?' Adrian levelled this in an exasperated tone, as if she was a petulant kid instead of the co-founder and one-time CEO of a million-euro online empire. She could feel herself glaring again. *Stop it, Lindy.*

She swallowed. 'Not at all, sir.' May as well keep it polite. 'I discovered the video clip during the course of preparing a prospectus for a new business venture of mine called The Snag List.'

She left it at that, heeding the advice of her own solicitor, Elise Enyi-Amadi: 'Let them do all of the heavy lifting. Only answer the questions they ask. Don't volunteer anything.'

'Riiiight.' More exaggerated weary patience from her husband's representative. 'And what did that prospectus entail? How did it lead to the discovery of the video and all that followed? Explain to us, please, what this venture, The Snag List, is?'

'The Snag List,' Lindy aped the man's patient tone, 'is a discreet service that allows people to address their regrets. With the support of my service, my clients can return to the things in their lives that they left undone. The chances they didn't take, the avenues left unexplored. With my help, they can tick them off the great snag list of their lives. For the last few months, I have been working with three individuals, trialling the service and gathering insights to present to potential investors. The client in this particular instance had voluntarily relinquished control of dozens of their social media accounts. And it was in one of these accounts that I found the clip. Believe me, I did not seek this frankly disgusting, not to mention hurtful and humiliating, material out.'

Over to Lindy's right, Elise was looking delighted – no doubt thrilled at the inclusion of 'hurtful and humiliating'.

'You have to humanise "Lindy Reid" for the judge,' she'd commanded that morning in the taxi on the way over as a nervy Lindy smoothed her dark blunt bob and dabbed concealer under her eyes. Sleep was in short supply the last few weeks, since her life had been laid out for public consumption.

'I *am* a human,' Lindy had said. *Can't be a good sign that I'm having to point that out. People mistake* appearing *detached with* being *detached. I wish I could be detached.* 'I *am* hurt and humiliated, Elise – more as every day passes and the internet continues to have a field day with this.'

'Great,' Elise pointed at her. 'Be sure to get that in later during your testimony.'

'It's absolutely desperate,' the taxi driver had thrown over his shoulder. 'My missus was having a real go this morning, saying you deserve what you got given how you make your money and all. And I said, "No, Bridey! Not even Bezos himself deserves to have all that put out there."'

Lindy had related this exchange to her Snag List WhatsApp group, the place where all this misery had begun – if they hadn't gotten together and started comparing notes on their millennial life crises, none of this would've happened. *At least it'll give Ailbhe and Roe a bit of entertainment*, she'd thought, watching their replies drop in.

> **ROE: On the plus side, the taxi lads are always a great barometer of public opinion. They're out there on the front lines of the national gossip. If he's defending you, that's a great sign.**

> **AILBHE: Roe's really scraping the bottom of the Reassurance Barrel there.**

Lindy had grinned in spite of the bleak destination. *How am I driving to actual fucking court right now?* If nothing else, she could count on Ailbhe for honesty and Roe for support. *Thank God I still have them.* They'd known each other less than six months, but communally decimating your lives really fast-tracks a friendship.

Her husband's solicitor cleared his throat, bringing her back to the present unpleasant moment. He was sweeping his hands wide, as if to dispel any empathy her admission of pain and humiliation may have elicited from the judge. 'Do you think it's a good idea to meddle in people's lives in this way?'

Lindy flashed on Ailbhe, Tom, Roe and Eddie all sitting in devastated silence around an abandoned dinner party. Across the table from her, Adam had looked livid.

Keep it simple, Linds: 'Yep.'

'Why do you think you're qualified to do this work? To fix people's lives?'

The question finally put words to the unformed dread that had lurked inside her in the weeks since that cursed dinner party. *Why do I think I'm qualified to rid people of their regrets?*

She tried to breathe deeply but it came shallow and did nothing to quell her anxiety. Her pretence at stoicism was becoming exhausting. She felt the judge looking at her – no doubt taking in her expensive silk shirt and tailored navy trousers. She looked rich, successful. Too aloof to be relatable, probably. He couldn't know it was her armour.

'I used to think I was qualified because I've gone after what I wanted in life. More or less. But now ...' She looked across the room to where Adam sat and tried to find his eyes, to bridge the fissure between them. He just stared at his hands clasped on the desk in front of him. *It's impossible, we're both too ruined – there's no blueprint, no script to follow for coming back from betrayals like these.*

She placed her next words one after another carefully and deliberately. 'Now, I think, I'm qualified because I can see that if our regrets remain unresolved, they trap us and define our lives. I'm qualified because I, myself, have so many regrets. So. Many.'

She breathed again and this time her lungs filled without effort. She felt a bit better because it was the truth. Pity the truth had ruined everything.

1

5 months earlier...

'HEY, GUYS, WELCOME ... UH ... WELCOME BACK TO my channel ...' Pale morning sun stretched languidly across Lindy's bed, where she lay propped on pillows watching her favourite old video of her son on her phone – the date in the YouTube description read 26 March 2017.

'Can it see me, Muma?' the little six-year-old Max on screen was asking.

'Of course it can – see the green light? That means it's working.' Her younger self was off to the side, out of shot.

'OK. You go and I'll call you when it's ready,' Little Max on screen instructed.

Lindy watched her younger self lean down into shot. 'OK. Can I give you a kiss?' The boy obliged and leaned slightly forward so she could kiss the back of his neck. It was a soft little stem of a neck and something of a special ritual between her and her son. Even now, five years later, if she asked to give him a kiss, he would do the exact same movement. On the screen, Max was talking to himself, acting out a story with tiny Lego figures and a Megatron toy so large only the legs were visible.

'This video is so embarrassing!' The now eleven-year-old, long-limbed Max lounged beside her. He had just brought her up a coffee because it was 26 March, her birthday – *How am I thirty-six years old?!* – and this coffee, along with watching this video, was their tradition.

She laughed at his disdainful face. 'At least production values have improved since then!'

It was the first toy video Max had ever made that they'd put on YouTube. Little did they know this little Lego melodrama would become a multimillion-hit channel. Five years on, Maxxed Out operated exactly like a TV station powered by ad revenue and branded content. The difference was every 'show' was created by her husband, Adam, their son was the star, and Lindy helmed the entire business end of the Maxxed Out juggernaut.

It was a life they'd stumbled into. On her birthday, the year she turned thirty-one, six-year-old Max had demanded to know what present *he* was getting. She'd explained that on other people's birthdays you got *them* presents. He announced that he wanted to make her a video like the ones on YouTube. Even though she could smell a kid agenda at thirty paces, she said she'd love that. *Little did I fucking know.*

Soon Adam was in on it too. They played together for the camera, and Adam would edit the videos and upload them to a YouTube account. The videos were unlisted – only people with the specific link could access them, and they only doled the link out to family and friends. It was a way to keep Adam's parents and brother in America in the loop and make sure they didn't miss out on Max growing up. It was also, Lindy suspected, an Adam-engineered opportunity for him to showcase his hyper-fun, super-engaged 'dadding' skills, for which he received lavish praise from the American contingent and a lukewarm, slightly baffled reception from Lindy's family. After about a year, Max became obsessed with a kid YouTuber called Axel who hosted his own show on the platform and had more than a million subscribers. Even though he was young, Max soon cottoned on that his videos weren't being seen by anyone other than family. He wanted to have a 'real' channel. Lindy was extremely wary. She'd sit beside her son as he watched Axel, and when Axel, who couldn't have been more than nine himself, reminded his viewers to hit the 'thumbs-up' on the video, tiny Max unquestioningly obeyed. It was unnerving, like wholesome, peppy mind control.

Adam was very pro the idea, reasoning that all kids now would be online to an unprecedented degree and this could be a safe kind of on-ramping for Max. With Max pleading, and without Adam's back-up, Lindy's resolve crumbled and she agreed to open up the Maxxed Out videos for public consumption. With hindsight, she felt the timing had a lot to do with it. Just weeks before they set Maxxed Out live, she'd lost a pregnancy. Lindy had been delivered the body blow of a silent sonogram on a Thursday morning, then gone back to her desk at the psychology practice, Heart Mind Solutions, where she had managed logistics, that afternoon. It had hit very hard. And because of the cack-handed way the world dealt with grief of this nature, she'd never taken compassionate leave from her job, never even told any of the actual therapists that she worked with, even though it would have surely helped immeasurably.

At home, Adam was as devastated as she was, and every moment with Max brought a two-pronged thrust of pain: he was a constant reminder of the child that wouldn't be; and he was her baby, bewildered at the recent shift in the atmosphere of his previously safe and cosy home. The channel made Max happy, and at that moment, from the depths of her grief and guilt, she'd clung to that.

And then it had made them money.

Four years ago, she and Adam had both gone full-time on the channel, and two years in they'd been busy enough that they'd needed to hire the extremely commercially minded Jamie Bell, who was now managing director. Adam's days were now spent literally playing with their son for their captivated fanbase. Hers were filled with sponsorship negotiation, financial negotiation and talent negotiation – tricky given the 'talent' was her husband and son. It had been four years of being the fun police in every single respect, from no to dessert on a Tuesday to a massive NO to a potentially lucrative collaboration with an alt-right YouTuber in Minnesota, no matter how big his audience was.

Adam's background in advertising was an advantage in the new venture, and she enjoyed running the business, though she'd also vaguely hoped it would eventually leave space for her to resume her abandoned psychology training and perhaps embark on a venture of her own – wishful thinking of the highest order.

When the pandemic hit, her misgivings about both working with family and putting her son to 'work' on the internet were instantly drowned out by terror at the fact that they had put all their financial eggs in one basket. She couldn't have known in early 2020 that, with everyone about to be under mandated house arrest and desperate for childcare in any form whatsoever, conditions were perfect for channels like theirs to thrive. Max and Adam were essentially babysitting swathes of children around the world while their parents clung to jobs.

And so she and Max rewatched this funny little video every year, and the coffee was historically bad but she was detecting an improvement with each birthday that passed.

'You were only six, Max! You were so creative.'

'I know, you're sooo proud of me,' he said, doing his bored pre-teenage voice.

'You're lucky you're sick of me saying I'm proud of you – that's a good sign, you know!'

'OK, I know, Granny and Grandad never said it enough and now you have *issues*.'

Lindy laughed. 'Oh, they said it! About as much as anyone's parents did in the nineties.'

'Can I go now, Mom? I'm setting up a safari video with Dad. Cannot wait for all the new kit we'll have in the new house – Dad says a whole room just for my Lego – the Lego *studio*.'

'Yes, amazing. Go! You're dismissed. Thank you for humouring me.'

Lindy stretched out and sipped at the coffee before immediately dribbling it back into the cup, grimacing. *By the time he's seventeen, I'll be drinking it*, she calculated, placing the cup on the sagging shelf above her bed.

It was her last birthday in the house – a slightly ragged red-brick terraced cottage with a cherry blossom in the garden. They could be gone before it bloomed; they had just over two weeks left. She'd miss this tiny bedroom under the eaves. It had been the attic; they'd converted it when Max was six months old. Even before he was crawling, the house had felt like it was shrinking around them, but Lindy loved the sash windows and the bockety wooden floors, not to mention being able to walk into town or around to her parents' house on the other side of the park. Lindy would have happily stayed, but she couldn't deny that both their family and the business had long ago outgrown the place. It was time. The channel was doing well, and what was it all for if not to live well too? A text interrupted the rationalising that had become a round-the-clock refrain in the lead-up to this move. It was Fionnuala.

Don't forget we moved your birthday brunch to 10.30. You're an old bitch now – don't be a late bitch too.

Lindy texted back a single middle-finger emoji and hopped out of bed. The café was only ten minutes' walk, but her sister was always so pass-remarkable about Lindy's clothes that Lindy had to factor in at least ten minutes of agonising before probably still just pulling on the same bland shite she always wore since leaving her office job – jeans, vaguely nice top, expensive but boring khaki jacket.

★

'You're jiggling again.' An hour later, Lindy was watching her sister shifting around on her seat on the other side of their marble-topped table outside Egan's, their favourite spot. Drumcondra was close to the city centre but still had a nice villagey feel. If someone could spot you in your school uniform having a cheeky smoke at the bus stop and report you to your mother, that had to be the definition of a village, no matter how close to the city you were.

She'd lived here her whole life and had indeed been spotted smoking at fifteen by Mrs Connelly. It was the best neighbourhood – all the families she'd grown up with were still around and cohabiting peacefully with the blow-ins, who could usually be identified by whether or not they'd had the windows done on their houses.

Finn's jiggling was intensifying. 'I can't believe I need to wee. Again,' she moaned. 'I'm worse than you after Max decimated your bladder control. The new serum formula we're trialling is throwing up some very random side-effects, but look, just *look* at my under-eye area.' Fionnuala thrust her face at Lindy.

'I'm not seeing anything.' Lindy examined her older sister's flawless, make-up-free, nearly-forty-four-year-old face.

'Eh, fucking exactly, Lindy. No darkness, no discolouration, no … *pouches*,' Finn pronounced with disgust. 'Skin Love is going to completely overhaul the industry – I can feel it. We've all been relying on the "no make-up" make-up for too long. Skin Love is going to liberate us. I haven't put on a scrap of base in months.'

'Yah, but you're an anomaly, a sideshow oddity,' Lindy remarked dryly. 'You've got the skin of an influencer's child avec Paris filter. The rest of us *need* the bit of base. We *like* the bit of base. Don't forget women use make-up for a lot of reasons. Be careful you're not alienating clients with the messaging.'

'Hmmm. Good point.' Finn's eyes narrowed, and Lindy instantly regretted wading any deeper into her sister's business than her usual vague *great*s and *well done*s. Finn was constantly trying to tempt Lindy on to the Skin Love team. Finn shifted to jiggle in a different direction. 'This is why I cannot understand your refusal to come on board, Lindy. You obviously have an interest. Our relationship to our skin is very rooted in our psychology. Having you on the team with your background would add a whole other dimension.'

'What "background", Finn? I didn't even finish my degree. I'm not a psychologist.' Lindy hated that she hadn't finished her BA, but you had to let these things go. Back when she was working in Heart Mind Solutions she'd fully intended to get back to studying, but then Maxxed Out happened and, well, her work now wasn't helping people in the way she'd once hoped, but that's what happened when you started a family. Responsibilities and kids and obligations started hijacking ambitions. It happened to everyone to some extent. Or every woman anyway.

Finn powered on with her job pitch: 'You are clearly better than me on the sensitive-approach side of things. You're right. I'm an outlier, my skin is incredible – always has been. I'm not the Skin Love client. You are. A woman desperately in need of "skinprovement" and some self-esteem.'

'Finn, I can't believe you think your approach isn't sensitive enough!' Lindy laughed.

Fionnuala was eight years older and, since they were kids, she had playfully cultivated a sort of faux pity for the (according to her) totally forgotten youngest child, Lindy – Séamus, in the middle, was the only boy and, as such, doted on. Lindy was fully immune to Finn's ridiculous narrative by this stage and mostly just entertained by it.

'You could be so good,' Finn bulldozed on. 'You never do anything for yourself. You've sacrificed your best years working for a narcissist.'

'Adam's not a narcissist. And anyway, I don't work *for* him.'

'If you don't get out now and go after your own goals you'll be left pissed off and resentful.'

'I'm fine with that – I'm not sure anyone *alive* doesn't wind up pissed off and resentful,' Lindy deadpanned.

'You're turning into Mum. A slave to her family and now a bitter old slag.'

'She's right there,' Lindy indicated mildly.

'I am.' Jean Reid sniffed, feigning upset.

'Of course you are, Mum. Always right there, judging and martyring away.' Finn could joke like this because Jean was the least martyrish Irish mammy since time immemorial. She adored her three kids and her husband, Liam, but also had a healthy detachment, giving as much time to her teaching career – she specialised in adult literacy – as she did her family.

'I *wish* I was a slag,' Jean mused. 'It sounds fun.'

'Jean, don't be giving me cheek!' Finn was unstoppable. *Does the woman even need oxygen?* Lindy wondered. 'Right, the pisser beckons. Mum? I presume you're coming? She's on the same new products as me,' Fionnuala explained as she grabbed her mask and her mother and marched towards the loos at the back of the restaurant.

Where does she get her energy? Lindy stared after them. *And her nerve? Don't call my husband a narcissist – only I may do that.*

As for calling Jean a slag? Jean would only take that from Finn – her devotion to her eldest never wavered. The Jean–Finn dynamic did sometimes leave Lindy feeling out in the cold. Her mother just didn't quite get what Lindy did – 'home videos but on the internet; all very strange but I suppose they're trucking along' – and she wasn't featured in the social pages of the magazines in Jean's hairdresser's like Finn was, so it was like it didn't count.

It was the problem with having a fairly recently invented job: you spent a lot of time at weddings, funerals and family gatherings explaining it and always leaving the conversation with a sense that your relatives were vaguely concerned about you.

Lindy picked up her phone to check in on things. *Life admin is becoming more work than work is.* She knew it wasn't just her. If you gave people a chance to complain about how 'behind' they were on their WhatsApp groups, body maintenance and dentist appointments, they'd whip themselves up into a stress-frenzy within minutes.

Everyone's favourite part of socialising now was the pockets of time when friends went to the loo and you could address some of the notifications stacking up in the phone, Lindy reckoned.

A text alerted her to a voicemail. What kind of tormenter would leave a voicemail in the year of our lord two thousand and twenty-two? She put the phone to her ear. It was a robotic voice confirming the 'Let's Get to Know *You*' interview for this Tuesday, 14 April

'Hello, future Monteray Valley citizen! A reminder to please send through an up-to-date CV ahead of your Monteray Valley life curator's arrival,' said the voice.

What is with the automated voice? Why do they have to make everything so weird? She guessed it was supposed to be more personal than an email, but it was coming off vaguely demented. She'd forgotten the interview – she'd need to move her nail appointment. Feck.

'Brilliant, just brilliant,' she muttered as Finn and Jean returned.

'What's brilliant?' Finn quizzed, slipping into her seat.

Lindy quickly slapped on a smile. 'Oh, just our new house!'

She was in permanent defensive mode since the plan to move to Monteray Valley had solidified. She couldn't bear the opinions of others because for the most part she fully agreed with them.

'Doesn't it feel a little soulless out there?'

YES! Lindy wanted to shout.

'It's a bit isolated, isn't it?'

It's not 'a bit' isolated, it's completely *isolated*, Lindy wailed silently. It was easily twenty miles from the nearest Penneys, which was as good a metric for distance as any these days.

'I wouldn't want to be so far away from everything.'

No one wants this, least of all me. The suburban exodus is like a tide taking me against my will. I'm married, in my mid-thirties and with a child so it's the law *that I must retreat to the confines of a gated town so my wealth can protect me from any unpleasant realities.*

Most families moved away from the city for gardens and more space for their children, and it wasn't that Lindy didn't want those things. Her aversion to leaving the city was specific to Monteray Valley. At the open day, Esme, the Monteray social director, had emphasised ecstatically how self-contained Monteray Valley was. 'No one ever needs to leave.'

The high gates kept residents in and the world out. *Monteray* was a 'living experience' that had originated in California and now had satellite towns around the world. Like a franchise. Monteray Valley was the first in Ireland.

'That place sounds creepy.' Finn drained her mimosa and performed a complicated gesture to the waiter, who then returned seconds later with another round.

'It's not creepy. It's gorgeous – you'll love it. We'll have a dinner.' Lindy smiled harder.

'Linds, we won't have the *time* to come out there. It'd be more convenient had you and Adam moved to another country. *London* is more accessible than the M50.' Finn waved vaguely across Drumcondra village in the direction of the airport.

'We have to move the Maxxed Out operation. We've completely run out of space in Orchard Avenue – I've told you this. Also, a free house is a free house.' Though it wasn't quite 'free' of course. They were now under contract to post Monteray Valley content until the end of time. But it was still an unbelievably good deal.

'Is it really a free house, Linds?' Jean looked concerned. 'Are you and Adam stuck for money?'

'Mum! No! We're really successful. I keep trying to tell you.'

'Finn, could you not give your sister a dig-out?' Jean looked imploringly at her eldest.

'Mum!' Lindy waved a hand in front of her mother's face. 'I'm rich! I'm the wealthy one. I could dig *Finn* out. I'm a millionaire, like.' Sort of. Lindy's face burned with the mortification.

'Hmmm, but is it all internet money, luvvie? I worry about you.'

'Mum, Lindy could buy and sell me.' Finn laughed. 'Maxxed Out is a huge thing. Dunno how many more times we can explain this to you and Dad. Look.' Finn unlocked her phone and brought up the Maxxed Out channel. 'See that number: 1,845,453? That's how many people have watched this video. Nearly two million people have watched Max and Adam play *Minecraft Adventures Volume XVII*. So even if a sponsor was only paying 0.01c per view, Lindy is still pocketing a nice chunk of change.'

'What's all the words down at the bottom?' Jean pushed her glass out of the way and leaned in.

'That's the bottom half of the internet, Mum. Best not go there,' Lindy cut in, glaring at Finn who hastily turned the phone away.

'But I saw Lindy's name. Show me again,' Jean demanded.

'It's nothing, just weirdos being weird.' Lindy tried to sound unconcerned. The bottom half of the internet – aka the comments section – was life admin she'd long ago stopped trying to engage with. Unlike the rest of her to-do list, there was no hope of ever getting on top of it. It was a shape-shifting, fathomless morass of opinion from hysterical proclamations of love to the most cutting of condemnations. Adam waded through it delighted with the praise and utterly unfazed by the detractors. Of course, it was easy for him to not care – they didn't hate *him*.

'Me and Lindy have to get moving, Mum.' Finn stood and gathered her Chanel shopper and caramel-coloured, butter-soft leather jacket.

'Of course, sweetheart.' Jean leaned up to kiss first Finn then Lindy. 'Love you girls. Thanks for the pre-noon boozing – I'll be able to tolerate Dad for the rest of the day now!'

On the street, Lindy and Finn made their way through milling throngs enjoying the unexpected March sunshine and turned up towards Finn's cottage, just around the corner from the house Adam and Lindy were in the process of dismantling.

'I can't believe you won't be able to stroll over whenever you want any more.' Finn could swing into sentimentality at the drop of a hat and it always made Lindy smile. 'Remember when you'd just brought Max home from the Rotunda and you'd wheel him over to me?'

'Yes.' Lindy grinned, knowing what was coming next.

'And then you'd say, "I just need a wee", and after a while I'd discover you'd fucked off back out the front door to your own house. It was like a drive-by babying.'

'I was very tired, and we didn't have a minder yet.' Lindy laughed.

It was the kind of thing you could only do to family. You couldn't benignly abandon a baby on even the closest friends without them freaking out. She'd just needed the occasional breather. Lindy was in love with the baby in that all-consuming, disorientating way, but she also worried constantly. Motherhood had felt to her like a new world had been revealed – a world of infinite love and infinite terror. Finn could always bring her back out of the anxiety spiral. Having Finn around made everything feel lighter, more fun and less on the verge of disaster. This was another thing that made Lindy uneasy about Monteray Valley. She would have no family nearby. No neighbours around that she'd known, however vaguely, all her life.

Lindy and Finn slowed as they reached the little black gate to Finn's pebble-dashed house with the pink door. 'Hiya, Mrs Caughlan!' her sister called to her neighbour as she pulled out her keys. 'I'll come over and do the bins for you later.'

When Lindy, Finn and Séamus were growing up, Jean and Liam would dispatch them on a weekly basis to knock in to the older neighbours who lived alone to see if they wanted anything from the shops or had any jobs that needed to be done. It was the kind of thing Lindy'd tried to get Max doing, but it's hard to trick your famous-on-the-internet son into helping out in return for pocket money. And Adam didn't back her up at all – he just didn't get it.

'We didn't have old folks in Indiana,' he'd say with a shrug. 'Once they hit sixty in the States, they're shipped to Florida.'

Finn gave Lindy a hug. 'You sure you won't come in? We could have tea or more booze?'

'Nah, I should go home. Booze'll just make me maudlin.'

'Linds, you're already maudlin. I feel like you've been maudlin for ages. Just look at what you're wearing. This is a cry for help!'

'Shut up! It's my uniform – I got a style consultant.' Lindy hated being read so easily. 'It was a load of wank. She asked me who the different "Lindys" were.'

'What did you say? Hassled mother? School-run devotee? Soon-to-be suburbanite spiralling emotionally?' Finn cocked a mocking brow but there was concern in her expression too.

'I said one Lindy was a supposedly successful CEO who never has to leave her house. One Lindy dislikes waistbands, and one Lindy is an occasional parent–teacher association attendee slash hostage.'

'And she prescribed bootcut jeans? It's an act of violence. And maybe a sign that you're down. Getting someone to dress you? This doesn't feel like you.'

'I'm just very under it with work. The Monteray deal is a huge amount of additional content to be planned and, ugh, I dunno, I guess I'm getting ... not *cold* feet but chilly feet? It's hard seeing our entire home being stripped and shipped off. I feel like *I'm* being disassembled. I knew we'd have to move some time but not so fast. This house opportunity came up and I'd barely blinked before we signed. Adam's now acting like our own house was this *millstone*. When *he* was the very one who carried me over the threshold when we went to the viewing. Adam told everyone there to take their pathetic offers elsewhere while I was still slung over his shoulder. He hit the estate agent's face with my foot. It was pretty embarrassing.'

Lindy felt a pang at Early Lindy and Adam. There wasn't much conspiratorial mischief between them nowadays. 'Max was a baby in that house,' she carried on. 'I cleaned his puke out from between the floorboards with a toothbrush. His height is marked on the kitchen door frame.' Lindy tried to keep a lid on her rising anguish. She was breaking all her own rules being this honest with Finn. Of everyone, Finn had been the least pro Lindy and Adam's shotgun wedding and, as such, Lindy hated admitting when things were less than wonderful. 'Look, I'd really better go. There's still so much to pack.'

They hugged and Lindy hurried across the street and homeward.

Finn had been very vocal – too vocal – when Lindy had returned from Australia with a tan, Adam and an obsession with Tim Tams dipped in Vegemite that was not the affectation of a twenty-something backpacker but something much more serious …

'Just because you're pregnant, you don't have to marry him, Linds. It's not the fifties,' she'd pleaded. 'How did this happen?'

Another memory swept into Lindy's mind. She was lying on Adam's chest on the mattress in the back of the van, the rear doors were open to the still night, and the only sound was the distant crash of the sea. They'd just embarked on a road trip across Australia after the briefest of encounters in a Melbourne karaoke bar. The twenty-five-year-old Adam was explaining the hardships of being a nerd in an American high school.

'Just like the movies, only worse.'

'But you're so ridey! Did that not count for something?'

'You just think I'm hot compared to potato-faced Irish people.'

'Adam, you will be stabbed in the face if you ever say that on Irish soil. I'll be doing the stabbing.'

'"I'll be dooooing the stahbbing."' He was already workshopping his extremely shite Irish accent. 'I'm just fuckin' with you. They're not potato-faced. It's more of a boiled-ham look.'

'That's cos you're only meeting the Irish abroad right now. We're not suited to being abroad. We don't know how to handle ourselves in a dry heat. If you ever come to Ireland, you'll see us in our natural environment – hair frizzing due to drizzle, souls destroyed by the infernal moistness.'

'Yah,' he'd drawled. 'I geddit. So can I come to Ireland?'

'Can you come to Eye-er-land? No. But you can come to Ireland, maybe. Some time.'

She had *so* not meant it at the time.

But Adam grows on a person. And then when a piss in a petrol-station loo miles from civilisation en route to Perth confirmed that a bit of Adam was now growing *in* her – well, it was a done deal.

And now, Lindy reminded herself as she turned left down the lane that led to Orchard Avenue, moving to Monteray Valley was a done deal.

It'll be good for us. It will.

2

'STORAGE. STORAGE. THAT ONE'S STORAGE.' AILBHE was walking Niall, the captain of the Walkinstown under-19s who'd been drafted in by her mother, Eileen, to help with the move, through the various boxes crowding the living room. 'This one is … Hang on, let's see. Box 4sbr008.' Ailbhe slightly rearranged her tiny daughter, Tilly, who was sleeping on her shoulder, so she could consult the iPad. She paused to zoom in on the spreadsheet Tom's assistant, Maia, had compiled to help with packing up his penthouse. *Our penthouse*, she corrected. She'd lived there for nearly a year but still hadn't gotten used to it.

In fairness, it'd been a year like no other. Acquiring a husband, a baby and a penthouse in just twelve months had been hectic. Though more accurately she'd actually acquired a casual fling, a surprise slightly-late-in-the-day baby, a penthouse and *then* a husband. In that order. Tom wasn't in Dublin all that much, which suited Ailbhe's approach to relationships very well. When they'd first got together, he'd fly in for meetings, they'd go out for dinner, have a lot of fun and a lot of very hot sex, and everything was nice and low stakes. Then, of course, the shock baby grenade had landed in the middle of her perfect set-up.

How am I someone's mam?! This time last year, she wouldn't have believed it. She knew lots of people saw kids almost as something inevitable that they would move on to at some stage, like wide-fit shoes or starting to irrationally hate twenty-somethings. Not Ailbhe.

It wasn't that she had *never* pictured having kids or a husband, but her last serious relationship had ended eight years ago when she was thirty-four – she cringed at the memory. She'd been on the precipice of a wedding. She'd been with Ruairí, her pal Áine's cousin, for about two years at that stage. Ailbhe could still barely think about that time. She'd been so excited. With hindsight, she wondered if she'd ignored the signs because she hadn't wanted to see them. They were tasting cakes and saving dates by the time Ruairí finally admitted he didn't want to be 'nailed down' – his words. It'd caused ructions in their gang at the time – no one knew who to side with, and Ailbhe found the pitying looks and everyone asking 'how *are* you?' all the time unbearably humiliating. She put on a very convincing show of indifference and immediately stopped letting relationships with men go beyond a few dates.

'Super-healthy approach to getting hurt, Ailbhe!' Holly, her best friend and business partner, had been loving but relentlessly sarcastic.

Then Ailbhe had broken her keep-the-men-at-arm's-length rule with Tom and things had majorly escalated – as evidenced by the brand new *human* on her shoulder! But things with Tom were different. She winced. Very different. *Stop it, brain.* She quickly shook off the twinge of uneasiness that so often flared when she thought of how Tilly came about and circled the boxes grouped in the middle of the living room of Tom's extremely male apartment in Dublin's fashionable docklands.

'Seriously, the walls are brown leather! It is gak,' she'd told Holly the first night she went there.

In the year since, she hadn't bothered to do much with it, but she'd have full interior-decorating control in the new house in Monteray Valley, even if they wouldn't be there for long. It was an investment property. *How am I married to a man with investment property?* Some stuff was coming with them to the house out there, but most would be shipped directly to California, where Tom was from and where they'd be moving full-time later in the summer, on the 4 July weekend. It was American independence day and Ailbhe independence day. Thank fuck. Ailbhe was sweating to get out of Dublin – regrets were crowding in on her here. One drunken misstep in the year she'd been with Tom and her life had gone into freefall. *Stop that!* Ailbhe silently admonished herself. *Nothing is in freefall. We are* solutions *focused.* A couple of more weeks and she'd be out in Monteray Valley. Everything would be fine. Tom would never find out. No one would ever find out. A fresh start was needed.

'Ailbh, pet?' Her mum, Eileen, leaning round the door mercifully interrupted her frantic mind spiral.

'Hmmm?' Ailbhe tucked her long red hair back over her shoulder.

'Do you want anything from the shop?'

'Ooooh, white wine, please! Holly's on her way. She's giving me the full spruce.'

'Are you supposed to be drinking when you're feeding, Ailbhe?'

'A glass is grand, Mam.'

'Right.' Eileen carried on down the plushly carpeted hall and out the front door, which closed silently behind her. That is wealth, Ailbhe thought. No door-slamming for rich people. The doors in the colossal new house out in Monteray positively *whispered* to a close.

'Maia's got this down for shipping.' She turned back to the brawny Niall. He stretched casually beside her and she caught a hint of maleness on the updraft. *He is a ride. Old Ailbhe would've probably ... never mind! That was old Ailbhe. Old Ailbhe had started this mess. Old Ailbhe has revoked her decision-making rights. Also he's on the under-19s, you randy bitch.* Anyway, her gee'd been recently savaged by the adorable Tilly.

Niall nodded, heaving the box over to another lot destined for shipping grouped beside Tom's vintage jukebox just as Holly walked in, dragging her wheelie bag of kit.

'Eilers let me in!' Holly was here to give Ailbhe the full NCT. Since giving birth four weeks earlier, all Ailbhe's energy for giving a crap had been redirected into Tilly, but it was time. Slobbing around with straggly hair was so not Ailbhe – she co-owned a salon, for God's sake.

'Oh my God, Ailbhe, your colour.' Holly shielded her eyes. 'It's dulled so much, I can't even look. You *know* redheads cannot take the foot off the pedal for even a second ... Where will I set up?' She shrugged off her silk red bomber jacket, revealing a faded denim shirtdress and orange Perspex earrings that looked gorgeous with her platinum afro. Her nails were fluoro-yellow and she had a streak of matching eyeliner on each eye. Beside her, Ailbhe felt like that weird white stuff that collects in the corners of your mouth when you're dehydrated.

'Thank God you're here!' Ailbhe flung her arms around her.

Ailbhe and Holly had started Beautify together nine years ago when the whole country was just beginning to recover from the recession. They were best friends from school; their first premises had 'Holly and Ailbhe are sluts' in icy-blue neon writing on the wall – a long-running joke dating back to secondary school when some jealous dope had scrawled this on the toilet wall. They'd expanded to three premises before Covid hit and killed everything. The pain of letting staff go and closing all bar one shop had been horrendous. Now, Ailbhe felt incredibly guilty. Moving to the States meant she'd no longer be involved in the day-to-day, although Holly was being very supportive. She really liked Tom, which was both great and terrible. 'Great' because if Holly didn't like something she could be hilariously savage, but 'terrible' because she wouldn't *entertain* Ailbhe anytime she tried to moan about him.

'Want to set up on the sofa? We're trying to decode the moving instructions,' Ailbhe explained to Holly as she scrolled further down the document. 'I don't even know what half of this means – "Pacman arcade game, 5sbr2_001". It's gobbledegook.'

'Yeah.' Niall leaned in to take a look. 'I can't deal with spreadsheets at all. Your husband's into it, I see.'

'You should see the riding spreadsheet he made her!' Holly gleefully deployed this characteristically blunt announcement as she set up her portable speakers and the foot spa by the floor-to-ceiling windows that overlooked Dublin's swish docklands.

'Holly! Shut up, thank you.'

'I'm not joking – he schedules sex,' Holly hooted over at Niall.

'Or rather his assistant, Maia, does. What does he call it, Ailbhe? Human docking procedure?'

'Stop!' Ailbhe yelped. 'Niall doesn't need that visual burned on his retinas.'

Niall awkwardly busied himself with a couple of coded boxes on the ground by the door, clearly desperate for the auld ones to stop talking about their dusty old-person sex lives. 'I'm just going to check if that missing box is with the ones in the office.' He slid swiftly out of the room and down the hall.

Ailbhe and Holly exchanged a grin.

'He's hot!' Holly whispered. 'I'd pencil *him* in on the spreadsheet.'

'Shshhshh.' Ailbhe giggled. 'Can you just let the spreadsheet go? I should never have told you.'

Speaking of the spreadsheet, they were due for a session that very evening. Scheduling sex definitely sapped the spontaneity of the thing, and she rued the day she'd joked to Tom that they should have a 'Sexcel spreadsheet' given the extended periods that he was away. One had appeared in her inbox from Maia the very next day.

'Please see attached' was the only text contained in the email, and Ailbhe had wanted to die. Die. Morto. *My dignity is over.* The attached document had not been called 'Human Docking Procedure' as Holly had joked. But it wasn't far off: 'Intimacy Exchanges June–July 2021'. She would never, ever be revealing to Holly that there was a key for the document too. Enter IE-P, for example, and you'd be logging a penetrative intimacy exchange; IE-RS was remote sex. IE-ANL was … *Well, let's hope it never comes to that.* Ailbhe winced.

Tom had been baffled at her embarrassment that Maia, a woman Ailbhe had never met, was privy to their sex life. All three of them had access to the spreadsheet, so Ailbhe got an alert every time an intimacy exchange was moved or cancelled due to Tom's schedule. 'Maia has made a change to your shared document' chirped the notification.

'What's the problem?' Tom had been confused. 'Maia's been married for three years and she thought it was an awesome idea. Her and Judd never do it, not even virtually! She said it was really great that I was taking pre-emptive action against the onset of the inevitable marital-sex lag. You have to keep sex on the agenda. Don't worry, honey, Maia is very supportive,' he had concluded, completely missing the point.

'This is not about Maia being supportive. I just don't want her involved. Look, just cos I rode you between floors in the Hilton International lifts the night we met doesn't mean I'm grand with you broadcasting our sex life.'

'Honey, Maia is my right hand – you'll get used to her.'

'You realise describing Maia as your right hand is particularly off-putting in the context of this conversation, right?'

'Ha,' Tom had barked a laugh.

Now Ailbhe eased gingerly onto the couch, careful not to disturb Tilly still lolling on her shoulder.

'She is so gorgeous.' Holly reached up and gently pinched the tiny pouch of peachy flesh under Tilly's chin.

'She is, but don't you dare wake her – she sounds like a chainsaw when she gets going.' Ailbhe grinned. 'Eilers is getting the wine. I am in dire need!'

'Ah, so I take it Tom's gone back to California?'

'God, yeah, he is not into me making White Russians with Tilly's tit milk!'

'I don't think that's just Tom, yanno – think it's more a medical guidelines thing.' Holly shook her head.

'A glass or two is fine. I read a study on Facebook. It is definitely way more grand than people let on,' Ailbhe argued, grinning. 'And, anyway, when Tom's around I am very good!'

When they were casual, Tom's absences had suited Ailbhe. He'd fly in to see her and every weekend was an event. They'd go out for dinners or head away for luxury breaks. It was all very sparkly, with just the right level of commitment for Ailbhe – i.e. none at all. They'd met the previous year on the weekend of Valentine's Day. Maia had contacted her and Holly to book out the salon for the entire day. It could only mean one thing: mystery celebrity client. Or recent *Love Island* contestant *convinced* they were a celebrity.

She and Holly had arrived early to prep, eager to discover who the client was. It turned out to be a somewhat disappointing tech entrepreneur who was in town to give a talk for Tom's company. The guy was just coming off a twenty-one-day screaming retreat in Donegal and in need of intensive grooming – nothing could be done about the popped veins in his eyeballs, unfortunately, but Holly valiantly hacked away at his woolly beard for hours while politely nodding to his relentless monologue about the benefits of screaming for releasing negativity.

Meanwhile, Ailbhe had offered Tom a mani-pedi – more to pass the time than anything. Over his nails – which were no stranger to a cuticle remover – they chatted idly about his business, Optimise ('A suite of personal betterment apps,' he'd explained), what he thought of Ireland ('Love your sexy Irish tax laws,' he'd winked) and what he was up to that night ('I have to entertain this guy,' he'd whispered, making a face). Ailbhe had a finely tuned craic detector and, considering what he was paying to make this lad fit for public consumption, she sensed a night on the lash funded by Tom would be worth the potentially tedious small talk.

'You should bring me and Holly with ye, make it up to us for the taxes we're paying to cover your stingy multinational arse,' she'd said, grinning, while massaging almond oil into his fingertips. And so he did. And they'd had a surprisingly good time.

Tom was a lot more upfront and no-bullshit than the lads she'd usually end up with. Perhaps it was because she'd grown up in Dublin that she'd tended to hook up with guys she'd known for years and with whom she could call all the shots. They'd all gone to school together. It was nice and familiar. During their twenties, they went to the same clubs and parties. In their thirties, she'd done the rounds of all of their weddings. And in their forties, she and Holly were now finding themselves on a spate of 'fuck him' divorce holidays, quietly congratulating themselves on bypassing the whole long-term monogamy fuck-show.

Then the dreaded emotional glomming-on began with Tom. The funny thing was, though, the emotional glomming when it came from him was kind of sweet. In every other relationship since her doomed engagement to Ruairí, if anyone tried to progress to more serious territory she would flee, but with Tom, she caught her thoughts occasionally drifting towards vague notions of future plans. It was massively un-her. Ailbhe didn't like the thought of getting emotionally entangled with a man. Nothing wrecked a woman's life more than allowing her happiness to become contingent on a man. Look at her own mother.

Eileen had started going out with Eamon when she was sixteen and he was twenty. At seventeen, she had Ailbhe, and for the next few years Eileen was tormented by Eamon. He'd started with the betting when he was eighteen and was always either flush or scrounging. He was in and out of their lives constantly. Anytime Eileen made any inroads into being free of him, he would suddenly reappear and reel her back in. He never committed but he kept Eileen on the hook. It wasn't until the year Ailbhe was eleven that anything changed. He stole the money Eileen had put aside for Christmas and didn't contact them again for five years. In that time, Eamon, in fairness to him, got a handle on his addiction and eventually made amends, but he was never going to be in their lives in any kind of normal way. Eileen was still very young but was left permanently affected by the ordeal of her first love.

Tom told Ailbhe he loved her on what he'd claimed was their four-and-a-half-month anniversary.

'That's not a thing!' She had laughed. 'And Tom …' Ailbhe had trailed her arms over his broad shoulders and whispered into the dark curls at his ear. 'You don't love me. You just think you do. You're thirty-two – you've just caught monogamy. Don't worry, it'll pass. You just have to wait it out.' She was trying to keep things playful.

Then, in predictable fashion, she'd gone straight out and made the worst mistake of her life. Well, not the worst. She looked down at Tilly. *She's the best mistake of my life. But also the most complicated.*

'Right, get comfy.' Holly had laid out some big fluffy white towels beside a little portable foot bath. She lit a lavender candle and was picking out some soothing music on her phone.

Eileen came in carrying a couple of glasses of white and set them down on the ledge at the base of the window.

'Thank you!' Ailbhe trilled. 'I just need a straw for mine.' She indicated her arms tied up with holding the baby. 'Or an IV.'

'It won't come to that, I'll pop her down in the Moses basket.' Eileen eased her granddaughter into her arms and padded back out.

Ailbhe rolled her shoulders gratefully and scooped up her glass. She drained half and topped it back up, ignoring the flicker of Holly's eyes. She gratefully settled back on the couch, recognising their Mellow playlist from Beautify drifting out of Holly's speakers. This coupled with the scent of the various products instantly transported Ailbhe back to their salon and the day she'd found out she was pregnant.

It was the end of July the previous summer and they'd just closed. Ailbhe had announced she was late so Holly was fixing some fortifying G&Ts while Ailbhe stood in the little bathroom paralysed with shock. Positive. Of all the stupid shit she'd ever pulled, nothing had ever had permanent consequences. Not like this. Fuck. She could have had a termination, of course, but even amid the jittery panic she detected not a longing as such but maybe a flicker of curiosity. While she would never have set out to make this happen, once she was faced with the possibility, she became consumed with how she would feel if she *didn't* just go for it. Would she regret not taking the chance when it was presented to her? Would she always wonder how it would have been?

'FOMO is no reason to become a mother,' Holly had said firmly.

'Yeah, well, I can't help thinking about it,' she'd argued.

Thinking led to more thinking until she'd thought her way right into keeping the baby. And so it was more by dint of a double negative – not wanting to *not* have Tilly – that she'd had her.

Eileen was more reassuring on the method of Ailbhe's decision-making. 'Not wanting to *not* have them is probably how 90 per cent of babies happen,' she'd said with a shrug.

Ailbhe wasn't big on regrets. Her reasoning was: You made the decisions with the information you have to hand and that's all you can do. The information Ailbhe'd had to hand was a positive pregnancy test and a man who was, let's face it, a very solid bet. He loved her and she did really like him. They had fun. The fact that there was a slight timing issue regarding Tilly's conception had to be put out of her mind. The other possibility didn't bear thinking about. For a myriad of reasons, it was just better if Tom was the father. They'd go to America and start their new lives afresh and Ailbhe could leave the soiled feeling of guilt here in Dublin.

Tilly would have a completely different childhood to Ailbhe's. Ponies and boats and holidays. Security. A mum *and* a dad. Really, it was all a lot simpler if she just put some distance, an ocean, between her and that niggling little doubt. And the doubt really was just a niggle. At night, she soothed the warm little body draped over her shoulder and she turned it over in her mind, interrogating the events. And each time, she'd eventually conclude that it really was way more likely that Tom was Tilly's father. Waaaaay more likely. Pretty much nearly definitely – 99 per cent. Or 89 per cent, maybe. Look, OK, she wouldn't bet *Tilly's* life on it but she'd happily bet *Eilers'* life on it. Eilers'd had a good life, she was a good age. Kind of. What more was she planning to do at fifty-nine?

'Well, Siobhán is getting on great,' Holly announced. 'I honestly think she's a good candidate to become manager now that you're leaving for good.' Holly's support made Ailbhe feel even worse. She had worried Holly would think Ailbhe was abandoning her for an easy life with a wealthy husband. Holly didn't know, *couldn't* know, that Ailbhe *had* to do it. For herself, for her daughter.

She wished she could tell Holly the whole truth – how every time she looked at Tilly she felt an overriding panic as well as a rush of love – but even Eilers didn't know. Ailbhe was alone in this one.

'So how am I looking?' She smiled as brightly as she could. 'Are we talking hours or days to get me back on track?'

Holly, crouched down by Ailbhe's former feet, now hooves, gave her an appraising look and picked up the left one. 'These are in bits.' She flicked at Ailbhe's heel. 'I should've brought the angle grinder!'

At that moment, Niall popped his head back in. 'I have an angle grinder down in the van, if ya need?'

'We're grand, Niall, thanks.'

Niall headed back down the hall to the office to wrangle with yet more cryptic instructions and Ailbhe leaned forward conspiratorially. 'Bang of the Paul Mescals off him.' She grinned at Holly. 'TG he's finishing up in the next few days – I need to get out of his sexy orbit.'

'Don't forget you're resoundingly off the market. I know what you're doing.' Holly was vigorously filing Ailbhe's toenails. 'You're trying to act like the old days. Like you're still rounding up dick for your collection. You are married now, Ailbhe. I know this is a part of your "pattern" or whatever, but seriously, if you try and pull your usual Ailbhe crap on Tom, I will absolutely go off. You guys are so good together.'

'I can still look!'

'Oh really … And you've *just* been looking?' Holly dropped

Ailbhe's foot, dried her hands and pulled her phone from her pocket with a flourish.

Ailbhe felt a tug of fear. She couldn't possibly know. She couldn't.

Ailbhe knew this was pure paranoia, but over the last ten months she'd come to learn what harbouring a massive, radioactive secret could do to a person's ability to be rational.

Do not look like a person fighting a mild to medium panic attack, Ailbhe warned herself silently. Out loud, she said, 'Can't imagine what you're getting at …' trying to sound bored with a touch of amused.

Holly shook her head looking exasperated as she scrolled.

If she knew she'd look mad. Or maybe not mad. Disgusted? Horrified? It didn't really bear thinking about.

'Aha, got it.' Holly swung her phone around and slapped it into Ailbhe's hands. 'Not you commenting on Aidan Murray's stag weekend post at two in the morning then?'

Ailbhe's hurtling thoughts immediately slowed: this she could handle. 'LOL, shut up, Hol. That was ages ago. And a very innocent comment. "Nice pic" is hardly salacious.'

Holly fixed her with a stern glare. 'A) it was not "ages ago", it was Monday. B) two in the morning, Ailbhe? What's that about, if not the lonely vagina of a new mother reminiscing about old hook-ups? And C) this is a historical post, Ailbhe, you absolute rookie. How long were you scrolling back on Aidan Murray's account to unearth it? Him and Sheila are at the marriage-counselling stage by now.'

'I actually never slept with Aidan.'

'If you never slept with him, then he's the only one on this Carrick trip you didn't.' Holly laughed. 'Oh, and of course Seb Knox – how could I forget the Forever Near-Miss.'

Ugh, just his name sent a spasm of anxiety through Ailbhe's chest. *Not a near miss any fucking more.* Ailbhe quickly swiped through Aidan's page looking for something to distract Holly. She could really run with an idea, especially if it was bugging Ailbhe – the downside of their whole sisterly bond thing.

'The marital rocky patch definitely suits Aidan,' Ailbhe remarked, clicking into a more recent post and turning the phone back to Holly.

'Oooooh, yes, brooding.' Holly leaned in. 'The eyes say "I've seen some shit" but the well-cut jeans and five o'clock shadow say "I've been upcycled by a previous woman – she's done the work so you don't have to".' Holly picked up Ailbhe's foot again and started massaging her arches. Ailbhe rested her head on the back of the sofa to fully appreciate the sensation.

'You should write that on his post,' she murmured.

'You know, I should.' Holly rolled her knuckles up and down the soles of Ailbhe's feet. 'Second-hand men are the best – some other poor bitch has had to break them in.'

They lapsed into silence and Ailbhe was grateful to dodge any more of Holly's commentary. This time next week, she would be out in Monteray. Then all she had to do was kill a couple of months and she'd be in America with an ocean between her and her Old Ailbhe Bullshit. She just needed to stay the hell off her socials.

3

'WE'VE BEEN LIVING HERE A WEEK AND I STILL DON'T get exactly where the hell Monteray Valley is.' Roe fiddled with the radio trying not to sound like a petulant child especially as Eddie, her partner, was driving her all the way back into Dublin for her shift at work. It felt like they'd been gliding over mile after mile of grey dual carriageway for an age. It didn't even feel like their city out here. 'Are we still actually in Dublin, Ed? I'm not getting a signal at all.'

He shot her a look. 'Don't be like that. Of course it's still Dublin – the westerly side of the compound tips the county border to the west. Also, so what if it's not Dublin? *You're* not even from Dublin.'

That could explain part of her aversion. These featureless, monotonous roads reminded her of going to her parents' house in Kilshannagh. The anxious, jangly feeling in her arms that accompanied her infrequent trips home was the exact same.

Home. Why did she even still call her parents' house that? Home was with Eddie. She reached over and brushed the soft auburn hair from the nape of his neck. Without taking his eyes off the road, he caught her hand and drew her fingers round to his mouth to gently kiss them.

'You just hate change – don't hold it against Monteray,' Eddie said firmly, relinquishing Roe's hand and changing lanes to take the exit for the south side of the city centre.

'Everyone hates change,' Roe persisted.

'You didn't want to move to Warren Street at first, and by the end you were desperate to stay, even though we were still having to cut through the toilet to get to the kitchen.'

'Opening the fridge from the loo is convenience personified!' Roe remarked. 'With an upgrade, Warren Street would've been perfect.'

'C'mon, babe! It was a pokey one-bed. Great location but remember we were hardly going to be out having brunch every weekend once you got pregnant. Monteray makes sense. It'll be our forever home.'

Why does 'forever home' sound so terminal, Roe thought darkly. *So stifling.* Warren Street had always felt a bit like camping. It was safe in its lack of potential, its impermanence. The heating was temperamental. It had been too small to even get a dog, which suited Roe. She didn't like the constricted feeling she got when anything, even a supposedly cute thing like a dog, threatened her familiar, secure routines.

'We've been living on top of each other since college,' Eddie carried on.

'Maybe I like being on top of you – *bawm chicka wowow ...*' Roe wriggled playfully in her seat doing cheesy seventies porno music. 'Also what about Liberatchi?'

The Warren Street yard was home not just to the patio furniture but a rat they'd christened Liberatchi, after Liberace, one of Roe's many musical heroes.

'The new owners won't understand that he likes to summer there,' Roe continued, only half-joking.

'Getting sentimental about the rat, Roe? Really?'

She shrugged unhappily and stared out the window. The monotony had at last given way to the leafy canal on Dublin city's south side. Their place. Their relationship could be mapped by the different landmarks they passed. Cans at the locks during summer evenings when they were younger. Strolling down Camden Street shopping for Friday night's dinner – shelling out for one single cheese at the counter in the fancy food store before retreating to the Aldi up in Rathmines because, let's face it, who could afford to do the full shop in Mayor's. Of course in recent years their money situation had changed dramatically. Not only was Eddie in constant demand as a barrister but a judicious investment of his in an online events platform years before had catapulted them into major money just as the rest of the world was going to shit.

The money had changed things between them. Eddie had always made more than her but had always insisted that his money was their money. However, in practice, it was hard to navigate, especially when it came to the house. From the moment Eddie had got the Monteray Valley plans up on the iPad, Roe had felt in her gut that these plans just did not seem to chime with *their* plans. Though, being honest, she knew that 'their plans' had always been Eddie's plans. When they'd got together in college, it had been a relief to have someone so certain of the next move, and Roe had gratefully followed. Eddie was finishing his law degree while Roe was fannying around with a half-hearted arts degree – a degree her parents had insisted on, having dismissed singing and theatre as being too unrealistic. Eddie was exactly the kind of prospect her parents would approve of. And they did, which should've made things easier for Roe after the difficult years in her teens, but, strangely, ending up with Eddie had somehow managed to make her feelings towards her parents even more thorny and complicated.

It was painful when Roe detected her parents' approval rating rising once she was with Eddie. Maura and Pat had palpably relaxed, dismissing her 'girl stuff' as a phase, and it confirmed for Roe that their love had conditions. They were relieved she had 'settled down' with a man, apparently believing this 'cured' her of her bisexuality. Though, as it began to dawn on them that Eddie and Roe didn't plan to get married, the tide of approval turned again. Whatever. Roe had spent years in therapy at this point trying to come to terms with the fact that their acceptance, particularly her mother Maura's, was an always-shifting horizon and not a destination she would ever reach.

'Roe.' Eddie was now parking in front of DeLacey's, the restaurant where she worked. Forward, forward, swivel the wheel, back, back, back. 'I don't want to be a dick about this, but you cannot pass-ag me out of a house we've moved into! I showed you the plans. You acted like you liked it.' Eddie paused to check the wing mirrors before turning the wheel for final adjustments to the car's angle.

'And now the decision is made,' Roe huffed. She looked up at Eddie. *Shit, he's definitely teetering towards pissed off.* 'Look,' Roe scrambled to add, 'I'm sorry. I guess when it was on paper it didn't seem so real, and actually knowing Warren Street is now

sold just seems so final. And being out there this week, it's so …'
Roe considered her next words carefully. Generic? Boring? Culty?
When their life curator, Yannick, had detailed the laundry service
that came into your home to gather dirty clothes and, by the
sounds of it, whip the knickers right off you for the wash, Roe had
nearly expected him to say 'April fool!' even though they were two
weeks into April already.

'It's so … uniform,' was the adjective she went with eventually.

'Uh-huh, so it's an aesthetic issue?' Eddie cocked an eyebrow
and Roe felt what little energy she'd had for this argument abruptly
ebb.

'No, I know they're nice houses. They're huge, though, and it's so
far from the restaurant. I'll be spending more on petrol than I earn
in a night.'

DeLacey's was on the canal, exactly three minutes from their
old front door. Roe had been there six years and manager for the
last four. She'd been steadily nursing the place back to health since
the strict lockdowns of early pandemic. She was quietly proud of
her introduction of what had become a permanently booked-out
supper club from Thursdays to Sundays. Roe searched for a way
back from her little strop. She hated going against Eddie – it felt
dangerous. In her own family, the slightest dissent was treated like
high treason, and she'd taken this into her relationship despite
Eddie's frequent reassurances.

'You know what, though,' Roe forced herself to perk up, 'it's
closer to choir so that's a plus!' The Life and Soullers, of which
she'd been a member for years, rehearsed in Craghanmor – a ball-
ache to get to from Dublin 8.

'But hun …' Now, it seemed it was Eddie picking his words

delicately. 'Realistically, how much longer will you be doing choir? Two rehearsals a week on top of the restaurant? Pregnancy can be very tough on a woman's body,' he ventured.

Roe's other least favourite topic: the apparently imminent baby. Roe wasn't sure about the ethics of her current contraception situation. She'd heard of women skipping the pill to engineer an 'accidental' pregnancy, and that was for sure beyond messed up, but doing the reverse – taking the pill without your partner knowing? That was surely not as bad ...

She considered the night ahead. Did she want to wade into a hard conversation about the house and pregnancy and choir? And then spend her whole shift fretting about the fallout from said hard conversation? Though, when did she ever feel up to these conversations? Eddie was not a barrister for nothing. Conversations with him verged on aerobic. She dredged up a smile, opting to ignore his look of concern. 'I know. I guess if I do get pregnant I'll have to cut back on choir. You're right.'

'Roe ... I don't want you to tell me I'm right. I just want you to tell me what you're really thinking about all this.'

'Nothing. Genuinely. I'm not thinking anything.'

Why did I start this? Roe thought, irritated with herself now. She wasn't going to derail Eddie's plans because of a few nebulous misgivings. If Eddie didn't *make* the plans, God knows where Roe would be right now.

'You're thinking *something*,' he pressed.

Roe cast around for 'a thought' to offer up. 'I'm going to be late for work.'

★

'You are so bloody weak, Roe.' Danny was polishing cutlery beside the till and looking disgusted. 'Why can't you just say "I actually don't want to be some baby-making Stepford Wife out in Pleasantville"? How are you going to get in and out from here?'

'I'm not weak! And it's *not* that I don't want those things. I do … maybe? I just … don't want … I dunno. I don't know what I want, but I do know that I don't want to disappoint him.'

'You never want to disappoint him and it has been the basis of your every life decision for the past decade. He's not your parents; he's not some "one strike and you're out" situation. He could handle you going against one fucking thing – especially something this important.'

'I know he's not my mum and dad.' She hated Danny's 'takes' on her life. They'd been best friends since school in Kilshannagh. He'd been there for her when Maura and Pat had treated her coming out like a bigger disaster than Chernobyl. But just because you witness something at close range doesn't mean you fully understand how it feels. His own parents, Johnny and Patrice, had been amazing when he'd brought Davey Connelly home after Junior Cert night and introduced him as his boyfriend. They'd also more or less parented Roe through those shitty years.

'You need to go put tables 9, 10 and 11 together for that party of fourteen coming in,' she announced.

'*You* need to talk to your boyfriend,' Danny countered but grudgingly stalked off to reset the tables.

Roe pulled up the DeLacey's FreeTable account to check there were no last-minute cancellations. Table 6 wanted to push their reservation to the later sitting. She opened a new tab and examined the table plan for the evening ahead. It was doable. Roe fired off a response to table 6 confirming their new time and picked up her phone, her SopranHoes WhatsApp group was pinging.

MAGS: @Roe Sooo? How'd the first week go in the new gaff? You've been totally awol.

The choir pals were keen for updates on Monteray. Maggie and her husband had just missed out on a house in the neighbouring crescent.

ROE: It was fine. Well, not fine, huge actually. The sheer quantity of bathrooms is obscene.

Danny – who was also in the group and clearly not remotely putting tables 9, 10 and 11 together as she'd told him to – added a gross toilet-related GIF. Mags was quick to admonish him.

MAGS: Jaysus, Danny, you're only an honorary SopranHoe – we could still evict your ass for lewdness and lasciviousness.

Danny responded with a *Great British Bake Off* GIF of someone piping creamy icing and Roe laughed quietly.

ROE: Danny, you are at work right now. I am literally your boss. Get off your phone.

AIDEEN: I am sorry, Roe, but OMG why are we even TALKING about this? Did ye not SEE Róisín's Insta post about the auditions?

Róisín was the musical director of the Life and Soullers and was feared and beloved in equal measure. Aideen shared a screenshot to the group:

> *Our big show this year is a musical based on Ireland's historic Eurovision sweep. And there is a special *Surprise Element* this year that could catapult us to the NEXT LEVEL in the world of amateur musical theatre!!!*

KAREN: Gawd. Will they never let that Eurovision streak go? *eye-roll emoji*

MAGS: Karen! High treason! One does not eye-roll the Eurovision. Everyone goes on and on about Italia '90 but it was really those years of Irish Eurovision GLORY that formed the backbone of Irish self-esteem. Plus next month we're coming up on the 30-year anniversary of the start of it – the iconic Linda in Malmo. That song, that one-shoulder dress.

Roe x-ed out of the app. Another audition they'd all become completely wrapped up in. Roe never went for them – she couldn't imagine it, standing up there completely alone on the stage. Danny and Mags generally tried out, and last year Roe and Karen had gone to see them in an endearingly amateurish production of *Kinky Boots*.

'Roe ... ROE?' It was Gina, the head chef, yelling through the pass.

'Sorry, G – yep?'

'Can I get numbers on tonight's bookings please? When you

have the time, obviously,' she added, glaring pointedly at the phone still in Roe's hand then clattering over to the stove to violently slash a spatula at some pans. Gina was a bit of a horror. Roe scrambled around, printing out the bookings info.

Hot breath on her ear startled her. Danny had slid back in behind the counter. He hissed, 'First-round auditions are at the start of May appara. Two weeks away, Roe.'

'You didn't need to mouth-breathe in my ear!'

'There's scant info available right now, but Róisín's warned the auditions are going to be *fraught*. I don't know what the hell role I'll be eligible for. It's pretty woman-heavy, but there's always Johnny Logan and they could beef up the John Waters role, maybe shoehorn in a few baritone TV execs, that kind of thing, I imagine.'

Resolutely ignoring him – he was forever pressuring her to try out – Roe located the printout and leaned into the pass, where Gina was now hacking at herbs like they'd mowed down a beloved pet of hers.

Roe cleared her throat. 'So we've had one cancellation for the first sitting, but otherwise a full house and exactly twenty-six diners for the second sitting.'

'Funny – didn't see a *word* on our socials about a last-minute early table going spare.'

'Doing it now, Gina.'

Danny was stacking clean glasses and filling carafes with water now. 'I think it's high time you tried out, Roe. So many strong female leads here. You're a Niamh Kavanagh to the bone. Beautiful and charismatic. You're a bit more voluptuous obvi…'

'I hate "voluptuous", as you know.'

'You ready for specials?' Gina snapped. 'Stop distracting her.' She pointed her tongs at Danny.

'Yep.' Roe swung back to the till. 'Hang on, I'll just grab my pen—'

'Mains,' Gina continued in a bored voice, not even bothering to wait for Roe. 'We have rainbow trout with pea risotto, charred scallions and fresh lemon and basil oil. Starter is a house-made boudin noir with poached rhubarb and toasted hazelnuts. Dessert is roast pears with a chestnut and chocolate tart.'

'Really? Is that not a bit—?'

'A bit what?' Gina demanded, suddenly snapping to attention. She hated any kind of interference from the front-of-house.

'Well …' Roe tried to hold her gaze without betraying the pounding in her chest. *I have to get better at feedback. I can't just roll over every time there's a conflict,* she coached herself. 'It's a bit autumnal for mid-April, like?'

Gina glowered. 'I am sick of you and your power trip ever since you became manager.' Now she was wielding a paring knife over the pass. 'Out there buried in your phone like you're—'

'Gina, I've been manager for four years,' Roe said evenly. It was better to try and de-escalate Gina – this was her pre-service nerves. 'I love your food. No one has your instincts. It was just a minor thought. Ignore me – I don't know what I'm talking about.'

'You don't!' Gina flung her tongs in the overflowing sink to her left and stomped off to the walk-in fridge, hopefully to cool off.

Roe wished *she* had somewhere to hide. It felt like she'd just survived an encounter with a wild animal.

'I'm sorry, but if you can go up against Gina when she's absolutely on one, I have no idea why you think you're not up to trying out?' Danny was persisting. He did this every year.

She taped the list of specials beside the till for the rest of the wait staff to copy down. 'It's too late for me to be getting into all that stuff,

Danny. I'm not a performer. I'd die up there – my corpse would have to be nudged off stage left while the show carried on.' She dropped her voice. 'Look at me, I'm shaking after just *talking* to Gina there.'

She loved her singing and, yes, one of her private pursuits was dancing, but she took the dance-like-nobody's-watching maxim extremely literally – she couldn't so much as tap her foot in front of someone.

'Well,' he looked furious, 'so long as you know that you'll be sentencing us to the un-fucking-bearable Denise. She'll be straight in. She's always the lead, Roe,' he whined. 'And it's so boring and predictable. Why are we endlessly punished with mildly talented tiny blonde women everywhere we look? You're the only person with the range that could challenge her, but I suppose we'd see the Brits win Eurovision sooner than you try out for something.'

'Harsh!' This, Roe knew, was Danny's way of encouraging her, but he didn't know what he was talking about. 'Look, even if I wanted to, I'll be stuck out in Monteray. Eddie's kind of been making noises about me … if I get … you know … duffed up that I might have to quit choir.'

'I'm sorry, what are you? A delicate Victorian lady?'

Ugh, I have to get him off this topic. 'Excuse me, I am much more a consumptive Victorian child! In which case, Monteray Valley is actually the perfect place for me. They literally do everything for you there. We met our "life curator", Yannick, this morning and he said he's at our beck and call now. No irritating task is too small, appara. He's going to arrange to have my handbag cleared out once a week and for our Christmas shopping to be bought, wrapped and stashed by June!'

4

'AT MONTERAY VALLEY, WE DON'T SIMPLY OFFER A lifestyle; we offer a life *styling*. We build your bespoke life according to your personal needs. This interview with your personal life curator is the first step into being inducted into the Monteray Valley vision for living.'

Lindy smiled blandly as their life curator, Pierce, delivered this strangely corporate explanation. Beside her, Adam was nodding vigorously between glancing up and down at his phone. They were all in the back room in the house on Orchard Avenue, sitting on the fold-out garden chairs that were among the last things to be packed up. Tomorrow morning they'd be gone for good.

'So,' Pierce smiled neatly, 'some background required for your on-boarding – how did you two meet?'

'I'll take this one, honey.' Adam pressed a finger to her lips and swung himself up to standing.

The 'how did you two meet' question was the Adam Show, and he'd long perfected it.

He spread his arms wide. 'Let me set the scene for you, Pierce. It was an Aussie karaoke bar and I'd sung the same song every night for nearly two weeks and every night I'd had home runs. With the ladies, to be clear. In my youth I was, as Lindy would say, "a fucking ride".' He paused to land an extremely cute grin, looking from Pierce to Lindy. 'You guys are supposed to say "You're still a fucking ride, Adam"!'

Pierce gamely parroted: 'You're still a …' He cleared his throat awkwardly. 'Ahemm … ride, Adam.'

Lindy shook her head, grinning. It was probably highly inappropriate to make him say that – he was, in a sense, their employee at this moment – but Adam thrived on highly inappropriate. It made her husband pretty Marmite – people were either utterly repelled by his bombastic, brash ways or, like Lindy, fell for them even against their better judgement. He was fun and, to be fair, as he'd said, a bona fide ride.

'Mrs Zelner.' Adam cocked a finger in her direction. 'I didn't hear you there?'

'It's Ms Reid and please just get on with the story.'

'OK so there was I, a young midwestern Brad Pitt, crooning to a room of beautiful women, one of whom – this one – pretending she wasn't interested. Galling.'

'I was embarrassed for you. You were singing 'Pretty Fly for a White Guy'.'

'I had a lotta guys rooting for me that night. They wanted me to bag lucky-thirteen but I was a goner. I knew it had to be her. I tried everything but I struck out with her that night. She broke my streak.'

'I should clarify, Pierce, when he says "tried everything" what he really means is he was gross and inappropriate *at me* for fifteen minutes and then staggered off to sleep in his friend's car.'

'"Give it to me baby, uh-huh uh-huh."' Adam made a beckoning gesture at her.

'The worst part is he thinks he's being obnoxious in an ironic way,' she told Pierce.

This was the way 'how did you two meet' always played. They had it down pat after ten years together. All couples did this to some degree, Lindy found, though not all meet-cutes involved karaoke re-enactments and regrettable white rapping.

'She came back the next night, though' – more cheeky grinning from Adam.

He is still very cute, she allowed. He kept his blond hair shaved now after the first signs of thinning. A good call. Sometimes Lindy would catch him from a random angle and be startled by the signs of age in him. *And he must get it even worse with me. I haven't bought a new bra since 2018.* Her mind strayed to her underwear drawer, so packed that every time she opened it to get the one wearable bra and knickers she owned, she had to wedge it closed. *I need to go through it, weed out the dross and start afresh with some decent underwear. Maybe there's someone who does that out in Monteray?*

'Eh, Lindy?' Adam was raising an eyebrow in her direction. 'I said: she came back the next night, though.'

'Right.' She did love his total lack of pretence that this was anything other than a highly engineered and rigorously rehearsed meet-cute story. She cleared her throat. 'The next night he was singing 'Zombie', which he dedicated to me.'

'And,' Adam picked up the thread, 'she screamed across the whole bar: "This song is not romantic, you dopey sap, it's about the

Troubles!" I could barely understand her cos of the accent but I was enchanted. Next night, I did 'Sunday Bloody Sunday' just to see her mad again. She's so cute when she's mad.'

Lindy rolled her eyes. 'I wasn't mad – I was irritated because you were a douche.'

'I was playing up to the obnoxious American stereotype.' He spun round to Pierce. 'And it totally worked.'

'The next night he did 'Nothing Compares 2 U', and I will admit it, he got me. I was at a very low moment. We had just eaten the last packet of Banshee Bones sent over from home.'

'We kissed.' Adam twinkled over at her.

'I was thinking about Banshee Bones the entire time,' Lindy finished flatly.

'And scene.' Adam bowed. 'A hand for my lady wife.' Adam clapped in her direction and then swooped in for a kiss.

Lindy was generally not one for public shifting but she let him for a minute before batting him off. He hadn't kissed her in so long. To be fair, she hadn't kissed him either. They never even cuddled now.

The beginning of the end of sex had set in a few years ago. It was probably around the time of the last bra purchase, so she couldn't even blame the pandemic. Working together had definitely changed their relationship. It had become so transactional. As time went by, she found that the less sex they had, the less sex they had. It was like an awkward silence going on so long that the thought of breaking it was becoming more and more remote. *If we suddenly did manage to have sex now, we would be forced to acknowledge that we hadn't had sex in months. Months and months. What are we averaging? Four times a year?*

'So here we are, twelve years later.' She ran a hand through her dark bob. 'In my defence, Pierce, I had no context for him. I thought he was probably cool and from LA cos that's where TV Americans were from.' She grinned. 'By the time I realised he wasn't, it was too late. I was pregnant. Surprise!' She laughed lightly.

Adam returned to the chair beside her and rubbed his hand along the sandy stubble on his jaw. 'Turned out to be the most lucrative surprise ever!'

'Pierce,' she cut in abruptly. She hated when Adam was glib about their son. 'You wanted to ask us some questions?'

'Yes, of course, of course. OK, so I usually start by asking what are the daily life tasks you find the most tedious?'

'Wiping my ass,' Adam honked. 'Can I arrange for someone to take care of things on that end?'

Pierce, while visibly repulsed, appeared to still make a note of this.

'Oh Jesus.' Lindy covered her husband's mouth without breaking eye contact with their life stylist. 'I'm so sorry.' She was laughing in spite of herself. They always did better when they were performing their relationship for others, rather than just on their own together. She'd never noticed this until the lockdowns began and they were no longer out all the time doing the Adam and Lindy Show at dinner parties and tech-industry events. It had been an unsettling realisation, and she was desperate to know if their friends had experienced similar; though, as they were pretty much all YouTube families themselves, it was unlikely she'd get an honest answer. As much as the group had in common, admitting that her marriage had washed up like wreckage in the wake of the pandemic felt too risky to reveal. 'Well-placed insiders' being quoted on gossip sites and all that could kill a family-orientated YouTube brand.

'Don't worry – this is all good stuff here.' Pierce batted away her apology. 'This is why we have these consultations. I'm here to really drill down into the different elements that will make Monteray Valley living a first-class experience for you both. Our researchers have spent years exploring the different facets of modern living that corrode human health and well-being. Many are obvious – loneliness, for example. Studies are now proving that loneliness can contribute to death.'

'Wow, really?' Lindy feigned interest. *Great, I'm already lonely at the thought of leaving my family and friends and now I'm apparently gonna die from it.*

'Loneliness is to the soul what smoking is to the lungs,' Pierce offered brightly. 'In Monteray Valley, our residents are never lonely, thankfully. Clients in other facilities report a summer-camp-like atmosphere in the population. You see, there's a mean age of thirty-eight among the adults; families have an average of 2.2 children; they come from similar socio-economic backgrounds and share a similar outlook on key issues. The cohort has a lot in common so it stands to reason that the social side gels well.'

Facilities? Population? Cohort? Frequently a strangely institutional lexicon bled into the Monteray pitch.

'Our researchers have found that often it is the low-grade irritants that can really undermine an individual's well-being. Kind of a "death by a thousand cuts" idea. Life is filled with annoying obligations and that's something we're seeking to eradicate for our citizens – in so far as possible at least! We can't take over *everything*, you still have to do all your own blinking and breathing and swallowing at Monteray,' he twinkled. 'But where we can, we want to deliver a polished existence. Thoughts, Lindy? What would make life smoother? Sick of the school run?' He glanced down. 'Ah, I see you're already signed up for that. Of course it's barely a "school run"! Monteray Academy is no more than eight minutes' walk from where you'll be in crescent C. Hmmm, what else?' he glanced down at his notes. 'Laundry service we have you down for too. What other annoying things do you have to do every day?'

'I hate changing the bins,' Adam announced.

Pierce noted this down. 'Check.'

'Unpacking the groceries – buying them, even! – all total ball-ache,' Adam continued.

'Oh, no one at Monteray does grocery shopping. Not in the old "weekly shop" sense anyway …' Pierce looked appalled at the mere *idea* of such drudgery.

'But how does this all actually work?' Lindy interjected.

'We have teams assigned to each crescent. They have access to the houses via discreet staff entrances. They do everything – the cleaning, laundry, replenishing groceries, meal prep, school lunches, you name it – all at night while the family sleeps so that you never have to interact with them directly unless you want to. Think of them like au pairs but for the adults. For you! They're there to take care of you and will do anything you need – provided it's legal. Take, for example, hangovers. Do you two drink?'

'Uh-huh but, obviously, being over thirty-five it's barely worth it.' Adam shook his head ruefully.

'Oh, I feel you.' Pierce attempted a chummy grin but it didn't match his general starched primness. 'So the worst part of a night out on the tear is the hangover, right? Well, not in Monteray Valley.

We have the Hangover Helper service. The helpers come, bring you food, hold your hair – they're even trained to insert an IV to rehydrate you and get you back from the brink faster. One woman in our Orlando complex books her Hangover Helper to come the morning after every book club, and all he does is hold her hand and reassure her that everyone doesn't hate her. That. Is. Living. Amirite?'

'Sounds … weirdly intimate. But, nice?' Lindy was trying to make an effort since Adam had told her she was killing the buzz lately with all her reservations about moving to Monteray. He'd been particularly shirty when she'd confronted him the previous week after the Monteray PTA mixer had resulted in not one but two lump sums from their savings being invested in new-neighbours' companies. He insisted it was all to get off on the right foot but she knew it was Adam's ego that got him every time. He wanted to show them how much he had to spare. Which, even though on the face of it Maxxed Out seemed to be on the up and up, was not as much as he liked to pretend. Money streamed in but also flowed out at an unnerving rate and Lindy just wasn't over the financials as much as she probably should be.

'Pierce, lemme ask you something.' Beside her, Adam leaned forward earnestly. 'We've been toying with getting a dog for my son for ages but we're not really dog people. So. You know the way people can get dogs but hire others to walk them? We kinda want the reverse of that. We don't really want the dog in the house – the mess, the noise.' Adam grimaced. 'Or it being, ya know, "part of the family". We want dog *interludes* – is that something that could be arranged?'

'Absolutely, Mr Zelner. We could find humane storage for the dog for the times that you are not walking it. Or perhaps find another Monteray family interested in doing a dog timeshare.'

Later, after Pierce had left and Max was in bed, Lindy and Adam sat, each plugged in to separate devices, with pizza boxes discarded around them. They'd barely spoken since Pierce had left. Lindy tried to focus on her favourite comfort watch – a YouTube channel called Closet Therapy. Mae and Ramona were two NYC psychologists who had retrained as professional organisers and every episode saw them going through an ordinary woman's wardrobe and dealing with her issues through the medium of sorting. It was very soothing. The combination of women emoting and Manhattan interiors was intoxicating.

Beside her Adam was scrolling on his phone and watching the Masters. She couldn't stop thinking about how they'd had more chat that afternoon with a third party present than they had in months. She hated the thought of bringing her lonely marriage to Monteray Valley, where surely their lapsed intimacy would be highlighted by proximity to other happy marrieds. Monteray, she was certain, would be exactly like the group holidays they took with friends – everyone watching and assessing how the other couples were doing ten years in. Giuliana and David were clearly still into each other but were generous enough to be lowkey about it. Miriam and Anthony looked pretty defunct, which Lindy couldn't help but be vaguely reassured by. Meanwhile Sigrid and Tomas were apparently still attracted to each other, audibly so, as a shared bedroom wall in the last Airbnb could, unfortunately, attest to.

Maybe Monteray could be a new start for her and Adam. She wanted to believe it was possible. Seeing the room around her dismantled brought her back to their very first night in the house.

It had been blank then too, but not bereft like this. That first night the empty space was full of anticipation for the potential life that could unfold there. Music was playing – Bell X1, Lindy was sure: she'd been schooling Adam on Irish music at the time. Baby Max was fast asleep in the only place he would submit to sleeping at that time: bound to Lindy's chest in a stretchy wrap. They had talked into the night and then, after stealthily transferring Max to his makeshift nursery, they'd had sex for the first time since he'd been born.

Lindy had been so nervous. After much sibling debate about how to approach the first post-birth screw, Finn had procured Lindy some Valium. Séamus, on the other hand, had jokingly presented her with two ecstasy pills. She'd availed of neither in the end. She hadn't needed to. Sex with Adam had always been hot and it was no different that night, despite her nerves. She'd pulled off her top and straddled him, and when he'd roughly pulled down her bra and her breasts spilled out, it had been just like it always had been. Now, stirred by the memory, Lindy glanced at Adam. *I need to just break the seal. We can't go to the new house with this desiccated sex life.*

Beside her, Adam was engrossed in golf, but she urged herself on, letting her left hand drift towards his upper right thigh. When she made contact he jolted.

'Are you OK?' He whipped off his headphones.

'Yeah, I just thought, you know … we could do … it?' Excruciating.

'Sure we could do it,' he replied, and Lindy tried to ignore that he'd said it in the same tone someone might say 'sure we could de-hair the shower drain'.

He leaned in to kiss her, a very polite kiss. They were out of practice. Then he leaned his hand on her hip, but it slipped off, pinching a wedge of her thigh flesh between his hand and the floor.

'Oww!'

'Sorry, sorry.' He tried to lean in again at the exact same moment she did, causing them to bash off each other. 'This is going great.' He smiled ruefully.

'C'mon, we can do this.' It was the most Lindy had ever acknowledged the no-sex spell. Though 'spell' was putting it mildly. It was more of a no-sex era at this point. Lindy pulled herself up into a squat and crabbed sideways to straddle him, grateful she was wearing a dress, which he started to hike up. 'Wait – my knickers.' She bent her knee up and pulled one side of her pants down, acutely conscious that she was flashing him quite a lot of undercarriage. Post-baby, Lindy had often quipped to Giuliana that she could wear her vagina as a sarong. Ugh. *Don't dwell on it, c'mon, other side now*, she coached herself and at last flung the knickers clear. She positioned herself over his erection, trying not to think about the fact that it could've been harder, *would've* been harder a few years ago. She gripped it to guide it into her. *Oh God, it's bending. This is mortifying.* At last, she managed to stuff it in, trying not to grimace. She avoided Adam's eyes, knowing instinctively that he was probably doing the same. If they looked at each other, it would be too obvious that this was not going well. She moved up and down. It was chafey because she was too self-conscious to be remotely turned on. She chanced a look at her husband; he was flinching slightly. *The chafing goes both ways.* She had to get wet. *Jesus, the pressure! OK, think of something, anything.*

She closed her eyes and one of her stock scenarios began to come into focus. Zane had been a TV presenter when Lindy was younger. A very hot TV presenter who interviewed bands and hosted proceedings backstage at Glastonbury. Now, like them, he had a kid-orientated YouTube channel called Zaddy Zane that she occasionally visited, especially when Adam and Max were away. She pitched up and down on Adam trying to concentrate on the storyline of her fantasy – she and Zane were fucking in his car in the underground car park of the kind of anonymous hotel where YouTube events were always held. She opened her eyes briefly; Adam's eyes were also squeezed tight. *Where is* he *right now? Same car park with some YouTube mum?* She shut her eyes again. *Come, Lindy! Come!*

'Ehm,' Adam quietly interrupted her fevered internal chanting. 'Are you going to …? Cos, well, I don't think I'm …'

Thank God he left it at that – to say the words would've been too damning. She slipped off him. They didn't speak, and after a couple of minutes, Adam put his earphones in once more and Lindy went to do her night-time Skin Love routine.

Later, after Adam had come to bed and Lindy'd feigned sleep, she lay on her side in the dark, and cold humiliation trickled through her, pooling in her stomach. Her perfectly silent tears streamed sideways across her face and onto her pillow. She wanted so badly not to see it, not to know that something was very wrong with her marriage. This aborted sexual encounter with the man she'd hitched her life to had caused a visceral breach in the iron-clad denial she tried to maintain at all times. Now all-too-specific worries were rushing in. *Does he not love me any more? Does he wish he was with someone else? How have I let this happen?*

5

AILBHE'S PHONE STARTED BUZZING AND SHE rolled over groggily to see a picture of grinning Tom glowing in the darkness. 'Tom calling' flashed on the screen. She loved their almost-nightly Tilly-life catch-up, but what time was it? Her phone said 23.43, 25 April – ten weeks to the day till they would leave Dublin. Her tongue felt woolly in her mouth and a headache throbbed behind her right eye. The fallout of three glasses was intense when you were already running on newborn-sleep levels. She eased herself up on the pillows and hit the green button.

'Hey, babe,' she whispered. Tilly was asleep just feet away in her cosy little bassinet. 'Guess where I am?!'

'Ooh, new house? How is it, honey?'

'Very cool, the front door said "welcome home" to me when I arrived and it told Eilers she looked fab.'

'I love all their personal touches. I see you guys have cracked the champagne already.'

'Eh … yeah. How'd you see that?' *Can he literally tell by my face?* She panicked.

'You ordered on the Monteray app – everything is tracked and logged. You didn't overdo it on the champagne, Ailbhe? Half a unit a week is the recommended amount.'

'Of course not!' Her eyes darted to the glass on the side table that she'd brought up when she came to bed and made sure it was out of shot. 'So any updates on if you'll be back over before we come to you?'

'I might be! Maia's still moving some stuff around, but I'm hoping I'll get over to you in June and we can all fly back together.'

'Ah, amazing!'

'Is your tourist visa all straightened out?'

'Yup, visa will be sorted.' *Ugh, gotta get on that.*

'The guys in legal are still researching what the best approach is for long-term, but the six-month one will be fine to start – it's not like you'll be working.'

'Oooh, speaking of work,' Ailbhe kept her voice low so as not to disturb Tilly or exacerbate the thumping in her head. 'Holly has taken on a freelance gig doing make-up for a reality-show thingy that's starting in a few weeks and I'm going to help her out, just for the last few weeks before we leave. I'm so excited to be back on a set. It's been *so* long.' She scooched back down in bed, getting comfortable, and propped Tom beside her on the other pillow, his angular, sun-bronzed face glowing in the dark. She tucked her hands under her cheek, her wavy red hair spilling away from her. They were so rarely in the same country that she'd gotten oddly used to just having his head in bed with her. At first, Tiny Phone Husband had seemed like just the right amount of husband for

Ailbhe, but more and more she found, to her surprise, she was missing him.

'You look so beautiful, babe.' The cute dimple under Tom's left eye appeared as he smiled. 'I keep looking at the photos from the birth. Every time I just get this new level of awe that you did that.'

At her birth, while Eilers gamely snapped photos, Tom had cheered Ailbhe on via OptimEyes, the Optimise answer to FaceTime. The midwives had been highly entertained. Not least because Tom had been on a plane with Seth Rogen pitching an investment opportunity for the duration.

Ailbhe's eyes drifted to her plump, rosy daughter tucked up in her pale-yellow sleeping bag. She was hers, yet Ailbhe didn't know who she was yet. Would she have an American accent one day? What colour would her eyes be? The thought jarred; her guilt snapped at her suddenly. That could be a problem. She chased the thought away and focused on Tom.

'Yes, I am awesome,' she agreed. 'Want to see our girl?' She slipped out of bed.

'Your mother? I'd love to.' He grinned goofily.

Ailbhe giggled. 'I'll bring you down to our fifty-nine-year-old bundle of joy in a sec – she's down the hall – but look at this little lamb first!' She turned the phone around and they gazed silently for a moment. Then Ailbhe caught a glimpse of the slightly bizarre scene in the window reflection. In her long nighty, with Tilly's wicker basket and Tom's glowing disembodied head, it looked like a demented nativity scene.

'Look, Tom.' She turned him towards the windows. 'We look like an episode of *Black Mirror*!'

He laughed and she nudged the volume down, hopping back under the covers.

'I definitely think Holly finds all this remote marriaging weird,' Ailbhe continued. 'She will not drop the intimacy-exchange spreadsheet.'

'I love Holly as you know, honey, but maybe she just has a narrow worldview, Ailbhe.' He was still pronouncing her name ALE-ve, she noted. *Tell me your marriage was a rush job without telling me your marriage was a rush job*, she thought. He ploughed on, 'I could have Maia do up a deck for Holly outlining how disastrously the conventional "in-person" marriage model has performed historically. Look at the dismal success rate – only about 50 per cent of marriages survive.'

Ailbhe grinned at the image of this. A deck on the efficacy of marriage would leave Holly *more* baffled, not less. Meanwhile Tom continued his impromptu TED Talk.

'If marriage was an app that had such low satisfaction among its user base, we'd have scrapped it or at the very least done some updates. Thanks to Covid, we now know remote working works. What's wrong with remote relationships? Anyway, we won't always be remote. In two months, we'll be toasting our new life here with Mom and Pop and you're going to love it.'

They'd hung up, and shortly after Tom followed up with a satisfaction report. No joke. It was one of the new additions to Optimise that Tom was trialling. Five statements – including 'My emotions were given sufficient space' and 'My discussion points were addressed' – were to be answered with a thumbs-up or thumbs-down emoji. Ailbhe couldn't even imagine how Holly would react to the information that Tom liked status updates on everything from money to feelings.

She dutifully ticked off the thumbs-ups and closed Optimise. Even though she was still feeling a bit ick from the champs, she reached over to retrieve the glass she'd brought up. *Medicinal*, she thought. It'll help the headache. Still lying down, she dribbled a little carefully into her mouth, and on autopilot opened Instagram next. She'd vowed to stop but it was so damn moreish. Despite how well things were going with Tom, she'd found it impossible to stay away ever since the night of Tilly's birth when, in a spooky bit of synchronicity, she'd received a DM from Seb. 'Still thinking about you …' he'd written.

Seb knew nothing of her pregnancy. For obvious reasons, she'd kept the news firmly off social media, abandoning her own Insta account the second she'd calculated her conception date. She and Seb had run in the same crowd back in their twenties but she knew he'd drifted. Plus she'd taken pains to keep the pregnancy as quiet as possible, telling Holly and her mother that she didn't want people judging how recently she and Tom had gotten together.

She'd never answered Seb's DM: it remained hidden in her phone but nagging at her like an irresistibly pushable red button. She avoided looking at the message, but still every couple of weeks the urge to check his account struck. It was like her hands were tapping of their own volition. Seb Knox was easy to find. She searched 'Seb' and it was the first account suggested. Easy to find, not so easy to lose. He was something she picked at – satisfying in the moment but ultimately knowing it could hurt her.

@SebKnoxTV's bio was frustratingly minimal.

Telly guy. Founder and director of Knox Pictures. Dublin sometimes, London mostly.

She looked down through Seb's profile. One picture showed him with his arm slung around Brendan Gleeson, who was gripping a BAFTA. It was clearly some champagne-soaked afterparty where middle-aged men swaggered and ingénues perched on every surface, hopeful to be noticed and lifted out of the struggling years. *No more struggling years for me* – her gaze drifted to her left hand and the rings (most likely chosen by Maia). No more struggling years for Seb either, clearly. For years he'd seemed so flaky. Always drifting in and out of TV work. Always seeming to have stuff 'in development', never getting anything into production. Now since their last encounter – *Don't go back there! God, it wasn't even good, Ailbhe!* – it seemed his star had ascended. He was doing well. Would that have changed her decision? She didn't like the thought and turned away from it.

She scanned Seb's profile. She knew all the pics. He hadn't updated in two months, not since March, when he'd shared the BAFTA Brendan Gleeson pic. *At least he's in London.* It felt safer that way. She could browse without fear of being forced to confront anything. She opened his stories. First up was a pint picture with some text proclaiming '9 a.m. airport drinkie, it'd be rude not to …'

A rush of adrenaline whipped through her. So much for 'at least he's in London'.

The next story calmed her. A selfie on the plane captioned 'Transatlantic calls for shots!' She pressed her thumb to the screen to hold the picture in place. He was Tom's polar opposite. Tom had a very cute goofy quality to him, whereas Seb was arrogant as hell.

Though why? He was nowhere near as successful as Tom, never would be. Tom had gotten into and out of hedge funds in less than five years with enough money to start up Optimise before he was even twenty-five. Seb was forty-five at least and probably didn't even own a *car* he could start up. They were both hot but again on opposite ends of the spectrum. Seb had a square build and Travolta-ish grey quiff, laugh lines and quite a toothy grin. Tom was baby-faced by comparison, with wavy shoulder-length black hair and gorgeous full lips.

Distractedly, she sipped from her glass and managed to dribble some on her camisole. She fumbled and dropped the phone. As she picked it up, she accidentally hit a reaction to Seb's story. 'Noooo,' she hissed as heart-eye emojis cascaded up the screen over his selfie.

Fuck fuck fuck. This is the most 2015 mistake ever, she lamented silently.

There wasn't a second to waste. She tucked the glass she was holding gently under her right elbow and began scrambling out of Seb's story and into her DMs, where she knew if she was quick she could delete the reaction before he saw it. She held her thumb to the traitorous little heart-eye emoji and the option to delete popped up. *Delete delete delete.*

The reaction disappeared and she exhaled, slumping gratefully back on her pillows and completely forgetting the champagne flute. The stem cracked clean off and champagne tipped everywhere. *Fuck's sake.* She rolled her eyes, picked up the broken glass and immediately nicked her finger. *Jesus! What am I like?* She suppressed a giggle and pulled off her cami to give the mess a cursory clean. *I'll get it in the morning.*

She leaned out of bed and pushed the damp top and the bits of glass under the bed – no need for her mother to come across it. She settled back down to sleep, Tilly no doubt would be up again soon demanding feeding. *I'd better defrost a bottle*, she thought vaguely as sleep started drifting over her. Just as she was about to drop off, guilt suddenly thudded in her chest. *Don't think about it.* That was the problem with moderate drinking: it wasn't enough to block out unpleasant feelings – if anything, three glasses just made them more heightened. *This is the choice I made*, she reminded herself. *I'll get used to it.* She knew that, in the future, on occasion the hangover of her deception would wash in like a foul tide. This is what she was signing up for, unfortunately, but her life with Tom would be easier and she couldn't forget that. He was a known quantity. He was sweet, he appreciated her and he wanted to make her happy. And she would be happy. *I am happy.*

6

EDDIE NUZZLED INTO ROE'S CLOUD OF CANDY-
coloured hair in bed on the morning of their third Saturday in
Monteray. Roe usually loved his big comforting arms around her
in bed. He would stroke every curve and dip of her body and she
felt desired but, lately, his hands on her body were motivated by
something much more complicated. He stroked her stomach.

'Maybe this month …?' he murmured sleepily.

'Maybe!' She tried to sound cheery, sliding away from him. 'I'm
gonna get the coffee on.' She smiled over her shoulder, pulling a
fine-knit cardi over her lilac silk chemise and made her way down
the three flights of stairs to the kitchen. Even though it was officially
nearly summer, drizzle coated the windows like lace and the light
was muted. It was matching Roe's mood. She was looking forward
to choir this afternoon, but it wasn't quite enough to balance the
rest of the day's drudgery. Brunch with their parents – Eddie's
folks she loved, her own not so much. Plus, when she got back
from rehearsals, they were off to the inaugural Monteray Welcome

Mixer. Kicking off the day with that nod to the baby question had dragged her further into her slump. As far as Eddie was aware, they'd been actively trying for two months now. With the move, he had effectively dismantled every roadblock to babydom that Roe had erected: space was no longer an issue, nor was her age – thirty-one was old enough – her career had never been something Eddie had accepted as a decent excuse, which was fair. Despite her dedication, Roe couldn't pretend she was passionate about DeLacey's.

Roe knew she hadn't been forthcoming about how she really felt, but telling Eddie she didn't want kids was huge. 'To kid or not to kid' was pretty much a deal-breaker in a relationship. *Anyway, I want a baby. Do I? Sort of. In theory?* The concept of a baby was so abstract – how could anyone understand it before it's dropped into their life?

'Are you OK, Roe?' Eddie had followed her downstairs. 'Are you annoyed that I brought up the baby thing?'

'No! Of course not! I'm putting coffee on.' Roe took a deep breath. 'It's just I don't want us to get our hopes up. Best not think about it all the time.'

'It's so hard not to! I'm just excited.' Eddie crouched in front of his cupboard of health bullshit and started pulling out the makings of his customary weekend breakfast. *Protein pancakes should be banned*, Roe thought. Sometimes she was tempted to vape for breakfast in defiance. God, she wouldn't be vaping if she got pregnant. Eddie resumed mixing flaxseed with water and tipped vanilla protein powder into a bowl. 'Are *you* not excited? Even a bit?' He glanced at her. He looked a bit nervous. Very unEd.

'I am excited. It's just a lot, isn't it?' She edged carefully around the words she was choosing. 'Like how does anyone actually make the decision to have a baby? Does everyone one day just think: I'm done fucking up my own life and want the opportunity to completely fuck up a whole other person's life?'

Ed laughed heartily, which was not the response Roe had in mind, and when he saw her face he shut up instantly.

'Ah, Roe, it'll be so much fun. We won't fuck up the baby ... Unless it's really asking for it.'

She laughed in spite of herself and circled Eddie's waist, smiling into his back. *We still have fun together.* This was why she couldn't go against Eddie. They fit. They'd always fit.

I'll stop the pill next month – he won't know ...

'So,' he turned to face her, 'you look extremely sexy in this little slip thing.' He fingered the soft material of her nighty, leaning down to whisper in her ear, 'And there's no such thing as too much sex when you're tryna make a baby, but unfortunately my mum and dad are actually on their way already.'

'So punctual – so Protestant!' She spun away, back to the coffee machine – a piece of equipment so minimalist it looked like a modernist sculpture. She was relieved to be off the topic, at least for the moment. She grabbed their two cups and handed one to Ed. 'Esther and Philip are going to freak out when they see this place. They hitting service en route?'

'Yep, they love a new parish. They'll be creaming themselves over the Prods in Kildare.'

'So you admit it – we're not in Dublin!'

'I'm admitting nothing. They'll be here around eleven. Mum cannot wait to see the Monteray retail block, so I said we'd do a little tour after lunch. Do you mind getting a taxi to choir? And I can collect you?'

'Yep, no probs.'

Upstairs, Roe stepped into the shower and mentally scrolled through the Rolodex in her brain of her favourite show tunes before settling on 'Anything Goes' to belt out while she washed her hair. By the time she'd finished both the oxygen-denying Sutton Foster version and the slightly more chill Lady Gaga/Tony Bennett one, Eddie had joined her in the bathroom and was trimming his beard.

'You're sounding incredible, babe. Breath work's really paying off.' He leaned in to the slightly fogged mirror.

'Cheers.' Roe towelled her hair. 'You know, with eighty-five bathrooms in this place you could probably find a mirror that's actually usable.'

'They don't all contain a gorgeous, soapy woman! When do you think you need to give Róisín a heads-up about stepping back from choir? I don't know any other club that makes its members schedule baby leave!'

'Well, Róisín takes it very seriously, as you know. But I don't need to do it until we're … ya know … preggers.' She carefully avoided Eddie's eyes, pretending to be engrossed in scrunching mousse into her hair.

'Oh my goodness, Roe! You are more of a beauty every time I see you!' Esther gave her a big cuddle. 'I adore this outfit.' She indicated Roe's white-with-black-polka-dot shirt dress and chunky-heeled Chelsea boots. Her curly hair was piled on top of her head, showing off her massive gold hoops.

'How are you?' Roe smiled, returning to her spot mixing Bellinis on the kitchen island.

'Good, very good. We caught a rousing service in St Ambrose's on the way over, which was a delight. No offence to the rev. in Monkstown, but service is like sex in a marriage – you need a change up or else it can get very stale.'

'Oh, absolutely.' Roe nodded sagely, suppressing a smile.

'And,' Esther dropped to a conspiratorial sotto voce, 'I hear Pat and Maura are coming?'

'Looks like it.'

'That's ... nice?' Esther and Philip were long privy to the attitudes of Roe's parents and were sweetly protective of her.

'You'd think so,' Roe replied just as the door went, signalling her parents' arrival.

'Fauxciutto, Pat?' Eddie proffered the serving platter heaving with hummus varietals, cured vegetables posing as meat and vegan smoked salmon and cheeses.

'I'd rather faux-shooto myself in the face.' Pat chuckled nervily, bravely ignoring the scowl Maura shot over.

'Pat! So crass.' Maura primly slid a piece of pickled carrot that really did taste like smoked salmon into her tight-lipped slot of a mouth. 'Just because you don't agree, don't make fun of other people's lifestyle choices.'

'Oh, not at all.' Esther waved away Maura's admonishment. 'You don't become a vegan and not learn pretty quickly how to take a joke. So, you two, the house is really something.' Esther valiantly strode on through the conversational wasteland that was any event with Pat and Maura. 'I cannot believe all this.' She swept her arms wide to indicate the massive light-filled upstairs sitting room where they were perched with plates on knees. The couches and rugs were all plush and white with pops of clashy orange and aubergine in the throws and pillows. The large, low coffee table was a sheet of smooth amber-coloured onyx resting on slender mid-century legs. 'I love the decor. Is that you, Roe? She's so creative.' She looked to Maura.

Don't waste your breath, Roe felt like saying. She knew the way to crack normal mothers was through complimenting their children, but this was not the case with Maura O'Neill.

'Creative?' Maura's mouth pinched into what Eddie and Roe always called her 'cat's arse'. 'She is, I suppose, though true talent is about how you *apply* your skills and I'm not sure Rose's ever bothered with that.'

Roe could tell from the look on Esther's face that this kind of cutting response about your own child just did not compute.

'Well, Roe's done a fantastic job on the restaurant since Covid. It's no joke keeping a business steady in a global crisis,' Philip cut in.

'Hmmmm.' Maura looked openly doubtful about this assessment. 'I suppose you'll hardly stay on there, Rose, now that ye're all the way out here.' Maura turned to Esther. 'She was always a great one for starting things and never seeing them through. It's amazing that this,' she nodded at Eddie and Roe sitting side by side, 'is still going on. Though still not married after all this time. Lib notions, I suppose.'

Esther looked stricken and, beside Roe, Eddie stiffened. Roe only sighed. 'Never change, Mum.'

'You're so *sensitive*. I didn't mean anything by that.' She smoothed her napkin and clenched the cat's arse even tighter, looking around the room. 'It's just a huge amount of space for two people.'

'Well, we're hoping it won't just be the two of us for long, Maura!' Eddie stood up in a move Roe recognised as his signature power assertion. 'We wanted to show you the house and raise a glass to the future we hope to create here.'

'Does that mean what I think it means?' Esther raised her glass, looking giddy.

'It means we're *trying*.' Eddie smiled broadly, crossing his fingers.

This statement had the effect of abruptly dividing the room. Philip and Esther leapt up and embraced their son, and Pat and Maura stayed frozen in their seats.

It was such a stark representation of the difference between the Kellehers and her parents, Roe thought sadly. Obviously noticing the subdued air emanating from Roe's side of the family, Eddie brightly suggested showing his parents the rest of the house before they sat for the main course. *Fuck's sake*, Roe thought. *Just go right ahead, Eddie, detonate the bomb and stroll off there*. This was Eddie all over – he had an ongoing obsession with seeing her stand up to her parents.

As Eddie and his parents filed out, she heard him say, 'You *have* to see the first-floor bedroom – we're not actually *calling* it the baby's room buuuuut—' The door swung closed behind them and the muted *thunk* of the door catch sliding home echoed in the silence of the room.

Finally Pat, who had barely spoken since their arrival, cleared his throat. 'You didn't go with blinds, Roe?' Pat fitted blinds and was passionate about the 'shading' industry. He stood up and went to the window to examine the angle of the sun. 'I would've sorted ye out, you know. As we get more into summer that sun will be blinding in here. I can still come and put something in?'

In a bland voice, she addressed him. 'The blinds are on the snag list. Our contractor will be back to sort them. They're included with the house.'

'I see. Well, it's a fine house at that. Very big.'

'Hmmm.' Maura was looking around the living room. 'Strange to have a living room upstairs like this. I suppose that's how it's done these days.'

The silence stretched on with neither of them commenting on Eddie's 'trying' announcement. Roe wondered if their problem was just that she and Eddie weren't married? Pat and Maura were religious, but it was hardly unusual to stay together unmarried these days. Whenever Roe felt the morass of her mother's judgement bearing down on her, it was impossible not to date it back to Roe's teens when Maura had found out about Roe's sexuality. They were on holidays in Portugal and Maura had walked in on Roe with a girl who was staying in the resort. Maura had freaked and seventeen-year-old Roe understood then and there what her parents believed was and wasn't acceptable, and this, *she*, was not.

Roe avoided the girl, Emma, for the rest of the holiday. The night before Emma's family was going back to England, she had handed Roe a letter. *I'm not sorry it happened*, the girl had written. *I wish we could have had more time together.* Roe was sorry it had happened. She couldn't help but be. She'd seen the disgust on her mother's face. They had never exchanged a single word about it since and she had kept her relationships completely hidden, until Eddie.

'On a second-storey room like this, I'd suggest going with a very fine sheer curtain,' Pat sat back down on the couch, 'given that you're not overlooked.'

'Right, Dad.'

I should feel sorry for them, Roe mused, trying to be dispassionate. *They don't know their own kids.* Her older brother, Connor's approach was to emigrate and engineer an elaborate fake life of reporting on fictitious dates with women, and Jenny, the youngest, operated on a need-to-know basis with her parents, all too aware that many of the particulars of her life – an abortion at twenty-four, no plans for monogamy or children ever – would never chime with her parents' goals for her. It was sad that Pat and Maura's children had reached such a desperate impasse with their parents' rigid views that they'd given up on having any kind of honest relationship with them.

And it was worse still that Maura and Pat themselves were largely unaware of it. As far as they knew, Roe was the outlier. The impossible one. *The freak, the fuck-up*, as Roe frequently thought of herself in her dark moments. That's what Eddie and Danny could never understand about her relationship with her parents. As much as she raged against their narrow-mindedness, so often the voice in her head parroted their rhetoric. *I am a freak, I am a fuck-up. I don't deserve anything.* They were the people who had raised her, and insidious remnants of their dogmatic opinions resided in her to this day.

Some years ago, Roe had realised that when you are emotionally estranged from your parents, it is near-daily work to go against them. Every day opposing them was a sustained effort, a fight. And it was a strange kind of battle, unseen, without bloodshed as such, but still a conflict that underpinned her life. Like subsidence in the foundations of a house, her well-being, her pursuit of simple things like love and security, all pushed constantly against her parents' rejection and disgust with her.

'What do you think of the baby plan?' She couldn't help it – a little part of her wanted some scrap of approval.

'Why do you bother asking, Rose? You've never done anything the way I wanted you to.' Maura's scathing eyes roamed Roe's body. 'And look at you, Roe. How will you take care of a baby when you clearly can't even take care of yourself.'

'I take care of myself, Mum.' Roe hated how weak her voice sounded. 'Bodies just look different.'

'Hah, that drivel again,' Maura spat. 'I know it's not "popular" to talk about weight these days. But you'll have a harder time conceiving. Though if you ask me, becoming parents without marrying is a recipe for disaster. And I'm sure you'll say "my mother is so backwards, stuck in her ways" but the truth of the situation is this: if you won't commit to a marriage then why do you think you're capable of committing to a baby? You don't have the slightest idea what it takes.' Maura laughed sourly. 'Can you even comprehend all the heartache you put *me* through? Going against me every way you possibly could since you were seventeen years old.'

Shame gushed through Roe, a silent plea in her heart. *Please go. Please go.* She always felt like a child when her mother unleashed like this. The punch of rejection landed fresh every time.

The living-room door burst open and Eddie, obviously having heard the tone if not the exact words, rushed to Roe's side. 'Maura, Roe does nothing but try to—'

'We're leaving, Eddie. I try and try to be accepting of this arrangement. But this baby thing. It's too much.' Maura held her hand up as if the very concept pained her. She pushed her way out of the room and clattered down to the ground floor. Pat followed meekly. Downstairs the front door opened emitting a cheery 'Have a lovely day!' and then they were gone.

Eddie tried to pull Roe close but she fought it. 'I need a minute, Eddie.' Her words came out sharper than she expected. She hurried out to the landing, ducking into the little guest bathroom to dodge Esther and Philip who were peering sympathetically up the stairs from the hall below.

Roe sat on the toilet lid and buried her face in the hand towel. The comedown from dealing with her parents always took as much of a physical toll as it did a mental one. She gripped the towel and pushed it hard into her face to muffle her ragged roar of frustration. The anger, when it was ignited, was like being taken by a wave in a dark sea. When she got like this she could become nihilistic and myopic in a matter of minutes, her entire life narrowed until all she could see was some bleak interior horizon upon which her failures marched, mocking her. Just as it was work to go against her parents every day, it was also work to be happy with herself every day. Or not even happy, just OK with herself. And one encounter with Maura and Pat could demolish that work in just a look and a few choice remarks. Roe doubled over, still chewing the towel, tasting soap on the crisp fibres. At these moments, she didn't know what to do with the rage. She often wondered if any woman did. She wrenched the towel away, satisfied by the thud of pain as it yanked at her teeth.

Don't, Roe. This is not a normal reaction. Stop this, just breathe.

It had been years since she'd hurt herself and she was proud of that. Seeing her parents was always a trigger.

'I'm coming in, Roe.' Eddie opened the door and gathered her to his chest. She relaxed into the familiar ease she always felt in Eddie's arms. Her breathing slowed and that claustrophobic tunnel she'd been lost in just moments earlier widened out. The bleak flavour of her life dissipated and she felt better. Safer.

'I'm so sorry.' He was gazing straight out over her head. 'I really thought it would be better to get the baby thing said. I thought they might even be normal about it.'

She pressed her face into his warmth. 'Let's go down to your folks. The poor things have to parent us both.'

'OK, gang, big news tonight. I know you are all buzzing over the announcement of *Eurovision: Voices of Glory* that I posted on the Insta page. As you know, I hinted at some news that'll even top that and I am finally able to tell you.'

Róisín paced on the stage hung with red-velvet curtains in front of them, eyes shining as the hundred or so choir members held their breath. What was coming? The Life and Soullers had done some cool stuff in their time. They'd sung with Hugh Jackman when he was playing Dublin three years before, but judging by the look on Róisín's face this could potentially be even bigger.

'OK, so first off, obviously as you know, I am musical director of *Voices of Glory*.' She paused for applause before delivering her next revelation. 'And as musical director, I have been in talks with RTÉ who have signed on to produce … are you guys actually ready for this?' Róisín, a born performer, was clearly revelling in eking out every last bit of tension and excitement.

A chant went up from the choir: 'Spill! Spill! Spill!'

'RTÉ are producing a reality show to go with the musical!'

All-out shrieks and gasps swept the assembled choir.

'Oh my fucking gee,' Danny cried.

'That is deadly!' Mags clapped.

'The TV show will be called *Glee Me*.' Róisín was clearly buzzed. 'They'll be following the whole thing from auditions through rehearsals to opening night. The ups and downs and the sweat and tears that it takes to get a huge show like this into production. It is going to be epic.'

Róisín grinned and turned to motion to someone just off stage, apparently hiding in the wings. The next moment, a man with a huge camera hoisted up on his shoulder emerged and the choir burst once more into whoops and applause.

'Everyone, this is Gavin, and he's just one of the crew working on *Glee Me*. Now, anyone who doesn't want to take part in the show or the musical can speak to me separately. Gavin is going to do a little shooting of our rehearsal tonight just to get a few shots – anyone who doesn't want to appear on camera can sit further back.' Róisín turned to Gavin. 'Just include the first three rows – that OK?'

He nodded but absolutely no one made a move to get out of shot. These were musical-theatre people after all.

'So annoying,' Danny muttered. 'Denise is down there front and centre and I'm stuck back here.'

'Relax, there'll be loads of opportunity to whore yourself out to the TV crew.' Roe grinned. The giddiness was catching, though she did feel a pang at once again sitting on the sidelines.

'The support of *Glee Me* is going to be huge for *Eurovision: Voices of Glory*. As we all know, only too bloody well, the pandemic decimated the performing arts. Depending on how things stand in a couple of months' time, we may be performing *Voices of Glory* to a drastically reduced in-person audience. This is where *Glee Me* will help us enormously. TV audiences will be invested in the show. Plus *Voices of Glory* will also be available to stream on the RTÉ Player after the first, hopefully sold-out, run. And there's even scope to bring this show on tour – we're hoping that some of the big Eurovision countries will be interested in staging it. In short, this is big. *Huge!* Way bigger than anything we've attempted before.'

Roe looked at Mags and Danny cheering and clapping beside her and, not for the first time, wished she had their guts.

Look at you, Roe. How will you take care of a baby when you clearly can't even take care of yourself … She was always a great one for starting things and never finishing them …

Maybe it wasn't guts she lacked, but someone that believed in her.

7

'WELCOME TO THE MONTERAY MIXER! I HOPE YOU all have been settling into your new town, and hopefully some of you have had a chance to get acquainted already.' Esme, the Monteray social director, was in her forties, as sleek and shiny as the brand new polished-concrete kitchen of cathedral-like proportions that they all stood in. 'Monteray Valley offers unprecedented luxury living for a long and happy life.'

Lindy shuddered involuntarily at the word 'unprecedented'. It was still too soon for anything to be described as being 'unprecedented'. Even though life had moved on significantly since the early days of lockdowns and uncertainty, Lindy suspected the word 'unprecedented' would always be shudder-inducing for people of a certain age: people like her, the ones with the vulnerable parents and needy young kids, who had just about weathered the lockdowns with sanity and marriages intact. Well. Technically intact, at least. She cringed at the memory of their last attempt at intimacy.

'A "long and happy life" sounds like an obituary,' a statuesque red-haired woman to her right was whispering to someone who looked to be her mother – equally tall, equally red-haired. 'An obituary for my freedom. RIP the sesh life.'

'No one made you marry him,' the mother retorted.

'Yeah, well, I was thinking more *Napa* Valley than *Death* Valley,' the daughter hissed back and they laughed quietly.

My new neighbours. Intriguing.

The 'him' in question didn't appear to be with them. *How did he get out of this sterile little shindig?* Lindy looked around, checking out the rest of the group. It was pretty much all couples, about thirty-five in total. They'd been described as the 'first wave' (another unfortunate call back) of Monteray residents. The initial phase of the development was more or less complete, but over the next months, and then years, more and more enclaves would be added to accommodate the 'mass suburban retreat', as it was described in the Monteray pitch.

'They definitely need a better copywriter,' Lindy'd laughed when Adam had read this to her. 'Middle-class people don't *want* to be reminded that we're on the run from real-world problems. We want to think we care while never having to engage directly. A far more accurate tagline would be 'Monteray Valley: A Shelter from Reality'. He'd laughed. It gave her a pleasant buzz whenever they had a good moment. Which then gave her a pang of sadness. Cataloguing the good 'moments' in her marriage? *Yikes.*

In the expansive open-plan kitchen-cum-dining-cum-living-room, Esme carried on with her Monteray Valley spiel.

'Everything you could possibly need is located here in the

retail block.' A sheet of dazzling blonde hair swung forward as Esme bent to indicate it on the large model displayed on a plinth before her. 'The coffee-bean roasterie. The organic grocer's, the artisanal mustard shop, the butcher's, the chocolatier, the fudgery – we know many of you are coming from a more urban setting and are used to having access to high-end products. We provide that for you here, without you ever having to leave the compound.'

'It's either very convenient or completely sinister,' Lindy muttered to Adam, who was standing beside her feverishly thumbing his phone.

'OK enough from me.' Esme clapped her hands together. 'I encourage you to take a look around the house, get a feel for what's going to be not only your new home, but your new *life* and your new neighbours – I'm here if you've any questions.'

'Adam Zelner?' A toned-to-within-an-inch-of-her-life mum of the yoga-babe variety had strayed in front of them and was trying to contain her excitement.

'Rachel! So good to see you.'

'Oh my God, this is so crazy! Are you living here?' Yoga Mum took a sip of her glass of bubbles.

'Yeah!' Adam had cranked up the trademark 100-watt grin. 'You are too! What are the chances? It's all so exciting, isn't it? The last two weeks have been awesome – a completely new vision for family living. They're paying me to say that! Though I did not know that the view out here in Monteray would be so good.' He winked, to Yoga Mum's practically orgasmic delight.

Lindy observed the exchange and tried to remain impassive. She was always amazed at the effect Adam had on women – it had to be the accent. An Irish man would never have pulled off this display. But somehow the American accent and the American polish and the American *teeth* made it work.

Yoga Mum drained her glass. 'Better refill.' She giggled. 'See you at the organic grocer's, I guess. Sooo good to know someone already.'

'Definitely.' Adam grinned.

'I might see you there too,' Lindy abruptly cut in. 'I'm Lindy, Adam's wife.'

'Oh! My God!' A nervous titter escaped Yoga Mum. 'I didn't see you there ... I'm so sorry.' Her verbal flailing was mildly satisfying given she'd just been conversationally fluffing Adam.

I don't care about the flirting but at least acknowledge I'm standing here! Lindy itched to say.

'Rachel and I met at the Tubecon in London a few months ago,' Adam offered languidly.

'I knew Adam had a wife, of course. I just didn't recognise you. I mean, why would I? Cos you're never on the channel,' she hurriedly added. 'You're so lucky you're not on camera, you don't have to make such an effort. You get the easy bit, following the talent around.' Mercifully, Rachel concluded her small talk fumbling before Lindy's already crappy mood could dip lower. 'Well, nice to meet you too,' Lindy replied in a clipped voice.

'We're having a party soon,' Rachel blurted. 'It's my son Fielding's fifth birthday in a few weeks. Please come! Bring Max! I'll be sending out invites.'

'Great,' Lindy said blandly. Not particularly wanting to be left alone with either Yoga Mum Rachel or her own husband, she decided to exit before the other two beat her to it. 'I'm going to check out the rest of the house, start imagining my life of "unprecedented luxury". She hauled up a smile and plunged decisively into the giddy crowd.

People never put her and Adam together when they were out. Lindy insisted it was due to what she called their 'hotness disparity'. Which Adam thought was a joke. And Lindy did not. 'They think your wife will be some really put-together, forehead-as-smooth-as-a-car-bonnet blonde stunner, and then I appear with week-old hair, face sagged to my tits, tits sagged to my knees and manky leggings.'

Lindy moved through the chic-though-blank, impersonal living space which had strong 'first-class lounge in the airport' vibes. She was careful to keep her gaze adrift, never alighting anywhere lest someone catch her eye and try to engage. Everyone looked nice, she observed. Attractive couples with the kind of style and sheen that a healthy income bestowed.

The kitchen-living-dining area occupied one half of the enormous ground floor. The other was given over to two more rooms and a generous hallway tiled in rose-veined marble and boasting a huge staircase sweeping up to the next storey of five in total. She pulled out the book from her neat little Mulberry shoulder bag to guide her. No PDF brochure for Monteray Valley – the house specs and imagery had come printed on a thick-grade paper bound in a navy cover with the gates to the compound embossed in gold with the words *Monteray – Living but Better* underneath. The rooms on either side of the hall were referred to as the 'cosy adult den' and the 'play and learning zone'.

Lindy leaned in to check out the play and learning zone, which was fully stocked with the kind of tasteful kid gear that Lindy saw on Insta but couldn't imagine using in real life: a tepee in 'oatmeal', a suspended wicker hammock chair, wooden train sets and shelves of tonally cohesive toys and books. Was that a sunken trampoline? *Mad shit.*

Lindy, spotting an opportunity to hide from potential small talk and more of Adam's 'meet the fans' phoniness, eased the door to the hall closed behind her. She crossed the plush carpet – carpet! In a playroom! – and, after first assessing that the bolt in the ceiling could take her weight, climbed carefully into the hammock chair. The front windows, occupying nearly one entire wall, looked out onto the two-car driveway and the five other identical houses on the curve of crescent A. In their own version of this house, they would be giving much more storage to toys than this 'zone' afforded.

Toys were the tools of their trade. When they'd first looked at the slender navy lines that demarcated their future home on the plans for Monteray Valley, they'd been able to make certain stipulations on the design for theirs, and Adam had opted to put a second structure in the back garden to warehouse the enormous quantities of toys involved in Maxxed Out and accommodate a fully functioning sound stage. Incredibly, this still left room for the above-ground heated swimming pool with retractable cover.

The top floor would also be given over to the Maxxed Out empire. The builder had created further studio space up there for filming the endless YouTube videos and TikToks – though they still hadn't completed the soundproofing of a studio and sound-engineering booth for Maxxed Out's planned expansion into audio. Another thing for the snag list she was compiling for the builder. He still hadn't replied to any of her texts – very unMonteray. Lindy's office was on the fourth floor, as well as a shared office space for Jamie, the managing director, and whatever unfortunate digital-marketing graduates were working with him at any given time.

What to do with the play and learning zone? *Maybe I could put a reformer machine here?* From the look of the crowd out there, the female population of Monteray were in very good nick. Keeping up with that would be a full-time job on top of her full-time job.

The windows were off-putting, though. It'd essentially be an exercise-terrarium, placing her thirty-six-year-old bod on display for the neighbours. Plus, incredibly, it was almost too big for just a home workout studio. The houses were American rich-person reality-TV proportions each set on large grounds with pergolas, water features and neat landscaping. Some of the top-tier ones had elaborate grottos.

I could quit my job, finish my psychology training, get some curtains and set up a therapy room in here. Letting some other poor dope deal with Maxxed Out was a fantasy she often played out in her head. No more working like a dog on strategy and merchandise or budgets and legal issues. Or being the buzz-wrecker when their plans and ideas didn't match the Maxxed Out ethos or bank balance. The business of fun was surprisingly unfun when you got down to the brass tacks.

And then when it's time to go on Ellen *or* The Tonight Show *or even just the annual* Late Late Show *appearance, Adam and Max get to play the father–son besties while I sit in the audience playing up to my bullshit role as the long-suffering, eye-rolling 'mammy'.*

And that's if she got to go at all. For the *Ellen* gig, they'd gone without her – the show would only foot Adam and Max's travel.

Still, cutting out felt impossible – she had to be involved for Max's sake. It was a pipe dream. Speaking of dreams, a strange atmosphere not unlike a TV dream sequence appeared to have settled in the room. The colourful decals on the walls seemed ever so slightly obscured. Was it smoke? She sat up abruptly, ignoring the creak of the hammock's fixtures. An odd haze was drifting from the tepee and, now that Lindy was paying attention, there was definitely a funny smell. Was it ... apples? Yes, fragrant apples.

Then the tepee quivered slightly.

Lindy was unnerved. 'Hello?'

A long silence and finally a reluctant 'hi' emitted from the tepee.

When there was nothing further, Lindy leaned out of the chair to peer at the tepee. 'Are you ... OK?'

Finally, a short woman with messy pastel-dyed pink hair crawled out. The vape clamped in the woman's teeth as she pulled herself up was obviously the source of the smoke. 'I'm OK, sorry.' A little flush of embarrassment was blooming in her cheeks. She was very pretty and definitely not in the mould of the other Monteray Valley women.

'You're probably not meant to vape in here,' Lindy said just as the Blushing Vaper said, 'You're probably not meant to sit in that.'

They both laughed. 'Uh-oh, one day in and we're already like the Stasi here!' Lindy grinned and started to struggle out of the suspended chair, which immediately gave way, ditching her abruptly on the floor in a shower of ceiling plaster.

'Oh fuck! My arse!' Lindy was winded.

'Shhhh, someone will hear.' The Vaper looked around nervously just as the door from the hall burst open.

'Was that from in here?' The redhead Lindy had overheard earlier burst in. 'It sounded like a stampede.'

'It's nothing, shhh! Close the door!' Lindy gingerly eased herself up to standing. 'Shite,' she muttered, surveying the mess. A good chunk of the ceiling had come down with the chair. 'Was that very loud?' she quizzed the redhead.

'Hell, yes. I'd say your one Esme is on her way as we speak. You probably shouldn't have been sitting in it. It must have been – whatyamacallit? – ornamental.'

'C'mon.' Lindy strode to the large window overlooking the front lawn and pushed it open. 'Let's go out this way and we can pop back in round the side. I'm not getting into a whole rigamarole about breaking the fucking ceiling.'

The other two looked doubtful and Lindy steamrolled on in her most commanding voice. 'Look, I don't want everyone talking about how Lindy in crescent C broke a chair just weeks into Monteray. I'm Lindy, by the way, crescent C.'

'I'm Roe,' offered the Vaper as she kept glancing at the door.

'I'm Ailbhe,' said the redhead. 'I don't get what the problem is. You broke a kid's chair – there's no shame in a fully grown woman not fitting in a child's swing chair. What's the big deal?'

Lindy could hear voices outside the door. 'OK, you deal with it then, Ailbhe. C'mon, Roe.' Lindy winked and nipped straight out the window.

'What the f—!' Ailbhe exclaimed as Roe scurried through the window behind Lindy. Lindy leaned back and slid the window back in place just as Esme and a couple of the wait staff walked into the room.

Through the glass, Lindy could see Esme staring at Ailbhe, stunned as she waved the residual vape fog from the air and took in the chunks of plaster everywhere.

'Just walk.' Lindy nudged Roe forcefully. 'Act like we're as shocked as anyone.' Lindy pretended to gape in the window at the scene before moving towards the side passage, shunting Roe along beside her. Once they were out of sight, Lindy burst out laughing. 'Oh my God! I'm sorry – that was so random. I didn't mean to drag you into it but we had to act fast and that Ailbhe one was asking too many questions.'

'But,' Roe looked doubtful, 'will she get in trouble?'

'Of course not, she's just shelled out 1.5 mill for one of their gaffs. It's not school – no one's getting in trouble. I just didn't want to be forever known in Monteray Valley as the fat bitch who broke the ceiling.'

Lindy spotted Roe wince at the 'fat bitch' comment and felt awkward. It'd just slipped out. Lindy realised how stupid and shallow she must sound.

'I'm sorry, I realise that "people will call me fat" is the most pathetic rationale for running out on breaking a chair and letting a complete stranger take the rap.'

'It is,' Roe agreed. 'Though it's also how most people think.' She shrugged in a way that made Lindy feel like she'd just completely plummeted in this woman's estimation. Great.

Casting around for a subject-switch, Lindy remembered the erstwhile builder. 'So how're you finding the house? Do you have anything on your snag list for the builder? I've been trying to pin him down on when he'll get back to sort some of our things.'

'Oh yeah, we have to get on that.' Roe sounded weary. 'Some of the finishes were a bit iffy, weren't they? Can't say a word against Monteray in front of Eddie, my partner, though.' She rolled her eyes.

'Oh?' Lindy snapped to attention. Any hint of spousal ambivalence was like her oxygen. Or maybe it was more like a tasty little Valium, as it calmed the anxiety that was unleashed whenever she thought about her own marriage. Unfortunately, just as she was about to gently but determinedly interrogate further, the words 'You absolute psychos!' rang out behind them and startled them both. It was Ailbhe, their fall woman, rushing towards them.

Oh crap. Lindy mentally speed-scrolled through about six different excuses for her odd behaviour – from 'I recently changed my meds' to 'I have IBS' – before she realised Ailbhe was actually laughing.

'That was pure batshit!' She gasped as she reached them. 'Yer one was so pissed off! She had to pretend it was all grand, of course, but you could tell she was fuming. I said "I barely tipped it!" just as another chunk of ceiling fell right on her – I was dead. Dead! Her hair was wrecked, dust everywhere. She was so snotty, but when she copped who I was she had to fake nice.'

'Why? Who are you?' asked Lindy, delighted Ailbhe was taking their treachery so well.

'Oh, I'm no one, like, but my husband is one of the original Monteray investors, Tom Russell.'

'Ahh.' *Interesting*, Lindy thought. Tom Russell was a tech megastar. They'd run ads for his wildly popular apps on Maxxed Out. The Optimise schtick was all geared towards self-betterment – a bit like couch to 5K for positive habit forming. The Monteray Valley 'Living but Better' thing was very much the Tom Russell MO. So this was the wife: they'd heard some mutterings about a marriage – and a speed-marriage at that – but nothing concrete. *She's gorgeous. As to be expected of a rich man's wife*, she thought cattily. Being around the shiny population of Monteray was proving hard on her self-esteem. Ailbhe had a touch of the Jessica

Chastains about her. If Jessica Chastain had a proper Dublin accent. She was dressed in loose cashmere joggers and a cashmere hoodie, looking exactly like an off-duty celeb doing the Starbucks run in New York.

'We're not really going to be living here long,' Ailbhe continued. 'Tom says it's more of an investment property. My mam is staying with me at the moment to help with the baby cos Tom is so back and forth with his work here. He's actually only met our baby once in person, LOL. Anyway, Mam'll go back to Crumlin when me and Tom move over to the *real* valley. Tom wants to go back to California – I cannot wait! Just eight weeks! No more Irish weather. Obviously, there'll be Americans, but we'll cross that bridge when we come to it.'

Lindy thought of her American in-laws and her husband and son with their mid-Atlantic YouTube accents. 'They're not all bad,' Lindy allowed. 'My husband's American. And the in-laws will love you. Red hair, Irish, a "lovely cawwwleeen",' Lindy adopted the voice of Selma, her own mother-in-law.

'Oh no, the Russells despise me. I haven't even met them but they definitely had *opinions* on Tom and me getting married. I think they're –' Ailbhe leaned in and Roe and Lindy automatically did the same '– Christians,' Ailbhe whispered meaningfully with her eyes wide. 'Let's just say these houses,' she jerked her head at the red-brick exterior, 'have been a thing longer than Tom and I have been a thing. And obviously Tilly – that's our baby – is a bit of a reminder of our sinful shenanigans. We'd only been together a few months when I got pregnant!'

'No way!' Lindy laughed. 'That's exactly how I ended up with my American too! Though my in-laws are very sweet.'

'You're so lucky. Mine think I'm a dirty bitch. Out for his sperm – I'm ten years older! The irony is I wanted no part of the sperm – no baby for me, thanks – but then one landed in my lap. So when they're not hinting that I baby-daddied him on purpose, they're playing the money card. He's loaded,' she finished with a shrug.

'Wow,' Roe breathed. 'That's … a lot. Of information, I mean.'

'Well,' Ailbhe shrugged, 'we're gonna be Monteray Valley inmates together – may as well get to know each other. Though I've gotta say I'm glad my incarceration isn't a life sentence. So how're ye all getting on here? The gaffs are beyond!'

'Yeah,' Roe agreed.

Lindy nodded. 'We were actually just talking about the snag-list stuff for the builder.'

'Oh!' Ailbhe perked up. 'I need to get ours sorted too before we hit the road. Cannot *wait* to get going. Not that there's anything wrong with Monteray,' she added. 'But, like, it's a bit …'

'Soulless?' Lindy murmured.

'Contrived?' Roe said. 'It's like Disneyland for middle-class families.'

'Where in Cali will you be?' Lindy needed to steer away from the Monteray moaning. She had to make the effort to stay on whatever message Maxxed Out was contractually tied to at any given time.

'Morgan Hill, it's basically the Howth of Silicon Valley. I cannot wait! It is so swanky – Michelin-starred restaurants, man-made lakes, wineries.' She beamed around. 'Everything this place's trying to be.'

Ouch, Lindy thought.

'Sorry, that came out wrong. I'm just dying to get going. I'm sort of in between stuff cos Tom's over there and I'm here with my baby and my mother. Feels a bit like purgatory,' Ailbhe groaned. 'Ugh. Sorry, I hardly talk to humans I don't share genetic material with any more.'

Lindy grinned at this attempt at an explanation. 'Why don't we set up a WhatsApp for the snag list?' She was warming to these two. She needed allies out here and they seemed comfortingly real. 'We could pool our grievances! He can't ignore all of us.'

'Yes! Come to mine next weekend.' Ailbhe beamed. 'I'll get my mam to take Tilly out and we can booze and bitch about the incredibly tiny, superficial things that are wrong with our mansions!'

Later that night, Adam was in their en suite deep into his pre-bed skincare routine – there were crystals and somehow saging involved – while Lindy undressed in her enormous dressing room. Having a dressing room for her vast collection of mum-casuals was definitely overkill, but she could hardly call it her 'hiding from my fucking life' room.

Along one wall hung every shade of striped tee in creation, underneath which hung her collection of grey and navy jeans. It gave the impression that an entire army of listless Lindys were hanging there, waiting to be dragged out and forced into action. A smaller section of the next wall was home to six gowns that she trotted out for the rare YouTube events and awards she agreed to attend with Adam and Max. She'd once read a comment on the internet saying she dressed like a 'noughties nightmare'. *Gotta love being vaguely known online*, she'd thought gloomily at the time. A rack of boots filled more open shelving, while the entire third wall was taken up by floor-to-ceiling wardrobes, with smooth mirrored doors – all of which were empty. Caring about clothes seemed to have leaked away as she got deeper into her thirties. Was it a cry for help as Finn had slagged?

She thought back to the women at the mixer and took in her reflection. She had good points. She had lovely dark hair, wide-set grey eyes, and Adam had always loved her freckles – he used to trace them across her cheekbones and marvel at the fact that they even scattered across her eyelids. But it was hard to ignore how perfect everyone else in Monteray looked. To Botox or not to Botox? She was grand still, but a bit of filler would get her in mint condition. Ish. She strolled back into the bedroom and peeled off her dressing-gown, draping it over the sofa by the window that looked out on Monteray's own ornamental lake.

'I can't believe this,' Adam muttered out the side of his mouth – she'd been filling him in on the accidental show-home trashing of earlier. 'Seriously, that's really embarrassing, Lindy! Thank fuck Tom Russell's wife was cool about it.'

'Relax, would you?'

Lindy dragged all the completely functionless throw pillows off the bed and hopped in. She pulled up her book on the Kindle to shut out his admonishments. Time was they would've laughed about something like that.

Of course the Kindle brought no escape from the bleak thought given she was reading *Mating in Captivity* – a self-help title she'd vowed to finish months ago. She glanced back over at Adam through the open door of the en suite; he now had a glowing Hannibal Lecter-style LED mask on his face. Should she try and instigate something? She sensed Esther Perel would have something to say about *their* mating. Or lack of. Adam removed the mask and picked up his phone from beside the sink – never more than two inches from his hand.

'I'm gonna hit my man-den for a while – I'm on level 34 on *WarWorld* so things are really heating up.'

'Great,' she replied vaguely and watched him pad out of the room scrolling on his phone.

Lindy picked up her own out of habit. The newly formed Snag List WhatsApp was already hopping. The girls were detailing their house woes.

ROE: Eddie and I will be paying our monster mortgage for the next 70 years, meanwhile the gaff's already falling apart! I just blinked too hard and a piece of skirting board fell off the wall.

AILBHE: Tom and I just sexted too hard and a shelf fell down.

ROE: Ailbhe! We have known each other for less than five hours!!!

AILBHE: Well, brace yourselves, this is me at my most reserved. Will we do lunch tomorrow week then? Some medicinal Sunday boozing is always good to round out a weekend?

After they agreed to meet at Ailbhe's at 2 p.m. the following Sunday, Lindy put the phone on night mode and turned off the light. Ailbhe was mating with her husband even though he was thousands of miles away; meanwhile Lindy's husband was downstairs and she hadn't been able to face trying again since their last aborted attempt …

She threw back the blankets. She had to do something. 'Nothing changes if nothing changes' had been a mantra of one of the therapists in Heart Mind Solutions.

She padded down the stairs, her footsteps silent on the silvery grey carpet, and quietly opened the door to Adam's den.

The scene before her unfolded in a series of baffling realisations. Her husband was hunched on the couch with his VR helmet on his head. The room hung with darkness, the only light coming from the flatscreen TV opposite, casting her husband in a vaguely blue glow. More baffling still, Adam was pulling ferociously at his crotch. As her eyes adjusted, she gasped as she realised he was yanking mercilessly on his own penis. *Oh my God*. She started to back away. There was no need to let him know she'd seen. What the fuck was he looking at inside the helmet?

Well, porn, obviously.

Lindy felt conflicted about porn. It was hard to know where to stand on the matter. She knew you could get ethical porn the way you could get Fairtrade coffee, but Adam probably just stuck 'threesome' into the PornHub search bar. The muffled sound of Adam speaking inside the helmet jolted her. For a split second, she thought he'd noticed her, but then a deeply unpleasant realisation hit her: he was talking to the porn.

'I love it when you shake your tits.'

Lindy strained to hear. More muffled words at a lower volume. Was that a response? What the hell was going on? Knowing he'd no clue that she was there, she moved further into the room and spied his phone on the coffee table. He was casting a video call into the helmet – he'd mentioned trialling a new VR technology they'd be advertising on the channel soon. This was probably not what they'd meant by 'trialling'. She peered carefully closer, unsure if the video on the phone was going both ways. On screen, an impressive pair of breasts were jigging up and down. Lindy felt sick. It was one thing to know that they weren't having much sex – *No sex: Lindy, stop lying to yourself* – but it was quite another to be confronted with the object of her husband's desire. He was still vigorously masturbating beside her when the owner of the undulating tits leaned down into shot. Lindy's chest seized at the sight of the fawning woman from earlier – Rachel – pouting into the camera.

'Uh, show … me … those … uh … tits agaaain. Oh God!' came from inside the helmet.

Lindy turned and fled before she could be confronted with any more unbearable truths about the state of her marriage.

8

AILBHE FUSSED AROUND TILLY'S PRAM, CHECKING the various gadgetry involved in transporting her tiny daughter anywhere. Sun visor, defrosting breastmilk in a bottle, white noise machine, the weirdo baby vibrator that buzzed Tilly to sleep for every nap. Check, check, check.

'You sure you don't mind, Mam?'

Eileen appeared in her finest Lycras. 'Not at all, pet. I've got my podcast. Dying to catch up with the boyos.' She was devoted to *I'm Grand, Mam* – a podcast by two young Irish guys living in London. 'You get all your bits done with the gals and have a few drinks – you deserve it.'

'I do.' She grinned, pecked her mum on the cheek and blew a raspberry at Tilly. 'No bullshit for Granny, Matilda, we need her continued support,' she warned.

Ailbhe waved them off and then flung the door shut behind them. *Freedom. Yesssss.* Who'd have ever thought she'd be so excited to just be alone? Not even going out on the tear but just sitting in her gaff with two near-strangers for some bureaucratic builders chat and a few wines. Lindy and Roe had just better be up for it.

Although who even cares if they aren't? I'm having nineteen wines and they can just deal. Ailbhe spun out of the hall and back towards the kitchen, which they'd still barely unpacked. Neither Eileen nor Ailbhe cooked and the Monteray Valley meal service – 'meals on wheels for spoiled yuppies' as Eilers declared it – had kept them in good grub.

'Alexa, what time is it?'

'It's 1.45 p.m. Calendar event "piss up with the Snag List" is scheduled for approximately 15 minutes' time.'

'Cheers, hun.'

Ailbhe pulled out the wasabi nuts and fancy crisps she'd ordered for their drinks and balanced a stack of serving bowls carefully under her chin. She made her way out to the front sitting room, identical in position and proportions to the room she'd met Roe and Lindy in a week earlier. Of course, in her version there were no artful displays of eco-sympathetic toys – that was still all ahead of her. Though Tom, possibly still not getting that Tilly couldn't even roll over, had had a shedload of OTT toys and paraphernalia delivered the week before – it was all stashed in the attic for now.

'It is totally nonsensical,' Ailbhe had said laughing to her mother as she heaved a veritable menagerie of stuffed animals up the stairs. 'We're leaving in a few weeks. She's not going to need a ball pit between now and then. And the next time we're back here, who knows what age she'll be.'

'Don't remind me!' Ailbhe's mother had wailed.

'Mam, don't worry – you'll be over to us non-stop.' It was going to be hard without her mother. They had always been so united – a by-product of having to weather Eamon's chaotic ways together. They weren't quite in the nauseating 'people think we're sisters' category, but they had a shared appreciation for the Art of Slagging and Eilers could bitch for Ireland when she got going.

'Maybe it's because Tom feels guilty about missing most of her first two months?' Eilers had suggested as they stashed it all on the top floor of the house. Tom, despite his unbelievably demanding schedule, was devoted to video calling her. It was very endearing. He set an alarm no matter what time zone he was in to wish his daughter good morning. Weird though it may have seemed to outsiders, they'd relaxed into their little routine: she'd prop him up somewhere he could see the baby and drift off to do her make-up while he chatted away to the barely sentient Tilly.

Instead of a playroom, Ailbhe and Eilers had made this front room a luxe retreat. A pale-grey L-shaped couch dominated, with a couple of outsized beanbags that had cost an arm and a leg completing the space. Tom hadn't even blinked when she'd detailed some of the spend on the house. And if he didn't care, Ailbhe wouldn't lose sleep – though it was a big adjustment going from keeping a fairly tight reign on her money to buying a couch for high five figures.

She arranged the snacks on the low glass and steel coffee table that rested on the fur rug, then she flopped onto the beanbag by the window to order a drink from Rounds All Round, the mobile bar that served all of Monteray Valley. The bell went just minutes later – Rounds All Round was extremely efficient – and Ailbhe rose to accept three Proseccos, each topped with a plump raspberry from a cheery barman whose name was Paul.

'We'll probably switch to cocktails when the gals get here. Will you come to the window on the next round?' She blew him a kiss as he retreated to the funny little converted bar-a-van that all the Rounds All Round guys drove around the estate, pulling pints and cocktails from the boot for the Monteray Valley residents.

She returned to the beanbag to watch for Lindy and Roe. It was weird to have drinks delivered when you could just open a bottle in your own kitchen. Still, half the point of Monteray Valley was this kind of full-service max-convenience life. It was a bit like living in a Club Med permanently. No one used cash in any of the shops or restaurants: everyone used either their phone or a chic bracelet (available in gold or silver) with a chip in it to pay for stuff.

A tentative knock on the window alerted her to Lindy's arrival. Ailbhe extended her left leg and stretched her foot to nudge the window open without getting up. 'I want to be polite but I'm just too shagged to get up and open the front door right now.' Ailbhe sensed Lindy would be game. After all, she was a great woman for a window exit – surely she wasn't above making an entrance via one.

'Haha, I remember that feeling.' Lindy hopped neatly through. 'Don't move a bloody muscle on my account, honestly. You're so good to have us over. The second you want us gone, just say – you can't be polite when you're running on newborn levels of sleep.'

'Oh, don't worry, I'm tired but I'm also gagging for a bit of socialising. I wish we could go out out but I guess we're old marrieds now.'

Lindy was clearly about to protest when the bell went. Ailbhe sighed and was about to haul herself up but Lindy just leaned back out the window and beckoned Roe in.

'I'm getting reverse déjà vu.' Roe hopped through looking like a teenage renegade sneaking in after an illicit night out.

''Course she couldn't look further from an auld one.' Ailbhe proffered Proseccos. 'What age are you, Roe? I was just saying how much I wish we could fuck off on the absolute sesh right now but we're too old.'

'I'm a baby, just thirty-one. But no sesh would age discriminate. I'd say our biggest problem is the fact that we're at least thirty miles from the nearest sesh.'

'Mmm, true.' Lindy nodded. 'And I definitely feel too old.'

'Not to worry.' Ailbhe raised her empty glass. 'The sesh comes to the door in Monteray Valley and I'm on the baby 'n' boozin' schedule. Lindy, you're familiar, I'm sure? It's where you day drink so you can be moderately drunk for the afternoon, hung-over by tea time and sober in time for passing out on the bed later. I've been perfecting it for the last couple of weeks and I think I've nailed it. Will we switch to something fancy? Paul does a lovely thing called a Monteray Fizz? Good to support local.' She keyed the order into the app without waiting for a response from the other two. 'Sorry I sound like a thirsty bitch, but a newborn'll do that to ya.'

'No resistance from me.' Lindy cheersed from her spot on the couch. 'Hate to be the bearer of bad news but my tween is still doing it to me. He can be moody one minute and then my sweet baby again. Very hectic.'

'Well,' Roe sighed. 'Our kid hasn't even been conceived yet and it's being a buzz-wrecker.'

'Oh? How so?' Ailbhe had been curious to note that Roe and Eddie had moved into Monteray Valley where there wasn't a child-free couple in at least a five-mile radius.

'Oh, ignore me. It's too much to even get into.' Roe shook her head.

Lindy sat up straighter. 'Let's get this snag-list stuff boxed off and then we can talk properly – how does that sound?'

'It sounds efficient, like my husband.' Ailbhe grinned as Paul appeared at the window behind Roe's spot on the other beanbag. 'That's not him, by the way.'

Ailbhe indicated, causing Roe to turn and bolt upright in surprise. 'Jesus!'

'Three Monteray Fizzes!' He beamed, passing the glasses through the window.

Bemused, Roe distributed the cocktails and pushed the window closed as Paul trotted off once more.

'Anyone else feel like the new normal is way weirder than the old normal?' Lindy offered, sipping at the pinky-orange drink.

'Yup.' Ailbhe angled the straw so she didn't have to sit up on the beanbag. 'Right, house snags. Just about nine hundred to go through.'

Ailbhe ordered more drinks after they'd finished the document and sent it to the builder. They then settled into more general life chat.

'Wouldn't it be amazing if someone could snag list your life? Imagine it,' Lindy said idly. 'Think of *that* list: Grouting in upstairs en suite; skirting in hallway; guy you didn't bang in Ibiza in 2007 … You'd get to do all the unfinished things, the niggles and half-baked things that never worked out. What would you guys get fixed in your lives if you could just farm it out to someone else? I really wish I'd finished my degree. I did three years then took a year off to travel. Got pregnant and never went back.'

'Did you go weird after having Max?' Ailbhe asked Lindy beseechingly. She'd been trying to figure out for weeks if constantly swinging from anxiety to euphoria was normal post-baby stuff or particular to her situation of nursing both a baby and a major betrayal at the same time. 'I just feel so fucking crazy.'

'Yeah.' Lindy sighed. 'You feel kind of wobbly in your head for the first year at least.'

'That's it – I feel so all over the place. And it's disorientating. I look in the mirror and I don't even recognise this person. My tits are in bits, ya know? Not even sore exactly. But they're like *long*.' Ailbhe gazed at her breasts dolefully.

'Oh yeah, mine are just so sad.' Lindy grinned. 'They were never big before or anything, but now they look like they've survived some atrocity. I have to practically roll them up to put them in the bra.'

'Yeah, *yeah*.' Ailbhe pointed emphatically at Lindy. 'That's it. I swear to fuck I stowed one in my armpit a few weeks ago when our hot moving guy walked in on me breastfeeding. It was so sad. I used to be hot. I was hot last year. I know it sounds shallow but it's so hard to accept that your hotness is over.'

'You're still hot,' Roe offered magnanimously. 'I mean, right now you're kinda drunk but—'

'You wouldn't say that if you saw the spatchcock chickens I have instead of tits,' Ailbhe lamented. 'I'm sorry, ignore me. I'm just still finding my feet with all this being a wife and a mother. You two are married – is it normal after you get married to be thinking about all the sex you're not having?' Ailbhe hoped she didn't sound too desperate. Or tipsy.

'Ehh, not really.' Lindy looked oddly embarrassed, which made Ailbhe think Lindy knew exactly what she was talking about.

'I'll probably get past it once me and Tom are on the same continent again.'

'How does that all work?' Roe ventured.

'We have a virtual thingy. It's totally weird, to be honest. He had his personal assistant do up a schedule. Keeps the passion ... I dunno ... consistent?'

'At least it's still a mutual activity. Give it ten years.' Lindy downed the last of her drink. 'We're basically in separate rooms on separate devices and we've never been happier.' The smile she mustered had no warmth and Ailbhe wondered what might be lurking in the Zelners' marriage beyond the happy-clappy YouTube facade.

'I do love a device.' Roe, tiddly and oblivious, was cradling her Monteray Fizz. 'No emotional demands. Not like a broody husband. This stuff is lethal, by the way!' She grinned, fumbling with her vape and lolling on the beanbag opposite.

'Our whole relationship – no, our whole family,' Lindy carried on, 'has this corporate structure. It's hard to have sex with Adam when all I can think of is how his first appointment in the morning is playing Zombie Nerf Rescue Mission with Max for the premium channel members.'

'I don't even know what that collection of words might mean.' Ailbhe was horrified. It all sounded so ick. How could Lindy find this child-man fiddling with his toys sexy? She and Eilers had watched some Maxxed Out clips after they'd realised their neighbours were YouTube royalty. It was extremely wholesome stuff. Lots of peppy urging to 'hit that subscribe button' and 'don't forget to like and comment below if you want to see more of Max and Dad's adventures!' Adam was a good-looking guy, but his preppy 'shirt tucked into shorts' aesthetic made him look like a virginal missionary type, though he was sexier in person – a man built for baldness.

'I *wish* I didn't know what that collection of words meant.' Lindy shook her head, turning to Roe. 'What about you and Eddie?'

'Are you asking if we still do it?' Roe blushed. 'We, eh, do. Though now there's a bit of an agenda. It's baby time, at least according to Eddie.'

'Oh! Amazing,' Ailbhe exclaimed and then, realising she didn't sound that enthusiastic, added another 'amazing' for emphasis. It was hard to fake it for Roe. *The poor bitch*, Ailbhe thought. She absolutely loved her baby, but at times of nihilistic exhaustion, she actually felt a stab of sympathy when she saw a pregnant woman lumbering around looking peaceful with no idea what was coming.

'Look,' Ailbhe cut in. 'If we're having the inspermination chat, I insist we get another round.' Ailbhe checked the time. Nearly 6 p.m. Tilly's bedtime was soon and Eilers had already put in a good few hours. Ailbhe desperately wanted to prolong this little shindig – she was feeling more like herself than she had in ages.

'Oh go on.' Lindy grinned. 'One more drink! Tell us more about the baby plans, Roe.'

'Well, it's really … exciting?'

'You just said "exciting" like someone planning a colonoscopy.' Ailbhe cocked her head at Roe, who laughed weakly then straightened up as if she was bracing herself.

'Well, OK.' Roe took a deep breath. 'It's completely terrifying. Every time Eddie brings it up, I get a tight feeling in my chest and can't take a full breath. I can't believe I'm saying this to complete strangers except sometimes it's easier to admit these things to complete strangers than the people closest, ya know? I guess what I'm saying is I'm not even pregnant yet and it's already making me feel like shit.'

'Maybe you should listen to your body on this.' Paul had appeared at the window with Ailbhe's last order. 'My therapist always asks how something is making me feel in my *body*.' His eyes widened to emphasise the word.

''K, thanks for the input, Paul!' Ailbhe pulled the drinks in through the window and quickly closed it over on him to signal the end of his contribution. 'If I'd planned Tilly, I'd say I'd have been exactly the same. It's almost luckier to have it landed on you out of the blue. Kind of takes the horror of the decision-making away from you. If I'd had to figure out if I was ready ... there's just no way I'd ever have felt ready. To bring a new life into the world? No fuckin' way!'

'Yeah, thanks.' Roe nodded, looking more spooked than ever, and Ailbhe scrounged around to come up with something a little more reassuring. Nothing was forthcoming.

'That's what I can't get my head around,' Roe continued. 'How do you know that you're not going to just completely mess up this poor person's life? And what about your own life? How do you know that you're done, you know ... trying to live?'

'Ha,' Lindy barked.

'Sorry, that sounded worse than I meant it.' Roe was back-pedalling furiously. 'I'm not saying that your lives are over. I just mean, when do you know that you've, ya know, done all the things you wanted to get done? How d'you know you've made the right decisions?'

Roe's words hung in the air, sending a spike of anxiety through Ailbhe. She felt the booze haze, so pleasant just minutes before, now settling heavier around her.

How'd you know you've made the right decisions?

The decision is made, Ailbhe. And it was the right one. Seb would not have been a good father. My future is with Tom. Stop thinking there's anything unfinished. When I leave Dublin, this stress will fuck off. In the meantime, a little medicating the guilt with booze isn't hurting anyone.

Out loud, she forced herself to sound more sure of herself. 'I've probably ticked off a lot of the things,' she offered. 'Started my own business. Travelled a good bit – the beauty business is class for that. I went on location to amazing places when I was doing movies. And after we set up Beautify, we went to trade shows everywhere.'

'Our lives aren't over.' Lindy sipped pensively. 'But you do kind of get the feeling of possibilities being out of reach after kids. I always thought I'd have my own business. When we got back to Dublin and I was working in the therapy centre, I did have an idea for a matchmaking app – your family did the swiping and matching with the help of a qualified psychologist. Anyway, when Maxxed Out took off, I felt like I had to pick Maxxed Out. So I did. I didn't want to be left out of Adam and Max's thing.' She shrugged and Ailbhe detected a strange bitterness in the way she said 'Adam', though maybe bitterness was just a natural accompaniment to working with your husband. 'Anyway,' Lindy carried on, 'Snag listing your life would be an amazing business. Everyone has regrets! What's your regret, Roe? What's the thing you're afraid of not getting to do if you have this baby?'

Roe gazed down at her lap, a little crimson flush burnishing her high cheekbones. 'I've never really put myself out there with anything so I probably haven't taken enough risks to even *have* unfinished business.'

Ailbhe was starting to feel protective towards her – she seemed so unsure of herself. 'What about the restaurant? You're the manager, right? Would you ever want to have your own place?'

'God, no, it's such a difficult industry even before all the Covid crap. I think the problem is I've never wanted anything for myself. I think when I was younger I was always trying to do the things that I knew my parents would be happy with. As futile as *that* was. And then after I met Eddie, I was working but his career has always been the bigger thing.'

'Would you go back and study?' Lindy asked.

'That's boring,' Ailbhe interjected. 'This is a hypothetical conversation. What is the thing you would do if the laws of time and physics and logic and, most importantly, *consequences* did not apply?'

Roe laughed. 'I don't know!'

'Of course you do.' Lindy was catching Ailbhe's enthusiasm. 'What's the thing you think about doing when you're in the shower daydreaming?'

'Probably sing professionally.' Roe was barely audible as she said this. 'I'm in a choir but obviously it's not the same.'

'Oooh, are you any good?' Lindy leaned forward. 'I was an alto in school.'

'I'm not bad.' Roe shrugged. 'I'm grand, but if we were doing your idea, Lindy, the life snags – that'd be mine. I really wanted to try out for things like the musical in school but I never had the confidence. And I know it's not like a baby is the only thing between me and my "life on the stage"'. She put on a booming voice. 'There are plenty more things working against me!' She grinned. 'But I suppose a baby would definitely be the end of the potential for that.'

'It abso-fucking-lutely would.' Ailbhe nodded solemnly.

9

'FIELDING IS 5!!!' BRAYED THE BANNER HANGING over the door of number 3, crescent F. Lindy felt drained just looking at it.

You knew it was going to be a long drag of a party when even just the invite was exhausting. It had been a video of Fielding holding a clapper that said 'birthday boy' in the middle of the immaculate garden in a crisp white shirt and little suit pants. 'Pwease come to my mama and daddy's house for my fifth burday pardee on Saturday ...' The end credits and cutesy blooper reel with 'mama' Rachel looking ludicrously dolled up while clowning around were truly unforgivable. The verdict in the Snag List WhatsApp had been damning.

> **LINDY: I realise my son is all over the internet but it's the laboured performance I find so offensive about this. At least we've never scripted the Maxxed Out channel – well, not that much. Apart from Adam's cringe catchphrases. And, OK, some of the more complex 'adventure video' narratives. But this poor child is being coached for a 30 second video.**

AILBHE: Horrific.

ROE: Outrageous that straights can subject their kids to this kind of shite while gay families are put through the wringer to have their kids.

And Ailbhe and Roe didn't even know the extent of Rachel's crap. Lindy hadn't told a soul about what she'd seen the night of the Monteray Mixer. Confronting Adam felt impossible. It had been two weeks and she had been utterly paralysed. Who could she even tell? No one would understand that she couldn't tackle something like this right at the beginning of the summer-content schedule. The Monteray rollout was only starting: she couldn't jeopardise that deal – it was worth hundreds of thousands of euro – she couldn't risk their literal home over some sexting. And that was definitely all it was. Well. Sexting with visuals. Whatever *that* was called. Her stomach clenched. The humiliation gripped her anytime her thoughts drifted back to that night. She'd been back and forth about confronting him. The problem was that, as with everything else in their marriage, Adam's recent betrayal felt somehow knit into the Maxxed Out world. More and more she was thinking she needed a plan B. Her thoughts kept turning back to the Snag List idea. Surely she wasn't the only one feeling snookered by her life choices. Starting a business like that could be a way to get away from Maxxed Out and back to having her own bit of independence. After all, would a normal wife have kept her mouth shut upon discovering her husband like that? She had watched him masturbate over another woman – their new fucking neighbour, no less – and then checked the company diary to figure out when might be a good time to address the issue so it wouldn't impact the Maxxed Out timetable too much.

As Adam rang the doorbell, Lindy fired off a quick text to the Snag List group:

LINDY: Please tell me you guys are already here …

The Snag List group had rapidly become the best thing about the move to Monteray. Since their boozy afternoon at Ailbhe's, the chat had moved far past boring house-related issues and they were more like proper friends, not just neighbours. Ailbhe and Roe were generally there for whatever moaning or bitchy observation she needed to offload at any given time and were equally forthcoming with their own. She wished Ailbhe wasn't leaving – her flight was just weeks away – though Lindy knew she was dying to get out of Monteray. At least she'd still have Roe.

The door swung open and Rachel Fitzsimon fixed them with a megawatt smile. 'The Zelners! You guys! Thank you so much for coming.' Rachel's pep and white bandage dress, which presumably she would need to be surgically removed from after the party, had the immediate effect of making Lindy tired and clearly invigorating Adam. Lindy stood swallowing back her rage as the two embraced warmly.

When Rachel finally released her husband and made to hug her, Lindy raised a hand to head her off at the pass. 'I'm not a hugger,' she said firmly. 'It's not germ related – just, honestly, why does every social encounter need to be book-ended with full body contact?'

'*Riiiight.*' Rachel's smile was dampened slightly but still clinging on. 'And, of course, this is Max.' She bent lower with visible difficulty: the dress was like a straitjacket, and Rachel's breasts were making a bid for freedom almost directly into Max's face. 'You're a pretty big deal around this house.' She winked. 'Fielding will be so excited to meet you at last.'

Inside, the house – a carbon copy of their own – was packed with the kind of demographic Lindy always felt like an outsider among: extremely well-to-do people, all preternaturally successful in their various industries.

She and Adam had only been to a few soirées in Monteray, but each one had reminded Lindy of the parties in secondary school. Even in adulthood, the cliques were demarcated by a nebulous social code that, twenty years later, Lindy still struggled to decipher. They all seemed to know each other, or if not *know* each other then be connected in tangential ways – golf club, secondary school, sailing. In a word, it was all very *Dublin*. And not a Dublin Lindy had ever felt a part of.

She took a glass from a passing waiter – *Seriously, wait staff? At a five years old's birthday?* – and slipped in to a circle of women, some of whom she knew from the few times she'd managed to drag Max out to the park.

'Lindy!' Clíodhna, the creator of a WhatsApp group, Monteray Mamas, that Lindy had fled the second she was added, greeted her. 'How are you?'

'All good, the usual really.' Lindy smiled. 'Work, house to-do list unending, impending summer-camp dramz! Anyone else's child like Damien from *The Omen*?'

'Oh yes, absolutely. Olwen is the fucking worst. I mean, I hate her. She's seven and I hate her.' Sinéad was a harried mother of four who was incredibly high powered – her architecture firm had offices in London, New York and Dubai – and, like all the other women in Monteray, seemed to be physically untouched by motherhood. They all had incredibly expensive athleisure gear, always worn with the perfect blow-dry and the requisite rake of diamonds on their fingers. When exactly did they get around to the athletic side of their athleisure? Lindy pictured Sinéad flying business class to New York, barking down the phone to subordinates while a personal trainer moved her limbs for her.

As the other assembled women piled in to bitch about their kids, Lindy scanned the room and spotted Roe beside Eddie, deep in a group that the Snag List had dubbed the Sports Casual Dads. Anthropologically, they were essentially the male equivalent of the Athleisure Mamas, only their look was extremely expensive surf gear and classic male brands like Hugo Boss for shades and watches. It went without saying that each cohort was extremely, but *tastefully*, tanned.

A frantic communication of head shaking and grimacing passed between Roe and Lindy as each tried to break away to join the other's group. Then Lindy felt her phone buzz. She subtly checked the message as Clíodhna and Sinéad waged an odd, pointless war over who had put on more rosé bloat since the start of May. Objectively speaking: neither of them. Tedious stuff.

ROE: I'm coming over. Believe me, the Athleisure Mamas could not be worse than Sports Casual Dads.

LINDY: I dunno, they're fat shaming themselves over here.

ROE: Yuck. Still, I'll take my chances – one of the Sports Casual Dads just asked Eddie when he'd be 'duffing me up'. Vom.

LINDY: Sheesh. OK, well, you were warned.

Lindy smiled as Roe ploughed through the crowd that was energetically downing canapés and booze as kids ran in and out from the garden, where at least nine party entertainers of different genres were directing proceedings.

'Hi, Roe!' Clíodhna welcomed Roe warmly.

'I love your … what are they … overalls?' Sinéad couldn't hide her visible confusion at Roe's aesthetic.

'They're shorteralls, like shorts and overalls had a love-child.' Roe smiled gamely.

'So clever,' Clíodhna echoed, in the tone normally reserved for commending an eccentric child – which was basically what Roe appeared to be to these women.

'We were just saying how *horrific* our children are.' Sinéad rolled her eyes ruefully as she tossed back her bubbles.

'Right …' Roe smiled mildly and Lindy squirmed a little in anticipation of someone inevitably putting their foot in it.

'Any sign of pitter patter for you and Eddie, Roe?' Sinéad leaned in eagerly for Roe's answer but Clíodhna was quicker off the mark.

'Of course there is!' she cut in. 'You don't buy a six-bed in Monteray Valley without some plans for reproducing, am I right, Roe?' Clíodhna winked at Roe, who was still smiling impassively.

'Have you started trying?' Annie, a film producer, piled in on the interrogation.

'We're taking it slowly.' Roe was being patient but Lindy knew she hated this subject.

'Cheers to that.' Clíodhna raised her glass. 'If I could go back and do it all over … I don't know if I would even have them.'

Lindy was surprised. From their brief interactions, she'd filed the Monteray Mamas under that category of women whose main schtick was complaining relentlessly about their kids but who would shy away from ever directly saying they regretted having them. Wanting to un-have your kids was not something you could put on a snag list, and Lindy looked around cautiously, checking if Clíodhna's kids, Taidgh and Milo, were in earshot. Luckily Rachel, who appeared beside her at that very moment, had more or less quarantined the children so the adults could have fun at this child's birthday party.

'Uh-oh …' Rachel grinned, her eyes shining. 'Is Clíodhna on a downer about life choices? Want to go powder your nose, hun? Use the en suite on the second floor.'

'Oh, really? I'll come too.' Sinéad perked up and the two made for the door.

Bizarre. Can they literally not even break away from the pack to fix their make-up?

'You gals are welcome to as well?' Rachel smiled kindly at Lindy and Roe. Before Lindy could answer this strange invitation, Ailbhe appeared from the hall in skintight black jeans and a grey marl tee, baby Tilly clamped to her hip. 'Rachel,' she said as she joined the group. 'You fucking legend. If I'd known this was gonna be such a rager, I wouldn't have brought the bloody baby.'

'Give her to one of the nannies.' Rachel indicated vaguely in the direction of the front playroom where, on the way in, Lindy had spotted a portion of the child contingent glued to a movie. 'Where are the Bellinis?' Rachel drifted off in search of a waiter.

'Oh my God, gals, hilarious, I thought this party was going to be stiff as fuck.' Ailbhe came to stand beside Lindy and Roe.

'And it's not?' Lindy couldn't quite name it but something was up with Ailbhe. 'Have you just had your Botox topped up?'

'Lindy!' Ailbhe crowed, startling both baby Tilly and Roe. 'I wouldn't put that shite in my face!' She leaned in conspiratorially. 'Rachel's set up a little pep station in one of the en suites upstairs.'

'Pep station?' Roe looked confused, while Lindy took in Ailbhe's gleaming eyes and the keyed-up jigging of the baby in her arms.

'Ailbhe! You absolute lunatic. Are you on coke right now?'

'Coke!' Roe yelped. 'Really? Where did you put the baby while doing the coke?'

Ailbhe grinned manically. 'One of the Monteray Mamas held her for me.'

'That is depraved.' Roe looked equal parts shocked and amused.

'Mam is making the most of her last hurrah, isn't she? Yes she is,' Ailbhe cooed at the baby.

'Ailbhe, aren't you breastfeeding?' Lindy tried not to sound judgemental.

'Yer wan Clíodhna says it's grand. It was only a bump anyway. Some of the Sports Casuals are absolutely rolling, sure! Relax, Lindy, don't be a buzzwreck.'

'Oh, sorry, I'm wrecking the buzz at this *child's* birthday party.' Lindy rolled her eyes and carefully took the baby. 'I'll mind *this* while you go do *that*, whatever *that* is. It could be bloody Lemsip cut with Epsom salts, ya know. You could be snorting anything, Ailbhe.'

'Don't be insane – these bitches have the best of everything. I was actually here when the taxi did the drop-off. Even the drug taxi was swish, a Tesla!'

Roe was shaking her head slowly from side to side. 'This is the most debauched party I've ever been to. Drugs! Magicians! Hired staff! Crazy!'

'It's exhausting.' Lindy sighed just as Morris, Rachel's husband, or Fitzy as everyone called him, started shouting over the din of the kitchen.

'Lads! Lads! Lads! Shots, lads!'

'Fitzy, you ledge!' a dad nearby shouted, nearly deafening Lindy.

'Eeeek, shots,' Ailbhe whooped, raising her arms to point at Morris. 'Yessss! You cool to hang on to Tilly?' she fired back at Lindy. 'There's a bottle of formula in the changing bag upstairs.' Ailbhe winked. 'Don't worry, I wasn't going to drink and boob.' She pushed off to where Morris Fitzsimon was lining up at least twenty tumblers of Red Bull and balancing Jäger shots on the rims between each one, leaving Lindy and Roe holding the baby. The crowd were chanting 'Trainwreck, trainwreck, trainwreck' as Morris tipped the first shot of Jägermeister into the first glass of Red Bull, setting off a domino effect of shots tumbling neatly into tumblers across the table. The chanting abated as the crowd fell upon the glasses like hyenas discovering a carcass.

'This is a lot,' Roe muttered to Lindy.

As people finished downing the grim concoction, a chant of 'Fitzy, Fitzy, Fitzy' took hold.

'This is giving me such intense school flashbacks,' Lindy returned.

Where is Adam? she wondered. *Do I even care? Nah. As long as he's not doing any coke.* Rachel was deep in hosting duties so at least he wasn't holed up with her anywhere. She hated thinking like this, but everyone was monitoring everyone these days and Coked Up Maxxed Out Dad would not be a good look.

'We can hardly leave already – we'll have to give it an hour at least. Let's go hide somewhere to wait it out,' Roe muttered.

After traipsing through every room on the first and second floor of the house (all filled with shouty Monteray parents), Lindy and Roe realised that the best tactic to avoid the endless booze-pushing and bleary emoting of people whose tolerance was on the floor post-kids would be to hide in plain sight. They ended up back downstairs in the playroom, where they sat on the floor with Tilly, among the kids who were watching both a movie and a performer who'd been hired to keep them entertained. This was definitely the last place any of the other parents would be venturing.

'What is their deal?' Roe jerked her head in the direction of the door and the muffled sounds of inebriated people. 'It's like four in the afternoon? They're acting like it's 3 a.m. on a Saturday in 2006.'

'No one cuts loose like a fun-starved parent.' Lindy shrugged.

'It's kind of depressing, though, isn't it? They all seem to hate their kids. Or hate being parents at least. This is why I just can't imagine me and Eddie going for it. I feel like I'll end up like one of these cynical women shooting up coke at a kid's birthday party. Is it coke you shoot up?'

'I know it looks bleak from right here, but I swear it's not all social climbing and bathroom bumps of coke. It's nice having a family.'

Despite her words, Lindy couldn't quite summon the enthusiasm to match the sentiment. She hadn't clapped eyes on Adam since they'd all arrived. For all she knew, Adam was off in some closet motorboating Rachel for real.

She tried to picture walking in on that scene and how it would feel, but all she came back with was a kind of unnerving non-feeling, a blankness. Adam didn't want her any more. She should be screaming and railing but she felt too shattered, too sapped by the despair. Did the others in Monteray Valley feel like this? Was the pervading numbness a middle-class, mid-life malaise infecting all of them? Maybe this accounted for the coke and the hard-edged, unsentimental attitude to their own children. Maybe they'd hit a wall with their self-advancement. They had the money, the houses, the cars, the clothes. They had the lives they'd always been working towards and now had to confront the fact that there was still something missing. Was it just the next obvious stage for restlessness to set in? The desire to hunt out the things left undone, the things still outstanding that needed to be ticked off? That is some level of privilege, Lindy knew. Her own incredibly hard-working parents wouldn't know what to make of having things so good – at least on paper – that you would actually go looking for something to be unsatisfied by.

Lindy's thoughts drifted.

If you could have a do-over, what would you fix?

Children truly did create a watershed in life, as Clíodhna's prickly words had highlighted. After kids, you weren't the most important person in your life any more. All your decisions affected them. Your dreams, if you went after them, even had the potential to hurt your kids. Her own daydreams of starting her career over would definitely not benefit Max. The idea of stepping back from Maxxed Out made her feel guilty. Would Max feel like she was ditching him? Maybe he wouldn't mind. She could still be on the board. Maybe he wouldn't even notice.

'Mad to think,' Roe interrupted Lindy's ruminations, 'all *these* people,' she indicated the children swarming around them, 'came out of *those* people. How do people just do that? Like it's no big deal?'

'You know, being uncertain about having kids is normal, Roe.' Lindy felt protective towards her. 'It'd be weird if you weren't giving it a lot of thought. To be honest, for me, having a baby seemed to open the floodgates of doing things out of a sense of obligation. Decision after decision just fell into place once that piss stick said I was pregnant. Getting married, getting a mortgage, putting my own things further down the list, getting out of the city. You need to do the stuff you want to do before a baby. Or else it'll sour everything with Eddie.'

Roe bit her lip as stray children bounded around her and two little girls openly marvelled at her halo of curls. 'I don't know what stuff I want to do. I never have. I've just never had real guts,' she finally admitted. 'Like, you and Ailbhe are just doers. You're a CEO! Ailbhe has her own business too and look at her out there, living it up. She's blitzed to the tits at a kid's party and she doesn't give a shite. I'm not that kind of person – I never have been.'

'What if I helped you?' Lindy could feel the thoughts in her head aligning in that exciting and hard-to-describe way that always preceded one of her ideas. 'I could ... maybe coach you? I studied psychology, or mostly did anyway. What's on your life snag list? The thing you regret leaving unfinished?'

'Remember I told ye at Ailbhe's I wish I had tried out for the musicals in school. I wasn't joking. Is it so dumb that that is my biggest regret? I think that really is it. My one that got away is the St Christopher's 2007 production of *Chicago*. I have never had the balls to put myself out there. I never even auditioned. I couldn't bear for people to know I wanted to do it and then see me fail when I didn't get it.'

'Well,' Lindy readjusted the remarkably compliant Tilly, 'that is hardly the most out-there ambition. I'm right in thinking you just want the experience of doing it, right? Getting out there. You're not expecting to become the next Idina Menzel?'

'No, don't worry, I'm not!' Roe laughed awkwardly and, looking down at her lap, added, 'I know it's not realistic to start a stage career at thirty-one. *Twenty*-one is old in musical-theatre years.'

'Well, never say never. We'll see.' Lindy's cogs were turning. This is what people of their generation needed: to feel like there was still a chance to change their lives. They were the children of boomer parents who'd raised them to believe they could be whatever they wanted, until a recession and a pandemic had ambushed them. That's where Lindy could come in.

She *was* a doer, as Roe said, when she wasn't wallowing. She could make things happen. She could do what she was doing here: consult with clients and help them to make a snag list of their lives. Then, when they'd focused on the one thing that had got away that they wanted to do, she would tailor an experience that ticked that box. 'I wonder if we could find a show you could audition for.'

'Well, my choir is actually getting ready to put on a show,' Roe said tentatively. 'But I've never gone out for a part before. Well, one year I put my name down but when they called my name I legged it … Auditions are literally tomorrow, and I guess with Eddie going on about the baby, it's been on my mind … It feels a bit now or never.'

'Roe! You have to do it. It *is* now or never. OK, tomorrow is a quick turnaround but maybe it's better – no time to psych yourself out.' Lindy pulled out her phone to consult her calendar. 'I will keep you from backing out and coach you every step of the way – I am a demi-psychologist! I half trained. We have to do this, Roe! We both need to step up and go for our snags. I am going to buy TheSnagList.com domain right now. Sure, everyone's a life coach these days. Or they have one. And I can bring you to the audition – any excuse to avoid my loveless marriage!'

'Lindy!' Roe snapped to attention. 'You are joking, right?'

'Yeah, yeah.' Lindy feigned interest in the magician who was trying to slide a sword down his throat while children stumbled into him. 'Kind of.'

'Lindy? What? Are you OK? Is it really loveless?' Roe sounded nervous and Lindy guessed this probably seemed like advanced marriaging to her, far beyond anything she and Eddie would have experienced.

'It's not loveless. It's not. But I don't know what to do.' She took a breath and leaned closer to Roe. 'I caught Adam having some kind of socially distant, non-contact affair-type thing with Rachel Fitzsimon.'

'No.' Roe exhaled. 'No,' slipped out a second time. 'What did he say?' she hastily added.

'Nothing,' Lindy said brusquely, clearly struggling to remain composed. 'He doesn't know I know.'

'Really? Shit, Lindy. What exactly happened? How did you find out?'

'I actually don't think I can even say it.' Lindy looked pained as she shook her head, attempting a weak smile. 'It wouldn't be fair to you – it's quite graphic!'

'Lindy!' Roe laughed. 'C'mon, I can take it. I've seen *The Human Centipede*.'

Lindy actually managed a laugh at this, then steeled herself to say it out loud. 'He was wanking over a video call. With Rachel. Or rather with her tits. Her face was in more of a supporting role.' Lindy sighed unhappily. 'He was wearing his VR helmet for the full, immersive, 360-degree effect.'

'God.' Roe appeared to be flailing for something, anything, to say. 'The helmet is quite an addition. Seems a bit like driving blind – it must be a mess when he … you know—'

'OK, Roe!'

Roe snapped her mouth shut.

Lindy's anger was just a brief flash before the abject misery returned. 'I'm sorry to snap. I know I brought it up. It's just so weird to be saying it aloud. I knew we were distant. I think I was just blaming it on us working together and becoming more like colleagues than a couple. How did he even get Rachel's number? Never mind get her to agree to some virtual porno? When was all that happening? Who has the time for these things even?'

Roe scooted closer on the playroom floor and put her arms around Lindy, being gentle not to squeeze Tilly. 'I am so sorry, Lindy.'

'No, *I'm* so sorry.' Lindy struggled to remain composed. 'We were talking about you! I'm so, so sorry – I've just been trying to go along as normal. It's been torture in the house acting like nothing's changed.'

'Please don't apologise,' Roe insisted. 'You need to talk this out. You need to tell Adam. And decide what you want to do.'

Lindy straightened up, swiped at her eyes and smoothed her shirt. 'You know what I want to do? I want to make The Snag List work. So that I don't fucking need Adam. I've never done anything of my own. I want to prove it to myself that I can.'

'Lindy, you don't have anything to prove. Maybe you need to focus on what's just happened. This has to be a major shock. You don't have to do anything for my sake. Maybe this is just not great timing?'

'No, no, this Adam snag is no reason to back out. It's a reason to go all in. I can't face the thought of this all getting out and everyone pitying me cos my husband has no interest in me any more and I have no life left of my own. I've devoted years of my life to his career! I'm a cliché.'

Roe was biting her bottom lip; clearly even she was thinking it sounded bleak as hell.

'Don't look at me like that, Roe! I can see that even you are thinking it: "Poor Lindy. Ditched by her husband and never did anything with her own life. Always put his career first." Well, fuck that. I'm onto something with The Snag List. I know I am. I'm gonna fucking show him. I am not going quietly into the night!' She finished with a laugh that she hoped didn't sound as bitter as she felt.

A sudden commotion over by the door to the playroom interrupted the Snag List plans. A nervous-looking illusionist was backing away.

'Get the eff out of my way, David Copperfield.' Ailbhe, glazed eyes, came in and started darting wildly among the kids. 'I'm trying to find my baby!'

'Oh Jesus.' Lindy hiked Tilly up higher to show Ailbhe. 'She's here! We've got her. Remember?'

Ailbhe blithely pushed a path through the sea of children that carpeted the large room.

'Uh-oh.' Roe kept smiling while managing to mutter, 'She's looking a bit, eh, over-refreshed.'

They both watched as a foolhardy child of about six strayed into Ailbhe's path proffering a balloon sausage dog. 'Look at my bawooon animal!'

'Can you just not!' Ailbhe shrieked at him, ploughing on to reach them.

God, she's edgy all right. Lindy took a breath as Ailbhe wrenched Tilly from her arms.

'Ailbh, hun. Are you OK? Why don't you let us mind her – she's no trouble? I can drop her home to your mum later. You stay.' Lindy made sure she said the next bit carefully, without a scrap of judgement. 'You're having fun.'

'Yeah, it's all good, Ailbhe,' Roe backed her up. Tilly was placid as ever in her mother's erratic embrace, but still, it was probably not the best place for her right now.

'Naw, babe, it's not all good.' Ailbhe was skittish, looking around at the sea of bewildered five-to-eleven-year-old faces gazing at them. 'Fucking Tom is on his way,' she hissed.

'Tom your …' Lindy was trying to focus on Ailbhe's words but couldn't help being unnerved by the jostling Tilly was receiving in Ailbhe's arms.

'Tiny little phone husband, yeah. He's "surprising" me.' Doing the air quotes nearly made her lose her grip on the baby altogether, but Ailbhe barely noticed. She whooshed the baby back up and shoved her phone at Lindy. 'Eilers just texted to let me know.'

The message from Eilers just said:

Heads.Up.Tom.on.way.for.a.surprise.

'She is shocking with the auld one text speak, yet her GIF game is immac.' Ailbhe shook her head, rolling her eyes and snatching the phone back, all the while slinging Tilly higher up on her hip, apparently not noticing that the strap of her handbag was becoming tangled in her daughter. 'Gals, I'm screwed. I've had a bit of drugs. Do you think he'll notice? WHAT THE FUCK ARE YOU DOING?' she snapped, rounding on a shocked Roe who'd been trying to untangle Tilly from the chain of the bag.

'I think he'll notice,' Lindy said, cautious not to antagonise her further. 'Look, he'll be grand. Let us mind Tilly. Maybe parenting his kid while high isn't the best look.' She reached for the baby.

'He won't be grand.' Ailbhe's words were tumbling out at a ferocious rate as she wrenched Tilly back from Lindy's outstretched hands. 'He's not into drugs. I've kind of downplayed some of the good old days. I told him I'd never been to America because I can barely remember any of my J1 so it was easier to pretend I wasn't there at all. All I do remember is the time I got spiked with Ket, painted my face pink and got busted bringing pills to the airport in California by accident.'

'Wait, what?' Lindy, despite finding Ailbhe's slight manhandling of her daughter hard to watch, was intrigued now. 'When did that happen? What's Ket?'

'I think it's horse tranquilisers,' Roe supplied helpfully.

'I wuv horseys!' The balloon-animal kid had reappeared, as persistent as ever. *Read the room, child*, Lindy thought as he chattered on. 'I have a bawooon horsey too!'

'Get your animal away from me,' Ailbhe barked. 'I'm in crisis. Tiny Phone Husband will be here any minute. I can't be coked up. I need to get un-high. Someone google "How long does coke high last".'

'I got a smartphone for my birthday.' Another child, slightly older than Max, had detached from the crowd and was proudly displaying his new phone. 'How long does coke high last,' he muttered as he typed carefully on the device.

'Ailbhe, this is getting less appropriate by the second.' Lindy leaned towards the baby again. 'Give us Tilly and go out the window again. Go home, have a coffee and a shower. We'll cover for you when Tiny – eh, Tom arrives.'

'Wait,' Roe piped up. 'When you say busted … do you mean you were arrested?'

'Yeah.' Ailbhe looked impatient at the interruption. 'Or fined or something.'

'Says here you could stay high for up to two hours,' the boy with the phone announced. 'Any time, I take my lil bro's addy medication, I'm buzzed for days.'

'Who are you?' Lindy squinted at him, trying to reverse engineer this kid's brown curls and freckled upturned nose to link him back to any of the Sports Casual Dads or Athleisure Mamas. 'Never play with my kid, please.'

'I'm Malcolm. I'm just helping – don't be a narc. Are you always agitated like this?' He quizzed Ailbhe further. 'Cos if you're not, the agitation could be a sign you're OD-ing.'

'OK, this cursed child is not helping. Be gone,' Ailbhe commanded.

'So were you arrested or fined or what?' Roe asked.

'Yeah, fined.' Ailbhe swung around to them to block Malcolm from the conversation. 'We were flying home at the end of my J1. It was a really early flight so we'd decided to stay out all night. It was deadly. Except for the Ket bit. Never take that stuff. We'd gone to a house party and I spent the entire time in a K-hole, staring at this guy's pet iguana, which never seemed to move. Then it turned out he was a taxidermy enthusiast so that was probably not the Ket. We lit out of there then and got a taxi to the airport. The whole time going through security I was convinced that everyone was staring at me. I started completely freaking out. Then I realised at some point in the night I must have covered my entire face with my pink lipstick. I was kind of relieved because at least I wasn't hallucinating the staring. People really *were* staring. Anyway, then I noticed that I was holding the iguana. It was about that point that the police turned up. Apparently walking through JFK with your face painted pink, clutching an iguana was a searchable offence. Fucking bullshit. They found a couple of "questionable" pills and fined me on the spot. I think I was kind of acting out a bit. I don't really remember. Anyway, joke's on them because I got on a plane about an hour later. And obviously never paid the fine. My old roommate sent on court summons stuff that had showed up when I didn't pay. But I was, like, "Fuck you, America!" So I wasn't arrested but when I didn't pay the fine I suppose there was a warrant out for my arrest? Maybe? How did I even get on to this story?' Ailbhe nervously checked the door. 'Here, my face looks normal right now, yeah? It's not pink, right?'

'Yeah, your face is grand, bit clammy but grand,' Roe reassured her. 'But, Ailbhe?' Roe's tone was serious. 'You're supposed to be flying to America in four weeks? If there's a warrant out for your arrest, that'll be a problem, no?'

'Oooh, that's not going to be a good look,' the boy muttered.

'Ail-veee!' The unmistakable sound of an American grappling with an Irish name interrupted them. All four turned as one. Tom Russell was waving from the doorway. 'Tilly! My girls! Surprise, honeys!'

Later that night, Lindy sat in her dressing room browsing the various life-coaching courses on offer. They pretty much all started in September, which was only a few months away. She requested the PDF brochures from two that ran their workshops remotely and promised certification in twelve weeks. That would leave her able to start seeing clients in January. She texted the Snag List group:

LINDY: Looking at some options for my Snag List idea. We'll fill you in properly @Ailbhe, but basically I was talking to Roe earlier about doing something with that ticking off the life to-do list idea. I bought TheSnagList.com earlier and I've been looking at courses to become a life coach. I have a

couple of months before they start so I'm thinking I could get the business all set up and looking really slick and then I'll be ready to hit the ground running in January. It's perfect – everyone's FULL of regrets in January! Roe's gonna be my guinea pig @Ailbhe! Her choir – the Life and Soullers lol – are putting on a musical and she is finally gonna try out! Aaaand there's a reality show involved too which will be brilliant for the testimonials page on TheSnagList.com! So if you think of anything you want to tick off, Ailbhe, let me know … Bout to chat to Adam. 😩

Lindy heard Adam come into the bedroom and froze. She hated bedtimes at the moment – every night it dragged her back to the night of the wanking. Also it was the time of day when the awkwardness between them was most palpable. They were more or less never alone together the rest of the time. She stood up and tried to shake off the apprehension. She wanted to step down as CEO, and she knew if she didn't set things in motion she could very well lose her nerve.

'Hey,' she said as she walked out to the bedroom.

'Hey.' He was pulling back the covers. 'My head's gonna be in bits tomorrow. Might order a Hangover Helper!' Her smile was taut and he sat up. 'What? Is something wrong?'

Just get it said, Lindy. 'I have a business idea and I want to pursue it. It's kind of a life-coaching service for people with regrets.'

'Uh-huh,' he replied, and she surveyed his face for any sign that he himself might be harbouring regrets about sneaking around behind her back.

'I want to step down as CEO.'

'O-K.' His eyes darted as he processed this. 'Ehm, I guess that's doable. Jamie's definitely qualified to step up though there'd be financial implications. We'd be paying him more and you not at all.'

'Yeah. I know.' Lindy moved to her side of the bed. She resisted the urge to say *it's the least you can do, you cheating scum*. Instead she kept her voice calm. 'Surely we could take the hit. For a little while. I could try for a year, see if I can build it up. I just think it's time I did something else. Something for me. And it mightn't be a bad idea to have something lined up in case the whole internet goes tits up. I can still be on the board.' Adam nodded at this, though truth be told the board was a bit of a joke. They called it a 'board', but it was in no way official: it was just them.

'So, this is exciting . . .' Adam said, sounding not remotely excited, but Lindy decided to try and give him the benefit of the doubt. She had to. Even though she still had no idea what to do about their marriage, she needed them to stay united for Max.

She checked in on the Snag List group before going to sleep. Roe had answered her.

ROE: Go Lindy!!! Hope the chat went well. I'd say we won't hear a peep from @Ailbhe for days! Last I saw her, Tom was trying to coax her down from the coffee table at Rachel's.

10

'AILBHE? *AILBHE*?'

Ailbhe jolted upright as her mother's voice pierced her cocoon of sleep. Ugh. Her head felt hot, her tongue was swollen and her neck was killing her from sleeping on … Oh! … The couch in the downstairs living room? Fuck. What was she doing down here? Where was …?

'Tilly! Mam! Where's Tilly?' Ailbhe's grogginess instantly evaporated as she feverishly raked through the last memories of the previous night. All she could grasp were fractured moments. A child telling her she was paranoid. Lindy and Roe looking uneasy. Tom arriving. Fuck. Adrenaline shot through her veins. She jumped up, ignoring the pounding that had started at the base of her skull.

'It's OK, Ailbh, she's fine. She's fine.' Concern marred her mother's features, along with a shadow of something else … disgust? The hammering in Ailbhe's chest calmed instantly. Thank God. Eileen picked up Ailbhe's boots from the floor where she'd kicked them off the night before. 'Tom's taken her for a walk. I wanted to get you up before he got back. You should go and get yourself together.'

'Yeah, Mam.' Ailbhe tugged on a smile. 'Sorry I was so tired last night. I must've—'

'Just tired, was it?' Eilers cut in sharply and Ailbhe was caught off guard. Eileen was usually pretty easy-going. How bad had she been last night? The hammering of her heart resumed – had she said something about Tilly?

'Mam—'

'Ailbhe, that was a bit much. Lucky the Snag List girls were there to help with Tilly. But Tom was shocked.'

'Ah Mam, I was just having a bit of craic. I didn't mean to get so drunk. I'm really sorry, OK?'

'I don't want an apology, Ailbh. You're a grown woman but you can't behave like that. Tilly could've been hurt. This is serious.'

'I know. I'm sorry, Mam. I don't feel like myself at the moment. I'm just—'

At that moment, she heard Tom's key in the door and abruptly abandoned her explanation to Eileen. She slipped through the hall and up the stairs before he could catch her. She needed to be fresh if she was to have any hope of convincing him that she wasn't hungover to feck.

In the big bathroom adjoining the master bedroom, she stood in the shower gulping water from the boiling hot stream thundering down on to her. Once she was out, she checked her phone. Instagram was her first port of call. Any time she was drinking lately, even just a few wines, she'd inevitably end up on Seb Knox's profile, so she had to make sure she hadn't left any disastrous likes or comments. Thankfully it was all clear. A couple of Reddit notifications alerted her to a question she must've posted in the depths of the night after the party. It was on the reddit.com/Ireland/American-visa-queries thread.

> Hey everyone, so I have an outstanding fine that kind of escalated into a court summons left over from my J1 (good times!). I am now forty-two and supposed to be going to America with my husband in a few weeks and I'm just working up the courage to send the application. I'm applying for a tourist visa and can't decide whether to just come out with it or try and style it out. Like, not sure if the old fine will crop up during this process. I'd obviously prefer it not to! My husband doesn't really know the old me.
>
>   He barely knows the current me. Hahahahaha.
>
>   Anyway, if anyone has any ideas/experience of this, that'd be class. I'm supposed to be sending my forms asap.

Jesus I do not remember writing this. I sound demented.

The post had a dozen or so comments and Ailbhe eagerly leaned in.

> **lg412**: Ooof this one's so hard to know. I've a friend who was just doing the ESTA visa for a week in New York and she had a J1 arrest warrant. She decided to risk it for a biscuit and it was totally fine. Never came up. Good luck, hope this helps.

> **MickyGreenEyes**: Ah the old J1 arrest is a tricky one. Know LOADS of lads who haven't been let back in since San Diego 2003!!! What a year. Carnage. The greatest horseplay of all time.

Ailbhe frowned. What if America wouldn't let her in? What would Tom say? Before Fielding's birthday party, she would've said Tom could handle the hangover from a bit of youthful high jinks. But given he'd witnessed the mild tear yesterday, she felt a Ket-addled run-in with the law resurfacing now would not be good.

Plus not getting into America would be a disaster. A key component of her new life being Tom's wife was putting some big distance between her and *past run-ins*. She'd didn't like to think about it, but she'd put a lot more eggs in this emigrating basket than she was comfortable admitting.

She smoothed serum over her face and sat on the edge of the bath to catch up with the Snag List WhatsApp. Lindy sounded hyped about Roe's show. She noted the reality TV element, maybe it was the same show she and Holly were going to be working on – that'd be fun! A new message dropped in at that moment.

ROE: How's the head, Ailbh? Is that what you say to coke fiends?!

A knock on the door gave Ailbhe a jolt. 'Yes?' She placed the phone face down on the little wicker table beside the bath where a collection of scented candles rested.

'It's me.' Tom peered around the door, cradling Tilly in one arm. 'Look at you.' His face creased into a huge smile and Ailbhe relaxed somewhat. Maybe he hadn't noticed his coked-up wife of the night before. *Maybe he just thinks I was being 'Irish'.* 'You are so beautiful – can I come in? We barely got a second last night.'

'I know, I'm so sor—'

He held a hand up. 'Don't worry. I know you must've been super overwhelmed having to manage on your own all this time, but I'm here now and we can deal with this together.'

'Deal with …?'

'Ailbhe, you're obviously in trouble with your drinking, but don't worry, we will get through this. I have loads of pals in recovery – I've got some links to some online meetings.'

'Eh, Tom, that is so not what's going on here. I'm grand – I just got carried away slightly.'

'Honey, don't get upset. I'm just trying to help. Think of it like the world's cutest intervention.' He held up Tilly's little hand to wave at her mother. 'Don't drink to excess, Mommy!'

Ailbhe snorted. 'I can't tell if you're joking or not right now.'

'I think being wasted at a kid's birthday party is not a joke.'

'I wasn't wasted. Or, well, I wasn't the only one who was wasted.'

Tom leaned down and, careful not to squish Tilly, kissed her. 'You'll try the meetings, won't you, babe?'

She inhaled deeply. It was hard to believe he was really there. During his absences, she was able to hold the reality of her situation at arm's length. It was easier to dismiss the guilty thoughts. But now his presence, his familiar, sharply masculine smell, was invading her and unravelling the veil of denial she'd drawn over her mistake. Guilt made her comply.

'I will,' she nodded. What the hell else could she say, given all the other things she was currently full of shit about. She could probably do with drinking a bit less, no harm.

'Well done, honey! Maia is going to get you on a schedule of meetings. They say ninety meetings in the first ninety days is the best aim.'

'Tom! What? I don't have time for that – I have a baby! And I'm supposed to be helping Holly out until we leave. I've got a meeting with her and the producer on set this afternoon!'

'Don't worry, I'm here now! And it's just an hour out of the day, Ailbhe – a really important hour. Plus, me and Tilly have so much catching up to do.' He wiggled his nose against the baby's.

Ailbhe sighed. 'I'd better get dressed. If I'd known you were flying in I wouldn't have arranged to meet Holly. The first official scenes for the show are shooting this afternoon. *Glee Me* it's called. I'm picking her up from the Luas in twenty minutes.'

'No problem, I'm gonna bring Tilly in to show her the Dublin offices.'

Ailbhe couldn't help but laugh. 'She is barely sentient! Are you gonna do the whole "one day all of this will be yours" speech?'

'Absolutely, never too soon to be thinking about succession plans. We don't want a Kim Jong-un situation on our hands.'

'Of course.' Ailbhe grinned, making her way to the sink to resume her ablutions. 'Take one of the bottles of pumped milk from the fridge.'

'If you have the forms for the tourist entry to the US ready, I can send them from the office. Great to get them sent in good time. The next four weeks are going to *fly* by.'

'Yep, I'll finish them before I leave. There are some *intense* questions on there. They ask if you've ever committed genocide. Could anyone possibly be answering that truthfully if they had?'

Tom chuckled. 'I love you, Ailbhe, you are one funny fucker! I can't wait for you to meet all the crew in Cali. It's finally feeling real.' He stood and put his arms around her again and lowered his face to hers. Ailbhe closed her eyes and allowed herself to relax. *I am so lucky. He loves us so much.* He was a gorgeous kisser, somehow gentle but also shot through with an urgency that was extremely sexy.

After a couple of minutes she pulled away, feeling him getting hard. 'OK, Tilly is way too close for this to be anything but yuck. You go walk that off.'

He laughed and jogged a few feet away to where the imposing free-standing granite bath stood, Tilly still flopped contentedly in his arms. 'Am I a safe distance? We're not going to traumatise her. You're the one who's always saying she's got the awareness of a handbag.'

'Well,' Ailbhe grinned, 'I was sensing things could have escalated very rapidly there. We haven't IE-P'ed in person in a very long time and you are an extremely hot kisser. Is it a Christian thing?'

'Oh yeah, cos we don't do anything *but* kiss till we're like thirty!'

'Right, we will resume later. Off you go, I have to get dressed.'

As she carefully applied her make-up – you had to look the part on set – she picked up the phone to check on the Snag List group. She replied to Roe's coke fiend message.

AILBHE: Shut up. Stop. 😊 Thanks for talking me down yesterday, I was all over the shop. Head's doing better TG. Though Tom is acting like I have a drink problem – he's talking about getting me 'some help'. So obvi now my fucking Ket-at-the-airport-arrest-warrant-mess – if it comes up – will look ten times worse. It was a bit of J1 high jinks and now it might totally screw me.

ROE: So you haven't told him yet?

AILBHE: No, are you joking? The man thinks I need AA meetings for a few drinks at a party. Don't worry, I'll be getting out of that one.

ROE: It was a *five-year-old*'s party. And it was coke not drinks. Just playing devil's avocado here.

AILBHE: Put *Fielding's parents* in rehab. I put the class in Class As! I'm a new mother, I was just thrilled to be out – what's *their* excuse?

LINDY: Of course you were over-excited. We've all been that woman. What are you going to do about the flights?

ROE: Wing it?!

AILBHE: Actually, yes. I've been bet into Reddit and the consensus is you've about a 50-50 chance of getting away with it. According to a one lad called @MeSoHarney, it's possible that the unpaid fine just faded away. I know there was some official-type letter asking me to appear before a judge but they'd hardly be bothered putting a warrant out for the arrest of some J1 student in high spirits?

LINDY: Ailbhe, hun. Is it not just better to explain it to Tom? He won't be mad. It's not like this just happened – it was years ago. You're an adult woman now. You're a business owner! A mother! Surely, just be honest.

★

At Craghanmor Community Centre, Ailbhe scanned the crowd for any sign of the *Glee Me* producer. She pressed through the packed hall, holding her breath to protect her from the fumes of hairspray and bald, feverish ambition that emanated from all musical-theatre people. The entire building clanged with singers tuning their vocal chords and holding nothing back on the high notes. As Ailbhe had neared the Luas stop, Holly had texted to say she was late and for Ailbhe to go ahead without her. Now, Ailbhe loitered in a quiet spot beside the water fountain and opened her emails to finally catch up on the brief for the show.

> Glee Me *centres around the Life and Soullers, a little community choir with BIG DREAMS. This reality show will take us from tense tryouts to the big night – the world première of* Voices of Glory, *a musical charting Ireland's historic Eurovision winning streak.*

Fuck off! Ailbhe laughed to herself, quickly firing off a text to the Snag List.

AILBHE: Too funny! I think I'm working on your choir thing, Roe! Are you here at the auditions?

ROE: Yes! Where are you?

AILBHE: I'm trapped in a group of people who are either doing vocal exercises or having a communal stroke.

In minutes, Ailbhe spotted Roe and Lindy emerging from the densely packed crowd. At the exact same time, she heard her name being called behind her.

'Ailbhe O'Casey, only the hottest girl in Dublin, how the hell are you?'

Ailbhe whirled round and narrowly avoided headbutting the tall and intensely handsome blast from the past who'd stooped to kiss her cheek.

'Seb? Oh wow, Seb Knox?' She recovered from their near-collision and quickly smoothed her pale pink T-shirt dress, carefully running her tongue over her front teeth. The thought: *Please God, I hope I look good* sped across her mind. *Stop that, Ailbhe!* What was he doing here? 'You're in London.'

'I'm … not?' He laughed, leaned in and brushed a kiss against her neck right below her ear. Fuck, that was some intimacy-exchange shit. She jerked back and checked to see if Lindy and Roe had seen. Roe was buried in her phone, humming to herself and tapping a foot anxiously. Lindy, however, was watching their greeting with interest.

'Lindy, this is—'

'Seb Knox? Yep, I got that.' Lindy smirked and Ailbhe tried to telepathically communicate: *Don't show me up, Lindy, and don't for God's sake mention the husband and baby I'm touting around nowadays.*

'Any news?' Seb was grinning down at Ailbhe. He looked different to last summer; his salt and pepper hair was shaggier. But he still had those distracting lips and that bulk and solidity she'd always loved. 'How's life?' He cocked an eyebrow. 'You're very quiet on socials these days?'

Oh God, all these months she'd been lurking around his Insta, he'd been looking at hers too.

'Life's good.' Ailbhe was breezy. 'Not much to report.' This elicited a snort from Lindy, which Ailbhe snuffed out with a sharp look.

'So,' Ailbhe continued. 'How are you? Back in Dublin? Are you here with work? Or a wife?' Oh fuck, that sounded playful in her head but psychotic out loud.

'A wife? God, no, nothing like that. I don't move on that quickly, even when someone doesn't answer my texts.' His hazel eyes were twinkling at her in a very, very cute way. She was glad she'd picked this dress: it showed off her legs very nicely, if she did say so— *Wait, no, Ailbhe, you do not want anything from him, remember?*

Suddenly, she became consumed with a terrible realisation. The pale pink dress was about to screw her royally as a troubling ache started up in her right breast – *no, please, not now*, she willed silently. The fucking breastfeeding. She seemed to have a very sensitive letdown, and the right boob had evidently misread her intrigue at Seb's taut upper arms as maternal instinct.

She crossed her right arm over her chest to cover any leakage and smiled as he continued. 'I'm producing this for RTÉ and handling the TikTok tie-in.'

'Ah yes.' Lindy perked up. 'Our friend Roe is auditioning for it.'

'It's not really our usual thing but it's a bitta buzz. I'm just delighted to be going into production on anything after the year we've had. And so glad you and Holly are doing the hair and make-up. I actually didn't realise – my production designer, Claire, booked ye.'

'Cool. Yeah. We're thrilled with the gig.' Ailbhe tried to focus on what he was saying. Shit. Holly working with Seb? What if he told her something? She'd need to keep Holly and Seb apart as much as possible. *I'll insist she needs to stay in the salon. Let Siobhán and me do it.* How was this happening? And on this day during the feariest hangover of her life?

Oh, shite, who cares? Tom and I will be gone. We will be gone, we will be gone, she self-soothed. The main thing now was to extract from this conversation before the deluge started.

'We're about to start getting some establishing shots. I won't need you prepping participants for about an hour. Once they're getting up to sing, I'll get you doing a bit of powder and whatever else you think.'

Ailbhe nodded vigorously, both arms now wrapped around her chest, while she clenched her whole body in a desperate (and illogical?) bid to control the letdown. Just then, an older woman swung in between them.

'You're the producer, right? I've had cancer twice, and we lost everything in the crash,' she shouted. 'You have to make me a main character. It's the perfect backstory – rags to riches and chemo to soprano!'

'Don't worry.' Seb adopted a soothing voice. 'We'll be shooting for two months – I promise you will get on camera.'

The woman beamed and hurried back to a gaggle of mezzo sopranos who were all looking hungrily at Seb.

Seb turned back to Ailbhe, shuddering. 'These am-dram ones are next level. See you in a bit – you can set up beside the stage through those doors.' He pointed at the double doors leading to the auditorium, then headed over towards a cluster of camera operators lugging equipment. Ailbhe exhaled with relief, turning back to

Lindy and Roe just as two wet patches, a darker pink than the rest of her dress, seeped out beyond the cover of her arms.

'What was that?' Lindy's eyes were gleaming with the intrigue. 'Good God, you're lactating.' Lindy shook her head.

'He started it!' Ailbhe was rocked to her core.

'Oh my God, is he your snag, Ailbhe? The one that got away?'

'Absolutely not, he's the one I want to get away *from*. I haven't seen him in … like … years. We used to hang out with lots of the same people. I hate Dublin. It's non-stop running into people you low-key hate slash are trying to avoid.'

'Why were you trying to avoid him? Also, you are aware that he asked if you had any news and you made no mention of your, oh, I dunno, husband? And baby?'

'Relax, Lindy, I hardly denied their existence. I just didn't bring them up. If he'd asked me directly, I'd have said something.'

'Just as long as you're not trying to keep your options open or something crazed like that,' Lindy remarked. 'He's a lash, isn't he?'

'Yeah.' Ailbhe nodded wistfully. 'Seb Knox. You can guess what we called him?'

'Yes, I can. Absolutely no need to tell me.'

'Gals.' Roe spoke for the first time since they'd come over. 'I'm going to wait it out in the loo, OK? I might do a little nervous puke.'

Roe skulked in the ladies of Craghanmor Community Centre. *Voices of Glory* would be rehearsing in the centre until opening night in Dublin's Liberty Theatre in ten weeks' time, and Roe sensed she'd be hiding in here a lot in the coming weeks, given the cameras swarming and the sheer intensity of a community musical-theatre production. Breathers would be key. The auditorium was in the new wing of the building. It was all white tiles and rubber floors and had the sterile air of a sanatorium. The halls outside clanged with practising Life and Soullers. It was all a bit nerve-shredding. Speaking of nerve-shredding, she'd decided to text her mother earlier just to add another fraught layer of angst to this day. *Why do I do it?* It was like a scab she couldn't hold back from worrying. As much as she tried to not care about Maura, it was so hard to unpick the tight, muddled stitches of a mother–daughter relationship. Despite the anger and resentment her mother triggered in her, she wanted the approval.

ROE: Hey Mum, I know we didn't leave things well last time. Just checking in. I decided to try out for the choir musical. Just a little project.

It was an innocuous message, she'd kept it light, and Maura'd finally gotten back.

MAURA: That's great, if you think that's a good use of your time.

It was the kind of message that might not have seemed like a big deal to some people, people with cosy, supportive mothers who had a wellspring of praise and encouragement for their kids. However, anyone with a mother in the mould of Maura O'Neill knew such mothers had an incredible knack of communicating years of dissatisfaction in literally ten words. As always with a message like this, Roe was tempted to explode. To demand to know why she was such a serial disappointment, to berate her mother's toxic bigotry, but when she had in the past, it had achieved nothing. She'd gaslight Roe and insist she did nothing to warrant the outburst. Maddening. And devastating. It was no good. There was no point in responding. She deleted the chat from her WhatsApp so she didn't have to look at Maura's words every time she opened it. She stood by the sinks and fiddled with her hair. *Don't let her ruin this*, she coached herself as Danny rushed in.

'There you are! Praise the good lord Johnny Logan, we thought you'd backed out.' He leaned back out the door. 'MAGS! I've got her.'

'Roe!' Mags joined them breathlessly. 'What are you at? Denise has them filming her "prep routine". She's brandishing some kind of yoni tuning fork. It's a nightmare. You need a prep routine – preferably not cringe or medically questionable.'

'This is it.' Roe laughed weakly and leaned in to the mirror to apply a deep purple shade to her lips, trying to ignore the nausea roiling in the pit of her stomach.

'We need to get you out of these God-awful plaits and in front of a camera.' Danny had started to fiddle with her hair, fluffing it out.

'Here.' Mags was all business, handing him some product. 'You desperately need some volume. Love the lippy. Now, how's the voice doing?'

'It's good, I'm feeling good.'

'Belting good? 'Defying Gravity' good?'

'Let's hope so.' Roe watched in the mirror as they fussed around her.

'Roe, hun, I love you but why did you do this whole utility

thing.' Danny shook his head sadly and made a sweeping gesture to encompass her denim shirt and dark tracksuit bottoms. 'It's like you're *trying* to upset me.'

'I'm camera averse, remember? I figure they're less likely to notice me like this.'

Mags ignored her. 'What bra are you wearing?'

'A bra that I would like to keep to myself,' Roe responded curtly.

'C'mon, hun, this is a visual medium. If you want to get up there and have a shot at bringing our queen, Niamh Kavanagh, to life you need to make an impact.'

'Danny's right, this is musical theatre. You can't be shy and retiring. Idina Menzel doesn't half ass *anything*. You have to go out there and own this moment. Roe, in five years of the Life and Soullers, you have never stepped up. But everyone is rooting for you.'

He was right. Putting herself out there had taken far too long; it had taken the prospect of having a baby and missing the opportunity altogether to push her.

'Now this outfit, Roe,' Danny said grimly. He himself was looking stun in denim shorts and an oversized sequinned bomber. 'Let's just tie up the shirt, undo a few buttons.'

Danny and Mags set to work making adjustments so that Roe's neon-orange bra was now partially visible, the shirt tied up to expose a slash of midriff.

'Gorge! You look so hot.' Danny snapped a pic on his phone.

'No socials,' Roe protested. She was still unsure how this whole idea would play with Eddie.

'Relax, I'm just popping it in SopranHoes.' He blew a kiss.

DANNY: Our lil Roe is ready for her close-up #ProudStageMom

Her picture appeared in the WhatsApp group and Roe smiled in spite of herself. It was sweet that they cared so much. Over in the Snag List group, Ailbhe, even after the high-octane twenty-four hours she'd just had, was sending good vibes. Tom had not looked pleased as he'd escorted Ailbhe and Tilly from the party the previous day.

It's actually hard to decide whose marriage is the bigger trainwreck right now. She flashed on telling Eddie that morning that she was working a double at the restaurant instead of the truth: that she was doing her first-ever audition. She just hadn't wanted to get into it with him and psych herself out before this, especially as she might not even get a role. Apart from the whole contraception thing, she had never lied to him. It did not feel good.

Just then, Lindy peered round the door to the toilets. 'Roe! You look fab – I love this.' Lindy gestured to the tweaks Danny'd made to Roe's outfit. 'Hi!' She waved to Danny and Mags. 'I'm Lindy, Roe's Snag List life coach.'

'And what in the shit is that?' Danny arched one brow contemptuously.

'Bold Danny.' Mags batted at him in admonishment. 'Don't mind him, he just wants to be Roe's only hype man. I'm Mags.'

Roe gathered her make-up bits and they all headed out to the large community hall reception area, still echoing with singers practising and members of the *Glee Me* crew rushing to and fro. The tension was building with every second. The soprano contingent were positively shrieking by this point, while the Altos formed an ominous drone underscoring Roe's mounting dread.

'Seriously, Lindy,' Mags continued, 'I love the idea of The Snag List. Roe's told me everything and, honestly, anything that's getting this one up on stage gets my vote. She is so good. I dunno what I'd snag list from my own life,' she pondered, 'probably … and now, I don't know how you'd manage this one … but my last baby wasn't exactly planned and I'd probably not have had him if I could've.'

Lindy laughed awkwardly as Danny cut in. 'She's not Dumbledore, Mags.'

'I know.' Mags sighed. 'He's just one of those no-craic babies.' She shook her head sadly.

'I'd probably suggest you spend my retainer on getting more childcare,' Lindy offered.

'Not a bad idea.' Mags nodded.

'I'm just going to go check my time slot.' Roe slid away from her friends. She tugged on her shirt, feeling exposed in more ways than just a sliver of belly on show. She couldn't believe she was actually about to get up on stage in front of everyone. Though, as nervous as she was, she also thrummed with anticipation. She might actually get a part, a prospect as thrilling as it was frightening.

She made her way to the call sheet taped up outside the door to the theatre and double-checked that she still had twenty minutes before she would be standing before Róisín and the film crew. A cheeky vape would steady her. Or make her feel even sicker – it was hard to decide – but Roe knew she didn't want to go back and make conversation with the others. She was finding it impossible to focus on what was being said. The anxiety was manifesting as a pounding roar in her ears, and she had a sudden, desperate urge to flee. She'd slept badly after she and Eddie had sex last night. Her pill had run out, which meant she'd had to dust off the diaphragm – not nearly as effective. The morning had been punctuated with spikes of anxiety. Continuing to take the pill without Eddie's knowledge had felt like way less of a betrayal than hiding in the bathroom to insert the diaphragm and hiding the case in the toilet cistern – probably overkill but she had to be careful. Then after they'd finished she'd had to slip back to the bathroom after she was sure Eddie was asleep to do the whole rigamarole in reverse.

She hated the deception, she wasn't built for lying, but she also knew that the alternative – to have rolled the dice and allowed for the possibility of becoming pregnant – was unthinkable.

In an odd way, sabotaging the 'trying to get pregnant' was cementing her decision to go through with The Snag List. She had paid a disproportionately high price to stand on the stage today. She owed it to that insane decision to give it her all. Eddie would never need to know what she had done.

She pulled on the vape and gazed across the car park, where she could see Denise improbably engaged in some boxing. Random, Roe thought. This must be part of the prep routine. She was sparring with a cowering tenor holding up her pads while the *Glee Me* crew captured every bizarre moment. Denise was smart; she was obviously thinking in terms of useful montages for the crew.

Denise was zealous about choir but at least she stepped up and went for it. She owned her crazed ambitions. Roe's problem was that she never allowed herself to fully acknowledge the things she wanted in life. She was too afraid of failure and rejection. *In my defence, maybe Denise would be afraid of failure too if she'd been more or less ditched by her parents for failing to live up to their expectations.*

'Here you are!' Roe jumped at Lindy's appearance around the side of the building. 'You're not planning a runner, are you? Because I guaran-goddam-tee that you would regret that.' Lindy folded her arms.

'I'm not running – I'm doing the opposite of running.' Roe exhaled a plume of smoke and smiled. 'I'm doing my own less-cinematic psyching up.' She nodded over at Denise.

'Hmm, yer one has definitely cornered the market on dramatic cutaways for the TV crew, but you're going to be defying gravity!'

'Sure am.' Roe pressed her lips together.

'Roe, you OK? You look extremely un-psyched.'

'No, I'm good, I am.'

'LOL, no you're not. You're not good, you are *brilliant*, Roe,' she added. 'You have the ability to absolutely nail this audition. All that's ever held you back is you. You've been a bitch to yourself, Roe, but you deserve this moment. You deserve to get up there and stand centre stage and show them this huge talent you have. These people are going to be blown away. Blown. Away. Do you believe me?'

'Well, I … I want to.' Roe shuffled uncomfortably. 'To be honest, your big emotional speech is giving me more performance anxiety than the thoughts of the audition.'

Lindy burst out laughing. 'OK, OK, I'm sorry. What do you want me to say? I have to justify my presence here. I need to provide a service otherwise The Snag List is just a fancy website.'

'The website is looking really good,' Roe offered encouragingly. 'Just tell me this isn't some notion. Like, I know it's not Broadway but this is worth doing, isn't it?'

'Oh my God, yes, Roe. Yes! It makes you happy, right? It gives you a buzz?'

'Yes.'

'Then it's so worth doing. Things don't have to be Broadway to make them worthwhile. Just think of this as off-Broadway.'

'Way, way off-Broadway.' Roe grinned.

'Yes.' Lindy laughed. 'And thank fuck, if this was Broadway you'd be doing – what? – eight shows a week!'

'Well, all going well this *will* be eight shows a week.'

'Well, see, same diff – it practically *is* Broadway.' Lindy was smiling but Roe could see she looked drained. Roe couldn't imagine how she was functioning with all that was going on with Adam.

'How are you doing, Lindy? Have you still not said anything to him?'

Lindy frowned and checked her phone. 'It's nearly time, darl. Thank God because that is literally the last thing I could cope with talking about right now.' She smiled miserably and Roe felt a guilty scrap of relief that at least things with Eddie were nowhere near as complicated.

Inside the auditorium, auditions for lead roles were about to begin and the atmosphere crackled with anticipation and a certain delicious frisson of bitchiness. Dozens of her fellow Life and Soullers were draped around the seats like jaded emperors sitting in judgement at a gladiatorial event.

Mags and Danny waved down from the back and Lindy made her way up to join them while Roe settled in the front row, behind the judges, along with the others waiting to be called.

Áine of the two cancers was up first. The format was very *X Factor*, with Róisín playing the role of a gently encouraging Louis Walsh, flanked by veteran musical director Michael Holland on one side giving his best Simon Cowell impression, complete with deep

tan and blazing white teeth. The *Glee Me* producer, Seb Knox, was
on the other side.

'I've chosen the Eurovision classic 'Why Me?',' Áine called from
the stage, 'because when Jimmy told me he'd remortgaged the house
in 2006 to rebuild the pigeon shed I said …' At this Áine drew in a
deep breath and positively shriek-sang, 'WHY MEEEE?'

Seb Knox visibly jolted and Róisín muttered, 'Jesus Christ.'

Áine caterwauled her way through the rest of the song,
occasionally singing directly into the camera that was capturing her
performance. By the time she was wrapping up, Michael Holland
was holding his head in his hands and Seb Knox's smile was stretched
so tight his face looked close to snapping.

'Thanks for that, Áine,' Róisín said in a bored voice.

Denise was making her way on stage and Roe's stomach clenched.
Denise was good. She looked relaxed as she took her mark at the
centre of the stage. She also looked the part of a leading lady. Her
hair was of the platinum, swishy variety and her limbs were long,
lithe and toned. She looked like the type of person to open a sharing
bag of M&Ms and partake of a handful without devouring the entire
bag. A psychopath essentially.

'I'm Denise Halloran and I'm doing 'Shallow' by Lady Gaga and
Bradley Cooper.'

'Of course you are.' Michael rolled his eyes. 'That's great,
Denise.'

The performance was flawless but perfunctory, and Roe sensed
a slight disappointment from the Life and Soullers who weren't
auditioning but had come to 'support' aka judge. Perfection was
boring – they weren't spending their Saturday in Craghanmor
Community Centre to enjoy perfectly serviceable cover versions.

They had a shared blood lust, Roe knew; they wanted a mighty fall and Roe couldn't help but fear that she was about to provide them with just that.

'Roe? Roe O'Neill?' Róisín called and Roe made her way forward and up the steps at the side of the stage. Her head felt oddly empty after the anxious scattershot thoughts of the previous hours. She tugged at her waistband nervously and wished she wasn't on stage right now so she could fix her knickers, which felt skewed after sitting down. *Oh God, please don't let me have VPL up here.* She hoped the judges couldn't see her knees shaking.

'This is a nice surprise, Roe!' Róisín turned to Michael Holland. 'Roe has never, ever tried out for a solo with the choir. Was it the lure of the TV cameras?' she called up to Roe.

'Eh no, not at all.' Roe squirmed uneasily; the camera on the stage to the left of her seemed to be focusing on her with increased interest. 'To be honest, I'm not that into the whole reality-show thing.'

'Oh? Why's that?' Seb Knox spoke for the first time since they'd started. Shite. Roe definitely didn't want to attract his attention for good or for bad.

'Well, I'm not *not* into it, if you know what I mean. I'm just not mad keen to be on telly, but it's obviously part and parcel of trying out so I'll happily do what I have to.'

'So good of you,' Michael Holland remarked dryly.

The camera appeared to zoom ever closer. Maybe TV cameras were like cats and the more ambivalent towards them you seemed, the more they focused on you.

'What are you singing today, Roe?' Róisín nodded encouragingly and Roe sensed she was rooting for her.

'I'm singing 'Defying Gravity'.'

Michael Holland gave something of a disparaging whistle at this, and Róisín shot him a look before adding. '"Defying Gravity'. It's a tough choice, Roe.'

'Yeah but …' Roe gazed around the auditorium until she found Lindy, Mags and Danny, who were all waving and, she knew, silently cheering for her. 'I know I can do this,' she added firmly, smiling at Lindy.

The backing track started up and Roe missed her first cue. Fuck. She scrambled after the music to pick up the thread of the melody and desperately tried to ignore Michael Holland openly wincing.

A few lines on and Roe had the song back in her grasp: she was OK. *Just be in the moment*, she ordered herself. *Forget about the crowd and just sing*. And she did, her voice swooping perfectly up the notes of the iconic number from *Wicked*. Even caught up in the song, she could see that fuckstick Michael Holland actually sitting up straighter. *Yes!* she thought triumphantly. *Maybe don't be so quick to judge next time, prick.*

As the melody hit its powerful conclusion, she sang with utter freedom and abandon. She was doing it! Róisín was beaming, and as Roe leaned into her final triumphant notes, a potent excitement engulfed her. She'd done it. And by the looks on their faces, not to mention the awed hush that had descended on the room, she'd be doing it again. And again and again. There was no way she wasn't going to get cast. It was just like the song said, everyone deserves a chance to fly and this was hers.

As the final line reverberated through the hall, the assembled crowd burst into extravagant applause and Roe finally stopped and caught her breath. She tried to smile but to her horror tears sprang to her eyes. Why had she never let herself do this? Why had she been so paralysed by the thoughts of failure?

'Very good, Roe. Thank you.' Michael was bland in his tone but Roe didn't care – he was clearly annoyed at her showing him up.

As she made her way back down the stage steps, other singers mobbed her.

'Holy mother of God, in the name of Patti LuPone, Roe! Why have you been hiding that talent all this time?'

'Roe, jaysus! That was epic!'

'You could be in the West End. Genuinely.'

'Roe!' Lindy was skipping down the auditorium steps. 'That was incredible. I filmed it so you'll have it forever. How do you feel?'

'A bit sick but maybe in the good way. Like I'm high. I think I need to get outside.' Roe put her head down and charged through the crowds congratulating her. She wanted to bask in their praise but she also felt under siege. The magic of performing was already draining away, and she was hit once again by disbelief at the betrayal she'd committed in order to stand on that stage. She broke free of the hall, fleeing across the reception area and outside into the beginnings of a downpour. She could feel Lindy following behind.

'Roe, it's raining. Come back inside. What's wrong? That could not have gone better, you do realise that?'

'I know,' Roe wailed. She wanted to tell Lindy what she'd done, how she was lying to Eddie, but with everything going on in Lindy's own marriage, she didn't know how Lindy would take it. Spousal deception was probably not something she'd be too sympathetic to right now.

'Roe, you absolutely nailed the singing audition. We're going to way-off-Broadway, I'm sure of it! I know you're nervous but I'll be here to coach you every step of the way.' Lindy pressed on with the encouragement. 'And this is so exciting, Roe. You're going to do something you've been dreaming about for years.'

She's right, this is huge and I do deserve it. And if not now, then it really will be never.

She had to put the pregnancy-dodging out of her mind. It was only a small secret, she wasn't lying as such, and after the show – if she did get it – she could stop with the contraception and try for a baby for real. *Maybe. Stop dwelling!* Eddie would never know she'd put it off for a few months.

'OK, back in for the dancing now.' Lindy hustled her back through the doors.

As they came back into the auditorium, Roe saw Seb clocking her. She turned away fast, giving herself whiplash in the process, but sadly not fast enough. *Shite, he's coming over.* She was not ready for her close-up.

'Hey! Ray is it?'

'Feck,' Roe hissed before reluctantly turning to the eager Seb. 'It's Roe, not Ray, short for Rose,' she clarified.

'Ah, Roe, my apologies. We'd love to catch you for a few minutes – we know you really nailed the singing audition and just want to get a sense of how you're feeling ahead of the dance tryouts.'

'Oh.' Roe searched for something to put him off. 'I don't really have any feelings.'

'Like at all?' He grinned gamely.

'Yep, none.' Roe nodded decisively. 'I'm dead inside. Sorry.'

'Haha, that works perfectly.' He leaned closer conspiratorially. 'Honestly, the rest of them are unbearably bubbly. We need a bit of contrast. Someone to bring the snark!' Seb gestured to a camera woman behind him, who gamely zoomed in on Roe. A boom appeared above her head. Seb was all business.

'Just look at the camera, not at me, when I ask the questions. Thanks. So, Roe, you gave an extremely strong performance during the singing part of the audition. How are you feeling about what's next? Is dancing a strong suit of yours?'

Roe looked into the camera lens and smiled tensely. 'Yep. Feeling OK.'

Seb gestured in what was clearly meant to be an encouraging fashion. Reality-TV producers were clearly used to strong-arming their subjects.

'Fine, yeah.' Roe wasn't offering up much and she could see Seb's frustration.

'You've seen the routine? You don't think you'll get too bushed, jumping around like that?'

Roe sensed this was bait but she couldn't help but take it. 'What are you getting at?'

'Oh, nothing, it just must be demanding. Fitness-wise.'

Roe narrowed her eyes. Did he seriously just say that? She sensed the lens of the camera dilate as the camera woman zoomed in on her irritation.

'Fitness-wise I'm well able, thank you. Has it occurred to you that I might be fitter than you? That my size doesn't actually dictate my fitness, Seb?'

He grinned eagerly – he was obviously getting what he wanted. 'This is perfect, Roe. Maybe don't acknowledge me by name in your comments, OK? This is great, keep going. Do you find people underestimate you a lot, Roe? Because of your size maybe?'

Goddammit, he was loving this, and Roe had fallen straight into his trap. Any bit of controversy was the bread and butter of even the most family-orientated reality show. Still, it suddenly occurred to Roe that she'd rarely seen a fat girl triumph on a reality-TV show before. In fact, there were entire TV shows dedicated to 'fixing' women like her. She momentarily forgot about her resolve to give them nothing. She'd give them something all right.

'I'm really excited to audition today. Lots of people at home are probably used to seeing women like me on reality shows like *The Biggest Loser*, and I'm here to show everyone that I am not and will never be the biggest loser. I sing and dance and act. I'm a triple threat and I'm here to nail this audition. And truly, from the bottom of my beautiful fat heart, fuck the *Biggest Loser* – wait, can I say "fuck"? Oh, who cares.' She glared directly into the camera and grinned. 'Also fuck anyone who thinks I can't dance because I'm a fat girl.'

Seb punched his fist above his head. 'Brilliant, Roe. That was gold. Can we try that again without the fucks?'

But Roe was already storming back towards the stage. 'No probs,' he called after her, 'we can bleep them out!'

'How did that go?' Danny and Mags rushed towards her. 'I love how you were all "no way" to the *Glee Me* idea and then straight in the second you got a chance,' Danny mugged.

'Well, someone's gotta rep the odd squad with all these normies around.' Roe laughed.

'Hey, sorry to interrupt.' Seb, clutching his clipboard, had apparently tailed her and was now looking at them all with interest. 'I'm looking for someone to give a pithy but savage run-down of the Life and Soullers – would that be any of you?!'

Danny gave a worldly sigh. 'I'll take this one. Mags would be too bitchy for network television. I'll need some blush though. I'll be over in a mo.'

'Divine.' Seb ticked something off on his clipboard and scurried back to the camera operator.

Danny vogued savagely. 'I am so ready for my close-up but is middle Ireland ready?' and then stormed over to Ailbhe's make-up station.

'Life and Soullers who are auditioning for female leads, back at your marks, please,' Róisín was bellowing around the room as the various hopefuls hurried towards the stage. 'This audition is arguably more important than the singing one, gang. Everyone here can sing, we know that. And acting is a skill I can beat into you, but if you can't dance then you will not be doing much more than shifting scenery and getting my cold brew. Right, in a line and from the top. This will be round one of the dance tryouts.'

Roe hurried to the back row. She wasn't a bad dancer but they were coming to the routine cold. Luckily they were dancing to the 1976 UK winner 'Save Your Kisses for Me', which was a pretty chill mid-tempo. It would, per the lyrics, most likely just involve a lot of blowing of kisses and waving bye-bye. The music began and, following Róisín's lead at the front of the stage, Roe snapped her hips back and forth then spun to the right during the 'ooohs' before landing back at centre stage for the chorus. The next verse involved an elegant drop to the floor, with toes pointed to lead in to a couple of tricky fan kicks. The whole company finished on jazz hands and Róisín looked satisfied.

'Right, I've seen enough. If I call out your number, you can sit down: 11, 23, 6, 14 …'

Roe nervously held her breath. She was number 13; Denise was

8. If Denise was told to sit down, she'd know that was the group that was getting through this round. Denise always got through. She was just the type.

'And 4, 24, 7 and 9, sit down. OK.' Róisín surveyed the remaining choir members. Seb Knox appeared at her elbow and leaned in to whisper in her ear.

Roe glanced around. About ten of them were still up. Was she going to have to sing on her own? Dance on her own? She didn't feel ready for that.

'Roe!' She jolted. It was Mags sitting down to her right and miming for her to smile. Her thoughts must've been playing out all over her face. She jammed a manic smile in place just as Róisín waved Seb Knox off and two more camera men took up positions at the front and side of the group.

'Right. Those of you still standing ... Buckle UP! As you know, musical theatre is about stamina. A musical is a feat of endurance. A test of strength both physical and mental. Musical theatre is tougher than childbirth, a marathon and sitting through the entire *Lord of the Rings* franchise put together. No one will be on that stage who hasn't proven themselves. These auditions are vital to weed out the weak, to suss who has the chops for the lead roles and who will be,' Róisín looked mildly disgusted as she finished, 'in supporting parts.'

Obviously Seb Knox had told her to ham it up – it wasn't really in the spirit of the Life and Soullers to denigrate people who play the smaller roles in any kind of production. This was clearly Róisín's version of the opening monologue of *Fame* and it was making Roe nervous. What was she going to have them do?

'We're going to do the same number again, only this time I want singing and dancing. At the same time.'

A gasp buzzed through the crowd.

'Wait,' Róisín shouted, one hand raised to halt the giddy murmuring. 'I wasn't finished. I want singing and dancing at the same time. And it's last man standing.'

'Oh my fuck,' Danny squealed from his spot beside Seb before being silenced by a look from Róisín. 'Sorry,' he called, clamping a hand to his mouth.

Roe's thoughts raced. Last man standing as in …

'You will sing and dance the number over and over until there is just one performer left.' Róisín glared at the group.

Shit. There was just no way she could out-dance and out-sing all the other girls.

'OK, we're doing this immediately. Floor-dwellers up and out of the way of the MVPs.' Róisín winked as she hurried the others off the stage.

'Róisín?' Ailbhe, armed with a powder brush, was approaching the choir director. 'As it's a key scene, Seb wants touch-ups.'

'Sure, be quick. We don't want to lose our momentum.'

Ailbhe bee-lined for Roe. 'You need a touch up on that strong lip.'

'I need something considerably stronger than a lip, Ailbh.' Roe was pissed off. 'I can sing and dance but the two at the same time and over and over while perfect ex-Billie-Barry-kid Denise will barely break a sweat. It's too morto.'

'Roe, go like this.' Ailbhe stretched her lips into an 'O'.

Roe obeyed and tried to calm her churning stomach as her friend swept the lipstick around her mouth.

Lindy hurried down from her spot at the back of the hall to Roe's side. 'Hey, pal, how're you doing?' She squeezed Roe's hand. 'You're looking amazing up there. Remember, this is not just about the show: this is about showing yourself what you are capable of. Don't get carried away worrying about the big picture – just focus on what you have to do right now, in this moment, to tick this off your snag list. You do not want to be lying on your deathbed and thinking "shite, I didn't even try to do that thing". Remember, failing is not a failure: failing is a sign that you tried in the first place. Plus, you are not about to fail. And if you're dying of self-doubt and nerves right now ...'

Roe listened, bracing herself for some kind of Brené Brown-style wisdom.

'Remember, Roe,' Lindy concluded sagely, 'everyone shits.' Roe and Ailbhe burst out laughing as Lindy continued. 'Kristin Chenoweth shits. Idina Menzel shits. Anna Kendrick massively shits. Audra McDonald. Jennifer Hudson. That Billie Barry melt Denise in your choir shits. We all shit. Now break a leg. We love you, Roe!'

Ailbhe was convulsing with peals of laughter. 'I thought you were going to say ... something profound.'

'Yeah, I think the Snag List script needs work.' Roe blotted her lips.

'I know.' Lindy grimaced. 'Don't worry, I've booked myself a place on the diploma course with the Irish Life Coach Institute starting in September. I'll only be coaching adorable guinea pigs like you until I'm qualified.'

'Good to hear it!' Roe turned back to take her place among the dancers. This was her chance. She was risking more than the others to be there. She was playing Russian roulette with her relationship. But Lindy's 'fuck it'-style pep talk was oddly effective, and as the music started up once more, Roe took a deep breath and began to move to the beat. The first round of the song saw everyone stay standing, but Roe kept her focus on her own performance. She realised as they headed into the second go, they didn't necessarily have what she had. It wasn't a given that they were better than she was. She was good. One of the cameras swooped in front of her and she gave a playful wink as she fan-kicked enthusiastically. She was enjoying herself, and Roe knew you didn't usually enjoy doing something that you weren't good at.

As they headed into the third rendition of 'Save Your Kisses for Me', the first dropouts began. By the closing bars only four of them remained, and Roe couldn't stop grinning as she spun, waving bye-bye. Denise was actually looking quite stumbly and Roe knew she probably only had another go in her. The singing was hard and Roe was starting to get breathless – bloody vaping – but she wasn't giving in. Finally, it was just Denise and Roe, and the whole auditorium was tense and silent except for the plinky backing track and their laboured singing.

Roe was hanging on by a thread and she knew it wasn't worth continuing if her vocals were suffering, but then Denise abruptly stopped and bent over, gasping for a breath. The stunned room burst into applause; Mags leapt up and hugged Roe. 'Oh my God, how did you do that? Seventeen straight minutes of singing and dancing!'

Roe could barely catch her breath to answer before she was being bundled in front of a camera and Seb was firing questions at her.

'How does it feel? No one thought you could do it, am I right?'

Roe laugh-panted. 'God, Seb, don't sugar-coat it.'

'C'mon, Roe, give 'em the goods – audiences love an underdog.'

Danny had appeared at Seb's elbow. 'In my talking head, I predicted you'd win!' he added. 'Well, we shot two versions and I predicted you'd win in one of them!'

Over on the other side of the hall, Denise was crying in front of a different camera with the production assistant nodding encouragement at her. What could she possibly be saying?

As though reading her thoughts, Seb leaned in and whispered, 'Denise is playing the old "not feeling 100 per cent" card, just FYI.'

Danny shook his head in disgust. 'I mean, we all know there's no excuses in musical theatre. It's like the majestic Maggie Smith says: "Never complain, never explain".'

Roe was still sweating but elated. She nodded decisively at Seb. Then she grinned broadly at the camera. 'OK, so I dunno how the hell I just did that. Maybe you're watching right now, sitting at home and being all "no big deal", but seriously that was *haaard*! I sense I might have looked like I was experiencing some light demonic possession at a few points but TBH I don't even care – I just cannot believe I did that!'

'Perfect!' Seb clapped his hands together. 'Right, can we just do a couple of talent-show filler lines about how this has been your dream for as long as you can remember yada-yada-yada.'

Roe smiled and looked down the barrel of the camera lens. She knew she'd gotten completely carried away. She was supposed to be low-key.

Still, the desire to revel in this success was strong. Feck it. She'd figure it out later.

She took a breath. 'This has been a dream of mine for a really long time. I just never believed in myself. Until now.'

11

TWENTY MINUTES BEFORE THE YOUTUBE MUMS were scheduled to arrive, the operatic chime of the front door blared. *For feck's sake.* Lindy picked her way through the latest deliveries in the hall. It was a Friday morning and the Maxxed Out crew, which consisted of Eric, the videographer, and Peter, the sound guy, were in the back garden filming. She was dreading the YouTube moms coming over. Adam had met Rachel at Tubecon in the spring. She knew Miriam and Sigrid had been at it too because she'd feverishly scrolled back on both their Instas to confirm, and a paranoia had begun to fester in her that they might know something about Rachel and Adam.

'I know I'm early!' Sigrid's muffled voice came through the door. 'Are you leaving me out here to think about what I've done? C'mon, Linds, if Irish people had their way no one would ever arrive anywhere.'

'Hi, Siggie!' Lindy swung the door back to reveal her first guest to the house in the two months since they'd moved in.

'Oh wow, Lindy. What a peaceful place. It's basically the middle of nowhere.' Backhanded compliment #1. Sigrid could often hit double digits with these in just a matter of hours. Lindy had to admit, she and Sigrid would not be natural friends. Lindy wasn't mad close to any of the YouTube mums, really. But they did ease her discomfort around her career of choice.

As Sigrid moved through the hallway, she dispensed another backhander. 'Love the stairs, Lindy. They're so *Real Housewives*!'

Sigrid was resplendent in asymmetrical sacking. *How does she pull it off?* Of the YouTube momagers, Sigrid was definitely the most image-conscious, probably because she was the only one who did front-of-camera herself. Her channel, This Scandi Life, was a full-service lifestyle brand with fashion and interiors, along with the usual kids playing for the camera. Her older daughters, Cali and Clem, were blonde, braided beauties like their mother – and at seven and twelve, they ensured Sigrid was capturing several key demographics: Aspirational Mum, Cute Kid and Mumpreneur. Clem was also hitting the Generic Tween market but, as she was ensconced in the awkward phase, Sigrid featured her less and less – 'for her own sake' Sigrid insisted.

'Are we getting the tour? Or do I show myself around, Lindy?'

The bell chimed again and Lindy directed Sigrid through to the living-room-kitchen where the morning sun was streaming in from the enormous glass concertina doors through which the dino-hunt shoot was underway.

'Hi, gals.' At the door, she hugged Miriam and Giuliana each in turn. 'Sorry about the mess, you know yourselves. Deliveries!'

'Oh, it's non-stop,' Giuliana sympathised.

'I wish we could get off some of these press lists,' Miriam

confided. 'Some of the stuff is just—' She mimed puking. 'Like, I have standards.' Miriam Sullivan's high standards were obvious from her channel, which adhered to a strict nude palette with occasional well-judged charcoal greys for contrast. The devotion to the aesthetic was seriously impressive. The Sullivan kids played exclusively with eco toys made from sustainable materials and delivered in 'conscious' packaging. Lindy cringed at the sheer quantity of toxic, garish plastic shite Miriam was currently being subjected to in her hall.

'Come through, Sigrid's here.'

''Course she is.' Giuliana winked. 'You look whopper, by the way! Is this for us?' She circled Lindy, admiring the dark wide-leg, high-waisted trousers and cream fine-knit top.

'Kind of? But also I'm going up to the office later. I've actually started getting dressed properly again.' She laughed. 'It makes me feel more proper while I sit there fretting that I won't get any real clients and trying to work out if dispensing business cards to people at social gatherings would be borderline offensive. Like: "Oh, hey! You look really beaten down by life. Any regrets I can help you address?"'

'Got to start somewhere.' Giuliana smiled. 'I think the new venture sounds so exciting.'

'I envy you stepping down as CEO, Lindy.' Sigrid shook her head in a world-weary fashion. 'I would so love to be popping off to do a little passion project. How many weeks has it been?'

A little passion project – there it was: backhander #3.

Lindy smiled. 'I hung up my YouTube momager pants in the middle of May. So, what's that – a couple of weeks ago now?'

'So how are you settling in?' Sigrid continued, accepting Lindy's proffered coffee and arranging herself elegantly on the enormous U-shaped teal velvet couch.

'Exhausted from the move but happy to have so much extra space.' Lindy plastered on a smile. God, if they knew something about Adam and Rachel it would be so humiliating. Tears pricked her eyes and she took a breath to steady herself. She hadn't wanted to move here and now she was trapped here in her screwed-up marriage. Regret stole across the pit of her stomach every time she thought of their old house in town. It would fade. Some regrets were just an immutable fact of adult life. You accumulated more year on year. After a while you got used to them, learned to live with them, and then eventually they faded. Or they receded, at least. She couldn't go back there. She really needed to decide what to do about Adam.

Phone sex was definitely not the kind of thing that would eventually recede but Lindy'd been utterly paralysed about the situation for weeks. Only Roe knew and any time she brought it up, Lindy had to cut her off. It was too humiliating. Lindy'd begun to see the end of the summer as a kind of watershed. Things were so up in the air right now with her departure from Maxxed Out and trying to get the Snag List going, she was hoping that by September, with Max starting in school and her course beginning, things would settle down and she'd be able to confront Adam head on.

'The space is amazing.' Giuliana was gazing around admiringly at the mint and navy kitchen to their left and the dining space dominated by a hanging copper sculpture trailing indoor ivy.

'I suppose the location is just the price you pay now for space like this,' Sigrid announced in the same tone she might have used had Lindy had to trade a kidney for her new house. Backhander #4. 'When This Scandi Life received the Monteray Valley pitch we were tempted, but ultimately, as I told Mark, we're Europeans, we're cosmopolitan – we belong in the city! I just couldn't picture us out here. We would stagnate. It would stifle me. And no offence but suburban mummy – or "mammy" as ye call it here – is much more your thing, Linds.'

Ouch. There goes #5, Lindy thought.

'I know!' Miriam chimed in, sipping her coffee and peering around. 'The deal was good but sacrificing the city – all the amenities, the galleries, the restaurants – I just couldn't.'

Yeah, yeah, I get it. You're all too urbane for the Monteray Valley thing. Lindy curled her hands into fists to resist saying this out loud.

Subtly, Giuliana gave Lindy a meaningful look to communicate solidarity against the never-not-condescending Sigrid and Miriam.

'Jeez, you gals are crazy,' Giuliana said. 'I would've jumped on it if we'd been approached. What package with Monteray did you agree on?'

'Oh, stings in the videos for the next bajillion years, info on Monteray Valley in all YouTube descriptions, some dedicated content. Max doing house tours, playroom tours, kitchen tours, bloody utility-room tours. It's actually kind of bonkers but, well, it made sense for us.'

In reality, Adam had been adamant: 'There's no *way* we can turn it down.' Maxxed Out was doing well, but they would never have been able to get the mortgage for Monteray Valley. Banks still had a hard time getting their heads around careers like 'YouTubers'. Plus they had no real capital. They made a lot of money but Adam's penchant for investing meant it drained back out at a troubling rate. He insisted it was investing in their future. YouTube channels, even ones as successful as theirs, struggled to have longevity.

'Anyone for more coffee?' Lindy barely listened to their answers as she drifted over to switch the coffee machine on, hoping they'd move on from the subject. She was uneasy about it all. The house represented in a very visceral way how locked in to Maxxed Out they actually were. She thought about the VR-helmet crisis constantly, felt it simmering just under the still surface at all times, threatening to spill over into their life. She just felt so trapped. Trying to ignore how much it hurt for fear of jeopardising Maxxed Out seemed to underscore just how warped her relationship had become.

'I see Adam and Max are enjoying the new set-up?' Sigrid watched out the window, checking out the filming that was underway.

Adam was practically prancing for the cameras. 'We're going on a dino hunt. Can't wait to use our super awesome Squirt Rocket 500s to snare some of the raptors. Right, Max?'

'Whatever you want, Dad,' Max replied with barely concealed boredom.

'Cut,' Adam yelled and gestured for the production crew, Eric and Peter, to reset. 'Max, we're really gonna need some better energy than that, buddy.'

Sigrid turned back to Lindy. 'We have Clem acting up all the time now. It is such a pain in the ass.'

Outside Max continued to look moody. 'Whatever, Adam.'

'This is really not him.' Lindy bit her lip. He'd been off since they'd told him she wasn't going to be the CEO any more.

'Buddy.' Outside, Adam was speaking through clenched teeth and clearly trying to stay calm in the face of Max's lacklustre performance. 'Squirt Rocket 500 is basically paying the entire car lease this month, so do you think you could play the scene with a bit more enthusiasm?'

'Sure, whatever.' Max shrugged, looking glum. Lindy spotted Eric and Peter exchanging looks.

'Can you please stop with the "whatevers"? Don't say that word again,' Adam warned.

'Wh'evs …' Max rolled his eyes, and Adam exploded.

'Max! Goddammit,' he erupted.

'Oh God,' Lindy whimpered involuntarily.

'Don't stress, honey.' Sigrid waved a hand airily. 'They're all at it. My kids are the pits at the moment. They're getting older. Thinking they're in control of the whole show.'

She could see Adam storming over to Eric and Peter. 'We'll take five, guys.' They retreated to the outdoor lounge area to vape and presumably bitch quietly at yet another disruption to the day's filming.

Max was stomping away from the house and down the garden, ignoring Adam.

'Gals, I'm just going to check on things – I'll be right back.' Lindy slid out the doors.

At the end of the garden, Max was doing haphazard push-ups, his skinny arms shaking.

'Hey, you're doing great!'

'Uh-huh,' he replied with a little difficulty. 'I'm on … twenty … five.'

'Wow, that's amazing!' She crouched beside him. 'Are you sure you're OK? You don't seem to be having as much fun today as you usually do. Is there something on your mind? You can ask me anything, you know, and I will always tell you the truth.'

He abandoned the push-ups and sat cross-legged considering this while nervously twisting his hands in his lap. Eventually he looked up. 'Are you and Dad breaking up? Is that why you're not in charge of Maxxed Out any more?' His brow furrowed, and seeing him creased with worry made Lindy's throat constrict.

'No! Absolutely not.' Her heart stuttered at making this promise that she had no idea she could keep. But what the hell else *could* she say to that? She frantically searched for words to reassure him, words that were less definitive. She wrapped her arms around him. 'And if anything like that ever happened, it would have nothing to do with you or the channel. We love you. So. Much. With all of my heart, sweetheart. I love you. You're the best thing that ever happened to me.'

He pulled back to look up at her. He suddenly looked so young again. Her baby. 'I just …'

'What is it, sweetheart? Is it Maxxed Out? Do you not want to do it any more?'

'I do wanna keep doing Maxxed Out! It's not that.'

'Are you sure it's not? Are you feeling down about something?'

Max looked a bit stumped himself and Lindy felt stricken. It was a lot for him to comprehend, this odd internet fame that none of them had set out to achieve. He still claimed to enjoy the videos, being goofy and creative in front of the camera, and he and Adam always seemed to love trooping off to conventions to meet the thousands of Maxxed Out fans. She felt so conflicted. *I'm the parent. If the show is affecting Max badly, I should be putting a stop to it regardless of what he's claiming to want. He's just a child.*

Finally, he asked, 'Why did you not want to be CEO any more? Is the channel not doing good or something?'

'No! That is NOT the reason. I loved being in charge of Maxxed Out. But I studied psychology before you were born and I had this cool idea for a business that could help people and I really want to see it through. Plus, I wanted to make sure that we had another job so that whenever you don't feel like doing the channel any more there'd be a fallback, well not a *fallback*. Another option.' She rushed to correct herself, not wanting it to sound like they were currently solely reliant on him and Maxxed Out. 'Sweetie, Maxxed Out doesn't really need me any more. But promise me, anytime you want to throw in the towel on Maxxed Out, you'll tell me, won't you? We don't mind. You know that, right, honey? Daddy is just being a grump today – I'll talk to him.'

'I told you I don't wanna stop the channel.' Max was emphatic. 'I just want Dad to care about playing with me, not just for YouTube all the time.'

'He does, Max – he loves you.' Lindy pulled him closer, hugging him tightly.

'Mu-um! Stop it!'

She smiled and felt some relief at his grumbling resistance. If he'd succumbed to the cuddling too readily, she'd know that he was really upset, but the fact that she was annoying him with her affection meant he was his usual self once more. For now.

'OK, I'd better go hang out with my friends before I have to go to my office. I have to meet my new business lawyer this afternoon! Sounds fancy, right?' She held up her hand for a high five and he obliged.

'I love you, Mom.'

She made her way back to the house. Adam was on his way back too, scrolling on his phone as he walked. She caught up with him. 'I think Max is OK, just a bit tired, maybe.'

'Hmmm …' Adam barely looked up.

Watching your other half mess with their phone has to be one of the most annoying things about marriage. Lindy felt like slapping it out of his hand. Interestingly, as soon as he spotted her looking, he abruptly shoved it into his pocket.

Rachel? From the way he's acting, it has to be. She hated being so paranoid, hated that he'd done this to her.

'You're on the phone so much these days,' she said, to see how he'd react.

'Just work emails,' he quickly responded.

'Oh, really? Anything I should know about?'

'Now that you're just a board member? No, Lindy. Don't worry, Jamie and I have it covered.'

She opted to ignore the petty tone. 'After Sigrid, Giuls and Miriam leave, I'm meeting Finn up at the Work Hub.'

'What time will you be home today? I have a work call scheduled for 9 p.m.'

'Oh? About what? Weird time for a call.' Why was she pressing him? It was like running a finger along the blade of a knife: dangerous but strangely irresistible. She wanted to see him sweat a little. She wanted to examine him as he lied to her. What was she looking for? Signs that he found it hard to deceive her? A sign that he still cared about her?

'It's just a preliminary call about an investment opportunity. They're in New York.'

You think you're so smooth, Adam.

'I guess I'd better start thinking about investors too!' Lindy smiled tightly. She'd need more than the lump sum from Maxxed Out that they'd agreed to put into her initial costs. The 10k would cover her office space and the course in September but she'd need to put a lot into advertising and social media come January.

'Right, sounds like this Snag List thing is really shaping up. I'm glad.'

'So am I.' She was grim. 'Maxxed Out has a shelf life, Adam. Max seems fine to go on a dino hunt now, but what about next week or next year?'

'We shoulda had more kids.' Adam didn't seem to get that this wasn't the time for jokey quips.

'We'd need to have sex to do that,' Lindy snapped. 'You should have a think about next steps too. What do YouTube dads go on to after they're put out to pasture? You could do a fitness channel, I guess, or gaming? You love your VR helmet so much.'

He looked startled, which was satisfying at least. She swept back towards the house.

★

'OK, the solicitor says he's running about ten minutes late …' Finn read from her phone as she and Lindy entered the enormous reception space of the Monteray Work Hub later that afternoon.

Lindy nudged the distracted Finn. 'Hello? Will you look at this place?'

Finn's eyes widened. 'Whoa! Are they real trees? Is that a waterfall?'

'It is.' Lindy smiled, glad to have time to give Finn the tour. It would hopefully help to shake off the edgy hangover from the tricky morning at home. 'It's the largest man-made indoor waterfall in Europe.'

The Work Hub was a beautiful if slightly eerie space. The entire thing was made up of five circular buildings, each three storeys high so as to remain unobtrusive and not rise above the surrounding homes. From the entrance you could see straight up to the domed glass roof while the offices on each floor circled the perimeter.

'Every office looks onto this "nature space". So you can hear the waterfall and look at all the green, see the sky. They've done all the research on how this improves productivity blah blah.' Lindy rolled her eyes and led Finn over to the sloping ramp that gradually rose up to the upper floors.

'It was inspired by the Guggenheim in New York, and the free-snack game absolutely slaps.'

'Hey, Lindy.' George, a guy from crescent F, greeted them as he passed going down.

'It's so crazy to be working near other people again. I left Heart Mind Solutions five years ago, like! And I was sleep-walking through the last one with everything that happened.'

Finn nodded gently. 'Of course you were – Christ, you didn't pause for a minute.' She shook her head. 'I always felt bad for not intervening and making you take a rest,' she admitted.

'No!' Lindy stopped just as they came to the first floor. 'I wouldn't have listened to anyone at the time. What would I have done? I was *afraid* to slow down. And, what? Be with my thoughts? Horrific.'

'Sis …' Finn leaned in for a hug and Lindy grabbed her arms.

'Absolutely not, Fionnuala! This is not us.' She laughed. 'Slag me quick. Say something cutting – you're weirding me out.'

Finn laughed. 'From behind I can see that these high-waisted pants are absolutely riding you. It's grotesque, frankly.'

'I know! What is the deal? Everyone just goes around never talking about this major issue with high-waisted pants.' Lindy feigned outrage. 'Especially the swishy ones. They just glide up there. At least with the jeans there's enough friction or something to keep them in their place.'

'It's got to be the patriarchy,' Finn said solemnly. 'I'm convinced they hold a summit every year to decide what debilitating fashions will be on trend next.'

They carried on, and a little further down the curved white corridor, Lindy opened the third door on the right. 'Here it is.'

'OK, this is gorgeous.'

'They have a crazed mandate that everyone's office is pure white but you're allowed to use an "accent colour" to give a personal touch. Obviously I'm going with the pink and red to match the Snag List logo.' Lindy stepped to the side to show off the large pink and red logo she'd had made and mounted on the wall behind the desk. 'The' and 'List' were done in cursive lettering in a dark red, while the 'Snag' was a pale pink with a few subtle cracks on the 'g' done in grey.

'Oh, that is slick, I love it.'

They sat down on the white chairs. 'A menstruating person's nightmare,' Finn remarked.

'I'll get the coffees.'

Finn watched with obvious fascination as Lindy tapped on the Monteray app. 'I know you told me it was like this, but it really is amazing. I didn't see a coffee place down there. I can't even *smell* coffee. Offices always smell like bad coffee, but this place smells like citrus and – what? – eucalyptus. And money.'

A man in a startlingly pristine white suit knocked gently and came in to set the coffees down.

'Thank you!' Lindy called as he left again.

'OK, *where* did he come from?' Finn was incredulous. 'That was creepy.'

Finn's going to have a field day with this, Lindy thought but carried on nonetheless. 'Sooo ... There's a network of underground tunnels—'

'They LIVE UNDER GROUND?' Finn thundered. 'Oh my God, this isn't an upper-middle-class enclave: it's an upper-middle-class *dystopia*. Jean and Liam's mildly socialist little hearts will give out when they hear this.'

'The staff don't *live* here,' Lindy argued. 'They live in their homes. The tunnels, subterranean corridors, are just so the whole place isn't swarmed with staff all the time.'

'The more you say, the worse it sounds—'

Lindy was immensely grateful when, at that exact moment, a compact man with glasses and very wiry dark hair ducked his head in through the door.

'Finn! Howya!'

'Hi, Patrick. Thank you so much for coming all the way out here. And well done for finding us – I thought you'd call when you got sucked into the beige maze out there.'

'Lindy! Patrick, great to meet you.' He waved across to Lindy. 'I found it grand. Lindy's website has very clear directions. The website's looking great, by the way – Finn says it's still early days with The Snag List.'

'Oh yeah, it's very early days. Pre-days really.' Lindy was dragging the other chair over so Patrick could sit. 'I'm working with a pal as a kind of trial run, and obviously I'm trying to get the necessary structures in place. I've a bit of experience of not getting things in writing early on in a venture, so I'm just very keen for The Snag List to be watertight on that front.'

'Of course.' He slung off his backpack and took his seat, pulling out his laptop. 'I had a good look through everything you sent me, and I can see what you mean about it not being a standard one-size-fits-all release form, but we can definitely draft an approximation of that and add and subtract clauses et cetera on a case-by-case basis. It'll mean a bit more money needed for contracts in general, but better paying money into the legals rather than the lawsuits. I've sent you over a draft to get us started. Do you need me to tailor this to the specific clients you're working with right now?'

Forty minutes later and Patrick had said his goodbyes and sent through an invoice in the time it probably took him to exit the building.

'Oh, he is very prompt with that stuff.' Finn laughed.

'His rate is really good, you were right – thanks so much for gifting him to me!' Lindy smiled. 'I can't wait to start the course and I'll be recruiting actual clients soon. It's getting real! Eek, *too* real!'

'I don't want to be compounding the too-real-ness but, Lindy, I'm getting vibes. Is everything OK? You've hardly been saying a word on the family WhatsApp since you moved out here. Is it the house? Adam?'

Lindy felt herself flinch. Oh God, Finn was impossible to hide things from.

'OK, Lindy, you just flinched at his name. What's going on? When ye were back home in Drumcondra, you didn't have to say it for me to know things weren't brilliant. But I thought you both just had Pandemic Traumatic Spouse Disorder after the lockdowns. I figured that it would *dissipate*. Are things worse? Are you two OK?'

Lindy took a deep breath and prepared to lie. She tried to smile in what she hoped was a reassuring fashion. 'Well—' she began, but then she cracked. This was Finn: she had to tell her. The idea that Finn would come here and not know immediately that something was wrong had been ludicrous.

'Lindy.' Finn came over to hug her and this time Lindy didn't stop her. 'Tell me.'

So she did …

'That effing bastard. Jesus, Lindy, I am so sorry.'

'I know.' Lindy had cried all the way through the retelling and now felt wrung out.

Finn looked at a complete loss. 'I feel so bad for what I said. I actually really do like your trousers.'

Lindy snorted.

'I do! I like seeing you dressed up, it feels like – I dunno – a good sign or something. And then you tell me all this is going on. How are you keeping everything together?'

'I'm keeping it together because I have zero other choices.' Lindy sighed. 'Like, what can I do? That is a genuine question, by the way, because I can't picture a way out of this that doesn't completely ruin Max. Earlier he asked if I was leaving Maxxed Out because it wasn't good any more and it just killed me. What would he do if I was leaving his dad?'

Finn looked helpless.

'You probably think I'm pathetic that I haven't confronted Adam yet—'

'I absolutely don't, Lindy, not for a second. Look at me. Two marriages, same man. Did I learn? No. Love is absolutely baffling sometimes. It's so hard. "Marriage is hard" as a phrase is so overused that nobody even hears the words any more. Marriage. Is. Hard. No two ways. I don't hold with that whole "if it's love then it should be easy". Lies. Fuck that,' she hissed and Lindy had to laugh.

'But it definitely was easy at the start – I remember it was.' Lindy picked up her now-freezing coffee and stirred it for something normal to do. Saying everything out loud to Fionnuala was reigniting the shock and sadness she'd been trying to keep buried.

'Of course it was easy at the start. In the beginning, you're all cocooned away in a sex den of pheromones. Then life forces its way in. And it came in on you and Adam very quickly. You had tough things to contend with in pretty quick succession. Adam moving to a new country; Max, the sweetie, charging along; the pregnancy you lost; the business taking off; the mother-goddam-fucking pandemic.' Finn stopped and silence swelled in the room. A lot had just been said.

Lindy pulled nervously at her bottom lip. 'What should I do, Finn? I've thought and thought and I really don't want to give up on our family.'

'People co-parent, Linds. People adjust. You know leaving him would not be giving up on your family.'

'OK, yes, I know that in theory. I just can't imagine confronting him. We could lose everything – our business, our home … I can't imagine being the one to strike that match. Is this enough to do that?'

'That is up to you, sweetie. Can you get past it? You don't even know fully what "it" is or was. And if you never ask, will that unknown eat away at you, or can you reconcile yourself to it? I am not judging in any way, by the way. I know I've been vocal in the past about you and Adam getting married quick and all that, but I know how complicated life can be, and working through or not working through something like this is so personal. Only you can know.'

'For fuck's sake, Finn. The one time I want you to boss me and you're all Switzerland about it.'

'OK, leave him.'

'What?' Lindy balked, jerking her cup and spilling coffee.

'Right, freeze.' Finn seized her shoulders from across the desk. 'How did it feel when I said that?'

'Oh, I see. You're good. My stomach plummeted when you said "leave him". You made me spill my coffee on the white rug. That's my answer, isn't it?' she added quietly.

Finn sat back. 'It's your answer for now. Maybe that'll change. Organised CEO Lindy would probably be looking for more information before making an investment, though, wouldn't she? And sticking with him is an investment of sorts.'

'What are you suggesting? Tail him? I really don't think they've been meeting. Between the neighbours and the staff, the surveillance here is pretty intense; someone would notice and it'd probably wind up on the Monteray Valley Concerned Residents WhatsApp.'

'I'm not talking about that. I am talking about you properly spending some time together. Trying to figure if what you have is salvageable. Remember in Drumcondra you and Adam used to do those sixteen-hour-date days. Leave in the morning, go walking and have breakfast. Spend the whole day away. I'll come and watch Max next week. You and Adam clear a window and have a mini holiday, a little trip back to the old Adam and Lindy.'

12

AILBHE SAT AT HER LAPTOP IN THE OFFICE ON THE third floor of the house on a Zoom Alcoholics Anonymous meeting. She was only five days in and already AA was a ball-ache of the highest order. As Tom had promised, Maia had connected her with some online recovery meetings, and despite feeling that AA was utterly unnecessary, Ailbhe had actually liked having the chats with Maia. At first, she'd been embarrassed at Tom insisting she needed help, but Maia was very non-judgemental and even confided that she herself was in recovery – she'd had a serious drinking problem when she was younger. She even came along to the first couple of meetings with Ailbhe as support, which was nice. Still, Ailbhe knew this wasn't the place for her; this gang at the meetings seemed to have drunk every day and lost jobs and families over their drinking. She was fine. She was going to go along with it all to keep Tom onside – after all, he was here from now until they left in July so she had to be on good behaviour – but really the AAers weren't doing much to sell the sober life. They wouldn't touch so much as a Solpadeine and they were endlessly stressing about going in for various surgeries and being prescribed tasty, delicious morphine.

'The wee lad is finishing up his fourth year in college.' Declan, the man currently sharing, was getting misty. 'He took us out for dinner. Paid and all. I said to the missus, did you ever think we'd see the day when *he'd* be treating *us*! And of course none of it would've been possible without AA and these rooms.'

Christ. Ailbhe checked the time. Twenty minutes left. The one bonus of Zoom was she could mess around on social media. She opened her DMs to check how many messages from Seb had racked up. He was flirting incessantly with her and it was extremely stressful. She was trying to maintain a delicate balance of responding here and there so he wouldn't think something was wrong and potentially ask Holly about her in rehearsals, but not respond to so many that he got the wrong idea. My God, what were the bloody chances of him catching up with her just weeks before her getaway? *Why does the universe hate me?* she wailed silently.

'Well, anyway, that's me.' Declan was wrapping up at last.

'Thanks, Declan.' Audrey, the secretary of the lunchtime meeting, appeared to scan her screen before addressing the group. 'Anyone in their first thirty days want to share? I'm not trying to put you on the spot.' She smiled and Ailbhe had the unnerving sense that Audrey was staring directly at her little window in the gallery. 'Remember, we listen to learn, but something you share as a newcomer can be just as valuable to those of us who've been here longer.'

Ailbhe scanned the other people in their separate boxes – no one else seemed to be new. They all looked so earnest it was painful. *Ah, I'll say something to get them off my back. I'll open with a joke.*

'Hi, I'm Ailbhe, and I am here because my husband is American and he doesn't understand how we do things in Ireland!'

'Hi, Ailbhe,' a few people chimed back at her, apparently willing to overlook the fact that she'd neglected to identify as an addict, as is the custom.

'So, anyway, I'm not doing down what you all do here, but I actually amn't an alcoholic. I'm just trying to reassure him. There was a little incident at a party like a week ago and he thinks I have an "alcohol problem" – which I don't, by the way. I was actually on coke at the time!'

Shit. That would not help her cause one bit. Thank God Maia wasn't at today's meeting.

She scrambled to smooth the situation. 'It's not like I was the one who *brought* the coke. All the other parents were having little bumps at this party too. I was just politely partaking. Plus, I don't know if any of you have been to a five-year-old's birthday party recently, but, seriously, how are you supposed to get through one of those *without* drugs? It would be hell totally sober.' Ailbhe gazed around beseechingly. *Oh God, just shut up, Ailbhe.*

'OK,' Audrey interrupted, shuffling pages in her little window. 'I'm taking a group-conscience decision to stop you right there. At this meeting we have to focus on our problems as they pertain to our addictions. If you're not ready to take this seriously, I'm not sure we can help you. We do this to maintain the integrity of the group, not to shame you,' Audrey explained. 'It sounds like you have some stuff to work through. You say that you don't have a problem, but there are some elements of your life that suggest otherwise. Not all people have troubles in their marriages after a child's birthday party.' Audrey smiled gently but her tone was firm. 'And maybe there are other troubles in your life as a result of drugs or alcohol too, perhaps?'

'No, as a matter of fact!' Ailbhe couldn't have Audrey reading her so easily as her mind immediately flashed back to the cursed night almost exactly a year ago that was now threatening to derail her plans entirely.

Last summer, when Ailbhe had walked into the Lord Edward to see if it'd be good for Eilers' fifty-eighth birthday, she'd had no idea what was coming. She was checking if their function room upstairs was back in action since the last lockdown and going back and forth in her mind over the conversation she'd just had with Tom. He'd told her he loved her and she'd brushed it off. She felt guilty. She knew her feelings for him were becoming more serious, but instead of being happy she was feeling out of control. Since the wedding debacle and the year afterwards, when a sea of depression had dragged her under, she'd dodged any relationship that seemed to be heading towards a deeper commitment; it felt too risky. Until now.

It had only been a couple of months with Tom and already he was trying to get serious, and Ailbhe was torn. One half of her wanted to trust him and take a risk, and the other half, the half that usually made her decisions, wanted to cut and run. She wanted to not care. Caring led to hurt.

She'd been assessing how many would fit in the function area when she'd spotted Seb at the bar. They had many drinks. *We're just catching up*, she'd told herself, trying to put thoughts of Tom sitting on the other side of the city out of her mind. Seb was over from London and staying in the Jurys Inn right next door to the pub. Ailbhe felt herself inexorably pulled towards the destruction that sleeping with Seb offered. If she slept with Seb then it meant that she was still in control. It was a hop, skip and a jump to his bed. Tragically, cracking into a €9 bar of Mint Crisp from the minibar was the most exciting thing that happened in that room. What a letdown. Of course, Seb seemed delighted with it – men always do. He was all for her staying over, clearly dying for another grunty go. *Ew*. Despite the powerfully crap sex – a lot of thrusting with no consistency in rhythm or pressure; if it had been a song, she'd have said it was a flaccid ballad – she'd found it quite satisfying to find that the one that got away wasn't so amazing after all. She'd made a lazy excuse – something, something, have to feed the cat – and filed it under 'It happened in a blackout so it DOESN'T COUNT!'

Had it not been for the desperate collision of events that unfolded soon after, Ailbhe would likely have never thought of it again.

She cringed. It was a filing system she'd completely abandoned since. She hated that she'd done that to Tom. And on the night he'd been trying to get closer to her.

She sat in silence for the rest of the meeting.

Look, I didn't know we were going to be long-term, she reasoned. *I will never do anything like that again. Just, please, God – I know I'm always coming crawling back to you, but please get me out of this one intact and with nobody finding out anything that could hurt them.*

13

'SOOOOO! HOW ARE YOU FEELING, BABE? Anything ... *different*?'

Roe stared at the traffic straight ahead, resolutely dodging Eddie's sidelong glance as he switched lanes.

'Different how? Different like ... I've been fertilised? Or different like I want to give up this whole crazy life and just get really deep into a wellness cult?'

He grinned. 'Don't give me a hard time. I know it's too soon for there to be "signs" – I'm just excited.' Eddie inched along the canal towards DeLacey's and Roe's dinner shift. At least Thursday nights were more chill. *I have got to learn to drive.* Roe sat fighting her angsty pregnancy-*un*related nausea. It had been a week since the auditions and their last insemination attempt, and she had been battling this queasy guilt every single moment she spent in Eddie's company. Seriously, how do cheaters do it? People who conduct months-long affairs while pretending to their spouse that they're perfectly happy and not off boning someone else must be sociopaths. How else could they cope with the daily lies?

She was counting the days until her period would come and Eddie would stop monitoring her. Next month she'd put him off trying altogether – it was too much on top of her edginess about *Voices of Glory*. The parts for the musical were being announced at rehearsals the next day, but anyone who'd landed lead roles would be notified by email tonight. This was because the *Glee Me* crew needed key cast members in rehearsals earlier to shoot talking heads and reaction shots ahead of the real announcement.

Being on a reality show was adding a whole other layer of fakery to her life right now. Dodging pregnancy was shady but it wasn't the worst thing. However, she hadn't mentioned a word about getting coaching from Lindy to Eddie. And when she'd told him, after the fact, about auditioning, he'd been lukewarm, so she had massively downplayed how well it had gone. Any other year, Eddie would have been thrilled to see her putting herself out there, but this year the baby plan was all he seemed to be thinking about.

'Here we go – take it easy in there now, Roe.' Eddie parked outside the delivery entrance in the lane beside the restaurant. 'You don't need to be running around. You're the manager, delegate. Get Danny to cover the upstairs section tonight, will you?'

'OK, firstly, relax. Women have won weight-lifting titles while in the throes of pregnancy. And secondly, I'm not even—'

Frenzied rapping on the car window startled them both. Danny. And by the looks of him, Danny at least 800 per cent more frenetic than usual. Her gut seized with a potent blend of anxiety and excitement. *The email has to have come through.* Her phone was in her bag on silent. She hesitated to roll down her window. She hadn't wanted to find out in front of Eddie. If she was cast, she needed a game plan. Unfortunately, Eddie was already opening her window from the button on his side.

'What is he on?' Eddie laughed as Danny's arm came over the retreating glass first, followed by his entire upper body.

'Roe, you Liza–Barbra–Bette love-child. Have you SEEN? You got it.' He grabbed her face and smooched her lovingly.

'Wow.' Eddie smiled tepidly and Roe caught a twinge of unease in his eyes.

Danny clearly didn't notice. 'Our girl is the lead, Eddie! The lead. I could cry but this mascara runs. Roe O'Neill *is* Niamh Kavanagh. Aaaaand I am none other than Michael Flatley baby.'

Something joyous and awesome whooshed through her. A feeling so big and beautiful, Roe couldn't help but also feel a shard of sadness as she realised it was one of the happiest moments she'd experienced in years. Maybe ever.

'Oh, Roe, that's … wonderful.' Eddie's words faltered as he leaned over to catch the tears she hadn't noticed on her cheeks. 'It's such an achievement. You'll aways have it.'

'Enjoy this moment, darl.' Danny was uncharacteristically solemn. 'I'll get in there and distract Gina. Give you two a moment to celebrate.' He blew a kiss and ducked into the restaurant.

'Wow, so you got it!' Eddie looked a bit stunned. 'Had to be this year, huh?'

Roe's big beautiful feeling was shrinking by the second but she was feeling defiant. 'Well, I'd hardly be doing it next year if we had a baby kicking around.'

'Yeah.' Eddie nodded, his eyes on the dash.

'It could take us years to get pregnant. I can't be tiptoeing around every month on the off-chance there's a zygote sloshing around in there, Eddie. Anyway, they are super protected in there – a bit of singing won't do anything.'

She flashed on the drills Lindy had sent her in the accountability Slack channel she'd set up called Operation Triple Threat. It was a sadistic tutorial for improving lung capacity – singing while doing some very hardcore stuff with skipping ropes. 'Eight shows a week, you'll thank me, you pathetic ingrates,' the instructor in the clip barked. 'Do you think Barrett Wilbert Weed would complain about this? This is conditioning for dancing and singing and keeping a goddamn smile on your face.'

'Yeah.' Eddie exhaled. 'I know. You're right.'

Roe sensed he needed more reassurance. She hated them being so distant. It made her feel untethered, a little unsafe. 'Look, if you duff me up in the next few months, I'll drop out. Róisín will have contingency for that kind of thing.'

She tried to ignore how satisfied Eddie looked at that suggestion. But it poked at her as she said goodbye and went through the dinner service set-up.

'He should want this for me,' she vented to Danny as they pushed tables for the supper club together.

'OK, you know I'll denigrate male entitlement any day of the week, but to be fair to Eddie, have you been honest with him?'

'Well …'

'No is the answer,' Danny snapped.

'Wait, I—'

'The question was rhetorical, Roe. You haven't. Have you said the words: I don't want your goddamn spooge spawn? Have you said: I actually think I want to shoot for the moon and get on stage? No. I'm sorry, but I'm getting a bit bored of this now, Roe.'

'OK. Ouch.' They pulled back the huge front windows of DeLacey's in silence. The evening was going to be beautiful. Early June nights in the dining room overlooking the water were very special. A warm summer breeze, ripe with possibility, drifted in and was enough to overthrow the upset Roe was feeling. At least for the moment.

I got the part!

14

LINDY AND ADAM WERE IN WICKLOW, STANDING IN waist-deep, sharply cold water, paddles in hand, with two long, wide boards floating in the water before them. The beach was beautiful in the pale Friday-morning sun; they'd cleared the day's schedule specially. The strand was deserted except for their bleached and weathered instructor, who was carrying the last board down from his van parked in the dunes.

'Are you ready for this?' Adam was squinting over at her. 'It's very complicated.'

'Stand-up paddleboarding?' Lindy grinned. 'I think it's the only sport where the name can double up as the instructions.'

'Duh, what about "foot" "ball"? Anyway, I wasn't talking about that – I was talking about *this*!' He lunged at her and unceremoniously dunked her head into the sea.

'Je*sus*!' She surfaced with a yell, spluttering and coughing. 'You don't know your own strength.' She pretended to nurse the side of her head.

'Aw, babe.' He pushed through the water towards her. She waited until he was well within reach and launched herself at him. The idea was to dunk him, but due to their differences in size and strength, he just caught her in his arms and didn't budge. They stood like that for a minute, her legs around his waist and her hands on his shoulders. 'You the catch of the day?' He smirked up at her.

'Corny.' She made to squirm away but then his hands slid from the small of her back and cupped her ass.

He leaned in, his breath hot on her cool shoulder. 'After this, do you wanna go do it in the dunes?' he whispered.

'Another sport where the name doubles up as the instructions!'

Lindy was feeling optimistic this morning. Finn was minding Max and she and Adam had the whole day. She'd booked the paddleboarding, hoping a bit of loitering around while wet and barely clothed might jump-start things.

He kissed her ear as the instructor called to them. 'You guys ready to go? The first thing we're going to do is stand up on our boards and then paddle!'

The lesson lasted an hour and Lindy was willing it to be over. She was thinking about Adam's words all the way through. In the sea, her senses felt heightened and there was a pleasant squirm of excitement in her belly, though trepidation was there too. She knew her nipples were hard, they pressed against her swimsuit, and she'd seen Adam looking. The knowledge that he was probably getting hard thinking about her nipples was exquisite but unfortunately jumbled in with a cacophony of conflicting feelings and intellectualising about their relationship.

She could not cope with another clunky ride. Her marriage couldn't take it either. One more botched job in that department and they'd have to acknowledge how bad it'd got.

Live in the moment, she ordered herself. She made a pact with herself that this day was to be a hiatus from the constant agonising.

At the end of the lesson, back on the beach, the instructor practically fled.

'You can't blame the guy.' Adam laughed, pulling her to his chest. 'The randiness was palpable.'

'Eh, speak for yourself. I was just minding my business, enjoying the wholesome water sport.'

'Uh-huh, of course.' He placed his hand between her shoulder blades and pressed her against him. His right hand trailed lazily up her ribcage, skirting her breast and tugging the strap of her swimming costume down until her breast was exposed. He didn't touch it; he leaned in to the dip of her shoulder and groaned. It brought so much back. They were once good at this. Now he was pinching her nipple, then his fingers were inside her. The cold was shocking and divine at once.

'We have to go somewhere, Lindy.' His voice in her ear was urgent.

They hurried back over the dunes and up the path leading to where they'd parked. There were trees on either side, though they wouldn't provide much cover. Still, Lindy was not going back to the car – it was going so well, and she sensed any return to reality would kill the moment.

'Here.' She pulled him off the path and through the low branches until they came to a depression at the roots of a large tree, slightly shielded from the path. He immediately pushed her up against the tree and pressed his erection hard against her. The bark was rough on her back. 'Fuck, Lindy. You're so beautiful. You're so hot.' His face was close to hers; he smelled like sea and his breath was hot in her mouth.

He says this to her.

'What do you want me to do?' He was staring at her intensely.

Don't let the thoughts in.

'I want you to suck on my tits,' she commanded.

He yanked down her straps. When his hot mouth found her cold nipples, she wondered how much longer she'd be able to stand; a luscious warmth was spreading through her. She shimmied her suit off.

He pushed his shorts down, grabbed her behind her left knee, raising it to push into her quick and deep. She cried out and he thrust again.

'I'm gonna come.' Her words came out strangled. It was building, an intense, deep burst of pleasure, and then with each push more and more and more.

'That's it, that's it,' he muttered in her ear.

She gasped and came hard again. 'Fuck,' she breathed. He stopped pushing into her for a moment. 'My back …' she whispered.

He understood. He pulled out and eased her to the ground.

'I wanna see you.' He laid her out on her right side. He stroked the small of her back over her hips. She liked the way he was looking down at her in a detached, almost appraising way.

And then: *He looks at her like this.*

She suddenly felt horribly vulnerable. *Is he comparing me to her?* He grabbed her thigh and pushed it up slightly to ease into her again. Barely a minute passed and he was gripping her hip and the small of her back, his face clenched, trying not to make too much noise as his body shook. 'Oh God. Oh God.'

After, he flopped down beside her, breathing hard. Eventually he spoke. 'So what are we doing for the rest of the day?'

'Well, first we need to de-pine-needle.' Lindy pulled her arm protectively across her chest and stood up, not looking at Adam watching her. She was now hyper-aware of her nakedness. Adam scrambled up after her and handed her the swimming togs. She accepted them and waited for him to turn so she could put them on, but he stayed looking at her.

'I feel like we never look at each other any more.' He traced a thumb along her hairline down to her neck. 'Do you feel that way?'

'I do.' She was quiet. She did not want to do this. If they said much more she would cry, and that was not what this day was about. 'Maybe it's just the life stage. We have so much on the to-do list every day ... So, I have a surprise but you have to be the gentleman and go get the towels and clothes.'

Once dressed they sat in the car and Lindy pulled out the notebooks and pens she'd brought.

'Right. One each.' She passed Adam his pen and paper and turned to face him, pulling herself into a cross-legged position with her back against the car door. 'So the game for the day is one of us asks a question and we both write our answers at the same time and hold them up to read at the same time. Got it? The question can be about anything but we have to both write answers. I'm going first: What do we want to have for breakfast?'

Adam grinned and tapped his pen against his bottom lip. Then he wrote something.

Lindy'd known what she wanted for breakfast since they'd left the house at six that morning. She scribbled her answer.

'OK, what do we want to have for breakfast?' she repeated.

Adam turned his page around. *YOU! Again ;)*

She turned her notebook over: *Sausage sandwiches, coffee and bananas with peanut butter on the beach.*

'OK, into it.' Adam put the car into gear. 'There's a garage a few miles back. I hope they have peanut butter.'

In less than twenty minutes they were back, devouring buttery sausage sandwiches on the beach blanket Lindy had brought. The coffee was notably crap, but it was amazing how the beach made everything taste better. She idly began spreading the banana with a smear of peanut butter.

'Lindy! I can't believe I'd forgotten that's how you eat that. Absolutely crazed, no vehicle, just peanut butter straight on it …'

'Only you ever fixated on it – no one else ever felt the need to comment. Anyway, it is objectively the best method of pairing the iconic banana–peanut-butter combo. If you use bread or whatever the whole thing is too claggy. This is more refined.'

'Of course, dead right. So what's next for the day?'

'Are you asking the notebooks?'

'Sure, OK.' He picked his up and thought for a moment before jotting something down.

Lindy quickly wrote her own answer. 'OK what's next?' She turned hers around to reveal: *Whatever you wrote*. He laughed and turned his around: *Go look at some … fish …?!?!*

'It's hard to come up with stuff!' he cried. 'And yours is a complete cop-out. You shouldn't be allowed do that.'

Lindy munched on her banana and pretended to nod gravely. Then: 'OK, I've given it some serious thought and I've decided that I'm fine with what I just did. Anyway, "go look at some fish" is a great idea. We can drive to Bray.'

'Yes! The aquarium there has a larger-than-life-size picture of topless Richard E. Grant holding a fish like a baby.'

'It's weird that you know that.'

'Well, there it is.' Adam uncovered her eyes – he'd insisted on covering them before the big reveal. 'Majestic, isn't it?' They were standing in the entrance to the aquarium gazing at Richard E. Grant, as promised, cradling a large fish.

'It's so incongruous – we should ask someone why it's here.'

'No,' Adam cut across her. 'I never want an explanation. The explanation will probably be boring. I want to hold this no-context Richard E. Grant fish-hugging image in my mind forever uncorrupted by reason.'

The rest of the aquarium tour was surprisingly fun. They'd done lots of this kind of stuff when Max was a kid. The zoo had been close, and seeing the deer in the Phoenix Park was a Sunday-morning regular. Then the Maxxed Out camera had started to come along with them and it became something else entirely.

After lunch (they'd both written down McDonald's), they walked down the pretty, wide streets of white Georgian villas back to the Bray seafront. They were on a vague hunt for an ice cream when Adam stopped and took his notebook out of his back pocket.

'I have one: What do we think are the best things about each other?'

'Ugh, no.' Lindy scoffed. 'Too saccharine.' Also, she was definitely afraid they'd struggle too much to come up with stuff.

'Nope, I'm insisting, Linds. It'll be good for morale!'

She laughed and retrieved her notebook from the large pocket of her navy rain jacket. 'OK, fine. Are we doing one thing?'

'How could you possibly narrow yours for me down? Let's do our top three.'

They walked in silence, thinking, and when they came to the promenade in front of the grey pebble beach, they sat at opposite ends of a bench to write. Adam was finished well before her, and Lindy twisted away from him slightly, scanning the horizon, willing something to come. It wasn't that there was nothing. It was more like there was too much: her head was like a washing machine. *You're hot, you're fun, you're energetic, you're lying to me, you're spending our money like it's your money, you're looking at another woman.*

God, get on track, she ordered herself, consciously pushing the clamouring thoughts out of the way.

She wrote:

Arrogance/confidence.
Funny (sometimes).
Smell.

She turned to show him and he rocked with laughter. 'Well, that has put me in my place.' He turned his to her:

> *I love your humour and your intelligence.*
> *I love the freckles on your eyelids.*
> *I love the way you smell.*

'Mine's like a love letter and yours is a shopping list.' He slid along the bench to her and put an arm around her. 'We are two good-smelling bastards.'

She settled back against him and watched the seagulls circling and swooping, crying and fighting over the occasional scrap of food.

Adam nudged her. 'Look,' he jerked his head over to the row of shops behind them, 'a tattoo place. No ragrets?'

She laughed. They'd actually tried to get matching tattoos once in Melbourne. 'Remember they said to come back when we weren't so shitfaced?' She giggled.

'Do you remember what we were going to get?' Adam frowned, trying to think.

'It could have been anything. It was, like, 2011 so it deffo would've been horrific.'

'Well,' he waved the notebook, 'will Adam and Lindy get their first tattoos?'

Lindy didn't immediately have an answer to this one. She didn't strictly not want a tattoo, but a permanent thing like a tattoo done during a date she'd proposed, in part, to find out if her marriage had any shot at permanence? It was either ... poetically fitting or completely tragic.

She wrote: *OK.*

He'd written: *Whatever Lindy says!*

She smiled and stood. She reached for his hand. 'OK, ice cream before or after tattoos?'

★

They got home at ten that night to find Fionnuala on her phone on the couch in the kitchen with Max lying against her, dozing.

'It is so nice when he sleeps on you, isn't it?' Lindy swooped down to kiss her son's ear.

'I'll bring him up.' Adam slipped his arms under Max, lifted him gently and carried him out.

'Sooo! How was it?'

'It was very teenage, actually. We got McDonald's, had fairly dodgy public sex and got tattoos.'

'Shut up! Please say matching.'

'Not matching. Mine's here.' Lindy pulled the neck of her top down to reveal her shoulder where a very fine red line joined a group of her freckles to make a drawing of a constellation.

'It's so cute. Is it Adam's star sign or something?' Finn's face was pained at the mere idea.

'Nah, it's Aries for me and Max!'

'Love it. New-age tattoo for your new-age life-coaching career is perfect.'

'Maybe it's a new-age tattoo for a new age of me,' Lindy countered.

'Does that mean you've made a decision?' Finn kept her voice low in case Adam returned.

Lindy curled up in the other corner of the couch. 'I don't know. Today was actually amazing. And I do keep thinking how I have no evidence that that time wasn't just a one-off. A horrible one, obviously. I just don't know. Like, taking it on today's terms – it was so good. We felt like us again. And that gives me so much hope. But then another part of me is like … it wasn't us in our real lives, you know? And can we bring whatever we had today back here to this?' She nodded, indicating the rest of the house.

''Sake, Lindy!' Finn mugged. 'I can't believe you didn't make the decision to end or not end your marriage in a single day! Jeez.'

Lindy laughed grimly.

After she said goodbye to her sister, she headed upstairs. On the second-floor landing, Adam was at the bedroom door of the apparently now awake Max.

'You better get to sleep, pal. You don't want to be tired in the morning. We've got the Awesome Slime Adventure series to shoot and loads of great content to work on through the weekend.'

Adam carried on up to their bedroom and Lindy tapped on Max's door. 'Can I come in for a sec?'

'Yep.' Max had his notebook on his lap, she noticed. She settled down beside him and looked at the figure he'd drawn on one of the pages along with the words 'free solo'.

'What's this?'

'It's this guy I saw on YouTube called Alex. He made a movie called *Free Solo* about climbing El Capitan in America but, get this –' he turned to her, eyes wide '– with no ropes.'

'Oh Jesus.'

'Can we watch it, Mom?'

'Yes, but you have to hold my hand – it sounds terrifying.'

'Yeah, he's a legend.' Max returned to his notebook.

Lindy subtly twisted her head to see that he was writing random words: arete, bomb-proof, undercling, smear.

'Are these climbing terms?'

'Yup.' Max turned to her. 'I figure if I want to climb, I have to know the words.'

'And you want to climb? I absolutely couldn't even imagine doing it. That's amazing, Max. But you mean with ropes, yeah?'

'Well, ropes at first.'

Lindy shelved the 'at first' part of that comment to argue with at a later date; an idea was hitting.

'Do you know there's actually a climbing wall at Monteray Vacay, the place we're going on holiday in August?'

'Really? Can we go? You and me, like? No offence to Dad but he'd probably turn it into a Maxxed Out thing.'

'Absolutely. I'll do it with you,' she said, despite the words immediately making her feel practically woozy with terror. 'It'll be so cool.' She smiled in a way that she very much hoped looked excited and not utterly petrified. 'I'll book the climbing right now.' She kissed his temple, knowing he'd tolerate it, distracted as he was by his writing. 'OK, now back to sleep, you.'

As she made her way out the door, he spoke again. 'Can't wait, Mom.' And she felt lighter than she had in weeks. It had been a good day. She'd felt connected to Adam and her sweet boy seemed happy.

15

'OH MY GOD, CAN YOU CHILL OUT WITH THE driving? You just took that corner in fifth gear – it's fecking raining, hun.' Holly clung to the passenger door beside Ailbhe. 'What is the rush? On the run sheet, Seb said he wouldn't even be arriving till later?'

The *Voices of Glory* rehearsals had been swinging (Flapping? Caterwauling? Flailing?) for three weeks now and Ailbhe'd successfully managed to keep Holly away from Seb the entire time – this was her first day on set since the gig started. Ailbhe had insisted Siobhán work with her but with Siobhán at a friend's wedding and Holly standing in, it was going to be tricky. Ailbhe was counting on them getting in and out before Seb even showed up. Ailbhe chewed the inside of her cheek as she swung a left onto the Dunshanley Road, passing Epic, a long-closed nightclub they'd occasionally frequented back in their twenties.

'The old haunt,' Holly yelped. 'The state of it now! Seb's a bit of an old haunt of yours too, of course,' she added conversationally.

'Shut up, please,' Ailbhe instructed. 'That hadn't even crossed my mind.'

'Yeah, right, I'd say you near-rode him all over Dublin back then and now you're just randomly all over this job.'

Ailbhe made the turn in to the community centre, relieved that Holly wouldn't have time to pursue this conversation. She was right, of course – Ailbhe *was* all over this job, just not for the reasons Holly was thinking. If Seb showed up before they got out of there today, she needed to monitor Holly and Seb's interactions. She didn't want them talking about her and comparing any notes on her activities of the last year.

Seb had stayed a serial 'what if' for Ailbhe throughout her twenties. They were friends with a lot of the same people and constantly found themselves among the last ones up at parties, drifting with seeming inevitability towards each other only for some irritating dregs-of-the-party creature like Drunk Friend or Crying Friend to interrupt them. They would reluctantly tend to the faux crisis, each looking wistfully at the other. She'd never imagined that when they did finally score they'd be in their forties. And as hot as Seb remained, it had been only … grand?

She pulled in to a spot beside the entrance. This over-analysing had never been her style, but apparently when your life starts coming apart due to your own terrible decisions, self-reflection is a dreadful by-product. Who knew? Holly was gathering her bag and jacket, getting ready to brave the downpour, when Ailbhe hit the central locking to trap them inside.

'Eh, sinister much?' Holly laughed, surprised.

'It's just that …' How to say this? Ailbhe didn't want Holly mentioning Tom or Tilly to Seb. She didn't want any calculations to be done. That could be disastrous. *Just be casual,* she counselled herself. Holly was looking impatient. 'It's just I think maybe it's best not to mention my situation to Seb or the production team in general.'

'Just checking, by "situation" do you mean your ... new family?'

'Yep.' *Keep it breezy, Ailbhe.* 'Just to ... ya know ... keep things professional. You know how women are treated in the workplace after they give birth – everyone acts like it's a buy-one-get-one-free on episiotomies and lobotomies.'

Holly laughed. 'I won't say anything, even though it is psychotic. You're not doing a classic Ailbhe here now? Trying to "keep your options open"? Because you realise that your options couldn't be further from open. The second that sweet maniac, Tom, fertilised you, the options *slaaamed* shut. Also, I happen to love that maniac – he's a real grower and you guys are so good. He gets you, Ailbhe.'

Ailbhe chose to ignore this entirely and unlocked the car. 'Cool, good talk! You can get out now,' she said graciously. They hurried across the glistening tarmac and ducked in out of the rain. Ailbhe's eyes immediately darted around the large glass-fronted reception area. There were giddy knots of people everywhere but no sign of Seb. A whack of nostalgia caught her off-guard. This was exactly how it had been walking into any party when she was younger. She'd arrive and immediately 'suss the sesh', as she and Holly had called it. It was her talent. Within moments of entering any shindig in Dublin in the early 2000s, Ailbhe would have a detailed breakdown of the exact demographic: percentage of ridey males to wouldn't-even-in-the-event-of-a-nuclear-winter types; who was sadly gay and which males were available versus which had a territorial girl prowling the perimeter. And while she resolutely refused to voice this at the time, in sussing the sesh, Ailbhe was nearly always checking to see if Seb was there just like she was now, albeit for very different reasons.

Ailbhe hurried after Holly across the entrance hall, threading her way through singers warming up their vocal chords, many riffing on the Eurovision aspect of the show.

'Nul points, nul points, nul points!' one woman ascended sweetly beside her.

Another group to her left were singing 'Rock 'n' Roll Kids' in pitch-perfect a cappella. Up ahead, she could see Holly stopped at the door to the auditorium with Gavin, one of Seb's assistants. Thank God, no Seb. She fixed a smile on her face and joined them.

'So just a reminder we need you to be mindful of current health and safety guidelines regarding all brushes and tools et cetera.'

'Absolutely, we are all over it – in a very hygienic way, obvi.' Holly smiled.

Ailbhe tensed, spotting Seb with Róisín in a sequinned T-shirt dress and high-top trainers coming towards them.

'Holly, hey! We finally got you here.' He beckoned her over. 'This is Róisín, the musical director of *Voices of Glory*.'

'Hi.' Holly smiled. 'You must be so thrilled to be staging such a big production.'

'Oh my God, yes.' Róisín's words raced out on the crest of a lilting Cork accent, and she clapped her hands in excitement. 'Now that we're on a firm timeline to opening night – middle of August is seven weeks away! – I have some materials for you and Ailbhe to look at. Obviously the show is set in the early nineties, so we're thinking over-lined lips, a lot of blush and next-to-no eyebrows. But make it look good. If you can.'

'It's what we do!' Holly laughed. 'So what's the plot of this thing?'

'Well, we've been a bit fast and loose with the truth and are just dealing with Linda Martin's legal team at the moment. Every musical needs a bit of conflict, see? Not a word of it is true but it's got everything: overcoming personal struggles, foes who become friends, sabotage by a hostile enemy – a Tonya Harding-type scenario. And with the entire Eurovision back catalogue to pick from, the numbers are fantastic.'

'Cool,' Ailbhe said. *Bonkers*, she thought.

'If all comes to all, we'll rename the characters and change some of the details. It doesn't affect the songs, thank God – we've got them locked in – and, of course, we have our ingénue Niamh Kavanagh on her rocky road to Eurovision stardom played by Roe O'Neill.' She dropped her voice so none of the other performers could overhear. 'This girl's going to elevate the production massively.'

'Ailbhe actually knows Roe!' Seb cut in. He turned to Ailbhe. 'She's spectacular, Ailbh. A world-class talent. I'm genuinely stunned she's never pursued this professionally.'

'Not yet!' Róisín widened her eyes meaningfully. Then she whipped round to bark at a tenor who was singing Dana at least thirty feet away: 'You! You're flat on that second line.' She spun away into the crowd.

'So that was the extremely type-A Róisín, as you gathered, Holly.' Seb was his usual playful self. 'She won't be satisfied until we're served legal papers over some libellous chorus or something. Gavin, my right hand,' Seb continued with his formal introductions.

'Cute nickname!' Ailbhe chimed. 'You should be *my* right hand, Holly.'

'Excuse me, I am *not* your right hand.' She turned to Seb and Gavin. 'You'd never know what her hand has been up to, she has a new baby—'

'Puppy!' Ailbhe quickly cut across her, smiling broadly at the two men and telepathically screaming at Holly. *You had one job, don't mention the bloody family!*

'Oh, class, any pics? I love a puppy.'

Gavin needs to shut up, Ailbhe thought darkly. 'I've no piccies,' she snapped. 'He's very new.'

'Weird, that's the first thing I'd do if I got a puppy,' Gavin mused.

'Jesus, Gavin. I'll email you some, OK?'

Seb snorted then calmly suggested they set up the make-up station. 'Here's the list of talking heads. All our key cast members are briefed and we'll send them over, starting with Linda Martin.'

'Yes, grand.' Ailbhe had a moment's relief that he was at least keeping it to business when, just before turning away, he leaned in close to her.

'You know, I can see you've read my messages, Ailbhe. As I said, I'm in the Jurys Inn again and I'd love to treat you to another extortionate Mint Crisp.' He winked and was gone, with Gavin streaking after him.

'Seriously, Ailbh, what are you doing?' Holly's voice cut through the din of singing. 'What's he on about Mint Crisps? Also, denying your baby's existence is extremely fucked up.'

Ailbhe felt a bit sick at Holly's words. She wished denying Tilly's existence was the worst thing on the list of fucked-up shit she was currently doing. Thank God she only had a couple of weeks left before she was on the plane and home free.

16

'SOOOO LET ME GET THIS STRAIGHT: YOU HAVE THE time to throw yourself a little goodbye party but have left Siobhán in the lurch with *Glee Me* three times in the last two weeks?' Holly swigged her Bellini, leaning against the kitchen counter. 'You insist that you do it and I stay in the salon then you bail – what's the story?'

'Please, please, don't be mean to me.' Ailbhe was putting last-minute touches to the boards of cured meats and cheeses that had been delivered that morning. Holly was right, Ailbhe had been avoiding any rehearsal that Seb was scheduled to be at. She knew she was being seriously unprofessional and even worse, she still hadn't told Seb that she was leaving. She was waiting until she was safely on American soil – from her reddit trawling she'd decided once and for all to chance it in that department.

'I'm not being mean to you! I'm just calling out your bullshit.'

'At my goodbye party?'

'If you'd fucking spoken to me over the last three weeks and not left me blue-ticked, we wouldn't have to be having this conversation right now. We'd have already gone through it and I'd have been able to be pleasant at this little shindig, and just hate you *quietly* as per the laws of long-term female friendship. But your ghosting me has forced my hand.' Holly shrugged wearily and Ailbhe knew she was thawing.

'I didn't mean to ghost, Hols … At least I'm a friendly ghost.'

'Don't be cute.' Holly was stern. 'You're not cute, Ailbhe.'

'OK, but in my defence, Tilly's still only three and a bit months old. I'm probably still hormonal.'

'Whore-monal more like.'

'I am scum.' Ailbhe nodded contritely. Appeasing Holly was Ailbhe's only shot.

'You are scum.' Holly nodded sagely. 'OK, c'mere. I'm done with the lambasting. This Bellini is very good.' Holly gathered Ailbhe in a consoling hug. 'Don't ever do that again, though. You're fifty not fifteen.'

'I am forty-two, you cunt!'

'Hmmm. How is your cunt doing these days? Has it re-formed yet?'

'Like a nineties boy band, baby.'

'Holly, you look sensational.' Tom came in from the hallway and spun around the island to welcome her. 'Beautify going well?'

'Yes, thank God – global crises or not people will always have hair and faces.'

'Just about,' he answered meaninglessly. 'Right, I'm off. Some of the Monteray dads are bringing me kitesurfing. Enjoy lunch.' He pecked Ailbhe, unclipped the baby monitor and handed it to her. He leaned closer. 'Not too many of these, Ailbh.' He discreetly glanced at her Bellini and Ailbhe messed with the lemons, aware that Holly was taking it all in. After the first two weeks of AA, she'd told him that while the meetings had been a huge help, she was certain she wasn't an alcoholic, she just needed to cut back and he seemed to have accepted this. She'd been on her best behaviour since. Tom grabbed his shades and headed towards the hall. 'Don't forget to parent ...'

'We will. We kept her alive for three months while you were in a different country, remember?'

Tom shook his head, grinning, then ducked out; the door slammed seconds later.

'He has no chill when it comes to the baby,' Ailbhe offered by way of explanation.

'I hear that's pretty common among parents,' Holly replied.

'Hey, gals.' Lindy appeared in the kitchen doorway carrying more bottles of fizz. 'Tom let me in there. He's been sworn in to the Sports Casual Dads fraternity, I see. Hi, Holly, is it? I'm Lindy. So nice to finally meet you.'

'Yeah, I finally got the invite!' Holly answered, and Ailbhe shot her a look. Lindy put the bottles in the fridge and settled herself on the couch by the open garden doors, wincing at the blood-curdling screams of the kids playing next door.

'It's the one downside of Monteray,' Lindy remarked as Holly joined her. 'Even if your own kid is momentarily not being an arsehole, someone else's probably is, and it's always within earshot.'

Holly laughed and Ailbhe felt a flutter of relief. She always dreaded bringing different friend groups together. It could be so awkward. But she'd figured Lindy's no-nonsense would chime well with Holly's no-bullshit. She did feel shit for neglecting Holly but she'd felt awkward introducing Holly to her life in Monteray Valley. She was sure Holly would rightly mock it for being the richest, whitest place in Ireland. It was all a moot point now, anyway, as this time tomorrow she and Tom and Tilly would be at the airport. She fixed another Bellini for Lindy and brought it and the board piled with mortadella, chorizo, prosciutto and pickles over to the large low table around which the couches were arranged.

'Nibbles,' she called brightly just as Eileen arrived in with Roe, whose freshly dyed candy-pink hair was woven into a pretty braid around her head and worked perfectly with her mint-green overalls. Also with them was Rachel, doing high-end casual in a drapey white T-shirt and Acne jeans. Ailbhe had run into her when she was bringing Tilly for her walk a week before and, desperate for something to say, had invited her. As the others did their various hugs and hellos, Ailbhe noticed Lindy looking annoyed. Was it because she thought it was just going to be them? She swiftly picked up her glass and launched into an impromptu speech to gloss over the awkwardness.

'I know I've complained a lot about Monteray Valley – but now that I am leaving in twenty-four hours, I really am going to miss you all. Especially Tilly's other mammy.' She gave Eileen a squeeze. 'I'm going to be completely fecked without you.'

'You will,' her mother agreed. 'I dunno what I'll be getting up to here without you. I'm not young or yummy enough to be in the yummy-mummy set, and I'm not old enough to hang around with the other grannies.' She wrinkled her nose in disdain. 'I suppose I'll be kept busy. I'll be finishing decorating this place – Tom wants me to furnish it fully. He's given me an insane budget. I'd say at least half of that'll be going straight into my face! You know you can have all the injectables delivered here, Holly!'

'Stop. That's amazing.' Holly spread gorgonzola on a cracker.

'It's so handy,' Lindy agreed. 'I never really thought I'd get into it but I gave in. Now, I think facial expressions are overrated! Look at me, for example. How do you think I'm feeling right now?'

Holly leaned in to examine Lindy more closely. 'I'll go with nonplussed.'

'No way, she's quizzical,' Ailbhe guessed.

'Nope!' Lindy was triumphant. 'I was annoyed. And you couldn't tell remotely. I'm telling you, it's so handy for being married. I'd say it's keeping every Monteray marriage on the road!' Ailbhe spotted Lindy throw a sharp look at Rachel and beside Lindy, Roe looked distinctly awkward. *Weird.*

'So, you do the Maxxed Out channel?' Holly wrapped a piece of prosciutto around a cornichon. 'My nieces are obsessed with your son. Is that weird to say?'

'Oh, not at all. I'm pretty used to hearing that, to be honest. Though I've kinda stepped back now.'

'Lindy is doing a cool new thing, though.' Ailbhe drained her drink and got up to grab another bottle. 'She's starting a new service for people to fix their regrets.'

'Oooh, how? That's genius.'

'Well, thank you.' Lindy smiled. 'It's called The Snag List. It's early days but I'm hoping to run it like a life-coaching service but with more practical elements. It's very … eh … bespoke, so I suppose how it works depends on the client. But, I guess, what I do is sit down with someone and go through their life and make a snag list.

Ascertain their unfinished business, figure out what things they didn't do that they wish they had. Then suss out how to let them experience these things without it negatively impacting their lives right now.'

'It's a brilliant idea. But isn't everyone's snag just people they didn't sleep with?' Holly asked. 'Are you not going to wind up arranging affairs for all your clients? Like an Ashley Madison vibe?'

'No!' Lindy looked dismayed. 'Not everyone's snag is sex-focused. Roe's snag is the show. And mine is this business. Before now I've always worked on other people's business ideas. And I'm going back to study – I'm starting a course in September.'

'I'm sorry – you're right.' Holly nodded. 'I actually can't think what my snag would be … Not that my life is perfect, but I just don't know if there's anything I feel like I've missed out on.'

'I've got one,' Eilers piped up, guzzling her Prosecco. 'This will sound mad but I've always wanted to try hallucinogens.'

'Mam!' Ailbhe yelped. 'You don't know what drugs are!'

'Go way outta that, of course I do. It's so funny you should bring drugs up, Lindy—'

'You're the one bringing up drugs.' Ailbhe was reeling, she'd always thought Eilers was kind of innocent about these things.

'Since that cocaine party for the chisler, I've been thinking about acid,' Eileen continued, ignoring her daughter while Rachel looked mildly abashed.

'Acid! No, Mam, you can't just suddenly do acid. You've never even smoked a spliff. That would be going from nought to ninety.'

'I have smoked a joint, Ailbhe! Of course I have. Though I thought it was just a normal ciggie. Didn't know what was happening, then I ate two boxes of Findus Crispy Pancakes. Would you do something like that for my snag list, Lindy? I'd pay your rate, of course.'

'Eh—' Lindy seemed at a loss for words.

'Mam, Lindy can't get you drugs. It's illegal.'

'Yeah,' Lindy agreed. 'It'd be tricky for the books. And Ailbhe's right, maybe acid might be a bit hardcore. What about magic mushrooms? That'd be easier to swing all round. We can just pick them and we wouldn't be, ya know, supporting criminality. And I could put your snag through the books as … foraging? Perfect!'

'Perfect, except my mam will be tripping for the first time and I'm gonna miss it,' Ailbhe whined.

'Well, a small price to pay for escaping to the real Monterey Valley rather than living in this bargain-bin version,' Roe remarked. 'The most escaping we're doing this summer is the dreaded … Monteray Vacay.'

Roe and Lindy both looked pained.

'What's that?' Holly asked Roe.

'It's a high-end prison like this one, only with sea views. It's basically a replica compound in Waterford with holiday gaffs. Me and Lindy are going with our various balls and chains for the August bank holiday.'

'So you all live here together and then go on holidays there en masse?' Holly looked baffled.

'Yeah.' Lindy nodded in a resigned fashion. 'It has its advantages, I guess. Like, at least you know the food'll be good. And there's no need to do any leg work. Babysitters, private chefs – all the stuff we have here, they'll have there.'

'Wow.' Holly shook her head. 'Monteray is really something, isn't it?'

Ailbhe was glad when her mother swung the conversation back to her apparently imminent drug trip.

'I am so excited!' Eileen gushed. 'I've never really cut loose. I had Ailbhe very young and there just wasn't the support there for younger single mothers at the time. So I never got out much during those years when all my friends were experimenting … Thank you so much, Lindy.'

'It's my pleasure, and the more case studies the better for when I launch. Though, let me do some research. I'm not even sure when mushrooms are in season. We could be talking about a major wait.'

'Maybe …' Rachel tentatively spoke for the first time since she arrived. 'Would you take me on too, Lindy? I have a snag. Though,' she glanced around at the others, 'it's confidential.'

Lindy looked wary but nodded slowly. 'Sure, I can book you in for a consultation, I guess.'

Ailbhe would miss the low-grade Monteray Valley intrigue. *Lindy and Roe had better keep me updated after I'm gone. Oh God, provided all goes well with emigration tomorrow.* Ailbhe downed her glass to subdue the nerves. She needed to get on that bloody plane if only to get this relentless anxiety to piss off.

17

AT THE AIRPORT THE NEXT MORNING, AILBHE STILL felt groggy. She wearily scrolled Insta while she waited for Tom to come back with coffees. The DMs notification was drawing her in with the pull of a black hole. Seb had already messaged twice asking why she hadn't been at the last few rehearsals, and she hadn't responded. She had literally two more hours until she would be free from it all. Tilly was graciously cooperating with her mother's hangover by sitting quietly blinking in her pram. Things had escalated at the goodbye lunch from giddy to nostalgic and tipsy. She was gutted she wouldn't see Roe's inaugural performance. She would miss Holly, and Roe and Lindy. They'd become so much more than just stepping-stone friends, and she was now feeling apprehensive about starting over again in Morgan Hill. Tom insisted that the wives and girlfriends of his various colleagues would welcome her with enthusiasm, but Ailbhe didn't like the idea of being essentially *given* to a group of women who were all only friends because of the men they'd chosen to sleep with and procreate with.

'Ailbhe? Honey, you think you should give Tilly her booby now before we go through the gate?' He handed her her coffee.

'She's totally fine, Tom. If she wanted a boob we'd all know about it, believe me.' He was constantly fussing over the baby – it was sweet. Tom, Ailbhe sensed, was just days away from whipping out some cue cards and trying to hothouse the child into being one of those spelling-bee children they had in America.

'OK, if you're sure, hon. Let's go through to departures then. Even with the gold-member fast track we're a little tight on time.'

Naturally, in the passport control queue, Tilly committed mother–daughter treason and began squawking in a demanding fashion. Shite. Ailbhe couldn't get over the insubordination. *We're supposed to be on the same team*, she thought as she furiously began pulling on the cloth wrap she used to carry her daughter. *Great, now I have to tit and emigrate – it's all very coffin ship all of a sudden.* Tilly was now crying hysterically, as though it'd been weeks rather than an hour and a half since she'd been fed, and Ailbhe was instantly sweating. It must be some weird primordial biological reaction that the fervent cries caused her to suddenly become so frantic and clammy – Ailbhe felt like ripping her clothes off.

'It's actually an act of societal violence that I'm supposed to try to breastfeed discreetly,' she raged to Tom. 'It's already the most awkward thing in the world – way to make it even harder by demanding that I keep it under a cover.'

'Ah, she's a hungry lil baby,' Tom cooed proudly into the wrap, as Ailbhe manhandled her right boob out of her top and into the baby's mouth. At the first whiff of nipple, the greedy little gob clapped over it and the shrieking mercifully ceased. 'Also, less of the violence talk, honey, we don't want to attract any more attention.' He smiled around at the various armed officials manning the cordoned-off queue snaking its way through the enormous vestibule. 'Welcome to the United States of America' was emblazoned overhead, flanked by the eagle emblem of her husband's home country. American flags were also dotted around the hall lest anyone be in any doubt that, while still in Ireland, they were officially on American soil.

'It's all so bombastic, isn't it?' she whispered, at last feeling a twinge of excitement through the haze of hangover.

'That's the States for ya. Wait till we get to Morgan Hill – everyone's got flags on the lawn. You'll be reciting the Declaration of Independence before ya know it. I'm so excited for your first Fourth of July weekend.' He gave her an excited squeeze. The queue shuffled along and Tilly continued sucking contentedly.

'Ma'am, can you step out of line, please?' A solid-looking officer in his fifties had opened the retractable belt that surrounded the queuing area and beckoned to Ailbhe just before they reached the booth they needed to pass through to get to the gate and board their plane.

Shite. This couldn't be the outstanding fine business, could it? Ailbhe smiled at Tom, who looked curious but not anxious, and stepped out of the queue.

'Ma'am, I need to ask you to please cover yourself.' The officer spoke out of the corner of his mouth and didn't quite meet her eye.

'What?' Ailbhe was momentarily stunned. She'd read things occasionally online about people being dicks about breastfeeding in public, but having conducted almost her entire career of being a mother in the contained confines of Monteray Valley, which was practically a manufacturing plant for human young, she herself had never encountered anything other than the wistful smiles of other mothers and benign awkwardness of scattered dads.

'Ma'am, please keep your voice down. We have a dedicated—'

'Keep my voice down?' Ailbhe responded, involuntarily raising her voice. 'What are you talking about?'

'Is there a problem here?' Another younger officer had joined them. Meanwhile Tilly, upon hearing her mother's tone, relinquished the nipple and began roaring inside the sling.

'No, there's no problem, Eric,' the original officer replied. 'I was just going to show this lady to the—'

'Oh, we have a fucking problem, Eric.' Ailbhe couldn't believe them. 'I am minding my business breastfeeding my baby, which is the WHO recommended method of feeding her. And this … this …' Ailbhe scrounged for something derogatory but not OTT. 'This *man* is telling me to cover up.'

'Your passport now, ma'am.' Another officer had joined them.

'Oh it's "ma'am" now, is it?' Ailbhe knew she was being a bit confrontational, but she was clammy and embarrassed and didn't quite know how to row back on the whole situation. She plunged through her bag hunting for her passport – tricky with Tilly still in the sling screaming and adding a further layer of stress to the interaction. As she came up with the passport, it flicked awkwardly from her hand. This looked most unfortunately like a throw, not helped by the fact that it glanced off the side of Officer Eric's head.

'Ma'am! Hands where I can see them,' the original officer shouted.

'Request back-up,' the latest officer spoke into his radio set as he checked on Officer Eric, who was cradling his head and had slumped to his knees.

'This is ridiculous.' Ailbhe held her hands aloft. 'It was an accident. It barely tipped him.'

'Do not throw items at an on-duty officer.' The original officer grabbed the passport from the ground and marched away to the booths.

'What the hell is going on?' Tom appeared by her side looking freaked. 'Ailbhe,' he murmured to her, 'American cops are serious. You have to show some respect, not throw your passport at them like a petulant kid.'

'I did not throw it—'

'Sir?' Officer Eric was recovered and now glaring at Tom. 'Sir? What's your business here?'

'I'm sorry, officer, this is my wife. She's Irish,' he announced, apparently believing this to be some kind of explanation. Ailbhe jigged the baby indignantly.

The original officer, whose name badge read 'West', arrived back brandishing her passport.

'This lad was trying to make me cover up the breastfeeding,' Ailbhe finally managed to explain. 'Like, it's not on. You can't have one lot of men in the World Health Organization being all "breast is best" and then this lot of men telling me to put my tits away.'

'No one was referencing your breasts in any way, ma'am,' Officer West spoke coolly. 'I was simply seeking to inform you of the breastfeeding facilities available to you.' He extended his arm to indicate a discreet booth bearing a mother and baby symbol. 'However, it's since come to my attention that this isn't your first altercation on US soil.'

Oh fucking fuck! Ailbhe could kick herself.

'I just ran a search on your name and I'm afraid there's an outstanding warrant for your arrest.'

'This has to be a mistake,' Tom interjected. 'My wife's never been arrested. She's never even been to America.'

'You might need to check your sources on that, sir. This is an outstanding warrant dating from an unpaid fine in the state of California in 2001.'

'Oh, hell, Ailbhe!' Tom rounded on her, looking furious. 'Did you know about this? Why didn't you tell me? Did you lie on the form?' He turned back to the officers. 'Didn't this come up when they processed the tourist visa application?'

'Sometimes those guys are sloppy,' Officer West cut in. 'Sloppy like your wife here back in 2001.' He laughed heartily until he noticed no one was joining in. 'Ahem.' He straightened himself out. 'According to our report she was suspected of being under the influence and was acting in an erratic and disorderly manner.'

'Officers, I have a plane to catch. I presume my wife won't be flying today?'

'No, sir, we'll need to process this arrest and discuss escorting her to the US to face possible charges.'

'What. The. Actual. Fuck. No. *No!*' Ailbhe instinctively started to back away before Tom caught her by the arm.

'Do not make this worse right now,' he muttered urgently. 'I can't believe this, Ailbhe. Under the influence? Disorderly and erratic behaviour? This is alcohol again. I should've trusted my gut. You clearly do need to be in AA or some kind of recovery programme.' He looked anguished. 'Anyway, this isn't the place – we need to discuss this properly.' He glanced back at the slowly advancing queue and checked the time. 'My lawyer's east coast office will be just about open. I'll make a call once I'm at the gate. It will all be fine.'

'Tom, what?' Ailbhe couldn't believe the swift reversal of fortune that had taken place between the start of this queue and the end of it. 'Are you going without me?'

'I told you, I'll call my lawyer. And your mother! I'm getting on this flight.' He leaned into the wrap to lay a swift kiss on Tilly's forehead. 'I'm meeting the Optimise board of investors in eleven hours. Look, maybe next time tell me there's an outstanding warrant for your arrest *before* we get to the airport.' He sounded weary. 'I love you, honey. But you need to look at your behaviour.' He shook his head sadly and jogged back to the queue and disappeared through the booths at the other end of the hall.

'I cannot believe this. He just left!' Ailbhe gaped.

'Yeah,' Officer Eric agreed. 'I've never seen anything like that. You guys? Ever seen a guy just cut out like that?'

Ailbhe could barely take in what was being said beyond all the officers being in murmured agreement that no one had ever witnessed a husband just abandon his wife to airport security before. She didn't even have time to form a coherent thought about how to get out of this shitemare when Tilly started crying once more. She wanted the other breast. Robotically, Ailbhe rearranged her on the other side as Officer Eric gathered her bags for her. She felt desperately out of control. 'What happens now?'

'We take you back to the holding room. Is there anyone – family, next of kin – you want me to phone? Someone who can come get the baby?'

'Oh, Jesus,' was all Ailbhe could say. She quickly pulled out her phone and texted the Snag List group.

'And I'm sorry, but when you're done I'll have to take your phone.'

'OK,' Ailbhe answered, her voice dull. 'I'll let them know.'

The holding room had cement walls and no windows and felt ominously like practice for prison. She'd never felt so helpless in her whole life. Panic coursed through her as she paced and swayed the baby, trying desperately to stay calm. *Why why* why *did I make a scene? What is going to happen?* She was so tense that when Officer Eric appeared at the door to tell her she was being released, she dissolved instantly into tears.

'I'm sorry I'm crying – my mind was going wild in here. I thought you were going to take Tilly away and put me in prison.'

'It's OK, it's OK, Officer West was being a major hard ass today, but your husband's lawyers have handled everything.'

'Like *everything* everything? Can I still go to America?'

'Eh, I doubt that. For now.' Officer Eric looked uneasy. 'I'd say there'll still be plenty of red tape around that, but I get the impression the arrest and fine have been settled. Good ol' US of A,' he grinned, 'money talks.'

Ailbhe quaked at the thoughts of how much her J1 Ket antics had just cost her husband. And if they had cost *her* a husband. Had they told him the full story? The drugs? Tom was going to hate that. Ailbhe tried to keep her panic in check. Disappearing to America had been integral to her giving Tilly a good life. *Tom* was integral to giving Tilly a good life. Now she was trapped in Dublin, and a dreadful certainty that this would be her undoing was creeping in.

In Dublin nothing could stay a secret.

'Your friends are here to collect you.' Officer Eric led Ailbhe and the sleeping Tilly through a series of empty low-ceilinged corridors that eventually spat them out in front of Arrivals.

'Ailbh!' Roe and Lindy rushed forward and Ailbhe burst into fresh tears.

'I can't believe this.' Roe gently hugged Ailbhe, taking care not to disturb the baby. Lindy took Ailbhe's suitcase from Officer Eric and thanked him profusely.

'I thought you were home free after the visa seemed to go through,' Roe said as they made their way outside, dodging happy travellers reuniting with their families.

'I probably *was* home free until this stupid altercation over the breastfeeding.'

'Only you, Ailbhe,' was all Lindy said.

The hours until Tom touched down five thousand miles from her sludged by. Ailbhe tried to keep busy and to keep out of her mother's way. Ailbhe couldn't bear her questions but Eileen was doggedly tailing her from room to room.

'Ailbhe.' She stood in the bedroom doorway as Ailbhe opened her huge suitcase and began to pull her clothes back out. Roe and Lindy had taken Tilly to give her a moment to recalibrate. She had packed the case less than a day ago – always last minute – and the rest of her possessions were in boxes in some shipping container somewhere being shipped to a life that was no longer starting. With just a suitcase of clothes in this whole mansion, she felt like she was on the run. In hiding from her past and in exile from her marriage. 'Ailbhe? What happened at the airport? I deserve the truth. Tom is in a state. I think he was in shock when he rang from the departure gate. He's worried about you and Tilly.'

'It was just a mishap, Mam. I'd forgotten to put some stuff on my forms. Tom is making a big deal out of it. He's just mad at me … because of the inconvenience.'

'He thinks you have a problem with drink.' She looked stricken and Ailbhe was relieved Tilly – the most tangible evidence of her occasional tipsy misadventures – wasn't there. 'I feel awful,' her mother continued. 'Your dad has his issues …'

'I don't, Mam, you know that.'

Eilers looked like she wanted to believe her.

'I know I've been a bit all over the place since Tilly came along, but I was just adjusting. I swear I am going to cop on now. I *promise*. Tom and I will get back on track. We'll have a fresh start. He's going to sort out the fine, arrest, whatever. I'll cut down, I mean, stop … for a while. Show him that I'm taking this seriously.'

Her phone rang. Tom. As hard as this conversation was going to be, she was happy to have a good reason to turn away from her mother's searching eyes.

'I'll leave you to it.' Eileen closed the door quietly and Ailbhe hit accept.

'Ailbhe, what are we supposed to do now? I can't believe this is happening. I feel like I don't even know you!'

'Yeah, well, when you get together post-forty, there's going to be some stuff you forget to mention.' Ailbhe tried to make a stab at being light-hearted, but seeing him shake his head, she knew it wasn't right.

He can't even look at me, she thought. His troubled gaze was trained on something off to the right. He took a breath and spoke softly. 'I don't think I am actually ready to get into this yet. I need some time to process this, to figure out where we can even go from here. Ailbhe?'

'Yes,' she whispered.

'I want you to really think about your drinking. Do you really think it's normal? Most people have hangovers after drinking, not legal troubles in other countries.'

Or two potential baby daddies. She pressed her lips together and avoided his eyes. They couldn't look at each other. *He doesn't even know about the drugs. He doesn't know the half of it.*

'I'm going to take a few days on this. Maybe longer, I don't know.'

Oh God, it was falling apart, and not even for the reason she'd been so focused on. *I didn't even need my little soap opera to ruin this – I'm more than capable of wrecking my life on my own. And now my daughter's too.*

After she hung up and cried on the floor in front of the mess of clothes and make-up until she was wrung dry, she picked up her phone and looked up 'Do I have a drinking problem?'

The first result was a HSE self-assessment tool. She clicked and duly began answering the questions presented: female, forty-two years of age.

'How often do you have a drink containing alcohol?'

The first option was 'two to four times a *month*'. Ailbhe frowned.

Who was taking this test and clicking that option? She hesitated over 'four or more times a week' and then hit the lesser option, 'two to three times a week'. To be fair, that was true *some* weeks.

The next question asked: 'How many standard drinks containing alcohol do you have on a typical day when you are drinking?' She selected two cocktails and three glasses of wine. Again, she was maybe rounding down but this was the HSE – they were bound to be a bit hysterical.

The next question seemed to suggest that the HSE were on to her game: 'How often have you had six or more standard drinks on a single occasion?' She considered the fact that she'd been pregnant for much of the last year. Did it count as not drinking when you absolutely couldn't drink? Even breastfeeding hadn't impeded her drinking that much, she hadn't allowed it to – she pumped and dumped and gave Tilly formula when she needed to. She tried to swerve this discomfiting realisation and re-read the question. How often have you had six or more standard drinks on a single occasion? How many times had she had LESS than six drinks once she got going?

'How often during the last year have you found that you were not able to stop drinking once you had started?' *Oh c'mon! Who stops until the night is over? Give a bitch a chance. I'm going with 'monthly'.*

'How often during the last year have you failed to do what was normally expected from you because of your drinking?' She flashed on waking up after Fielding Fitzsimon's birthday party. That icy shock when she didn't immediately know where Tilly was. She couldn't hit 'never'. She looked at the next option down, 'less than monthly', and clicked it. It wasn't a lie. Though there had been other nights when

Eilers had done bath and bedtime, but Eilers had wanted to, and Ailbhe hadn't been *drunk* drunk those times. Not really.

'How often during the last year have you needed an alcoholic drink in the morning to get yourself going after a heavy drinking session?' At least she could confidently reply 'never' to this one! She enjoyed a brief, bright second of relief only for the next question to stamp it straight out.

'How often during the last year have you had a feeling of guilt or regret after drinking?' She regarded the two most extreme answers: 'weekly' and 'daily or almost daily'. The Tilly guilt throbbed virtually all the time. She selected 'weekly'. The same for the next question: 'How often during the last year have you been unable to remember what happened the night before because you had been drinking?'

To 'Have you or somebody else been injured as a result of your drinking?' she tapped 'no'. Not unless you count 'emotionally' – she had an unpleasant flash of Tom's reproachful gaze.

'Has a relative, friend, doctor or other healthcare worker been concerned about your drinking or suggested that you cut down?' She tapped 'yes'.

She hovered over 'See result'. Did she really need to see it? Was taking the test proof enough? Never mind that she was currently on the brink of losing Tom. She tapped the button.

18

LINDY AND RACHEL WERE IN THE SNAG LIST OFFICE, sitting side by side, with Rachel's computer on the desk in front of them. Lindy had only said yes to Rachel's Snag List request out of awkwardness at the goodbye party, but when Rachel had texted to follow up, Lindy realised that, even though things were much better with Adam, she was curious about this woman.

They'd been going over Rachel's chief regret for an hour now. It was not cyber-motorboating random husbands, as it turned out, but obsessively trolling Sigrid for many years. This insight into a pretty pathetic side of Rachel's character was definitely soothing Lindy. *She isn't even that hot.* Plus, since their date, Lindy and Adam had had sex two more times. OK that wasn't a lot of sex in four weeks and it was a little bit sad keeping count but, whatever, it was a big improvement. Lindy refocused on the comments about Sigrid rolling up the computer screen.

> *@RealTalkGal: I actually cannot even look at your smug face. Seriously, how does a person actually get to the point of being so goddamn self-satisfied?*

@RachyRantz: Ugh delete this woman PLEASE.

@RealTalkGal: If you can't earn money online without exploiting your children then you need to leave the FUCKING internet. Can't stand you.

@SigridTruther: You are a vile person. You need to wash your smug bitch face once in a while, not just layer over fake tan and hope no one notices what a self-obsessed mess you are.

Replying to @Sigrid Truther

@DontBelieveTheBS: Ugh Sigrid = Absolute Headmelt.

Replying to @DontBelieveTheBS

@EmilyCares: Someone needs to start regulating these YouTube families, they are sick abusers.

Lindy continued scrolling with increasing anxiety. She knew the Maxxed Out channel had plenty of similar comments. Though thankfully not directed at Adam and Max. She was certain this was because Adam was a man and therefore the people of the internet barely expected him to parent his son. More often than not, if the comments were critical, they rooted her out to direct their ire towards. 'Where's the mother in all this? Why doesn't she put a stop to this?' That kind of thing.

Jamie had a dedicated intern working practically round the clock to delete comments and block users. Lindy tried her best not to dwell on the comments. It was easy to dismiss a lot of them as trolling. The gratuitously cruel ones she wrote off as crazies. At first this had been a way of reassuring herself. *They're just crazy*, she'd think. And then she'd begun to consider the words: They're just crazy. They're crazy. They watch my son and they're crazy. She shook off the thoughts: they were safe here in Monteray. Maxxed Out was under control. Right now she needed to get back to Rachel's snag.

'So which of these accounts is you?' Lindy frowned at the screen.

'The thing is, Lindy,' Rachel ignored the question, clearly eager to explain herself, 'back in the day, I was really, eh … let's just say I had self-esteem issues, and I think looking at This Scandi Life just really got to me. And it's something that really feels unresolved.'

'OK … and why now?'

'I know it maybe doesn't sound like much, but my own daughter, Evie, is starting to act up and leave comments on the accounts of people she doesn't like, and I thought if she saw me taking responsibility, she would see how toxic it is. It was like smoking or something – I knew it was bad for me but I just fell into a habit and then I couldn't stop. I'd hit "dislike" on all her videos the second she'd post them. And then I made up more accounts so I could dislike the videos I'd already disliked to give them even more thumbs down. It was ridiculous. Then I started commenting loads. And getting into rows with other commenters underneath the videos. I was compulsive. I'd be raging back and forth with some other internet person about God knows what, under a video of a crown-braid tutorial. It was becoming unhealthy.'

'So when did you finally stop?'

'A few months ago.' Rachel looked mortified.

'O-K …' Lindy had been expecting this to have been a youthful folly, but no. There was, it seemed, no end to how crazy grown adults could act on the internet.

'I'm so glad I'm doing this with you. It's really uplifting to see Roe and Eileen seizing the day and fixing their snags. I've made up excuse after excuse to avoid facing it head-on. I need the accountability of another person pushing me.'

Lindy nodded. 'OK, c'mon, Rachel, enough stalling: how many of these are you? This doesn't work unless you are honest.'

Silence. Finally Rachel exhaled. 'I know. OK, I'll call out the handles but what are you going to do exactly?'

'I'm going to trawl the activity on these accounts and put together a presentation for Sigrid detailing every one of your sock puppets. She deserves to know it was all you behind them and not an army of people who share these opinions of her.'

'But loads of people agree with me. I do have a bit of a point here.'

'Rachel, do you want to fix this or do you want to continue wasting your energy hating her and criticising her life choices? Up to you.' Lindy was getting impatient as Rachel lapsed back into silence, staring at her lap. 'Regardless of whether you have a point or not, anonymously hurling abuse kind of undercuts that point, Rachel. Also, I just don't think this is about some crusade to protect these children. I'd say you don't give a shite about these kids. If they were running around screaming in a restaurant while you were trying to eat, you'd be wishing you could taser them. You called the one in the overnight-chia-pudding-recipe video a "pudding-faced bitch". She's six.'

'I know, Lindy! I'm sick.' Rachel looked up with a beseeching expression.

'Rachel, give me the full list of accounts and the passwords so I can do the leg work.' Lindy tried to soften her tone. She wanted Rachel as a case study – she couldn't let her feelings towards her get in the way. 'How many of these handles are yours?'

'Quicker to say which isn't mine,' Rachel muttered. 'RachyRantz isn't me.'

Well, that *is embarrassing*. 'OK.' Lindy hid her disdain with what she hoped was a gentle nod. 'So the rest of it here, @SigridTruther, @EmilyCares and @DontBelieveTheBS, is all you? You replying to you?'

Rachel nodded; she was blinking away tears. 'I was really unhappy in my own life. I'm not trying to make excuses. I know claiming to care about the kids' welfare is total crap. They're actually really annoying kids. Especially the youngest.'

Lindy snorted. 'Ugh, I know, I've met Narnia in person!'

Lindy spent the next half an hour creating a full document compiling all of Rachel's YouTube accounts – twenty-seven in all.

'OK that's it.' Rachel read the last one off her phone.

'Right, passwords? Do you have a list you could email me?'

'No, they're all the same password.' Rachel looked sheepish.

'I'm not even going to lecture you about the folly of one password for everything. What is it?'

'Em it's …' Rachel shifted, avoiding Lindy's eyes. 'I'll just spell it for you. S-i-g-r-i-d-C-u-n-t, caps on the S and the C.'

'Right so.' Lindy summoned an impassive smile. 'We are a no-judgement organisation, Rachel. I'll get straight on this. In the meantime, I've done some research around compulsive behaviours and created a roadmap for how we're going to deal with the root causes of this. Also as I am not qualified just yet, I've reached out to another coach who specialises in confidence building, and she is going to come on board and act as a consultant. Do I have your permission to share some information with her regarding your snag?'

'Yeah, of course.'

'Brilliant, I've pencilled our meeting with her for early August, so that leaves me a couple of weeks to bring together a comprehensive overview of your actions online. I think seeing it all laid out will show you the extent of this problem and help you to leave it in the past.'

19

HER BLOODY OVULATION WINDOW WAS BACK. IT seemed to come round faster every month. Also Eddie appeared to be hitting new heights of excitement. It'd been a week since they had minded Tilly after Ailbhe's *Banged Up Abroad* moment in the airport, and Eddie had not stopped going on about the baby since. As she tidied the kitchen after dinner, she could sense him in the corner of her eye. Now, he was advancing on her with a broody boner.

'I am sorry, but you are so hot, Roe. I think we're going to need to action this right here.' He pressed his hard dick against her hip, running his hands over her ass.

She turned and put her arms around his neck and he dropped his head to her cleavage, moaning a little.

'You'd better not be just after my eggs.' She pretended to sulk, and he immediately covered her lips with his own, his hand slipping up her floral-patterned baby-doll dress. She leaned back against the counter as he dropped to his knees and tugged at her panties.

'Hang on,' she whispered. 'Let's go upstairs. I want to get' – *my diaphragm!* she screamed mentally '– more comfortable.'

In the bedroom, Eddie unbuttoned her dress tantalisingly slowly, but Roe was too agitated to enjoy it. She needed to get into the bathroom. 'Wait, I just want to grab a glass of water—'

'I'll get it for you.' Eddie grinned gamely. He nipped through the bathroom door before she could protest and was hunting through the under-sink cupboard for a glass when he exclaimed, 'Well look who's still hanging around!' He emerged grinning and holding her diaphragm case. 'No need for this cock-blocker these days!' He chucked it in the bin behind him and turned back to the press, coming up with a glass this time and filling it from the tap.

Roe's thoughts galloped as she accepted the glass and took a drink on autopilot. *Crap, crap, crap.* She set the glass down. Should she pretend to be sick? Dizzy?

Eddie was already slipping his hand between her legs and nipping at her ear. She stared over his shoulder at the bin just visible.

Risk it? What were the odds? It was only a 30 per cent chance. Eddie had reported every scrap of intel the minute they'd started 'trying'.

He pushed her gently back onto the bed, running his hands over her breasts.

Fuck it. It won't happen. And if it does, so be it. It's just a community show in Craghanmor.

★

Ailbhe consulted the list: Roe was next. She started prepping her kit when she clocked Seb Knox making his way through the mêlée of crew and performers. Now that she was stuck in Dublin for the foreseeable, she had once again taken on the *Glee Me* work, insisting she needed the distraction and Holly needed to be in the salon as they were well into July and wedding season was hopping. What Ailbhe really needed was to keep Holly and Seb apart. It did seem unlikely that Seb would suddenly come out with anything, but she couldn't risk it.

And despite the discomfort of the situation, she really did need the distraction. In the ten days since visa-gate, she hadn't had a single drink. And she found she was thinking about it constantly – her mind spinning around the issue, raking back and forth over the last year. Without the booze to stifle the anxiety, she found it was hitting an all-time high. Tom was keeping her at arm's length and his absence was cementing – too late? – just how much she cared about him. She was afraid to say 'love', especially now that she might lose him. She wanted to tell him about her ten days of not drinking, but it seemed way too minor. It was hardly such a huge achievement by any normal person's standards. Though Maia, who she was back in touch with now that she was serious about getting better, insisted she was doing amazing.

'What do you make of the show so far then?' Seb stood before her, grinning. 'Too ridiculous or just right?'

'Well,' Ailbhe twisted her long hair over her left shoulder, 'TBH reality TV jumped the shark a *long* time ago. I'm a fan of the *90 Day Fiancé* oeuvre, so this feels kind of tame in comparison. Not boring-tame!' she swiftly corrected herself. 'It's got kind of cosy *Bake Off* vibes.'

Seb nodded, laughing. 'I know what you're saying. This isn't my usual gig. Gavin's much more experienced in reality stuff. He has an Excel spreadsheet of all the contestants and who's cried yet and who he's trying to get to have an outburst, that kind of thing.'

'Well, my money is on Róisín.' Ailbhe laughed and turned back to her kit. She didn't want to prolong their chat.

'Seb!' Gavin was gesturing urgently from behind a monitor.

'Coming,' Seb called, his eyes remaining fixed on Ailbhe. 'You know, it's funny you showed up here. A year later … Right after I gave up texting you. I actually thought we might have had some time to ourselves, but of course you'd actually have to reply to my messages. I know you – you're playing hard to get, aren't you.' He held her eyes for a beat longer and then turned to make his way over to the crew.

Oh God, he thinks I'm doing this for a fling. Should I quit? Try and get Holly to drop the job? But she'd want to know why. She might suspect that something's happened. The opening night of *Voices of Glory* was 17 August, a little over four weeks away. She could hold the line until then, right? She might even get another shot at America before then …

'Roe, I love this look on you! It's very … not you.' Roe laughed as Danny grabbed her hips and turned her from side to side so her sequined cropped jumper glittered under the brightly coloured stage lights illuminating the almost perfect replica of the 1994 Eurovision stage that had been erected since Tuesday's rehearsal.

That had been the final year of Ireland's sweep of the contest. Now, it was most memorable for the iconic original performance of *Riverdance* during the interval. The members of the Life & Soullers who'd been cast as chorus were on stage flinging legs and wigs of tumbling, tight curls everywhere. They'd been perfecting an incredible version of arguably the proudest (and most lucrative) fourteen minutes in the history of Ireland. The tapping was deafening; beside her Danny adjusted his leather pants as he waited for his cue. True to the era, they were an aggressively unflattering bootcut. He was playing Michael Flatley, and Ailbhe had done an amazing job of creating an odd little mullet of tight curls with his formerly dark now bleached-blond hair. Danny raised a leg ramrod straight out in front of him, extended his arms out to the side crucifix-style and mince-danced to the centre of the stage.

Roe made her way down to the auditorium and sat a few seats away from Róisín.

I love this. The thought made her smile; an unexpected gust of happiness swept through her. She didn't just mean the show, though it was incredible to be finally performing. It was the freedom of her budding confidence. She wondered if her parents would come and see her. She didn't want to care.

Róisín suddenly loomed into her field of vision, shouting to be heard over the thunderous clacking of Irish dancing. 'Roe! You are sitting there grinning gormlessly when you could and *should* be polishing your second-act closing number. It's a pivotal moment: we need it tighter and punchier for opening night.'

'On it!' Roe jumped up, pulling out her phone to bring up the lyrics. She turned away, spotting a text from Eddie. She opened it reluctantly, trying to ignore how just *seeing* his name could deflate her so rapidly at the moment.

EDDIE: Do you think choir will be running late again? Just wondering if I should go ahead with dinner?

A new text dropped in as Roe read.

EDDIE: Also please can you take it easy. I'm afraid you'll shake those sperms from last night out before they even get a chance to take! (This is 80 per cent a joke, FYI, and 20 per cent I love you and don't want you doing too much.)

She typed out a quick message telling Eddie to go ahead and eat because rehearsals would be a few more hours. It was a lie. She'd be finished up here in less than an hour, and then it was off to Ailbhe's for her inaugural drug experience courtesy of Eileen's mushroom snag.

After forty minutes studying the script in Róisín's eyeline, Roe sensed she could reasonably slip away. She ordered a taxi, pulled on her jacket and was shouldering her backpack just as Seb came over. *Oh shite, he wants yet another talking head.* She was rapidly becoming something of a focal point for the *Glee Me* narrative – her, as Gavin called it, odds-defying rise. The last time he'd referred to this, she was withering: 'It's not against the odds that a fat woman could be good in musical theatre – we're just never cast because—'

'OK, OK,' he'd cut across her. 'Let's not bog the viewer down with too much activism – remember, *Glee Me* will be airing in the 8 p.m. Sunday-night slot right before *Operation Tiny Nation.*'

'Hey, Roe.' Seb fell into step with her. 'You are looking amazing up there. How does it feel?'

'It *feels* amazing, but also weirdly sad. Like, I am so happy my friend Lindy coached me into doing it. I would never have followed through if she hadn't pushed me, but I keep thinking about how I could've done this years ago. I just never thought I was good enough.'

'You're good enough now, Roe. Seriously. I've been doing TV for twenty years. I've spent time around some really talented people and you are on a par.'

'Thank you.' Roe felt a little lump rising. Sometimes, she found praise very hard. Either the bitch voice in her head would immediately snuff out any compliment with *They're only saying that to be nice*, or it would press the bruise the absence of praise from her parents had left. Eddie, of course, was loving – Roe knew he thought she was gorgeous and smart – but never hearing the words from her mother had left a mark.

'I actually wanted to tell you something,' Seb continued. 'A friend of mine is casting a show in the West End. Auditions start in about six weeks. It's a big show, the new run of *Newsies*. Most of the people trying out will be veterans. But I immediately thought of you when he told me about it and, well, I hope you don't mind but I sent him some of the footage I have of you.'

'Are you serious?' Roe reeled. This was simultaneously the most incredible, terrifying, thrilling and inconvenient thing she'd ever heard.

'Yeah, of course.' Seb laughed.

'You didn't have to do this,' she told him. 'If you were just, you know, trying to be nice or whatever.'

He gave her a weird look. 'I know that. I'm just tryna help out my pal. He needs a cast!' He laughed, looking her over. 'Crazily talented woman lacking in self-confidence? Now I *know* you're a star! Anyway I am super relieved you don't mind that I sent it because …' Seb paused for effect, 'he was *bowled* over by you and wants to invite you to the auditions.'

'What!' Roe gasped, the shock and thrill causing her breath to catch. 'Oh my God, really? Really?'

'Really! You can't be that surprised. You *are* excellent. You have a three-octave range.'

'I know but I'm not a professional. People train for years—'

'Lin-Manuel Miranda got a late start, he didn't début *In the Heights* on Broadway until he was nearly thirty.'

'Yeah but he wrote the first draft at nineteen, Seb!'

'Look, you may not be "trained" but you're clearly "schooled". Anyway, I'm giving him your details – I got them off Róisín.'

'O-K …' Roe's elation was already spiralling downwards. The roll of the conception dice the previous night was suddenly a way bigger problem than it had seemed when only *Voices of Glory* was at stake.

'Listen,' Seb's voice had dropped and now had a vaguely urgent edge, 'I know this is all very "will you score my friend" but will you give me Ailbhe's mobile number? All I have for her is the Beautify contact and I think Holly has that phone most of the time. I've been trying Ailbh on the DMs on Insta and she never gets back. Anyway, I was hoping to catch her before we wrapped for the weekend but she's got away from me.'

'Eh.' Roe was perplexed at the 'will you score my friend' part of his request. It seemed really unprofessional to be joking about scoring a colleague. Unsure of quite what to do, she pulled out her phone and searched her contacts.

'Thanks.' He grinned. 'This is probably totally inappropriate but … does she ever mention me? We got together a year ago or just over. First weekend of July – I remember cos I'd come over to produce this Irish–American Fourth of July show. Anyway, I was gonna invite her to this charity thing I've been invited to, try and maybe get something going again.' He gave a nervous smile.

'Eh …' Roe froze. *What the fuck?*

'What?' Seb looked concerned. 'Is she seeing someone?' Shite, that *What the Fuck* was clearly visible all over her face.

'Nothing.' Roe stared down at her phone, speed-scrolling past Ailbhe's number. 'I'm so sorry, I thought I had it. I just changed phones. My contacts are all messed up.' Roe started slipping towards the door. 'I'll see you over the weekend. And thanks again about your friend.'

Out in the car park, Roe reeled. What was Ailbhe up to? How was she with Seb a year ago? What age was Tilly? She pushed the thoughts aside. *I don't have the bandwidth for Ailbhe's shit right now – what about the West End thing? I could be pregnant.* She struggled to breathe as a swamp of feelings churned inside her. *I cannot be pregnant right now. However slim the odds are, I cannot miss this opportunity.* Thoughts of the chance at the West End had her feeling kamikaze. She checked her taxi app. The driver was still a few minutes away. She googled the Craghanmor pharmacy opening hours. She had twenty minutes till they closed.

20

ON THE ATTIC FLOOR OF AILBHE'S HOUSE, LINDY
was laying out the boxes of mushrooms and the carefully worded
release forms, which she'd had Patrick draw up on her newly
designed Snag List headed stationery, on the carpet in front of
three miniature brightly coloured chairs. Up here they'd created an
insanely elaborate playroom for Tilly, the child who'd yet to sit up.

In front of Ailbhe's spot, Lindy placed a tea-pot and some milk
and sugar. She'd never brewed mushroom tea before and wasn't
sure how you took it. Ailbhe must know. She'd texted Lindy the
day before to say she wouldn't be eating the mushrooms but that
she'd have tea. Lindy didn't blame her – the mushrooms in the
box looked like gnarled bits of tree trunk: *gross*. In the end, they
hadn't been able to pick them as they wouldn't be in season till
the autumn. A bit of digging online and she'd actually managed to
order some using Discord. It felt way too iffy to have them sent to
Monteray so Finn had kindly stepped up. Lindy was a bit nervous
about the mushrooms but Eileen and Roe were so enthusiastic and

Sophie White 249

had insisted that if anything went awry, it would never come back to The Snag List. Lindy added some to Ailbhe's tea-pot and then added boiling water from the kettle she'd relocated to the corner of the attic for the evening in case Ailbhe needed a top-up.

'This place is amazing!' Lindy called as Eileen bustled in.

'I know, it's bonkers when we may not even be staying here, but Tom wants Tilly to have everything.' She gestured to the veritable zoo of huge stuffed animals grouped just beyond the vast ball pit, mini bouncy castle and a swing set. 'Mad altogether – if any child actually played with them and they fell, we'd probably be looking at a serious injury.'

'Well,' Lindy arranged Snag List branded pens beside each form, 'I'm not sure if you are aware, but this is basically the single greatest location for a mushroom trip of all time. Things can get very playful!'

'Love,' Eileen came and gave Lindy a little squeeze on the arm, 'thank you so much for this. I am so excited!'

'Yeah, I can imagine. Though drugs were never really my thing. Adam and I did ayahuasca one time when we were still travelling. I didn't love it. I threw up and sharted at the same time. I can still remember Adam's horror. But, sure, barely a year later he was watching me doing the exact same thing in the delivery room giving birth to Max!'

'Oh, Christ, I'm glad we're all girls here!' Eileen said. 'Should we be donning incontinence pads? I'm too young for that.'

'Nah, nah, mushrooms are way less intense. You'll have a fab time, and I'm here to mind everyone. I'll be the designated non-high chaperone, ready to keep you all safe while you enjoy some good, clean fun in this child's playroom.'

'Right,' Ailbhe called as she bounded up the stairs two at a time. 'I've settled Tilly with the babysitter. Same lad who does the bar. He double jobs all the time for a bit of cash in hand. He tells me the Monteray parents don't like the Monteray babysitting service because they're paro that they're taking notes! I mean, we know the parent piss-ups can get a bit Jude Law–Sadie Frost. I'd say he's seen it all at this stage. Nice to know we're not the only ones in desperate pursuit of our youth.'

'Speak for yourself! I am very young.' Ailbhe turned to find Roe behind her on the stairs, grinning up at her indignantly.

'OK.' Lindy clapped her hands together and herded them to the three tiny chairs. 'We're all very young and vital. No matter how old we are or how stagnant our relationships feel, life, as The Snag List shows us, is still full of possibilities for adventure, for getting to know ourselves better, for righting our wrongs of the past.'

'She's a pro, always on message,' Roe whispered as Ailbhe poured some tea from the pot.

Ailbhe was surprised she wasn't feeling at all envious of the other two doing their shrooms. Things had been so messy lately, the last thing she wanted was to add drugs into the mix. She'd been working hard at avoiding the wine. Things were so tense with Tom. It'd been nearly two weeks since he'd got on the plane without her. He said his lawyers were smoothing things with her visa, but there were still no plans for her joining him in America. It felt like everything was in danger of teetering towards disaster, and Ailbhe had taken to avoiding his calls just so she couldn't make anything worse.

Roe, she spotted, had already cracked open her box of shrooms. 'You are eager, little Roe!'

'Yeah.' Roe looked a bit sheepish. 'Eddie thinks I'm at choir so I need to get high and then not high in time to get home later on. Listen, Ailbhe …'

Ailbhe couldn't make out Roe's tone. *Concern mixed with*—

'You and Seb had a thing, didn't you?'

Suspicion. Fuck, it was concern mixed with suspicion. Ailbhe sipped her tea for something to do. It tasted bizarre but she swallowed it back, trying to form an answer for Roe. 'Oh, that was years ago.' Ailbhe was careful to keep her tone as casual as possible.

'He said it was *a* year ago,' Roe whispered. 'Thirteen months to be exact.' Roe held out her phone open on a post from Ailbhe in the Snag List WhatsApp. It was Tilly beside a teddy cuddling a heart that Tom had bought for her. The heart read: 'I am four months old today!' 'Got a bit of a life snag yourself there, Ailbhe?'

'Roe …'

'I'm not judging, Ailbhe. I am *definitely* in no position to judge. I don't know what the hell you have going on. But I just wanted to warn you that he was asking me for your number and … I dunno … I guess I'm here? If you need to talk.'

'Take up your boxes, gals!' They both started at Lindy's booming voice. 'And your tea, Ailbhe!'

My tea? What the fuck. Ailbhe sniffed at the mug. *Oh no …* She pulled the tea-pot closer and peered in: no tea-bags just some ominous, oozy mushrooms stewing at the bottom. *Oh. Shit.*

Lindy was walking around the perimeter of the huge room. 'Are we all feeling prepared for several hours of altered consciousness?'

No! Ailbhe felt helpless. *Should I try and make myself sick? Gross. It's probably already too late. Oh God, what the hell.* It could be an official last hurrah, she decided. It didn't have to derail anything.

'Send any last-minute texts now and then phones on airplane mode, please. To give you all a little idea of what's coming, I've done some research.' Lindy began to read from her phone: 'At lower doses, the mushrooms will provide a pleasant, mind-altering trip. In higher doses, they can open the doors of perception.' Lindy adopted a mystical voice and Ailbhe had to stifle a giggle. 'Mushrooms can give valuable insights into the surrounding world, the reality in which you exist and the one beyond. Stop laughing, Ailbhe – I'm setting the scene here,' she scolded from the other side of the colourful ball pit.

Ailbhe straightened up. 'Sorry! Absolutely right. My bad.'

'So,' Lindy carried on. 'If you want a milder trip, you can eat half of your box and that should— Oh.' Lindy had made her way back in front of them to find both Roe's and Eileen's boxes empty.

'We may as well go all in,' Eileen announced.

Forty-five minutes later, Ailbhe was swimming breaststroke through a river of balls. Her animal friends from the jungle were smiling beatifically at her from the banks on either side.

She spread her arms out in front of her, propelling her forward towards Eilers, who was standing just beyond the river, her upper body entirely slumped forward, swinging her arms back and forth as she muttered incantations.

'Mam.' She pulled herself from the river and slithered over to Eilers' feet. She reached up to touch her mother's hands, and briefly their fingers connected and blurred together. Looking up above her mother to the dark sky, she saw stars streaking overhead.

Aeons passed, and from her mother's half-whispered, half-sung words, Ailbhe learned the meaning of life, and the joy of it swelled inside her until she floated up, up, up and grasped her mother around her waist. 'I have to find a pen before I forget what you said. You are so wise.'

'I know my daughter.' Her mother drifted down to sit beside her. 'But you are in danger of fecking things up right now.'

The joy balloon started to deflate.

'Mam, please, no life talk – don't kill the vibe.' Ailbhe looked round, desperate for a distraction. Across the huge space, Roe was smiling with her eyes closed as she stood cuddling and petting a stretch of wall. Ailbhe couldn't even see Lindy. Who would rescue her from the dark turn this mother–daughter communion was taking?

'I'm doing the opposite of buzz-killing. I want to tell you about the day I fell in love. It's a beautiful story.' Eilers lay back and Ailbhe joined her. Hands behind their heads, they looked up at the sky, which was a lovely neat little square. Ailbhe snuggled closer to her mam.

'I was watching *Grange Hill* at your nanny's house one day when these horrible pains started up. I wanted to see if Doyle was going to be caught out in his light-bulb bootlegging scheme and if anyone would find out about Alan's smoking behind the bike shed, but the pains were getting worse and worse and eventually I had to admit that the baby was coming. I didn't want to tell Daddy and Mam because they had barely looked at me as I'd gotten bigger and bigger. Your aunty Philo was home from London so I asked her to bring me to the hospital. The birth was murder: the epidural seemed to only work on one side but the doctor wouldn't listen to me, I think because I was only seventeen and because of my accent. Snotty little shite was probably not that much older than me. Anyway, I was pushing this stubborn little thing for ages and eventually the doctor said he was doing a vacuum-assisted delivery. I thought he was talking about a hoover but then they came in with – no joke – what looked like a plunger to suck your big huge head out of me! It was hysterical. Me and Philo were in bits. In the end, I think the laughing helped you pop out better than the plunger. And that was the day we met. When I first saw your face, scrunched up and pissed off, I was laughing and I couldn't stop for days because I was so happy and in love.'

Ailbhe smiled but the story made her sad. Had she felt that way about Tilly? About Tom?

'Everyone feels it differently.' Eilers on shrooms apparently read minds.

'Do you think I shouldn't have married Tom?' Ailbhe whispered. 'I think I do love him, but I've been scared of letting go of my freedom. And I feel bad because the truth is I haven't been honest about who I am. He's overreacting about the drinking and stuff because I never let him see that side of me. I deliberately kept it from him. That's bad, isn't it?'

'Ailbhe, I think when it comes to Tom you are one foot on the dock and one foot on the boat and, to be honest, staying on the dock is not an option because you have Tilly now.'

'I feel like a teenager still, though.'

'Ha,' Eilers barked. 'I actually *was* a teenager, Ailbhe. That's not an excuse that'll work with me!'

'But I don't think I know how to do this,' Ailbhe wailed.

'Ailbhe. Let me tell you something that my father told me …

Look at the stars. The great kings of the past look down on us from those stars.'

'What?'

'Yes … So whenever you feel alone …'

'Wait, is this—?' Ailbhe sat up to look down at her mother. 'Is this Mufasa and Simba from *The Lion King*?'

'I need a good big drink of water.' Eilers vaulted up to standing. 'Maybe a bath,' she added and strode purposefully towards the big multipacks of Ballygowan that Lindy had brought.

OK, she is very high but she is also right. I need to grow up and step off the dock.

Across the room, Eilers squealed like a child as she tipped a bottle over her head and lapped at it. 'It's so fizzy!'

Ailbhe made her way across the playroom to Roe who was now, it seemed, whispering to the tiny ballerina in a small musical box. *God, they're all so high.* Then Ailbhe noticed that she herself was crawling and not walking. 'Roe!'

Roe looked up, startled, then immediately shushed the ballerina. 'Not a word,' she warned it.

'I know what I need to do now … Eilers was amazing – she told me all this stuff about why we're here and shit. Aaand she made me realise that I haven't fully committed to Tom. I've been lying to Tom.'

'That's right, you have!' Roe's eyes gleamed as if this was some exciting news she was just discovering.

'No, not about that.' Ailbhe grabbed her friend. 'Or not *just* about that. About my drinking and stuff. I've been trying to clean up my act. I want to show him I am committed to being a family. It's really hit me – everything wonky that's ever happened to me has been when I was high or drunk.'

'OK but … you're totally high right now!' Roe started laughing. 'Talking about not being high any more while being high is such high talk!'

'No, I'm serious, I am going to do this. I think I have to, for Tilly and Tom.'

'Did you ever notice Tilly's a really weird name? Tiiilly. Ti-leeee.'

'Roe, I am so excited. The second I come down I am going to get my shit together.' Ailbhe felt fabulous. Who knew her mushroom trip 'come to Jesus' moment would be so tragically vanilla? And that she'd be so happy about it?

21

'HI, GUYS, IT'S MAX HERE FROM MAXXED OUT – welcome back to my channel.' Max was jigging on his chair, delivering his spiel and drumming his palms on the edge of the dining table where, just out of shot, the cereal bowls from breakfast still lingered. 'If you haven't already, don't forget to hit the subscribe button and ring that bell for notifications … So in today's video I am showing you guys how we're going to pack for our Monteray Vacay with thanks to our awesome sponsors Monteray Life Limited and Samsonite!'

'Cut,' Adam boomed from the other side of the camera. Lindy took this gap in the filming to gather her phone and keys, keen to escape being sucked into any content. She needed to wrap up a few Snag List bits before the weekend away. Also, Finn had demanded a mysterious meeting at the office and would be there at noon, which didn't leave Lindy much time.

'Max.' Adam looked exasperated. 'I will *pay* you to stop drumming. We need to get all these intros filmed before we leave tomorrow.'

Two weeks after the trip in Ailbhe's attic they were going on a more family-orientated one. Apart from the day in Wicklow, they hadn't left Monteray in over three months, and Lindy was sure it'd be good for everyone, even though the set-up was a little, well, Monteray Valleyish. Monteray Vacay was yet another cult-like facet to the Monteray Valley life – virtually a replica estate built along the coast in Waterford that everyone could decamp to for six weeks a year. There were some bonus features: a golf course, a more extensive spa, water sports and activities for children. But going on holiday with everyone you live with was bananas.

'Take the money, Max, he's good for it!' Lindy called playfully as she headed for the door.

'Oh ho …' Adam picked up his phone and turned towards her. 'If *anyone* is good for it's Ms Just Got a Write-Up in the *Indo* over there.'

'What? About The Snag List? Why are they writing about it? The press release isn't even written yet.'

'It's the 'Industry Incoming' column, so just a short mention that you've lately left the CEO position at Maxxed Out and there are "whispers" that you're "spearheading" a new project.'

'Oh God.' Lindy did the wince-face emoji at Max, who gamely did it back to her. 'What's the worst thing they said?' She leaned against the door frame.

'Lindy Reid,' Adam read, 'perhaps best known as the wife of Adam Zelner.'

'Nooo!' She laughed.

'Absolute shade,' Max added.

'Well, that just looks bad on them. What's the best thing?'

'The stunning Reid could easily have gone the classic YouTube matriarch route into lifestyle endorsements but has instead opted—'

'Shut the fuck up!'

'Mom!'

'Lindy!'

'I'm sorry – it slipped out.' Lindy laughed at their identical looks of outrage. 'But you made that bit up!'

'Actually, no, it's right here. You *are* stunning.' He hopped down and came over to hold her face to the light like an appraiser. 'Marion Cotillard-esque I would say.'

'Shtap that.'

'Who do you think Dad looks like?' Max was looking at Marion Cotillard on his phone.

'Dad looks like a young Dr Evil.' Lindy rubbed her husband's head playfully.

'Excuse me, I am in much better shape than Dr Evil,' said Adam, slipping his hand around her waist and kissing her deeply.

She left them filming their intros. They had a lot of content to do over the weekend, and pre-shooting these bits was a bid to make the weekend feel less like work for Max. She walked through the bright, cloudless Friday morning feeling buoyant. Things were righting themselves. Adam's slip was just that, a slip; it didn't have to be a marriage-ender. She was feeling so much better in so many respects. The Snag List was coming to something. She'd snuck a look at the rest of the *Indo* write-up before she left the house, and it had called her a 'zeitgeist surfer' joining the 'swathes of savvy entrepreneurs spotting, in the wake of the pandemic, potential for new services and business opportunities'. They said The Snag List was hugely prescient, as people were re-evaluating their lives after the crisis.

It was certainly incredible seeing Roe doing so well. She was literally transforming because of the push she'd gotten from The Snag List. Eilers had been thrilled with the mushroom trip, and Ailbhe seemed to have got some new clarity from the escapade too. She wasn't drinking and said she was going to give AA another try.

Helping Rachel make her amends to Sigrid would bring an interesting dimension to the slate of testimonials. She was nearly finished getting all the data together.

Once at her desk, she typed out a suggested road map for Rachel's snag. She'd borrowed slightly from the twelve-step recovery programme and tailored it to create worksheets for Rachel.

1 August – Soul Searching: Rachel to review her online activities. For each hurtful comment, Rachel to examine and detail the fear or upset that motivated her to make that statement. E.g. 'What was happening in your own life, Rachel? Is this comment really about Sigrid or is it about you?'

Poor Rachel. Lindy wasn't a big believer in God or the universe, but she had to admit sometimes things in life had a habit of lining up right when you needed them to. She hadn't been overjoyed to work with Rachel but, ironically, seeing this side of the woman her husband had betrayed her with had helped her come to terms with the whole thing. Rachel was a sad person, and seeing this had made her realise it was not worth throwing away her marriage or business over one tiny, stupid thing.

On the laptop, she continued making her way down the

comments sections on Sigrid's account, grabbing comments here and there to paste into the worksheet document. Next she made a final sweep of all the troll accounts Rachel had given her, double-checking that each one was now disabled. Then something odd caught her eye under a Sigrid Kitchen Transformation video. It was one of the handles Rachel had given her, but the words were reversed. @NeverGoingAway was Rachel's handle that Lindy had disabled, but here in the comments section was @ GoingAwayNever. It couldn't be a coincidence. Lindy input the handle into YouTube's login page and entered Rachel's ridiculous password. The login screen gave way to the account's dashboard. Same password again. *The woman's an idiot.*

Immediately, Lindy could see this account was different from the others. The rest of the accounts had nothing on them, but there was a video posted here from 20 May, the day of Fielding's birthday party. The video was labelled 'test' and it had exactly two views. The thumbnail was black, and when Lindy played it, it was just a couple of minutes of blank screen. Then she spotted something deeply unnerving. There was one comment. 'Perfect,' it said.

The comment was from the Maxxed Out account.

Lindy's heart pounded as she frantically searched through the @GoingAwayNever account. No other videos were visible on the channel until she hit the 'manage videos' button and nine unlisted videos appeared. Unlisted videos were only accessible to someone who was given a direct link. The most recent one was posted on 24 July, barely a week ago. All the videos had the same black thumbnails.

You do not want to see these …

But maybe they were just more trolling nonsense?

She withheld this handle for a reason, Lindy!

Her thoughts raged, but she knew she was clicking on the videos. It was a big-red-button situation. Had to be pressed.

She hadn't gotten past the first few seconds of the very first one before she slapped the computer shut and the wave of nausea hit. Before she knew what was happening, she was on her hands and knees, vomit spraying across the carpet in front of her.

'Fucking hell, Lindy! Are you doing a new accent colour in here?' Finn was standing at the door, gaping.

Lindsay had never vomited from shock before and had always thought it was only something that happened in movies. 'Oh, Jesus.' Her eyes were streaming.

'Christ!' Fionnuala hurried in and closed the door. 'Did you eat something? Are you pregnant? Oh my God, this is disgusting.'

'Thank you.' Lindy spat the words out with difficulty. The sour taste clogged her mouth. She remained hunched on the floor, the sight of her own sick nothing compared with the images crashing over her again and again. Adam between Rachel's thighs, his grin, her hands on him. Her moans. His hard-on. The camera had captured it all. Well, not everything. Adam was clearly visible but Rachel was not. Still, it was undeniably her. Lindy felt the shock settle on her, pressing her to the floor and paralysing her thoughts. Then the shaking began. Her teeth chattered and she wondered was she actually unwell. Did she need help?

'What is going on?' Finn was freaking and Lindy tried to grasp at some words to explain but her brain wasn't cooperating. Nothing made any sense.

They were sexting or cybering. Not this.

'I'm calling emergency, Linds.' Her sister was holding her shuddering shoulders, crouched down beside her. 'Don't worry. It's gonna be—'

'Don't. Please. I just need a minute. I'm OK.'

'Ah, now you speak. After I knelt in your vom you're OK!' Finn U-turned on her sympathy immediately.

'I'm not OK. I just don't need an ambulance.'

Clearly sensing the undertow of despair in her words, Finn pulled her close again. 'What is it, Linds? Is it Max? Did you see Max in the comments—?'

'I saw something on that woman's YouTube.' Lindy indicated the laptop on the desk above. 'Just open it, Finn.' Let her watch it. Saying the words was just too unbearable.

Lindy realised that before this moment she'd managed to downplay her hurt because she'd demoted the infidelity to 'just a virtual affair'. There was nothing remote about this video. This was full contact, skin on skin. The thing that was so staggering to Lindy was how physical this hurt was. *I thought I didn't care.* She hugged her body to try to quell the shaking. *I remember that grin,* she thought as she buried her face in her arms, heaving dry, futile sobs. *He grinned at me like that, he held me like that, he loved me like that.*

'Lindy. I have no idea what to say.'

'Me neither.' Lindy pulled herself up to standing.

'I thought it was a —'

'I know.' Lindy regarded the floor. A curdled mess on the otherwise perfect white carpet. She found her way to her chair, torpid and hollow from the trauma of the moment. 'This is very … I'm … I dunno. I'm finding it hard to catch up with this. Everything has been so much better, Finn.' Tears at last breached the strange numbness. 'We've been so good since—'

'These are dated all through the summer,' Finn said quietly.

Lindy nodded her head. It was a reflex. She was nodding but she couldn't believe it. In the troubled quiet, Finn's question from a few minutes earlier returned to Lindy's mind: *Did you see Max in the comments?*

'Finn. What did you mean did I see Max in the comments?'

A wary look took over from Finn's shock. 'Oh, nothing, that's … we can talk about that later.'

'Finn?'

'Linds—'

'In what comments?'

'OK.' Finn was visibly trying to compose herself, clearly gearing up for something. 'I don't want to stand on your neck and spit on your soul while you're obviously already down, but I did come here to talk about something.'

Lindy clenched as Finn pulled her iPad out of her bag.

'I'm really not sure now's the time to get into this. We haven't even cleaned the—'

'What is it, Finn? If it's about Max I need to know this second What. Is. It?'

'The bottom half of the internet, sis.' Finn flipped open the cover and propped the tablet on the desk so Lindy could see. A couple of taps on the screen and a screenshot appeared. It took Lindy a minute and then the realisation of what she was looking at landed like a punch. The Maxxed Out comments section. She swiftly unfocused her eyes so the words about her couldn't penetrate, as she had trained herself over many years.

'Lindy, this is serious. I have some real concerns. So does Mum.'

'OK, OK, I can see how this probably looks, but I swear it doesn't bother me.' Not a complete lie. 'I know they seem to hate me, but that just comes with being a woman and being anywhere near the internet. I know you guys care about me but you just don't get it. You're not in the industry. It's fine. I am fine with it.'

It was a strange phenomenon that Lindy, despite never appearing on camera on the channel, was the main focus of the comments section. YouTube families were frequently up for dissection, and Lindy had spent the first couple of years of Maxxed Out engaged in a futile full-time game of whack-a-mole with the channel's detractors. No sooner had she crafted a carefully worded response to a vicious reply to a video than another would appear in its place. The trolls were easy enough to ignore and block; it was the people who she feared had something of a point that ensnared her and kept her awake at night. Was her son comfortable with being on camera? they asked. Was she ruining his childhood? Didn't he have a right to privacy? Had she no shame?

When she lay in bed, blinking into the dark, her mind racing towards agreeing with some of them, Adam would haul her back. 'They don't know what they're talking about. They don't give a shit about Max – they're just high on self-righteousness. Maxxed Out is giving Max an amazing childhood. What kid gets to go skiing and to Disneyland and on safari all in one year? What parents get to spend this much time with their kid? He'll have a deposit for a house before he even leaves school!' And in this way, Adam routinely talked her down.

Still the endless 'feedback' was exhausting. The questions in the comments section soon morphed into out-and-out accusations. She was a child abuser, a money-hungry fiend, a monster, a selfish bitch who should just go and kill herself. Lindy had long since stopped reading. She'd placed the task of managing follower engagement firmly in Adam's hands. *You want the YouTube channel so badly, you deal with the hate.*

Then when Jamie Bell, their MD, had joined the business two years in and assembled a dedicated team, she'd tasked him with collating the hate and providing a breakdown. It came as no surprise that 88 per cent of all Maxxed Out 'feedback' was vitriol directed at Lindy for her apparently dire and downright evil mothering. Concern for the child was how the viewers justified telling her to kill herself. Ugh. If she wasn't wholly dependent on it for their income, Lindy would really rather just turn off the internet at this point.

'I know it looks bad, Finn, and they are bizarrely fixated on me, but I can take it. I've made peace with it. I never ever go there.'

'You may not go there, sis, but Max does.'

'What? He can't – we have Cyber Nanny.' Lindy snatched up the iPad to examine the picture.

> **Sea Breeze Lover:** *Lindy Reid is nothing but a child abuser. She is exploiting that poor boy and robbing him of his innocent years #JailForYouTuberFamilies.*

> Hide 54 replies

> **The Real Max:** *My mom is the best mom in the world. You don't know anything about her. You're just a saddo online.*

Sea Breeze Lover*: I'm afraid that you are being gaslit by that mEgaLOmaNiac cUnt and you're much too young to see that right now. Luckily there are services in place to help children like you.*

The Real Max*: I don't need any help. I love my mom and I love doing my videos so ... FUCK You ;)))*

Oh God. Lindy flipped the cover back over the screen. She couldn't bear to read any further. She placed the tablet on the table in front of her and brought her head down to rest on top of it.

How can this have happened? I have completely failed him.

More fuel for the ever-blazing guilt fire in her head. Stealing his childhood, not spending more time crafting, too much screen time. Now Max was sneaking online and defending her. Defending their life. *He is eleven years old.*

'Lindy. Do you not have internet controls to keep him off there?'

'We do. But you have no idea what it's like.' When Maxxed Out became a limited company they'd created guidelines to protect their son but now, five years on, they seemed laughably naive. 'We try to keep Max's access to the channel restricted, but kids are way more savvy about the internet – what can we do?'

'More than you're doing, obviously.'

'Finn ...' Lindy could barely speak. This was bad. So bad. She felt hollow; the image of her son in his room at night carefully typing out these words to vicious strangers rose before her like a nightmare. Did he cry reading the comments? *How could I have done this?* 'Jesus, everything is turning to shit. An hour ago I was all buzzing about some stupid write-up online. How fucking selfish am I?'

'I'm sorry, Linds, I know the timing couldn't be worse …'

'That doesn't matter.' A flashback to Rachel and Adam still caused a lurch of humiliation inside her, but Max was the only thing that mattered now.

'I'm going to fix this, Finn.'

How will I fix this?

There really only seemed to be one way, but it felt so extreme … It would change everything.

★

After Finn left, Lindy killed the next few hours in her office cleaning up and going back and forth on her next move. They were supposed to be leaving first thing in the morning. Was it right to still go?

She tried to send a voicy to the Snag List WhatsApp, but getting the words out was impossible. After a few minutes grappling with typing a text, she scrapped the effort and instead sent one of the unlisted video links. She didn't need to explain further; the level of vitriol they came back with said it all. They insisted they wouldn't go without her. And Lindy was grateful. Being with Roe and Eddie and Ailbhe would be a distraction – way preferable to spending the long weekend in a house with Adam. She needed to spend as little time as possible alone with him right now – she just couldn't trust that she wouldn't scream into his face the moment she saw him. She had texted him to say she was working late and then slipped into the house after dark, relieved that he was asleep. By then the initial shock and pain had receded. For the moment, at least. A productive rage had taken their place. Lindy drank a glass of Malbec in the kitchen while googling 'divorce' – she sent a selfie to the Snag List captioned: Most Monteray Valley Activity of All Time?!

She would do nothing and say nothing. She would get legal advice. This wasn't about her marriage right now. She couldn't confront Adam about the videos: he might get defensive or angry. This was about Max and getting him out of Maxxed Out. If she didn't manage things right, it could be nuclear and she couldn't do that to Max. She needed time to try and claw together the ability to be rational for his sake.

She went upstairs and brushed her teeth in the en suite. Her eyes burned, and applying her night serum felt like preparing for battle. Adam was asleep but he shifted and muttered groggily when she slipped under the covers beside him.

He turned to hold her from behind and fell back asleep. She lay in his arms rigid with fury. At him, at the horrible people on the internet, but mostly at herself.

22

IT WAS NEARLY 4 P.M. THE NEXT DAY BY THE TIME Ailbhe, Tilly, Roe and Eddie, who was driving them, arrived at the first sign for Monteray Vacay and took a right, bringing them to a road running parallel to the ocean. Ahead was the Monteray Vacay private beach full of Saturday crowds enjoying the late afternoon sun. Loungers and wooden pergolas were arranged at intervals, each, Ailbhe knew, with a discrete number corresponding to a summer house – no morning dash for a spot on this beach.

Ailbhe pulled up the map on the MV app. 'Another ten minutes,' she announced. The relief. She was edgy with Tilly snoozing in the car seat beside her. She'd never brought her on any long journeys, and it felt like she was playing Nap Titty Tetris – when to feed her so she'd nap in the car but not nap so late that she wouldn't go down that night but not so early that … and on and on and on. It was a baffling game with no prize other than things just not going to shit. *A metaphor for parenthood as a whole!*

'I'd love to be getting straight into the hot tub when we get there.'

Eddie sighed. 'Pity Adam and I said we'd get nine holes in before dinner. Roe, you have to admit that this is gorgeous.'

'I wasn't saying it wouldn't be nice – I just said it'd be more *Truman Show* weirdness. Ailbhe, you agree, right? It's a middle-class Jonestown-on-Sea is all I'm saying.'

'With Tom an original investor, I won't be agreeing with anything. That'd be high treason and I don't need any more reasons for him to be mad at me.' She glanced guiltily at her phone, where yet another five missed calls from a California number had racked up. Just two more days and then she'd be able to surprise him with her progress. Twenty days of no drinking or any other bullshit – except the unfortunate brush with magic mushrooms, which wasn't technically drinking and wasn't technically her fault. She'd had a white chocolate Magnum every night while watching *Call the Midwife* with her mam. And if that was what it'd take to keep her from the wine then that was fine. Especially as the alternative – lose Tom and ruin Tilly's chance at having a dad – was so very *not* fine. It was a small price to pay to keep everything from falling apart. She had also, it seemed, finally gotten the message through to Seb that nothing more would happen between them; she hadn't had any more flirty DMs on Insta and he had said nothing more to Roe about getting her number.

Lindy, Adam and Max had been at the beach house since the morning. Adam and Max were filming for YouTube and, judging by the updates in the Snag List WhatsApp group, Lindy was just about keeping herself in check. With pharmaceutical help.

LINDY: The Valium I took at breakfast is about the same age as Max but I think if anything that's made it even stronger.

ROE: Fermentation?

**AILBHE: Just don't drink on top of it … until we get there. I'd
hate to miss whatever shitemare would ensue.**

ROE: Ailbhe! No mocking Lindy right now, it's too soon.

**LINDY: No, it's not. Please make jokes. It's fitting, my whole
life's a joke.**

Fuck! What can we even say to that? Ailbhe thought, peering at Roe
in the front seat. Roe glanced back at her and made a helpless face.
By silent mutual agreement they hadn't said a word in front of Eddie
– just lots of wide-eyed meaningful looks passing between them as
Eddie had steered them down the motorway, keeping up a cheery
commentary all the way. Before they'd got in the car, Roe had filled
Ailbhe in on the horrible cyber wank Lindy had walked in on earlier
in the summer. Poor Lindy. Ailbhe looked back down at the phone
and started to type: L-i-n-d-y. The text at the top of the screen was
flickering …
  Roe … typing
  Ailbhe … typing
  … as they each tried to scrounge together something to say.

**LINDY: Whatever placating responses ye're coming up with,
please don't bother. I just want to rage and wallow. Do you
know what I keep thinking? A sex tape is just so passé. At least
when they were doing it in a VR helmet it was imaginative. More
current, yanno? Zeitgeisty. Anyway, feck the Tommy Lee–Pam**

naffness, the main thing is talking to Max. When Adam and Eddie go golfing I'll have time. Ugh, I've to go. They need me to wear the chest cam. Just GET HERE.

As they reached the house, Tilly started bitching for booby and Ailbhe lifted her from the seat, smiling. 'We survived! Thank you for not being a complete D-bag in the car!' Tilly was working her perfect little cherry lips around her tiny fist and giving a cute little agitated cry. 'I've to feed this,' Ailbhe called back to the other two.

'Cool, we'll bring in your stuff.'

Ailbhe started up the steps leading to the large wooden wrap-around veranda. It was a white clapboard lodge, set just back from the dunes that bordered the resort's private beach.

'This is stunning.' Eddie and Roe followed behind.

Inside the house, Ailbhe, cradling Tilly, located Lindy upstairs unpacking Max's suitcase in the smallest of the six bedrooms. Ailbhe sat on the bed and unhitched the left side of her nursing bra. Tilly latched gratefully like she'd never been fed in her life. 'How are you?'

'I'm taking Max rock climbing!' She seemed unexpectedly energised. 'You're too young to come, sweetie,' she cooed at Tilly.

'Lindy!' Roe had joined them and immediately pulled Lindy into a hug, which Lindy tolerated for a couple of minutes then resumed her stacking of T-shirts in drawers.

'Are you sure you're all right?' Ailbhe peered at her.

'Yes. No. Who cares?' She slammed the drawer closed and roughly wiped her face.

'Aw, Lindy.' Roe made to hug her again but Lindy held her at bay.

'I'm not upset. These are rage tears. Everything will be fine. I'm going to talk to Max and figure out what he needs. It will all be fine – at least I know the truth now. No more being lied to,' she insisted. 'I have to go and climb a sheer rock face. Fuck the world!'

She clattered down the stairs calling for Max.

Ailbhe and Roe exchanged concerned looks. 'At least she sounds like herself? Kinda.'

Obviously Lindy was destroyed by the videos of Adam and Rachel, but even for Roe and Ailbhe, witnessing it had been destabilising, inciting, as it did, a fair bit of reflection on the state of their own marriages. It was like being in a leaky boat and watching the *Titanic* go down in front of you.

Roe looked worried. 'I can't stop thinking about it.'

'I know …' Ailbhe breathed. 'You heard what she said? "No more being lied to" – poor Lindy, Jesus. What must that feel like?' She fussed at Tilly's bib, suddenly aware of Roe's eyes on her. 'I know, I'm a hypocrite. But my lie is a lie to *protect* people.'

'Ailbh—'

'Really, Roe. It is. And not just protect me. It's for Tilly. And Tom. He loves her. Whatever I could've done differently – done better – at the beginning, it's too late now. He loves this child. Regardless of biology, she *is* his child. And I have to live with this lie. I cannot ruin her chance of getting to have a father like Tom. And I am making myself better for Tom – nearly twenty days booze-free over here!'

'Ailbhe, you giving up drinking doesn't cancel out the lie. You know that, right? This not drinking isn't some kind of penance, is it?'

'OK, yes. I think when I first thought of it it totally was. I thought it was how I could maybe make myself worthy of him. But since I've been reading about this and going back to AA meetings, I've actually been finding things in common with the people and their stories. Lots of people with lots of chaos behind them in the years they'd been drinking. And I guess, that is me to a degree. I'm still not sure if I'm a full-on alcoholic – maybe more of a "problem drinker"? Though there's one question that keeps coming up: "If you have a drink do you find it easy to stop at just one or two?" That struck a nerve. I was, like, "Of course not. But no one can!" But now I'm thinking maybe some people can?'

Roe laughed gently. 'Yes. They can, pal.'

Ailbhe nodded and smiled tightly. 'Yep, I'm gathering that. Anyway, wanna come help me give Tilly her bath? It is so cute. Baby-sloth levels of cuteness.'

In the bathroom, Ailbhe poured baby bubbles into the water.

'Are you sure it's OK for me to have this?' Roe cocked her G&T towards Ailbhe.

'Of course, I am a reformed woman, remember? Ish. Hopefully? LOL, I'm, like, ten minutes without wine in my system and I think I'm a saint.'

Roe was perched on the edge of the bath while Ailbhe knelt on the floor, leaning over the side to soap the little chubby limbs, eliciting squeals and chortles from Tilly. It was the highlight of every day. Ailbhe gazed down at her daughter. 'This kind of makes up for that midnight howling you're so fond of, babes. Kind of.'

'It's nice seeing you in mum-mode.' Roe took out her phone and snapped a couple of pictures.

'Thank you. I think I'm finally getting the hang! But it's going by so fast – I can't believe how big she is already compared with when she was born.'

Roe gulped back her G&T so quickly she managed to slop some into the bath. 'Sorry, sorry.' She wiped her chin and reached down to swill the bath-water a bit. 'That'll be all right, won't it?'

'It'll probably be a sleep aid.' Ailbhe shrugged. 'Why are you Thirsty McHoundTheBooze tonight?'

'I can't drink in front of Eddie.' She stared down at Tilly for several seconds before she added, 'He's really on the whole trying-for-a-baby thing – we're supposed to be taking a pregnancy test in another few days.'

'Oh. Wow.' Ailbhe couldn't believe it. Roe had never told them they'd taken the next step. But she'd taken mushrooms only two weeks ago? Did shrooms and early pregnancy mix? Definitely not, but maybe it'd been after the trip?

'And what about the show? Isn't kick-off in, like, two weeks?'

'Eighteen days,' Roe replied. 'When I got the part, I told him I'd quit if I got pregnant. But it's all fine. I won't get pregnant.'

Ailbhe didn't know what to say. 'But, Roe, look at me and Lindy. It only takes one sperm.'

'I reeeally don't wanna talk about it, Ailbh.' Roe looked beseeching.

'Sure, of course. I understand.' *I really don't, though*, Ailbhe thought. *Why do something so massive that you're so uncertain about?* 'What was I saying again?' she mused, dodging Tilly's splashes – her legs were going like two little pistons.

'Something, something, childhood is a many splendoured thing … savour every precious laugh and shart and yada-yada-yada.'

'Oh God, tell me I didn't sound like one of those.' Ailbhe carefully regripped the slippery little Tilly. 'I guess I was saying how it's really just hit me that there won't be any Snag List fixes for the things you don't do when your kids are young. If I miss it now I miss it. You couldn't at sixty turn to your thirty-year-old and ask to give them a bath and put them to bed one last time. Or you could but …'

'It'd be … troubling.' Roe was nodding.

Ailbhe scooped Tilly out of the fragrant warm water and onto the fluffy white towel she'd spread on the floor. 'Watch, Roe, this is cute.' Ailbhe gently rolled the baby up in the towel then perched her on her lap with just her little face peeping out the top.

'It's a burrito baby!' Roe cooed.

'You will only be my baby for so long,' Ailbhe told Tilly solemnly. 'And then you'll be a savage bitch teenager, so I need to Soak. You. Up.' She nuzzled the nape of Tilly's neck, where a few wispy coppery curls were starting to grow.

'I'm sorry,' Roe interrupted, 'but you do sound like an internet mom. I have to be honest with you. Friends don't let friends go around sounding like saccharine assholes!'

'Oh, relax, my slut-heart is still beating.'

'I'm gonna get ready for dinner.' Roe made for her room down the hall as Ailbhe made her way up to the next floor to dress herself and Tilly.

★

'OK, Lindy, are you ready?'

No! 'Yes.'

'OK, go, Max. Lindy, keep feeding that rope out gently and remember, if Max has any issues, you just pull down hard with your right hand. I'll be just over here.'

Lindy nodded and kept her eyes fixed on Max's progress as he made his way up the sheer grey wall studded with brightly coloured hand- and foot-holds. He was so confident. No hesitation. He made a lunge for a grip that was inches out of his reach and Lindy's heart lurched. He smoothly righted himself, gripping it firmly as his focused face relaxed into a smile of proud delight.

'Did you see that?' he called down to her.

'That was amazing, sweetheart! I wish we had the camera!'

'No way,' he shouted back, already looking up to choose his next move. 'This way it's better – it's just for us.'

This offhand remark was, to Lindy, like the slice of a paper cut. It'd be barely noticeable to anyone else, but to her it was a sharp shock of pain. *He wanted this moment to be just for us.*

My mom is the best … you're just some saddo on the internet.

She fed the rope out as smoothly as she could, her whole body flexed and ready to act should he need her to take up the slack on his belay rope. *I will keep you safe.* Coursing beneath her skin was her guilt at Max reading the comments and defending her even while she was the one who'd left him so exposed.

She'd emailed Jamie immediately about turning comments off videos but there was no telling what Max had been seeing up to then. God, why hadn't she done it sooner? She'd thought because it was all directed at her it didn't matter. She had never imagined Max looking at it. He hadn't even been reading all that well for long. He'd been slow getting the hang of it anyway, and then of course the Bloody Pandemic™ further hindered him.

★

'Max? I have to ask you something. And please don't be mad at me.'

They were sitting outside the climbing centre having Cokes. She needed to navigate this carefully. He tensed a little and seemed suddenly wary, years older than eleven.

'It's nothing bad,' she carried on. 'Or, well, it's bad but it is *so* not your fault,' she quickly added. 'I've seen you in the comments on the channel. And I know you're trying to defend me and protect me. And I just want you to know, that's not your job, sweetheart. It's my job to protect you.' She stroked his cheek, still baby soft for now. 'And I haven't been doing my job right because you should never have seen that stuff and I am so, so sorry.'

'But … they're being so horrible about you, Mom, and I just—' He paused, pushing away the angry tears that had already gathered.

Lindy pulled him close, feeling sick at his anguish. 'They are mean people, Max. They don't matter. I used to mind and then I realised that they're just sad in their own lives. And now I never look at them. Ever. And I want you – no, I *need* you to do the same.' She leaned down and touched her forehead to his. 'Promise me.'

He looked up at her. 'I promise. I won't do it again. I swear.'

Finding out that people possess infinite ability to harm one another was a lesson he was way too young for. And finding out you have harmed your child despite your best intentions is a lesson no parent is ever ready for.

'Do you still like doing Maxxed Out?'

'Yah! I do, of course I do. You're not going to stop the channel, are you? Cos I know we need it and I like it, I totally like it.'

'We don't need it, Max. Really. Daddy and I have loads of other things we can do.'

'No, no,' he was firm, 'I want to keep doing it. I swear. I don't mind at all.'

His vehement reassurances cemented it for Lindy. He was so young. She realised she'd done her best to hide her regrets about Maxxed Out from everyone, but especially herself. *We work so hard at not seeing the one thing we don't want to see.* His pretence at enthusiasm pushed the door she'd closed on her fears further open.

Back at the house, Max immediately cornered Ailbhe and Roe to give them a detailed account of the climbing session. His words tumbled out over one another in his excitement, and Lindy remembered when he was this thrilled with a new toy to play with for Maxxed Out. He'd detail the new subscribers at the dinner table, his words slipping around each other in his elation. He'd known many by name back then. She hadn't seen him this buzzed in a very long time. He'd been going through the motions because he thought they wanted him to. And even if he still thought he enjoyed Maxxed Out, it was probably because he barely knew life without a camera and a vast invisible audience. She had to talk to Adam. She couldn't delay any longer. There was still time to repair things.

She found Adam in their bedroom, just out of the shower after golf. She was nervous. The mutation of Maxxed Out from low-key hobby to a fully fledged business had been so gradual that she'd never even thought to put anything legal down on paper. A lot was hitched to Maxxed Out. The house in Drumcondra was long gone, the money absorbed into their chaotic finances.

'How was climbing? Did Max get into it?'

'He loved it.' Lindy stared out the window at the precise and arrow-straight horizon line that bisected the bright blue of the sky and the deep navy of the ocean. It was a metaphor so on the nose that she'd have dismissed it in a movie for being too obvious. The line she was crossing would be final. A lot was going to change. She had to shelve her own feelings of soul-sick humiliation to make a clean break. For Max's sake, Adam must not know what she'd seen on the tapes. She sensed he was not going to go quietly in terms of Maxxed Out. He loved the status of playing the devoted, hot internet dad. If he realised she knew about his affair, he'd accuse her of ending Maxxed Out to get back at him. As much as she wanted to scream into his face, to raze him to the ground, she had to hold herself in check. There would be time down the line when Max was safe.

'Awesome that he loved it.' Adam snapped the waistband of his underpants and started to pull on his shorts. 'Some climbing vids would be fantastic. If Jamie can hook a sponsor fast, we could even get away to the Alps, maybe, before the end of summer. I haven't climbed in years.'

'I don't think so, Adam.' Lindy kept her voice steady and continued to gaze at the horizon. Wherever you stood it was always about five miles away. You could try to move forward and close that gap but it would keep receding. It was how her life had felt for the last few years. Always beyond her control and out of reach. 'I think Maxxed Out has to end.'

Now, she felt like she was catching up for the first time in forever.

'What, Lindy? C'mon. Everything is going great. We don't need to stop. We can't anyway – we're contracted to the hilt.'

'It doesn't matter. Max is more important than contracts and it is time to stop. For him. For us. We have to get back to being a family.'

'Lindy.' He looked furious. 'You don't seem to grasp that we're not rich. We don't own a home. We don't have millions in ready money. We don't even own the car. It's all on the Maxxed Out dime.'

'We have the proceeds from the house.' Lindy turned to face him. 'We'll go back to normal jobs. It's what most people do. The money from the Drumcondra house will be our cushion.'

'Well, that money isn't just sitting in an account. It's tied up in investments.'

'What investments?'

Adam was clearly uneasy. He turned and yanked his sweatshirt over his head, seemingly for something to do with his hands. 'Different bits and bobs. I put a bit in Optimise with Tom. Little nuggets here and there into up-and-coming technologies.'

'What's a little nugget in Adam-speak?' Lindy's dread was building. Was there no fallback?

'A few thousand. Sometimes more.'

'What's in the bank, Adam?'

'It fluctuates. You don't know how these things work—'

'Neither do YOU!' *Shit, shit, shit.*

'I've picked stuff up. The YouTube circuit has been very fruitful for the investment portfolio. It's a full-time job just *having* money nowadays – where to invest, what to endorse. Do you go the altruistic route? How do you stiff the taxman? It's a waste just having money lying in a bank account – it should be out there generating more.'

'Are we in trouble with this, Adam?' Lindy reached for a full breath but it was obstructed by a growing morass of fear.

'No! Not trouble, just now's not a good time to wrap up Maxxed Out.'

'It's a good time for Max,' she replied flatly. 'It's overdue, in fact. He's been reading the comments on the channel, and he's seen some pretty dark stuff on there. Protecting him is more important than money or your ego.'

'My ego?'

Shit! She instantly regretted saying 'ego'. 'Sorry, not your ego.' *Placate him, placate him.* 'I meant your ... pride ... in your work, in being such a good father. So fun.'

It killed her to pander to him, but it was dawning on her that this is what was necessary when you shared a child with a person you no longer trusted. *Will I have to manage his behaviour forever? Probably.* Max was a part of them both. They both loved him. But it was undeniable: they had very different ideas about what was good for him.

'I think you are completely overreacting, Lindy. Anyway, Max won't go for it, believe me.'

A knock on the door silenced them. 'Guys?' It was Eddie. 'Dinner's on its way?'

'Coming,' Lindy called, hoping they hadn't been too loud.

23

'IS THIS TILLY'S FIRST OFFICIAL DINNER PARTY then?' Lindy was uncorking a bottle of chilled Albariño, and Ailbhe searched her feelings, happy to find no real longing. She had a new purpose: no more jeopardising the things that were good for her. Ailbhe watched Lindy pouring three glasses, and when Lindy looked at her with a questioning expression, Ailbhe gave a subtle shake of her head. Roe also declined, she noted. She had to tell Lindy what was going on with Roe – they needed to talk sense into her before anything untakebackable (like a baby!) happened.

Everyone sat for their starter of grilled prawns in chilli butter with fresh sourdough. A private chef, who'd arrived with the entire meal just a few minutes before, was discreetly placing the covered main-course tray in the oven on a low temperature and leaving a neat printout of instructions on how to serve the rest of the meal.

'Thanks a million.' Eddie tipped him as he slipped out.

'This looks amazing.' Ailbhe finished settling Tilly in the

newborn attachment of the highchair and pulled out the seat beside her. 'And yes, this is Tilly's first soirée – fingers crossed she can keep her chill for at least a few minutes. We should make a toast.' Ailbhe pulled her Coke towards her. 'I feel like any baby milestone should be celebrated in a big way. Especially after she tortured me with the colic for the first couple of months.'

'Oooh, wait, Ailbhe!' Eddie was rummaging in a bag propped against his chair. 'We can't toast Tilly before our special guest joins us.'

Special guest? Confusion gave way to vague dread when Eddie pulled out an iPad and settled it at an empty space at the end of the table. *Has to be Tom*, Ailbhe thought. *Oh God.*

'He wanted to surprise you!' Adam grinned over at her. 'Got me and Ed in on it.'

Ailbhe sat back, drawing a smile over her clenched face. *This isn't him surprising me: this is him cornering me. He thinks I've been avoiding him cos he's mad. I just wanted a couple more wine-free days behind me to prove how serious I am.* Reaching a round number felt meaningful to Ailbhe, so she'd placated him with videos of Tilly and avoided any face-to-face contact.

'He's so cute,' she said sweetly. *Great, now I have to have my first conversation with Tom in weeks right in front of our friends.* She didn't want to have to tell him all about her new clean living at a dinner party. Awkward didn't even cover it. *Though being tense and secretly fighting at a crowded dinner party is probably the most 'normal couple' thing we've ever done*, she thought wryly.

'Oh, here he comes.' Roe turned to Ailbhe and slyly poked her tongue out.

'Hi, gang! How's my connection?' Tom's smaller-than-life-size face appeared on the screen. He was in a white shirt, looking relaxed by the beach.

'Perfect, man.' Adam pretended to high five the iPad, and Ailbhe spied identical pained expressions crossing Lindy's and Max's faces.

'Hi, Ailbhe!' Tom's formal greeting to her seemed pointed but maybe she was projecting.

'Hi,' she echoed.

'You guys notice anything?' Tom looked around him, one eyebrow cocked.

'You're at the beach?' Lindy delicately peeled a prawn.

'Wait! Wait!' Max leaned forward to peer at the screen. 'That's here. You're at *this* beach. Are you? How?'

'Yeah, it's cool, isn't it?' Adam interjected. 'I sent Tom snaps and he's made them into a virtual background.'

'I wanted to make this feel as close to being there with you as possible.' Tom straightened up and fiddled with something on his computer. 'I'm actually in one of the Optimise nap pods!' His background flickered to reveal a dark space with the word OptiSnooze emblazoned above him.

He is sweet. Ailbhe smiled with real feeling as the beach returned behind her husband. *This is his way of being with us. He cares enough to attend a dinner party remotely in the middle of his working day. This is his way of showing me that he wants us to work too.*

'Look, I know you're all only on starters but I have a 2 p.m. so I need to get down to it.' The tiny face peered up at them; the iPad placement made it look like Tom was a small child at the table. 'This is an intervention.'

'Is it?' Lindy's voice was muffled as she hurriedly swallowed a hunk of bread.

'Yes, Lindy, it is.' Tom's tone was clipped – he was like a hectoring little toddler at the top of the table. 'You in particular, Lindy, know exactly what I'm talking about. The events of the night of 16 July – a couple of weeks ago in case you're too "hopped up on goofballs" to recall the timeline.'

'I definitely am not, Tom. And I don't know what you're talking about.' Lindy was withering but Ailbhe was freaked. What the hell was Tom saying? He surely couldn't know about ...?

'I'm talking about drugs, Lindy, and from what I've seen you were the one supplying them.'

This statement rippled round the table.

'What?' squeaked Eddie, while Max said 'MOM!' in a vaguely admiring tone. A baffled 'Lindy?' was all Adam could muster. Ailbhe and Roe clearly had nothing to say – though Roe, obviously thinking on her feet, said, 'Well ... Lindy, I am shocked!' and Ailbhe, despite the dire situation, had to suppress a bark of laughter. Oh God, there was nothing funny about this, though. How did Tom know?

'Eddie, Adam, I'm not sure of your stances on recreational drug use, but I am vehemently opposed. With careful management microdosing can, I admit, be a good performance tool in a work situation, but magic mushrooms, in a child's playroom and in the doses I saw these women ingesting, is not good. Not good.'

'Mushrooms?' Eddie stared at Roe in abject horror. 'You didn't do this, Roe? A couple of weeks ago? What's he talking about?'

Roe looked stricken and Ailbhe leapt up. It was one thing for Tom to confront *her*, but he had no right to mess with Eddie and Roe. 'Please, Tom, this is between us and I can explain.' She strode round the table to try and grab the iPad, but Eddie snatched it up just as Adam stood to block Lindy's matching attempt on the other side of the table. Roe just sat in her seat looking ambushed.

'Ailbhe,' – Tom, she could see, was struggling to maintain his composure – 'I am sure Adam and Eddie want to know exactly what their wives have been up to as well. There are, after all, children involved.'

He is not enjoying this. The realisation landed like a blow. *He is upset, of course he is … He watched you get off your head with Tilly just downstairs.* Ailbhe sat back down beside Roe and Lindy. *But I was off my head by accident, for feck's sake.* She imagined they looked like the front row of a funeral. *It didn't seem that bad. We were just cutting loose.* Ailbhe resisted the urge to defend herself, knowing that wouldn't help anything. She pulled Tilly, who was starting to fuss, into her lap. *Please let him forgive me.* After everything, she knew this could be her 'third strike and you're out' moment. *Please don't let this ruin us.*

'Hold on one sec, Tom.' Adam lowered himself back into his chair, training his stern gaze on Lindy. 'Max? Please give us a minute, sport. Grab some potato chips from the kitchen and go watch TV. I'll be right in.'

Max stood and walked reluctantly towards the kitchen, clearly straining to hear if anything else was being said yet. They all watched him go.

'Go on, Tom.' Eddie rested his chin on his hand and looked impossibly weary.

'I chose to tell you this all together because, as I said, all of our wives are involved but also because,' Tom shifted uncomfortably, 'I am aware that I don't actually know my wife that well and I just wanted to make sure that she wouldn't do anything—'

'Tom! I would never!' Ailbhe cried. 'Please, I swear Tilly was totally safe. We were just doing this thing because my mam never had … and… and… I actually didn't even mean to—'

'Let's just hear what Tom has to say, Ailbhe,' Adam snapped. She felt like decking him. Of all the people at this table *he* was the one doing shitty things behind people's backs.

'It's probably quicker if I just show rather than tell.' Tom messed with his computer and his screen was replaced with a still of Tilly's playroom. A small Tom was still visible at the bottom right of the screen and he continued to speak. 'Before I left Monteray, I installed a prototype of some hardware we're rolling out in the fall. It's an add-on to the OptimEyes app, OptimEyesOnU. It's a discreet multi-purpose camera. It's going to be huge. In terms of home security and surveillance, it will blow Ring right out of the market. You never know, could be a good investment opportunity, Adam?'

'Yeah, bro, I'll keep it in mind.'

Lindy scowled across at this.

'Anyway,' Tom continued, 'I put an OptimEyesOnU up in Tilly's playroom because I figured it was a handy way to check functionality from another continent. I didn't really think anyone would be up there, so I wasn't trying to spy before anyone starts up about privacy breaches blah blah blah. I am sick of users being so paranoid.'

'Tom, can you get on with this?' Eddie was barely keeping his patience in check.

'Sorry, sure. I had an assistant speed it up and edit it down. The original is at least four hours long, mostly garbled gibberish, but this will give you all the gist.'

The frame unfroze and Ailbhe could see them opening their boxes of mushrooms and that stupid cup of tea. She could see her and Roe having the whispered conversation about Seb, but luckily Lindy's Snag List run-down was all that was audible. Then it fast-forwarded and they went from sitting in their chairs to varying states of highness in a matter of seconds. She was writhing through the ball pit in the foreground towards Eilers, who was standing swaying and clapping under a skylight. Roe was off in a corner laughing with her hands clapped over her eyes, and Lindy was scrolling on her phone looking bored.

'Lindy, I cannot believe you were getting them wasted with a baby downstairs.' Adam looked livid. 'And for your … "business"?' He pronounced the word with disdain but Lindy just shrugged impassively and Ailbhe, despite her own distress, was impressed with Lindy's new zero-fucks stance. She should get an Oscar. Or a Nobel Prize for husband-fuckery.

More minutes sped by and Ailbhe watched herself and her mother lie under the skylight for what must've been hours. Then there was an interlude of some synchronised swimming in the ball pit, during which Roe leaned over the side and vomited into a wicker toy box full of stuffed animals and then carried right on rolling around with the others. *Gross.* Ailbhe barely remembered that. She could see some kind of vom run-off was seeping out from the bottom of the box – wicker was not ideal for containing fluids.

On the screen, Eilers vaulted energetically out of the balls and slipped straight over in the mess.

Christ, I must've blocked loads out. This does look a lot more degenerate than it felt in the moment.

'I think that is everything we need to see.' Tom ended the clip and his face filled the screen once more.

'I'm sorry, Tom, Tilly was completely safe. I swear.' Ailbhe held her daughter even closer. 'Can we just talk about this in private, please? I've been making some really big changes since that night and—'

'Ailbhe, I actually *wanted* to talk to you in private. If you hadn't been avoiding my calls, we could've discussed this without involving everyone. I was angry but I wanted to work this all out. The visa thing, the outstanding warrant. Everything. I wanted to know you. I love you. I did marry you, didn't I? But it's you, Ailbhe. It's you who's kept me at arm's length for God knows what reason. I don't deserve this. I never wanted to break up our family. I love you and Tilly. I don't want to start fighting over our baby girl. But you are giving me no choice.'

'Tom! Stop. Please. We can't break up.' The situation was slipping from her grasp. She'd thought she'd been in charge of taking her foot off the dock, but now the boat was pulling away without her. Everyone else at the table was silent. Eddie had his head in his hands and Roe was staring across at him looking absolutely destroyed. Adam's foot was tapping nervily against the table leg as he chewed on the skin around his thumbnail. A dejected Lindy was looking at Roe and Eddie, then she turned to Ailbhe and mouthed 'I'm sorry'.

How had everything fallen apart in a matter of minutes? On the screen, Tom looked the most desolate of everyone. 'You say we don't have to break up, Ailbh, but did you ever even want this in the first place? Because now I feel like all of it adds up. The stuff you never told me, the drinking and the drug use. Maybe you were never ready. Maybe the "you" I'm in love with isn't you at all. You thought you'd try me out. But Tilly and I are not accessories you can return.'

'I never treated you like that! I love y—'

'Tom, Ailbhe?' Eddie had emerged from behind his hands looking exasperated. 'We are all digesting this, Tom. You don't get to lob a bomb from across the Atlantic and then have all of us do some fucking group therapy for you and your wife. Or maybe you want us all to unravel right here in public as well? Is that it? So you two can feel better about your weird excuse for a marriage?'

Ailbhe flinched. Eddie was usually so diplomatic and controlled. It was horrible to see him so shaken. So angry.

'Well, excuse me, Eddie, but I presume you didn't know your wife was high as hell a couple of weeks ago either. And from the look on your face, it seems like this might be saying something about *your* marriage too.'

'Everyone,' Lindy was calm but serious, 'I have to explain. This is my fault entirely. Eileen wanted to do magic mushrooms; I was facilitating it for my new life-coaching company. And I said to Ailbhe and Roe that they should come and do them with her because it'd be too mad for Eilers to trip on her own, and I needed to stay sober for health and safety reasons. So I asked these gals – no, *told* them to join in. And Ailbhe had only wanted tea but I made her mushroom tea by accident. So it's all my fault. But everyone was safe.'

'Everyone was not safe, Lindy.' Eddie's eyes flashed; his neck was so flushed with rage it was nearly purple, his features so contorted he was unrecognisable. 'Roe might be *pregnant*. We are waiting to take the test. So actually everyone was not safe – you and your little project have endangered a child.'

'It's not Lindy's fault,' Roe spoke quietly, not lifting her eyes from her lap. 'She didn't make anyone come along.'

There was silence except for the sound of Eddie's ragged breaths. Finally he spoke again. 'Why did you do that, Roe?' Ailbhe could see that his anger was shot through with confusion and hurt. 'Did you not think "taking drugs might not be good for the baby I might be carrying"?' He shook his head slowly. 'What on earth possessed you? I can't believe you've done this. You realise our baby might be damaged. Oh God. I can't believe this is happening.' He sagged in his seat.

It was excruciating to watch, but just as Ailbhe was about to stand and suggest they get the hell away from each other for a moment, Roe spoke. 'Our baby isn't damaged, Eddie. There is no baby.' She was blunt.

Eddie looked up, his eyes glassy. 'You don't know that, Roe. You don't know that it didn't work. The success rate is 30 per cent. We could have gotten lucky. You could be pregnant right this moment. You could've been pregnant while you were puking out the side of that ball pit. I never believed you capable of something like this.'

'Eddie,' Roe spoke slowly, her voice quiet but firm, 'I am not pregnant. It's not a 30 per cent likelihood, it's a 0 per cent likelihood – pretty much a medical impossibility. The last time we had sex, I took the morning-after pill.'

24

LINDY WASN'T SURE WHOSE CAR JOURNEY BACK TO Monteray Valley would be the most horrific. In the end, they hadn't even lasted eight hours at the beach house before the whole thing had disintegrated spectacularly. Right after Roe had announced there was definitely no baby, Eddie began storming around, throwing things into their car. He pulled Tilly's car seat out of the back and flung it over by Adam's Range Rover. Then without so much as a wave or nod to any of them, he got into the driver's seat and turned on the engine. This, Roe seemed to know automatically, was her cue to say goodbye and go with him.

'Are you going to be OK?' Lindy leaned in to hug her goodbye as Ailbhe joined them, jiggling a very fretty and overtired Tilly. Adam hadn't even come outside.

'I don't know.' Roe's face was taut and pale. 'I can't believe what I did. I knew as soon as I had that it was a crazy thing to do. I thought I'd just wait it out. Get the negative test and finally talk to Eddie properly about the baby thing. Ever since starting the musical, I'd been feeling so much more confident about doing theatre and more sure that a baby doesn't fit,' Roe whimpered, and Lindy rubbed her upper arms trying to soothe her. 'Then Seb put me forward for this *Newsies* revival on the West End. I know it was selfish but I didn't want to miss that opportunity and regret it forever.'

Lindy felt utterly helpless and more than a little responsible. 'It's not selfish to want what you want, Roe.' She dropped her voice so Eddie wouldn't hear. 'But letting him think you were trying and then taking the morning-after pill …'

Why didn't I force her to talk to Eddie? I should've insisted they straighten everything out. Where was the sense in her meddling with the lives of other people when her own life was so off the rails? Goddammit, this weekend had nosedived and she had barely begun to address her own issues.

Roe pulled back from Lindy and gave her a weak smile. 'I'll call you later.'

'Whatever you need, Roe, we're here.' Ailbhe stepped forward, nodding emphatically. 'Call me any time. Middle of the night. I mean it.'

'Yup.' Roe swallowed hard and hurried down the wooden steps, but as she approached the car, Eddie revved aggressively, pulled back and hurtled off down the driveway, out of sight.

'Oh fuck,' Ailbhe exclaimed as Lindy rushed forward to hold the blindsided Roe, who looked like her legs might give way.

'So,' Roe croaked, 'we're having a sleepover, I guess.'

'Back inside,' ordered Lindy firmly. 'We need wine and sad-bitch tunes. Everything is going to be OK. Eddie will be OK. Let him process.'

They trooped back indoors.

'I'm going to put Tilly down.' Ailbhe was uncharacteristically muted, and Lindy felt a fresh spike of remorse over the mushroom tea. She'd been doing so well and Tom would probably never believe it'd been an honest mistake.

Tilly was grouching but Lindy couldn't resist leaning in for a kiss of the delicate hair at the baby's temples.

'Want to put some of the chicken parmigiana on plates?' Ailbhe suggested, looking doubtful.

'Not sure I've really got the appetite any more,' Roe replied. 'I may just ingest the rest of the day's calories in booze form. I'm going to get the limoncello I brought.'

Ailbhe nodded. 'I can provide moral support on that. I'll just eat seven white Magnums.'

Lindy carried on to the kitchen as Ailbhe and Roe headed down the hall, Ailbhe humming quietly to soothe the baby. *Fair play to her*, Lindy thought. *If that disastrous dinner doesn't drive her back to the wine, she must really want to make it work with Tom.*

In the kitchen, Adam was returning his and Max's empty plates to the sink.

Will he have the nerve to lecture me? Lindy picked at the crispy-cheese edge of the oven dish resting on the counter.

'Hallucinogens, Lindy?' He turned and folded his arms. His voice was low – Max was still watching TV next door – but his tone was disapproving.

Ah, it seems he will.

'Yeah.' Lindy shrugged and glugged the rest of the white into a tumbler she found by the sink. 'It'll definitely add colour to the Snag List prospectus. Though, obviously, I'm not thrilled Max heard some of that. Or that Tom's stunt has caused Roe and Eddie trouble. But, yeah, drugs. It's hardly like you've never done drugs, Adam. You can drop the whole Maxxed Out image right now, you know. It's just us here.' She arched an eyebrow. 'You pretend you're so wholesome for the cameras – well, some of the cameras anyway.'

His features momentarily tightened and Lindy beamed over at him sweetly.

Oh, it is fun to fuck with you, Adam.

He turned back to the sink to finish rinsing the dishes and then placed them in the dishwasher. 'No investor in their right mind will go for something illegal.' He straightened up to look at her.

'Ugh, that was a joke. Sheesh, in the prospectus I'll be listing it as a girls' trip! See? Not a lie. Cos I am not a liar.'

Adam was rubbing his hands together – something he did when nervous – but when he spoke he was his usual confident self. 'Did it occur to you at all that this getting out could hurt the Maxxed Out brand?'

'Oh my God, what?' She aped horror.

He scowled. 'You are unbelievable. Up on your high horse about finishing Maxxed Out and protecting Max. You think this shit is protecting Max? He just heard that his mother was doing drugs.'

'He did not, Adam. Calm down.'

'I cannot spend another second here. I'm postponing tomorrow's filming and taking Max home.' He yanked the kitchen door open to reveal Ailbhe and Roe, who jumped apart to let him storm through.

Roe hurried into the kitchen followed by Ailbhe, who swung the door closed behind Adam with aplomb. At the counter, she unscrewed another bottle of white.

'I heard everything. What a cock.' She pulled Lindy's glass from her hand and replaced it with the new full bottle. 'The glass would only slow you down.'

From the freezer, Ailbhe grabbed two Magnums, unwrapped one and upended it into a wine glass, unwrapped the other and shoved it into her mouth. Through chocolate and ice cream, she said, 'Cheers to hands down the least boring dinner party I've ever been to.' She looked absolutely beaten as she raised her Magnum glass.

Roe held the limoncello aloft.

Down the hall, Lindy could hear Adam calling Max. Usually she would be straight down there to talk to Max, but after the last two days she was spent. He'll be fine, she reassured herself. Let Adam deal with it for once.

Lindy offered up a gloomy little smile and raised her bottle. 'Cheers to that.'

★

Three hours, a bottle of wine, an Irish coffee and a couple of sneaky cigarettes later, Lindy was kneeling on the floor hunched over her phone. She squeezed one eye shut to better focus on the screen. This had to be about her twentieth rewatch of the Adam–Rachel clip.

'Stop looking at it.' Ailbhe lay sprawled on the couch above her, eating her fourth Magnum. She swiped lazily at the phone but Lindy batted her away easily enough.

'I'm doing exposure therapy,' Lindy snapped. They didn't understand – nothing could make this more painful. Watching it or not watching it didn't matter: it was out there; it existed. At all times, somewhere out in the ether Adam was kissing Rachel's breasts, pushing into her, whether Lindy was seeing it or not. Thank God Adam had left with Max after dinner. With this much wine sloshing around in her system, she couldn't have guaranteed that she wouldn't have unleashed on him.

'Please stop, Lindy,' Roe echoed. She was also watching a clip on her phone: herself performing the opening number from *Voices of Glory*. 'I am good, right? Like, is this a crazy thing to wreck a relationship for?'

Ailbhe sighed. 'This might be the sobriety talking, but I kinda think you're both crazy. *Lindy!* Stop watching!' she ordered.

'I need to watch. I'm trying to see if I'll get to the point where I feel nothing. I want to feel nothing.' The booze was a mistake, she realised, albeit too late. It was compounding the misery not assuaging it, and she was already regretting the Irish coffee – post-thirty-five they were lethal. She'd be awake till Tuesday for that one. 'I just thought we were getting back to the way we used to be. But I think deep down I knew something like this was coming because look at us. Look at our life. It's artificial in every way a life can be. I had the creepiest thought earlier. All my memories of Adam in the last few years are actually from the Maxxed Out videos. Him smiling at me in the sun at the beach is actually him smiling into the camera in the sun at the beach. Isn't that so strange? And, fuck me, this hurts.' She waved the phone and then flung it away across the carpet.

'I know it does, hun.' Ailbhe reached down and rubbed Lindy's back.

'You don't think there's any way the video is some kind of a deep fake? Like in *Line of Duty*? They're always deep faking in *Line of Duty*.' Lindy knew this was ludicrous.

'It's a deep fuck, Lindy.' Roe sounded mournful.

'Oof, don't try to sugar-coat it or anything.' Lindy crawled up onto the couch beside Ailbhe, who cuddled her close. 'Obviously, I don't want Adam any more. I fucking hate him but I feel like I have to try and keep us together for Max's sake. He could fight me on the Maxxed Out thing. It kind of sounds like he will. I just feel so powerless.'

'Lindy, you are the opposite of powerless – no wronged woman ever had more power than you right now. 'Cept … probably Hillary.'

'Not a woman I relish being compared to.' Lindy slumped back into the couch.

'You need to put that video on the internet.' Ailbhe was matter of fact.

'No.'

Roe nodded firmly. 'Yes.'

'I can't, it would destroy—'

'Adam? Yes. It would absolutely annihilate him. So deserved.'

'But, Ailbhe, it would destroy Max as well. And Maxxed Out.'

'Kill Maxxed Out – that's the best thing for him.'

Like she's the authority on what's best for a child, Lindy griped silently. 'I don't know that. If I killed Maxxed Out, Max might hate me for it. It's been his world for years. All his memories are wrapped up in it. I want it to end but I have to do it right. And it's not like Adam will just let it go.'

'OK,' Ailbhe relented. 'What if you just threaten to release the footage?'

'That threat wouldn't work on Adam. He knows I'd never do that to Max.' Lindy slid to the floor and grabbed her phone again. 'I'm screen recording it.' She fumbled a bit trying to hold down the buttons to capture the clip. 'I'm going to be in bits tomorrow.' Then it came to her. The perfect way to scare Adam.

'Wait, gals! I know what to do. This is perfect. I'm going to upload it to the Maxxed Out channel but keep it saved as a draft. It wouldn't ever go live but he'd have to confront it.'

'What'll that do? Beyond traumatising a Maxxed Out intern?' asked Roe.

'It's the weekend – they'd never see it. Adam would see it first.' She jumped up and started pacing as her plan came into focus. 'He'll freak. He'll know he's been found out but he won't be sure who's on to him. It'll be like an anvil hovering over his head, poised to drop at any moment. I'll be able to set the terms of our split, come to an agreement on winding down Maxxed Out. Obviously, I'll need to work things out with Max, but at least Adam won't be pushing him to continue any more. Adam will realise that with someone out there with a sex tape, the channel will never be safe. Any time, any day that person will have the power to destroy it.'

'OK, that *is* perfect.' Ailbhe leapt up to join her. 'Thank God one of us is getting their shit together. We need some Mary Black! When your life is in a shambles, she's really the only woman for it.' Ailbhe messed around with Spotify until she found 'Only a Woman's Heart' and turned it right up. She swayed with her Magnum, singing along.

Roe howled over the music about how low her heart was and Lindy laughed – even in drunken despair Roe sounded amazing.

When the song ended, they sat in silence.

'You really are an incredible singer,' Ailbhe remarked.

'Yeah.' Roe flopped down onto a cushion on the floor. 'Pity I didn't get over myself years ago and just go for it. The second I met Eddie I was so relieved because I never felt qualified to be in charge of my own life, and here was this guy who was so accepting of me and so loving.'

'He seems kind of controlling, Roe.' Ailbhe, Lindy could see, was wary. Criticising a friend's other half was like edging through a field of landmines, and Lindy wondered how Roe would take this.

Roe messed with her hair, winding a strand around her index finger. 'I don't think I ever relaxed,' she murmured. 'I was always scared that if I disagreed with him or did something he didn't like that he'd ditch me altogether. Danny thinks I've never even given him a chance to be supportive because I've never been honest with him about what I want. Or don't want.' She finally looked at them. 'The morning-after pill was pretty bad ...?' It was a statement but she said it like a question.

'Hmmm, yeah, not great,' Lindy agreed.

'This is a mess.' Roe looked like she was barely keeping her tears in check. 'And, like, now there's no way I can go through with the musical. And then I feel bad for caring about the musical when I've just destroyed Eddie.'

'Roe, that is insane.' Ailbhe grabbed her hands. 'You just blew up your relationship for this musical. You owe it to yourself to go through with it. If you don't, you'll always wonder.'

'And,' Lindy cut in, 'it's not like Eddie will take you back just because you've renounced the musical. You took the morning-after pill. Like, that's how badly you didn't want his baby.' Lindy winced. She didn't want to make Roe feel worse and quickly carried on, 'Maybe if he saw how amazing you're doing? Some footage from rehearsals or something, it'd help him understand. Let me email Gavin and see if there's any clips. I can send it to Eddie. I'll do the explaining, you've got the *Newsies* audition to prepare for. We still have Amanda the Confidence Calibrator booked for Rachel this week. We'll use her instead. You have to stay focused. Don't walk away from this, darl – you have to see this through.'

Roe said nothing for several minutes. She looked tormented.

Finally she spoke: 'If only completely fucking ourselves over had been on our snag lists, we'd all be done by now.'

They all burst into shrill, frantic laughter. *The laughter of desperate women*, Lindy thought.

'Maybe we only thought our snags were being in a musical and changing careers.' Lindy took another gulp of wine. 'Maybe, The Snag List should've been about getting honest with ourselves …'

'Maybe you should have done the training *before* opening for business.' Ailbhe raised her eyebrows at Lindy and then burst out laughing again.

'Eh, Ailbhe?' Roe, Lindy could see, was giving Ailbhe a somewhat stern look. 'Maybe you're not the person to be talking about timing issues?'

Ailbhe abruptly sobered up from her bout of giggles. 'We are not talking about that.'

'What?' Lindy couldn't imagine what else Ailbhe was hiding. She could see Ailbhe hesitating. 'C'mon, Roe knows.' Lindy pressed. 'Are you seriously worried about telling me? We are all terrible people here!'

'Well.' Ailbhe was avoiding Lindy's eyes as she chewed on the stick from her Magnum. 'I'm not sure, I guess, how to put this—'

Roe immediately jumped in. 'Ailbhe let Tom and Seb Knox spooge in her during the same weekend, so Tilly's potentially not Tom's.'

Oh. Lindy looked from Roe to Ailbhe. *Whoa*. 'So you don't know which one …?' Lindy could barely form the words. 'This is like *Brookside*. Jesus, Ailbhe, you are like a deception multitasker! Ms I Have Nothing for a Snag List.'

The next morning, Lindy turned over to find Roe in the opposite bed looking like the most awake person of all time. She was sheet pale and her tired eyes looked haunted.

'Well,' Lindy said, exhaling through her mouth.

'Well,' Roe answered with a similar defeated exhale.

Lindy felt shattered. She'd gone to bed convinced putting the video in drafts was the best course of action, now she wasn't so sure. It felt reckless. *I need to get the big picture in order. Properly.*

'I think I know what I'm going to do,' she said to Roe, pulling out her phone to email Patrick – even though it was Sunday, she still put 'Urgent' in the subject line. Next she went back to the Maxxed Out account and deleted the clip in drafts.

'I actually think I do too,' Roe answered. She rolled onto her back to stare at the ceiling. 'It's for the best but it's going to be so hard.'

Lindy nodded. 'Mine's for the best as well but I sense it's going to be messy. Like cutting-the-shark-open-in-*Jaws* messy.'

Downstairs, the doorbell rang and Ailbhe raced to get it. It was a one-woman cavalry in the form of Eileen.

'We're abandoned women,' Ailbhe wailed, throwing herself at her mother for a hug. Ailbhe had texted the night before as she was going to sleep and Eileen was here now to drive them back to

Dublin. 'Thank God you're here. Tilly is still asleep. Last night was a disaster. Oh my God, you brought McDonald's – I love you.' She pulled her into the kitchen and began filling Eileen in.

As Ailbhe was finishing bringing her mum up to speed, Roe appeared.

'Look, Eilers! More casualties from the Dinner Party Intervention.'

She steered a shell-shocked-looking Roe to a chair in front of some curly fries. *We look like the people who've survived to the end of an apocalypse movie,* Ailbhe thought as she guided Roe's hand to a chip.

'You poor pet.' Eilers came round the island to hug Roe. 'I heard everything. We'll pick up a few McFlurries on the way home – they're medicinal. Don't worry – Eddie will come around. It's good that this happened, luv. You can't hide from issues in a relationship. You better be listening to this too, Ailbhe, you scallywag.' She straightened up, pointing an admonishing finger at Ailbhe.

'I wasn't hiding from issues, I was hiding MY issues! There is a difference. Anyway, I was dealing with them in my own way.' Ailbhe took a morose bite of a chicken nugget. She couldn't believe how efficiently Tom had managed to bomb everyone's relationships apart. It'd almost be impressive if Roe's stark, troubled face wasn't sitting across from her at that moment.

'Where's Lindy?' Ailbhe checked the baby cam on her phone: Tilly was stirring.

'She's on to her solicitor.' Roe had barely lifted her head but was managing a few chips.

'Good on her.' Ailbhe dipped another nugget in the sweet 'n' sour. *They should bring out a condiment form of Valium – they could call it Vaioli.* Not that she was partaking any more. No more comforting booze or pills to dull the anxiety; she'd be rawdogging life from here on in.

'Good girl, eat up.' Eilers was rubbing Roe's back encouragingly.

'So, Tom's coming back.' Ailbhe waved her phone. 'He's already been on.'

'Wow, he is quick. Eddie's blue-ticked all my messages but not responded.' Roe chewed morosely.

'That's so shit, hun,' said Lindy, who'd just appeared in time to hear this gloomy update. 'Absolute torture,' she added, rooting in the brown paper bag Eileen was proffering. 'Did you actually speak to Tom?' Lindy asked Ailbhe, unwrapping a cheeseburger.

'Yup.' Ailbhe nodded. She felt bad that her marital problems had kicked off this whole fuck-show, yet she and Tom were the ones still speaking. 'We already did an OptimEyes call at 6 a.m. And he's flying back tomorrow. Couldn't be leaving his precious baby in this dungeon of debauchery, could he?' Ailbhe shrugged unhappily. 'He's acting like we're the Manson Family or something. Just for some friendly little magic mushrooms.'

'I feel terrible.' Eilers sighed.

'You should,' snapped Ailbhe. 'It was all your fault.'

'Ailbhe!' Lindy and Roe admonished her in unison. *Thank God I still have them*, Ailbhe thought, *even after telling them the sickening truth about Tilly*.

'Ailbh?' Eilers piped up. 'Can I go in and get Tilly? She is so adorable first thing in the morning,' she told Lindy and Roe before trotting out to the hall.

Once she was gone, Lindy leaned over the island and dropped her voice. 'She doesn't know, I take it?'

'No one does but you guys.' Ailbhe grimaced. If Roe hadn't figured it out, Ailbhe would never have said a word to anyone, of that she was certain. The only way to keep a secret was to pack it away deep down inside. Anyone you ever told made a crack through which that secret could one day seep out.

'Do you have any idea what the hell you're going to do?' Lindy offered her the curly fries as she spoke, which Ailbhe gratefully accepted. She couldn't conceive of having this depressing conversation without some salty carbs.

'Tom and I are going to have a big heart-to-heart tomorrow. He didn't tell me this, obviously – Maia just added it to our calendar.' She pulled up Monday 4 August and turned the screen to Roe.

'Wow,' Roe breathed. 'It literally says "Heart 2 Heart".'

'To be fair, the call this morning actually went pretty well. He seems to have calmed his tits significantly, which is a relief. And I told him about my whole new "grow the fuck up, Ailbhe" plan. He was encouraging. Sort of. He seemed to want to believe me, thank God. Last night scared the shit out of me … I came so close to fucking this whole thing up. And not even over my REAL betrayal, like – the actual irony if he'd ditched me for being dosed with shrooms.'

'To be fair,' Lindy's voice leapt up into a higher defensive register, 'you've never turned down a substance the entire time I've known you. And I've never seen you drink tea!'

Ailbhe laughed. 'Yeah, I know, I know! Relax. It was a mistake – you think I'm going to be a bitch about other people's mistakes?'

'Listen, Ailbhe.' Lindy was now giving her the full Brené Brown look and Ailbhe wasn't looking forward to the inevitable accompanying psychoanalysis. 'The thing with Seb … doesn't it seem a bit like subconscious self-sabotage? Didn't you say last night that it happened just hours after Tom told you he loved you for the first time?'

'Hmmm.' Ailbhe shoved in more fries so she didn't have to answer, but both of them were staring at her now. 'OK, fine, it probably is self-sabotage. Lindy, I was near-jilted when I was thirty-four! It made me a textbook never-get-attached person. I was scared that Tom'd get over his little phase with me and leave – find some wellness hun who sages her arsehole and matches his whole "lifestyle" thing. Then after the pregnancy he was so excited, and I think I was able to lie to him because we were hardly ever on the same land mass! I thought we'd be safe from it all once we got to America. I guess I had kind of convinced myself that the thing with Seb hadn't happened or didn't matter as long as I never saw him again. But when she was born, having her in my arms really stirred it all up. But last night, it just hit me. If you love someone, you give up some of your own power. You kind of have to. No matter what, Tom will always have this power over me because I love him and Tilly and I want us to all be together. And it's just made me realise that you can't be commitment-phobic about your own family. It *reeeally* doesn't work. I can't be a mother and a wife and stay totally independent.'

'But, Ailbhe, are you actually going to stay his wife?' Lindy asked. 'And never tell him the truth about Tilly's father?'

'But he IS her father. Basically. He's been there every moment of her life, albeit as Tiny Phone Dad sometimes. He loves her. It would kill him to find out. And it would kill our family. You both have to take this to the grave. No one can ever know. I am changing my ways and I will atone for this in my own way.'

Eileen bustled back in to the tense kitchen and Ailbhe was desperately grateful for the reprieve. She took the baby from her mother and buried her face in her daughter's soft, wispy hair to avoid the dismay on her friends' faces. And to hide her own shame from them.

25

ROE'D BEEN HOME FOR MORE THAN FOUR HOURS, and in that time Eddie hadn't once met her eyes. The day outside was oppressively nice in contrast to the still, clotted atmosphere in the house. Since Eileen, Ailbhe and Lindy had dropped her off that morning, he had walked out of every room she'd followed him into trying to talk.

At last, around six, as he poured a beer into a tumbler in the kitchen, he spoke. 'I can't take this any more.' His words clattered into the dead silence.

'Eddie—'

Abruptly, he hurled the glass into the sink and stormed out of the room. Incredibly, it didn't actually break – Monteray perfection could not be easily shattered – but the noise sent a dart of panic up Roe's spine and into her skull. She gave him a few minutes before she followed him up to the third floor.

She hovered just outside the door to the dressing room in her bedroom, confused at hearing her own voice, breathless with joy, coming from beyond the door. 'I have never been this happy in my whole life. If anyone out there is thinking it's too late, it is never too late. The musical is the most joyful expression of a story. I can use my whole being – my heart and my body and my soul – to create this human experience.'

'Roe O'Neill is without a doubt the beating heart and towering talent of this production. Just listen to her take on 'Waterloo' at the end of Act II.' Now it was Róisín's voice Roe was hearing, and she realised Eddie must be watching the footage from *Glee Me*. Lindy had sent it, she was very efficient when she had an idea.

Roe held her breath as the opening bars of her last number of Act II started, while Róisín continued to speak over it. 'In musical speak, this is the Big Gloom, the moment when Niamh Kavanagh believes Dustin the Turkey is going to take her place as Ireland's 1994 competitor. Roe brought me the idea of slowing 'Waterloo' right down and creating this beautiful a capella composition to convey the moment where all is lost.' Róisín's voiceover faded out and Roe's song swelled at the crucial line that promised love for evermore. Maybe Eddie would see now why she'd done it. See how important the show was and how well she was doing. It didn't make up for what she'd done, but maybe he would understand better.

The audio cut abruptly and she heard Eddie sigh heavily.

Roe wet her lips nervously and tugged at her hair to smooth it, then she entered the room. Her appearance seemed to send a charge straight through Eddie, who sprang to his feet.

'No, Roe.' He marched to the far wall and started to tear through the drawers in the walk-in, refusing to look at her as he savagely grabbed underwear and T-shirts and flung them in the general direction of the weekend bag flopped open in the middle of the floor.

'Eddie, please,' she said. 'You can't leave.'

'Roe!' Eddie whirled around. 'I'm not the one leaving, sweets,' he snarled. 'This is for you. I don't care where you go, but I can't be in the same building as you right now. If you have any opinions on the shit you wanna bring with you, I suggest you get moving. Esther and Philip are coming over.'

Ah, of course they are. Nice to have a commiseration squad that will fly in at a moment's notice to take your side in a bust-up.

She swept the catty thought aside. She needed to do something: she was watching her relationship disintegrate.

'Eddie, please. I want to talk.' She'd barely finished the sentence when Eddie slammed the pair of trainers he was carrying onto the floor between them.

'Now *you* want to talk so we'll talk, is that it?'

'I just, I feel like I need to tell you—'

'Nah, I'm not listening, Roe.' Eddie reefed Roe's kimono off the back of the door and rolled it up. 'Your turn to see how insanely frustrating it is dealing with someone who will not be honest. I gave you every chance to tell me what you were thinking about the baby thing. I begged you to tell me how you felt.'

'I know. And I didn't. I know that.' She grabbed the kimono back. 'Can you go easy? This is vintage.' She gently refolded it and placed it in the suitcase. 'I'll go, Eddie. I know you need space. But can you please hear me for one minute? The baby thing was freaking me out. And I was scared to be honest about that. Being honest with the people I love hasn't always worked out so well—'

'Nuh-uh.' Eddie was back at the drawers, drop-kicking socks and underwear towards the suitcase. 'You don't get to blame everything on your cold, repressed parents, Roe. Everyone has stuff. At some point, you have to be your own person and own your own bullshit. And fucking tell a guy that you don't want a baby with him.'

'I wasn't ready, Eddie.' Fear tore through her. 'Eddie, I'm so sorry. I know it's probably not the time to be saying it, but I think something good has come from this.' Her words rushed out. 'I feel so much more confident now. I know it sounds silly, but being in the musical has really made me feel much more sure of myself. You don't understand what that has meant for me.'

'Roe, you've just destroyed me and our life. And you're talking about that musical?' Eddie ceased his rage-packing and dropped abruptly onto the pouffe in the middle of the room. 'Am I really such an unreasonable asshole that you had to lie to me and pretend to "go along" with me?'

'No, babe, I love you.' Roe moved to stroke his hair but Eddie flicked her hand away.

'All your Snag List friends and the Life and Soullers were laughing at me, no doubt. Dumb prick Eddie trying to get Roe pregnant.'

'They didn't know!'

'Who does this?' He threw out a bitter laugh.

Roe debated answering. *Someone who's scared*, she wanted to say.

'Seriously, did you get this idea from somewhere? Did Lindy suggest it as part of her ridiculous life-coaching schtick?'

'*No!*'

'I googled it, you know.' He held up his phone. 'There was no one on the whole goddam fucking internet searching "my wife took the morning-after pill without telling me".'

'Did you try rephrasing it?' The joke came out in a thoughtless rush. 'I'm sorry.' Roe dropped her gaze. 'That joke was a reflex.' She shook her head – *This is so grim.*

'Roe.' Eddie's voice was measured but still taut with anger. 'Do you know what I've gleaned from the last twenty-four hours? People-pleasers are the true psychopaths. In theory, a people-pleaser could be a good person to have around. They'll "go along" with things. They seem amenable. But people-pleasers never take responsibility for their own lives. They never assert what it is that they want, so then when something doesn't go their way, they can blame everyone but themselves. That's handy, right, Roe? It's never your fault because you were just trying to do what I wanted. Perfect. Perfect fucking strategy.'

'I'm sorry,' Roe whispered, willing tears not to fall. Crying, she sensed, would not go over well with Eddie right now. She wrapped her arms around herself. She'd have to go somewhere. To Ailbhe's maybe? Though with Tom arriving the next day it may not work. And Lindy had enough on her hands. Maybe Danny would have her?

The doorbell rang and Eddie stood, irritable. 'It's my parents.' He looked at her bag at his feet. 'Will you just leave?'

Roe pressed her lips together and gazed at the floor. 'Yeah.'

The doorbell chimed again. Eddie's eyes flicked to the bedroom door. He seemed torn, rooted in place. 'There's something I need to know before you go.'

'Yes?' A fresh dread unsettled her.

'How?' Eddie asked.

The word hung before Roe like the blade of a guillotine. Why was he making her say it again?

'Eddie, you know. I took the—'

'Roe,' Eddie roared over her. 'I didn't mean "how did you do it". I meant how *could* you. How. Could. You. Do. It?'

Roe dragged air down into her lungs but still felt like she was drowning. She had no answer to this. Nothing that would make up for what she'd done.

'We had sex,' Eddie continued. 'I tried to make it special. I thought it was special. I was so excited, Roe. Every morning, I have woken up bursting at the idea that at that moment, inside you, our future could be growing.' Eddie came to stand in front of her and Roe wondered for a second if Eddie was softening. But then Eddie placed his hands on Roe's shoulders and delivered his final blows in a tight, strangled voice. 'Roe, from the bottom of my heart, I hate you.' Then he turned away, his face shuttered and blank.

26

ON THE MONDAY MORNING AFTER WHAT SHE, Ailbhe and Roe would (eventually) come to affectionately call the Donner Party, Lindy arrived back to her house at ten. After Eileen had driven them home the day before, she'd spent the night at Finn's strategising with the help of Patrick who, in a true though costly display of 'above and beyond', had come straight over when she'd asked him.

She looked at her door, took a deep breath and walked into her house and straight into a wall of shrieking and screaming. Shite! She'd forgotten she'd arranged for some kids who would be in Max's class at the Monteray Academy to come over to play and make a video. Amazing. There's a tragic irony to be found here somewhere. She was breaking up with Adam in the midst of eight hyper eleven-year-olds corralled by the Maxxed Out interns making a Pirate Shipwreck Adventure movie on the soundstage in her back garden. The ship was sinking and their marriage had run aground.

As she started towards the kitchen, she was snatched into the front living room by a freaked-looking Jamie. Oh shit. Could he have seen the video over the weekend? It was only up there for a matter of hours.

'Lindy,' he looked stricken, like the man in Edvard Munch's The Scream only more despairing. 'Get in here. We have to talk. Close the door.' He was sweating and frantically dragging his hand through his massive grey quiff. 'I don't know how to say this ...'

'Jamie.' Lindy checked the door was fully closed behind them. 'Stop. Calm down. I put it there.' His mouth fell open. Actually fell open. She carried on. 'I was kind of tipsy – well, shitfaced – when I did it. I blame Ailbhe. And Mary Black. I took it straight down the next morning. I didn't think anyone would have seen it! They didn't, did they?'

'No. But, Jesus, Lindy, you can't leave something like that lying around. I haven't seen a woman's vulva in seventeen years. It put the heart across me.' He made the sign of the cross. 'I would take a case against you if you didn't have enough to be dealing with.'

'I really am sorry. I was in a rage-haze. I don't even know what I was thinking. I was never going to put it live.' She felt sick at the thought. 'I just thought if he saw it he'd know that someone was on to him. And he'd let me just take Max and leave. I know that would be bad for you, I'm sorry.' She glanced up at Jamie, who looked awkward. 'But I don't want to do it that way, I want to confront him properly.'

'It's OK. He hasn't seen it. When I saw that it was gone this morning, I double-checked Adam's activity on the account and he hasn't logged in all weekend. Another thing, Lindy?'

'Yes?' Oh God, he must be furious that our bullshit is going to cost him his job ...

Quite out of the blue – and definitely out of character for Jamie – he gathered her into a hug.

'I am so, so sorry. I cannot believe what he's done. He is scum. It was all I could do not to spit in his face when I saw him this morning. I've always had my feelings about Adam, especially in the last couple of months. There's something off there. He's too smooth. I'll be honest, I've been looking for another role since the restructure. Working only with Adam has been—' Adam's voice outside the door cut Jamie off.

'Lindy? Was that you?' Adam opened the door. He'd obviously heard her come in. 'Well, you deigned to come back. Hope you had a lovely weekend.' He was clearly raging.

Jamie smiled broadly, sliding past Adam. 'I'll be off back to the office.'

Adam pushed the door closed behind him. 'We need to talk, Lindy. I heard you were drunk with your friends, blaring music after I left. The mushrooms, Lindy? If it got out that this is what your "new venture" is, that would seriously hurt Maxxed Out. You better sit down and explain to me right now what the hell you're doing.'

Lindy pulled her shoulders back and was about to let the rage rip out of her when the front doorbell chimed over the pounding of her heart.

Momentarily deflated, she marched out to the hall and pulled open the door to find Esme, the Monteray social director, and Pierce, their life curator, there beaming. 'Hel-lo?' Lindy couldn't imagine what they were doing there.

'Lindy! May we …?' Esme slid by her before Lindy could respond.

'What are you—?'

'Great to see you, Lindy.' Pierce gave a neat little wave as he too slipped in to the hall.

'What's this about?' Adam had appeared at the door of the living room.

'Will we go somewhere private?' Esme raised her voice above the shouts of 'Arghhhhh' and 'Matey' coming from the back garden.

'It's a matter requiring discretion,' Pierce yelled, causing Esme to flinch beside him.

'C'mon in.' Adam glanced at Lindy as he ushered their guests into the living room. From his face, she could tell he didn't know what was going on any more than she did.

'Right, sit, sit, everyone.' Esme stood before them, opening the cover of a tablet. Lindy joined Adam on the couch, feeling distinctly cheated. She'd been about to unleash on her husband and now these two had completely derailed it. Pierce perched on the furry footstool, holding his own tablet with a digital pencil poised above it. Esme gestured towards him. 'Pierce is just taking notes,' she explained.

'For …?' Adam folded his arms.

'The report.' Esme smiled firmly. 'We've had some concerning readings from the Harmony Gauge these last couple of months and felt it might be time for a check-in.'

'What's the Harmony Gauge?' Lindy asked. It sounded familiar but where had she heard it before?

Adam, she noticed, was recoiling slightly. 'It's the thing for monitoring the mood in the house,' he muttered. 'It was in one of the early Monteray promos we had on the channel.'

Oh God, a memory of Max came back to her. He was speaking to camera, reassuring an unseen audience of kids that in Monteray Valley 'Mom and Dad are always happy because the Harmony Gauge makes sure that every fight is resolved by third-party intervention before escalation'. He'd had trouble with the word 'escalation', she recalled.

'The Harmony Gauge, as I'm sure you remember, takes the emotional temperature of the relationship and we've seen some concerning results in the last six weeks—'

'I'm sorry, how exactly are you getting these results?' Lindy knew there'd been something about this in the contract but the particulars escaped her, though it couldn't have been that alarming if she'd signed.

'Well, it's a cumulation of different data: how many meals are the couple sharing at the dining table versus on the couch; vital signs; frequency of coupling versus onanism – that kind of thing. At Monteray, we see the success of our citizens' marriages as a reflection of our entire community, our way of life. We want to keep our Monteranians on track – we want to keep you two on track.' Esme smiled encouragingly.

'Often,' Pierce picked up the thread of explanation, 'by the time a couple realises they're in trouble, it's too late for reconciliation. The Harmony Gauge helps us see the early signs of rot.'

'So the house is telling on us?' Lindy replied. 'Great. Like a poltergeist but an overly interfering one that only wants the best for us.' She rolled her eyes.

'Lindy, I know this process can be very confronting – we've had quite a few marriages requiring the Monteray arbitration already this summer. It's not easy, I know.' Esme, to Lindy's horror, tilted her head to forty-five degrees. *No! The international symbol for pity. I do not want this pristine waif's pity*, Lindy wailed internally.

'But you have options,' Esme carried on, evidently undaunted by Lindy and Adam's lack of enthusiasm. 'We have all the usuals: couples therapy, reflexology, sex courses. But even better, we have the Monteray Marriage Pause – a place to take stock and get perspective.'

'Wait. A place?' Lindy perked up.

'It's a cluster of replica homes for spouses to retreat to during troubled periods.'

'What?'

'Yes!' Pierce beamed. 'It's so no one has to leave Monteray, even if things are less than perfect in the marriage. It's temporary, until the couple coalesces. And the Marriage Pause is discreet. The cluster is accessible via the subterranean network, so any signs of marital fray are undetectable.'

'And what if the pause needs to be permanent?' Lindy asked, sensing Adam's sharp glance in her direction.

'Well, that really doesn't happen.' A slight frown rippled across Esme's earnest expression. 'The divorce rate in our other Monteray developments is non-existent. Monteranians stay together.' She flicked a finger over the screen of her tablet. 'Especially Monteranians under contract to sell the lifestyle,' she added, a subtle, steely edge creeping into her voice.

Aha. Lindy felt her rage reignited. Never not thinking about the bottom line, any of them. She turned to Adam. 'Will we do rock paper scissors to see who has to go to Exile Valley?' she spat.

'Lindy,' he glanced tensely at Esme and Pierce and then back to her, 'we don't need to be hasty. No one needs to go anywhere. We can work on our, eh, coupling and stuff here, together.'

Lindy was so sick of him, she was going to tell him what she knew whether Esme and Pierce were there or not – she was past the point of caring. Even if she waited till they were gone, they would no doubt receive an update within hours. 'Adam, I know—'

'Before you two start getting into things, let me direct you to the marriage-rescue app, Monteray App-ily Married.' Pierce was tilting his tablet to show them the icon. She could see his notes off to the right of the screen: 'subjects are subdued'; 'body language suggests serious dearth of intercourse'; 'subjects have been reminded of their contractual obligation to embody the Monteray ideology'.

After agreeing to 'explore their options in the app' just to get them off her back, Lindy managed to edge Esme and Pierce back into the hall and eventually out the door.

Christ. Where does it end? Lindy thought, leaning back against the closed front door.

'They're right – we need to coalesce.' Adam had appeared in the doorway to the living room, adopting what he presumably thought was a reasonable tone. 'I'm willing to move past the dinner-party stuff.' He clearly thought this was an incredibly charitable gesture.

'No.' She walked towards him and he started to shuffle backwards into the living room. 'No, no, *no*,' she repeated in time with her steps.

Adam was clearly wrong-footed by her fury, but only for a moment, then he seemed to be about to speak again. Before he could, she felt the dam she'd used to shore up her grief burst. 'You're going to speak to me?' she shrieked – it hurt her throat but it was so satisfying to savage him. 'How *daaare* you think you have the right to say anything to me. You sit down right now and you explain to me—' she paused and then hissed the next words between gritted teeth, her knuckles white as she clenched her fists '—*you* explain to *me* how you can be such a cold, conniving, cunty fuck.'

He did sit down then, on the sofa, and slumped back, his head flopping against the headrest. It might have been a posture of defeat, but he looked to Lindy like a fed-up teenager.

She slammed her fist on the sofa beside him. 'You look at me! You look at what you have done. Look what you have ruined.' She was dry-eyed and grateful for that. She never wanted him to see her crying over this, over him. She glared down at him and felt nothing but disgust. No love and no pity. She leaned down and pushed her face right up to his to bellow the next words: 'I hate you. I *haaate* you. You are pathetic.' She pushed each word out with a deliberate, potent force. He looked terrorised and it was darkly satisfying.

She stood up and retrieved the large white envelope from her bag. 'It's all there. The way our split will go. And it's all on my terms. I'm giving you joint custody because it's better for Max, but if you so much as quibble about the *grammar* in this letter, I will annihilate you. I will screw you. Or rather you'll have screwed yourself with your stupid little video. What an ego, Adam, you can't even have sex without filming yourself. Be terrible for that to get out there. That whole thing with the tail is pretty embarrassing ...'

Adam's entire body froze except for his eyes, which were darting in a frenzied fashion, clearly trying to process what she had just said. In a matter of seconds, however, he'd obviously metabolised the news that she knew everything and was recalibrating his argument. 'You wouldn't, Lindy. It would wreck Max's life too, you know.'

'You mean *you* would wreck Max's life. Sign that agreement. Do not be a bigger prick than you already are. We are not getting into costly court shit. Patrick says this can be settled between us as long as you don't fight it. And if you do … well, you know what's coming.'

'But Lindy—'

'No, Adam.'

'Lindy, please. I … I'm sorry you … found that. I know it's unforgivable. I don't know what I was thinking … except that …'

'Yes?' She couldn't believe he was actually about to trot out some excuse.

'We got together so young. I hardly had any girlfriends before you. All the years on the road with Maxxed Out, with YouTube moms throwing themselves at me, and I never did any—'

'Adam.' Lindy held up her hand.

'You're not the only one with regrets,' he blurted. 'I never got to—'

'I don't want to listen to this,' Lindy fired back. 'You've humiliated me. You've broken our family. The least you can do is spare me the pathetic sob story you've come up with to ease your conscience.'

'Look, maybe this Marriage Pause isn't a bad idea.' Adam was looking desperate. 'We can't just break up. We have obligations. Max has obligations—'

'Yeah and he shouldn't. He is eleven. I know I helped put him in this situation but it's got to end.'

'But he loves it,' Adam protested.

'Does he? I don't think so. And even if he does, it's not the point. He's a child: it's our job to decide if it's good or bad for him. He's been in the comments – he's so exposed on there. Enough. I'm calling it, Adam.'

'Lindy, the money, the house. Max's trust fund. It's not a good time. We're tied up in so much. I know you're angry but don't do this to Max because you're mad at me.'

Lindy stood and scraped together what little remained of her energy for this conversation. 'Adam, I'm not mad. I am over it. I really don't feel anything for you. On Friday, we'll sit down with Jamie and go through all the clients who need to be contacted. They'll be pissed off but they can't make us do anything. If they get legal it'll only look bad on them – toy companies trying to force a child to honour a contract? Shite optics. Same with Monteray. We leave the house – what can they do?' She glanced around, feeling not a shred of regret at leaving it behind. Finn had offered her and Max the spare room in her place for the time being, and Lindy had felt the first glimmers of optimism at the changes that were about to unfold. Cosy autumn nights in Drumcondra with her sister would be restorative after the intensity of the last few months.

'Lindy! This is a business. You can't just fold and box everything off overnight. We need a period to wind down.'

'Well, fight me if you want.' She shrugged. 'I know you think I wouldn't put that video out there, but what if I decide Max knowing his father is a shit person is better than him being lashed to this YouTube channel?'

She turned and left, hearing the crash of what sounded like Adam kicking the footstool in the room behind her. She headed out to the garden to see Max and watch the last of the pirate adventure unfold. She was sad at what was about to happen to them, but she knew it was the only option. She pulled up one of the loungers and ordered a coffee and a plate of pastries from the Monteray app. She threw in cookies and some decaf iced mochas for the kids. She wasn't hungry, but if Adam came by, she wanted him to see her looking unruffled.

She was actually shattered from the confrontation. She had never screamed at someone before. Except for Max scooting out into the road. Or when he was really wrecking her head at bedtime when he was younger. But that was all normal screaming. What had just unfolded was the true definition of apoplectic. Adam was right, of course: she would never allow those videos to be seen by anyone. She couldn't believe how kamikaze she'd been putting the screen recording in drafts – thank God Jamie had found it. Bloody Irish coffees. The fallout for Max would have been unimaginable. No, she would just hold it over Adam's head like a bomb. Forever ticking.

27

'AILBHE?' HER MOTHER'S VOICE THROUGH THE bathroom door startled her. 'Are you hiding? Tom's back twenty minutes already and you've yet to appear. Skulking up here in the loo is not helping your case.'

'This is not a skulk.' Ailbhe pulled the door open. 'I was just delaying – very different.' Ailbhe ran a finger under each eye to take care of any rogue mascara. 'I'm just putting on make-up, trying to look good. How does he seem?'

'Why don't you ask him yourself?' said Tom, who'd appeared at the top of the stairs, shirtless and manhandling Tilly into a complicated sling stretched around his chest.

'Well, now.' Eileen clasped her hands together, her voice sugary. 'Isn't this lovely?' She paused for a split second before adding. 'I must go.' Then she fled the landing, clattering down to the ground floor and out the front door. *Thanks, Mam.* Ailbhe'd been hoping to use her as a human shield while pleading for clemency from Tom. She, at least, had better be getting dinner. It was nearly 6 p.m. and

Ailbhe'd barely eaten; the whole day had been a nervy countdown to Tom's return. Roe had kept to herself since she'd arrived the night before and was holed up in the guest room two floors up. She'd been notified of a place in the Monteray Marriage Pause Community but Roe'd no desire to be annexed to the holding pen of ousted spouses. Ailbhe had no idea how Tom would react to her presence – but as she'd told Roe when she messaged her, Roe's situation was semi Tom's fault so he'd have to put up with it. Also, Ailbhe was hoping having a guest in the house would keep everyone on their best behaviour. Not including Tilly, of course, who was fully kicking off in Tom's arms.

'So, how are you?' Ailbhe raised her voice over Tilly's indignant shrieks. The child hated the sling, but Ailbhe sensed opening with a parenting tip was not the best choice right now.

'Honey, honey, shhhh,' Tom soothed the baby, dodging the chubby windmilling limbs that were in danger of hitting him. 'I've got to do more skin to skin with her,' he told Ailbhe, before finally replying to her question. 'I am good,' he said firmly. 'Obviously, I've had a couple of days to think and calm down. I realise what I saw on OptimEyesOnU wasn't the full picture. Oooof.' Tilly finally landed a punch to his throat. 'Jesus, she's not crazy about the sling, is she? I don't understand it – I smeared breast milk on my chest to help lure her.'

'Of course you did.' Ailbhe pressed her lips together, trying to keep her laughter in check. 'Please say it was mine?'

Tom grinned. 'I helped myself to the freezer stash.'

'I should be annoyed.' Ailbhe edged nearer to him to disentangle Tilly's foot and ease her properly into the carrier. 'That stuff takes a lot of time and a shit-ton of calories to produce. It's not for men to give themselves sponge baths with.' She smiled tentatively up at him. 'I'm so sorry, Tom. The mushrooms were an accident. I swear. I wish there was some way I could prove it to you. But I am begging you to believe me.' If only she could tell him to ask Maia, who knew Ailbhe was attending meetings again. But Ailbhe knew that was out of the question.

'Ailbhe,' Tom was jigging slightly now and Tilly'd relaxed for the moment, 'Maia told me. About the last month, I mean. About how committed you've been. I was using the OptiDecide app around what to do about us, and she could see from what I was inputting that I was thinking the mushrooms were just the latest in the whole Ailbhe shitshow.'

Ailbhe flinched. He wasn't wrong but it was still so raw. All the messed-up stuff she'd been doing – she hated being reminded of it. It made her want to drink, which made no sense. Why would thinking about her past drunken fuck-ups make her want a drink? To kill the shame, she was beginning to realise. But, as she knew from experience, when she sobered up the shame would roll back in twice as murky and dread-filled. It was a relentless cycle.

'Maia's been a really big help.' Ailbhe desperately wanted to put her arms around him and Tilly, but she couldn't tell what he would do, and the thought of him pushing her away was too painful. She looked at them both – her family – and they were right there within reach, but she'd no idea how to hold onto them. The threat of Seb, of being found out, always circled even though only she could see it. 'Maia's guided me.'

He nodded. 'When we get to California, she'll be nearby.'

Ailbhe's heart surged. 'So we're doing it? You still want—?'

Tom wrapped his arms around her and pulled her gently close so both she and her daughter were nestled on his chest. 'I want you. I want this. Us! I was so happy when Maia told me how seriously you were taking your new direction. I want us to get back on track. The lawyers have smoothed the visa issue. I love you.'

'I love you too.' Ailbhe closed her eyes and breathed deeply. Despite the relief flooding her, adrenaline hummed through her as well. She'd come so close to losing it all. She'd never be so cavalier again. They would get away and she would never let things get out of control. She pushed the always-present dread deeper down. She would do whatever she had to do to protect her family: this was too precious. She pulled back to find Tom's eyes. 'You're very sticky.' She grinned.

'Hmmm, yes. Breast milk is very sweet.'

'I am not asking how you know that.'

He laughed.

'Listen,' Ailbhe continued quietly. 'Roe is staying here. Things are not good between her and Eddie.'

Tom looked troubled. 'Yeah. I had no idea that in confronting you I might kick off something even worse. I didn't realise the others were all so close to the brink. She hates me, I presume?'

'Ehhh, well ... no. I think she's mad at herself more than anything. She's been shout-singing along to *Spring Awakening* all day. Which isn't as cheery as the name suggests.'

'I should go up.' Tom started jigging towards the stairs but stopped on the first step. 'Jesus Christ, Ailbhe. Is that her? When I was downstairs I actually thought the neighbours were having construction work done. She sounds very distressed.'

Ailbhe joined him and listened. 'I think she's moved on to Sondheim.'

'It sounds like she's speaking in tongues.' Tom frowned.

'Yeah, that'll be the Sondheim.' Ailbhe nodded sagely. 'It's '(Not) Getting Married Today', I think.'

Tom looked stricken. 'Is Eddie … OK? Are they breaking up?'

'I have no idea, Tom.' Ailbhe shuddered. Speaking about Roe and Eddie's situation gave her the guilts. *It is not the same thing!* inner-Ailbhe had taken to chanting on repeat.

'Yeah, it's worse,' Lindy had remarked on the drive back the day before. *Lindy is not the audience for spousal betrayal right now,* Ailbhe reminded herself.

'Maybe I should do something?' Tom looked earnest. 'Broker a meeting, some kind of reconciliation?'

'I don't think they're there yet. Or if they'll ever get there.'

'Well, she can stay here as long as she needs – it's the absolute least I can do.' He grimaced as, above their heads, Roe started in on a particularly demented take on 'Everything's Coming up Roses'. He spun back to Ailbhe. 'We need to get ourselves organised for flying out. Maia has us on a 10 a.m. on Thursday. No airport hassle this time: everything for your visa is sorted out until Christmas, and in the meantime, I have a guy in legal assigned to working out full citizenship. How does Thursday sound?'

It sounds like a huge fucking relief, Ailbhe thought. Seventy-two hours until *Freedom: The Sequel.* She just needed to lay low until then. No goodbye parties this time, no going anywhere *near* the Voices of Glory production: just get out and thank the actual Lord for this second chance.

'Thursday sounds *so* exciting.' She reached up to stroke his face. It was all coming up Ailbhe. 'Dinner will be here soon. I'll just text Roe – I think she has rehearsal but she might have time for a quick bite.'

28

LINDY STOOD AT AILBHE'S DOOR ON WEDNESDAY morning. She rang the bell and Tom's voice emitted from the discreet intercom to her right.

'Two secs, Lindy. You're looking good!'

Lindy shifted uneasily. *Eyes fucking everywhere in this place. Yet I didn't see what was happening with my own husband.*

She steeled herself for Tom. From Ailbhe's texts, she knew that he was somewhat over himself now and feeling bad about effectively lighting a fuse under everyone's marriage – not that she could blame him for her own current predicament.

Incredibly, Adam was strong-arming the hell out of her. Apparently her catching him cheating was not inspiring a scrap of guilt in him but rather the reverse: as he knew things were irretrievably wrecked, he was now digging in majorly. He wanted an agreement that they would keep the channel going for eighteen months and, for the duration, keep up a pretence at their relationship to placate the Monteray board. *Jesus.* In a weird way, it was hardly less dishonest than how they had been living for the last three months. The only thing making her consider it even slightly was the financials. It had now emerged that Adam had been flinging money at tech bros like knickers at a boy band, and they were not in a good place. They had a sit-down with their respective solicitors scheduled for the next day, and every time her mind strayed towards it she felt shaky. Finn had reassured her there was a place for her and Max to stay and a job for Lindy at Skin Love, but the thought of being in debt after everything they'd worked for in the last few years killed her.

She'd handed over years of Max's life to this beast and now it seemed like it would be for nothing. *Fucking Adam. Be careful what you wish for*, they tell children. *Be careful who you reproduce with* is what they should be telling them.

'Hi!' Tom appeared before her. 'The two gals are inside.' He ushered her into the hallway, which was crowded with luggage. It looked like Ailbhe, after everything, was the only one going to make a clean break from Monteray Valley.

Lindy traipsed after him as he continued: 'They're talking about some confidence coach you arranged for Roe?' He rounded on her, dropping his voice. 'Are you proceeding with The Snag List?'

'God, no. I just feel like I need to see it through with Roe.' She'd already emailed Rachel with a terse explanation that she was hitting pause on The Snag List and deleted Rachel's reply without reading it. She hated that woman. 'I think Roe needs to get *something* positive out of it all,' she said. 'I had this confidence coach booked already and so … you know, we'll go through with it. It might be helpful to Roe. She's got a meeting with some producers about another show so this will get her in the right mindset.'

'Maybe you shouldn't drop The Snag List altogether. It could be an opportunity Optimise could get involved with? There's definitely something in the idea, even if your execution has been a little bit … haphazard.'

'Hmmm.' Lindy searched for something to say to this. How to explain to a cheery, can-do American the extent of her nihilism right now? 'I feel like I've done enough damage, no?'

'Lindy! A few glitches in early trials is totally normal. After all, the first hundred lung-transplant patients died!'

'Ehhh … yeah, that's a totally reasonable comparison!'

He laughed. 'Have a think about it. In a funny way, I kind of owe you, Lindy. If it hadn't been for The Snag List, I wouldn't have … you know … seen Ailbhe's problems. And we might never have gotten to this great place of radical honesty.'

Oh Jesus. Lindy cringed inwardly. She didn't like what Ailbhe was doing, but from where Lindy was standing, Ailbhe having to live with the lie was a bigger ordeal than simply being honest. Incredible that, in the midst of everything with Adam, there was still a situation worse than hers playing out right in front of her.

'Thanks for the offer. I'll keep it in mind. I'd better get in to Roe and get her prepped for the coach.'

In the living room, Ailbhe was pacing around holding up different outfits pulled from Roe's open suitcase while Roe moaned despairingly from the couch.

'What about the pink boiler suit?' Ailbhe displayed it hopefully.

'I hate everything I own. If it wasn't so stupidly hard to get clothes in my size, picking outfits for an audition would actually be fun.'

Lindy shut the living-room door behind her. 'Don't worry, we'll get something mega for when they invite you over *to London*! Today's just a Zoom interview.'

'Yeah.' Roe shuffled over to examine the boiler suit. 'They've seen the video of my scenes, they've heard me singing, so this Zoom is mostly about them getting to know me. Which is fine except that lately "me" has been a complete whack job.'

'You should tell them the whole thing – it really illustrates your commitment to the business of show!' Ailbhe chirped.

'Oh, look who's advising someone to 'fess up.' Roe cocked an eyebrow.

'Now, now.' Lindy slid between them. 'No one here is in any position to be lecturing anyone else. We're all dumb bitches together.'

Roe smiled wanly and pulled out her phone. 'You're right ... Look, Lindy, my mum sent me a super encouraging text earlier.'

'What?' She grabbed the phone. 'That's amazing— Oh,' Lindy blanched as she read the first line.

Rose, I am disgusted with you. Eddie has done everything for you for—

'Jesus, you need to block her.'

'Well, for once I am in wholehearted agreement with her.' Roe was morose. 'Maybe this is how we'll end up "reconnecting" – bonding over what a shitbag we both think I am for doing this to Eddie.' She pulled off her sweatshirt and tried on an orange cashmere sweater.

'This is very good.' Ailbhe nodded decisively at the top and started fussing with different jewellery options.

'What exactly does she know?' Lindy scanned the rest of the message: she got the gist. It was very generalised ire. Not even imaginative. 'You always do this.' 'You have no ability to commit.'

'I told her Eddie and I were taking some time apart.'

'How can she say "you always do this"? You've been with the guy for ten years!'

'I don't know why I even made contact.' Roe stuck the chunky gold hoop Ailbhe had handed her in her right ear. 'Well, OK, I do. I thought she'd be happy about us deciding not to try for a baby any more. So stupid. In the middle of *all* of this, some tiny part of me was still, like, "ooooh, maybe *this'll* make her happy". God, I need to be put down.'

'Roe! Stop it.' Lindy tossed the phone back on the couch. 'You are on the verge of a massive breakthrough. A West End director wants a follow-up meeting! This is real. Yes, on a personal level things have,' Lindy applied her next words delicately, 'been better. But on a professional level this is the biggest moment of your life. This could be a turning point. Maybe the fact you've lost everything is actually liberating. This opportunity is all you have left!'

'Do you think saying "you've lost everything" is comforting me right now?' Roe asked archly.

'Look,' Lindy said, 'let's see what our confidence coach, Amanda, advises. Wanna come, Ailbhe? We're on the countdown to our last few hours together … We can get pizza after.'

Ailbhe faked a sob. 'What am I going to do without you two? Who will make my own life seem like less of a shitemare over in California? They won't even know what a shitemare is.' She stopped and grinned. 'Yes, I'll come. Maybe I can ask Amanda for pointers about recruiting friends who have their shit together.'

'You'd hate that.' Roe gave a grim little laugh, putting on a gem-studded velvet headband. 'I cannot believe this West End meeting is really happening. It is happening, yes? I'm not in a fugue state right now? Or eaten some bad cheese or something?'

'It's happening. And –' Lindy checked her phone '– it is happening in ninety minutes so we need to go. You ready, Ailbhe? We have our consultation with Amanda, and then you'll do the meeting, Roe, and we will sit cheering you on in the corner in complete silence! Sound good?'

At the Work Hub, the early afternoon bustle was in full swing. Lindy led Ailbhe and Roe through the verdant reception area and up to her office – the Snag List headquarters as she had been calling it. *Ugh.* The logo above her desk stirred the sickening humiliation in her chest. *How did I think this would work?*

'So this is where you've been working! It is so slick.' Ailbhe looked out the windows overlooking the atrium.

'Yeah, this is where I've been playing make-believe business lady,' Lindy said in a bitter sing-song. 'Here's where I vommed when I saw Adam and Rachel doing a Kim K and Ray J.' She indicated the carpet by the desk. 'And here's the logo I paid eight hundred fucking euros for.' She swept her arm across to the opposite wall. 'What a waste.'

'Ah, Lindy, it's not a waste. Not at all.' Ailbhe looked distraught and Lindy could see she was about to say something else when Amanda of Calibrating Confidence knocked on the open door.

'Hellooo! Lindy?'

'Hi, Amanda.' Lindy rushed forward to shake Amanda's hand, and she was comforted by how unpolished Amanda seemed. She'd been afraid a confidence coach would be some kind of perfection Terminator, a white suit with silk shirt or something equally foreboding, but, no, here she was looking reassuringly normal in a denim jumpsuit and scuffed trainers with her thick shoulder-length dark hair held back by an orange knotted scarf.

'So! This is Roe, my client. Or your client. Whatever!' Lindy stumbled over her words, feeling suddenly embarrassed in front of a bona fide coach. 'When we started this work, I thought we'd just be asking you for pointers on Roe performing in a local musical, but things have really progressed and now Roe is meeting with the producers of a West End show who are really interested in her.' Lindy had no idea how much else she should tell this woman. Did Amanda need to know how ballsed up The Snag List was at this point?

'Congratulations, Roe! That's great news.' Amanda smiled broadly. 'Though, don't forget, external validation is just one piece of the puzzle – confidence is very much an inside job … Not to get all new-agey on you just yet.' She grinned, her hazel eyes gleaming.

'This,' Lindy carried on, 'is Ailbhe. Probably the most confident person I've ever met. I would say she is confident to a reckless degree, frankly.' Lindy winked, ignoring Ailbhe giving her major evils. 'I hope you don't mind us sitting in. Ailbhe is leaving for America tomorrow and this is our last day together,' Lindy explained.

'Of course, I don't mind at all!' Amanda unshouldered a large teal gym bag and settled herself on the white armchair. 'I think the bigger the group, the better this process works, to be honest! It's very powerful sharing our stories.'

'Oh, I don't have to share anything,' Ailbhe cut in. 'Like Lindy said, I am obnoxiously confident. I don't need aaany coaching.'

'Really.' Amanda tilted her head curiously at Ailbhe. 'I'm always interested in people who are insistent that they would have *nothing* to gain from chatting to me. They always end up being the ones most riddled with insecurities!'

Ailbhe looked outraged and Lindy fought back a laugh. She loved Amanda's delivery: she said everything in the most gentle, casual way but her words were fierce.

'I do not have any insecurities, thank you. I'm forty-two, I have a successful business, a lovely baby and a mansion, and I am hitting my zenith of hotness,' Ailbhe pouted triumphantly.

'You are very attractive,' Amanda said conversationally. 'But insecurities are not only connected to our looks. They can be about our abilities, our relationships, our fears for the future. The way I diagnose insecurities or, ya know, a lack of confidence is by asking clients if they are currently lying to anyone.'

Ailbhe's look of blazing conviction abruptly clouded with dismay. 'What?' She looked deeply disturbed. 'Lying? What would that prove?'

'C'mon, sit down, sit down. I'll kick off, shall I?' Amanda pulled over her sports bag and unzipped it to reveal a host of random craft kits, colouring books and pencils. 'Right, first, everyone pick a "buffer activity". These are to give us something to focus on if the discourse is making us uncomfortable. You can do a jigsaw or make a beaded necklace while we sit here and do the work. I've found it helps people to stay present even if the explorations start to get tough. Sorry if my woo-woo speak is a bit much. When I started out in life coaching, it used to make me squirmy too, but then I realised I was just obsessing over the lingo as a way to not hear the messages.' She twinkled a little smile around at them and then announced that she would be making a pasta-shell necklace.

She unbuttoned the collar of her jumpsuit to display many such necklaces with a rueful look. 'As you can see, all the work I do with clients I've done on myself already and continue to do because being confident is not, unfortunately, a static state. It's one we have to accept will ebb and flow. I think it's interesting where our two disciplines intersect, Lindy, because The Snag List asks what's missing from our lives, and Calibrating Confidence looks at what's missing in ourselves. And one is certainly connected to the other. We can't *acquire* confidence because any acquired confidence will always be contingent on who bestowed it. We must find confidence in ourselves and *build* on it. So, Roe ...' Roe had rooted out a colouring book of mermaids and, at the sound of her name, feverishly began to fill a seashell bra cup in a pretty lilac colour. Amanda didn't ask her to stop, just carried on in her gentle, melodic voice. 'From your files, I know a bit about your mother, and there's stuff to look at there for sure, but that's for your therapist. As your coach, I deal only in the now and the future. And I believe you've had a bit of a breakthrough in the last few days? You were lying to your husband about trying for a baby to protect your role in the show and to protect your relationship?'

'Yes,' Roe muttered, scribbling furiously.

'And how does it feel to have told the truth at last.'

Roe still didn't look up at Amanda but she paused in her colouring. 'It's shit and it's a relief. I feel like I've taken a claw-hammer to my relationship. And I know I'm really exposing how much I want this career in theatre and I feel very vulnerable. I'm so scared I'm not going to get anywhere.'

'Oh.' Amanda's tone sharpened. 'Hold that fear for a moment. What does that fear tell you?'

'That ...' Roe was still, and as she thought about it, Lindy turned inward and applied the scenario to her own life. How did it feel to have the truth out at last between her and Adam? As Roe said: both shit and a relief. And Lindy also felt potent fear any time her thoughts drifted too far into the future. But what did that fear tell her?

Roe looked up at Amanda. 'I think the fear tells me I care. That I want this. If I didn't care, I wouldn't be scared.'

Amanda nodded. 'The fear is a very important emotion. It can be motivating. The fear is telling you this is a high-stakes moment, and fear will also be the thing that helps you rise to it. Let's all try to work with our fear from now on. Buddy up with it, realise that fear is not something to be avoided at all costs, it is productive. Let's harness it! And let's be spurred on by it. Remember, nothing changes if nothing changes.'

Oh, she is good, Lindy thought with reverence. Walking away from a marriage was as high-stakes a moment as they come, but if nothing changed, nothing changed, and she would stay miserable and fearful.

'OK, let me bore you about confidence for a minute. Ailbhe? Do you need help with your macramé?'

'No,' Ailbhe shot back defensively despite the knotted mess in her lap.

'O-K! So Ailbhe, you said you've got more confidence than you know what to do with – that's nice. And is there anything you're hiding or lying about right now?'

Ailbhe's head snapped up and she immediately whipped round to Lindy. 'Did you put her up to this?'

'Of course not,' Lindy protested.

'You don't have to tell me what the lie is,' Amanda reassured her. 'Just think about why you cannot be honest about this thing. Maybe it's something about yourself that you feel you cannot be truthful about because you're not confident that it will be accepted by those you love? We hide ourselves, we hide our hopes, we lie about what we need. We say we are fine when we're not. All because our confidence has dimmed. Often people think "oh, I'm confident" because they can wear a suede jumpsuit or chat at a party, but that kind of confidence is usually a cover, an artifice. True confidence is being honest about our most vulnerable selves, our dreams and our desires.'

None of them spoke. The silence, it seemed to Lindy, was the sound of sudden clarity engulfing three flailing women.

'I take it some of this is ringing a few bells?' Amanda picked up a handful of penne and added them to her cord. 'So, Lindy, as I said, I think our respective coaching focuses of confidence and regret are very entwined, don't you?'

'I do.' Lindy was grateful that Amanda was willing to pretend that their work was even in the same category. 'Regret is born from that lack of confidence,' she said and Amanda clapped her hands, rattling the pasta shells.

'Yes! Exactly. I think we could have something very exciting if we played around with merging our stuff.'

'Yeah.' Lindy swallowed the unpleasant queasiness of failure. 'I'm not sure that I actually will … keep going, though.' She hadn't selected a buffer activity yet and quickly grabbed a stress ball to mess with.

Amanda just nodded at her gently. 'We can look at recalibrating your confidence when you're ready, Lindy.'

Next, Amanda smiled placidly at Roe. 'Right, Roe is ready to recalibrate, or at least you'd better be – we have forty-five minutes till you get on this call! You have already achieved so much in the last few months. Oh yes, a word on why I call it recalibration … I know it sounds like something from a cult but, basically, I don't like to think of confidence as something we can "lose" or "gain". We all have it, it's always in us, just sometimes we need to recalibrate it. So, I keep things extremely simple in the initial stages …'

'OK, she was amazing,' Roe gushed after Amanda had wrapped up the session and left. 'Not that you're not, Lindy,' she hurried to add. 'It's a very different approach.'

Lindy couldn't agree more. She opened the computer on the desk and started to get Roe set up on Zoom. She felt like her own perspective had shifted more in that hour than it had in ten years. She'd been lying to herself and then by extension to everyone else for years, demoting her own needs to make everyone else comfortable and make sure she didn't lose their love. *And now I've lost Adam anyway.*

'She wasn't that amazing.' Ailbhe was sulking on the couch.

Lindy went over to join her. 'You're just pissed cos her no lying philosophy doesn't suit your game plan,' she told her firmly.

'Nothing is served by telling Tom,' Ailbhe shouted.

Woah! Lindy hadn't realised that Ailbhe was feeling quite so touchy about the situation. Amanda must have gotten to her too.

29

'*COFFEE!* THANK YOU!'

The next day, Ailbhe was in the airport. She gratefully accepted the takeaway cup from Tom, who popped back to the counter to grab the rest of their breakfast – Danishes and creamy porridge.

She texted a selfie to the Snag List group with the caption:

On the day you're skipping off to America, even airport coffee tastes amazing!!!

ROE: Lindy, Eilers and I have a pool going about how long till we get a phone call that something ridiculous has happened requiring us to collect you/bail you out.

AILBHE: LOL fuck you. So touched you are all rooting for me.

She put the phone down and bit into her Danish, eyeing up Tilly twitching in the pram to her right. *Do not wake up, you monster,* she willed silently.

'You're doing the telepathic threats again – don't think I can't see you.' Tom grinned over at her, stirring his porridge – or oatmeal, as he called it. She glared again at her daughter: *Don't you be saying oatmeal too, it's porridge. And it's not sidewalk, it's path.*

'We'd better finish up soon.' Tom checked the departures board above them. 'Are you sure you don't want to wake her and give her a feed before we go down to preclearance?'

'Tom, are you a psychopath? Never. Mess. With. A. Sleeping. Baby.' Ailbhe crammed in the last bit of Danish and started to gather her things. 'I can do it after take-off.'

Down in the queue for preclearance, Ailbhe tried not to think about her little altercation there back in July. She'd deliberately kept her eyes down when passing the uniformed officers flanking the entrance. She was hoping to avoid any of the lads who'd witnessed the previous debacle.

Tom was furiously typing on his phone. 'Mom and Pop are so excited to meet you finally! And Tilly, of course. I've just told them we'll go to their place for a welcome dinner tomorrow night.' He slipped his phone into the pocket of his bomber jacket. 'I told them it was just a paperwork issue back on the Fourth of July,' he added quietly.

'Great!' Ailbhe rocked the pram for something to do. Being back in this hall was giving her a seasick feeling. The line zigzagged back and forth through the low-ceilinged room so that they were packed in by people on all sides. Low conversations droned, punctuated with the occasional staccato cough. Ailbhe concentrated on keeping her breathing even. *It's just having people so close.* She tried to quell the rising dread. It was still weird being in a confined space after the last few years.

Yeah, it's nothing at all to do with getting on this plane – right, Ailbhe?

Why did everything suddenly feel so drenched in dread? Ailbhe felt blindsided by this sudden rush of fear. She'd been counting the days until she could get out of Dublin. She'd thought this moment of escape would bring relief not amp up her stress. She looked ahead to the booths through which they would soon pass. Why did this feel like crossing the Rubicon? Going to America was hardly the point of no return on this lie. The point of no return had been many, many months ago. The queue shuffled another few feet forward and the sense that she was being funnelled towards some unknown disaster intensified.

Telling him when we get to America or telling him here makes no difference.

Wait! Her racing thoughts slammed to a halt. *Telling him? NO ONE'S TELLING ANYONE ANYTHING.*

'Why do you look so miserable, Ailbh?' Tom gazed down at her. 'Is it because I said no jet? You know it's bad optics these days. I can't justify jets for family travel. Business class is epic, don't worry.'

'No, no, it's not the jet. It's not anything. I'm really happy.' Oh God, just saying 'I'm really happy' had set off that awful fizzing feeling she always got in her temples when tears were near.

'What is it, honey?' Tom looked alarmed, immediately pulling her close.

'Hey again, you two! It's so great to see you guys together!' Officer Eric appeared on the other side of the cord, beaming. 'Hey, Westie, get over here. Guess who won the bet? Yours truly, my man.' He turned back to Tom and Ailbhe. 'I had a good feeling about you guys. Of course, we weren't sure we'd ever find out who won the bet! But when we figured out you were the Optimise guy, we thought, hey, this might be one bet we actually get closure on.'

'My man.' Officer West had joined them, tapping on his phone and shaking his head at Officer Eric. 'I am Revolting you right now.' He smiled at Ailbhe. 'I'd be pissed at losing, but I'm a sucker for a love story.'

A love story? Oh God, don't call us that. Why is everything in the world conspiring against me right now? This building is cursed. She looked around at everyone else in the hall. How many of them were on the run from something? And why did her getaway, her flight to freedom, suddenly feel like she was in the steerage queue for the *Titanic*? Beyond the booths felt like the end of the line somehow. *Every second I don't tell him makes it worse.*

'So, a secret arrest?' Officer West dropped his voice to just above a whisper. 'How does a couple come back from that? My wife and I are having some stuff.' He glanced at Eric, who leaned in to rub his back encouragingly, before continuing. 'You do all this betterment stuff.' He looked at Tom. 'What do I do? She's been keeping this from me …' He gazed down, obviously summoning the courage to tell them.

'You don't need to tell us,' Ailbhe blurted. She wasn't sure she wanted to hear Tom's thoughts on buried betrayal.

'No, no, to be honest, I'm so torn that I'm looking for guidance everywhere I can get it. And you two have been through something like this. I've just found out that when we first got together she got pregnant, and she had an abortion. She says she was afraid I would try and make her keep the baby. She says if she'd known that we would fall in love and stay together and eventually have kids – they're nine and ten now' – he flashed the lock screen on his phone to show two auburn-haired boys sticking their tongues out – 'it would've been different, but she panicked, and she figured she would never have to tell me.'

'Oh wow, dude, very tough.' Tom rubbed his jaw and shook his head. The line edged forward, as did the officers, Tom and Ailbhe.

Ailbhe didn't want to prolong this conversation – it felt radioactive to be talking about something so close to their situation – but she had to ask. 'How did you find out?'

'She told me. Nothing happened, she just started crying one night and said that it had been eating her up inside for years. That she couldn't go another day of loving me and hurting me all at the same time.'

'She should have told you back then,' Tom said firmly. 'But she made a mistake.' He pressed his lips together, furrowing his brow. 'This is a toughy.' He took out his phone and tapped the Optimise icon. 'We have one feature, OptiDecide, that may help. But it's more for calculating practical decisions – moving jobs, having more kids. It offers projections on how your quality of life might be impacted.' He put the phone away again and sighed. 'To be honest, it's not for this, I'm afraid.'

Maybe this is an opportunity, Ailbhe thought. *I could float a possible outcome and see how Tom reacts.*

'Officer West.' All three men turned to her. 'I have another angle you mightn't have thought about. Could you maybe see how this lie is actually proof of how much she loves you?'

She was careful not to look directly at Tom's reaction but kept him in her peripheral vision. *He's not rushing to argue*, she thought hopefully.

Officer West was thoughtful. 'Maybe? Yeah, I know what you're saying, I guess.'

'I think Ailbhe is right.' Tom sounded decisive, and the hope flooding her confirmed something that a few months ago she would never have believed: *I want to tell him. I don't want to lie to him every hour of every day for the rest of our lives.*

With the realisation came two overwhelming feelings. She was scared and she was exhausted. Keeping a secret was so draining and lonely. *I am wrecked from the sheer admin of it. If he leaves, he leaves, and I'll have to accept it.*

She thought of Lindy and Roe and Eilers and Holly. *I have friends.* She thought about the life she'd made after Ruairí and the wedding fiasco. She looked down at Tilly. *Whatever happens, she's mine and I won't lose her. And she'll understand one day that I drank when she was a baby and that I had a problem. She'll forgive me for losing her a dad because I'll stay sober and I'll never let her down again.* She thought of her sad, crappy dad and all his problems. *If Tom leaves, we'll make it. We've done it before.*

'Tom?' She tapped him and he pulled back from the bear hug he, Officer Eric and Officer West were now locked in.

'Yeah? Honey, why are you crying?'

She looked at his face full of concern and love and wished she could know for definite that he would one day, after all this, look at her like this again. 'I need to go to the breastfeeding booth. Will you come with me?'

He glanced up at the monitor displaying departure updates. 'Needs must but she's not even awake, honey. I'm just a little concerned re time …'

Officer West cleared his throat. 'Go, you guys – we'll escort you right to the top of the queue the second you're done. You've really given me some clarity today, thank you.'

Ailbhe pushed Tilly through the crowd towards the booth, prattling nervously to Tom about how a 'dream feed' might keep Tilly relaxed on the flight.

When they reached the booth, she pulled Tom through the curtain and sat him down on the two-seater couch. It was tight in there but Ailbhe figured this could work to her advantage. She parked the pram in front of his knees, effectively hemming him in. At least he wouldn't be able to escape, he'd have to listen. She hoped.

'Tom, I don't need to feed Tilly. There's something I have to tell you before we get on the plane.'

'OK.' He looked worried. 'You're freaking me out. I've never seen you cry before.'

'Tom,' she summoned every scrap of resolve. *Do it, Ailbhe*. She breathed deep and looked him in the eyes. 'When I conceived Tilly, I had sex with you and with another man in the space of a couple of days. I cheated on you. There's a chance she's not yours.' She closed her eyes because she knew if she saw his reaction she would think about it until the end of her days. Her tears continued to stream from beneath her lashes. 'I can't believe I did it. There is no way that I will ever be able to express how sorry I am and how ashamed I am that I am hurting you like this.'

She braced for Tom's anger, his rage no doubt building and about to hurtle towards her. She deserved whatever happened next. She squeezed her eyes further shut but there was nothing, only the sound of impatient people beyond the curtain moving through their perfectly ordinary lives. She looked across at Tom and fought to keep her sobs in check. After what she'd just done to him, it felt obscene for *her* to cry. He looked somehow collapsed in on himself, as though instead of an explosion he was being pulled inward, sucked down by a force deep inside.

'Tom, I know I can't ask for forgiveness. And I know any excuses would be an insult but please … Can I just say that Tilly is your baby, you are the father she loves, the only father she knows, and you are an amazing father. It would kill me … to know that I ruined her shot at being your daughter.' She swallowed, her throat tight, and then she too crumpled, feeling that same strange, contained implosion she detected in Tom. Finally the gasping cries rose up and she couldn't hold them in.

Tom stood slowly, shakily. He still hadn't uttered a word. He looked into the pram and ran a gentle hand over the baby's face. Then he edged around them both and walked out.

'Ma'am?' Officer West was outside the curtain. 'Ma'am?'

Ailbhe felt like she was hearing him from the bottom of a deep lake. Sapped from the emotional crash after telling Tom, she wondered how long she'd been sitting motionless in there. She pulled back the curtain. 'So sorry officer … I …'

I what? I just ruined my daughter's life? And Tom's? And mine?

'I saw him leave … You guys back at square one?' he asked gently.

'I would say we are hitting an all-time low,' Ailbhe replied, standing wearily. 'We're in the minus squares. So he didn't get on the plane?'

'Nope, it's left by now. Your stuff's on its way to America.'

'Great. Doesn't matter.' *There's some kind of heavy-handed metaphor here about getting rid of my baggage,* she thought as she reversed herself and the pram out of the booth. 'Good luck with your life, officer.'

She drifted back out through the double doors. Unlikely she'd ever be back here again.

Officer West called after her. 'Good luck with your life too, ma'am.'

30

AFTER WAVING AILBHE OFF TO THE AIRPORT THAT
morning, Lindy had driven straight to the hastily arranged
mediation that had been fast-tracked due to the complicated nature
of dissolving a family and a business in tandem. Lindy and her
new solicitor, Elise, who'd been recommended by Patrick as she
was better versed in family matters, sat across from Adam and his
solicitor, Adrian.

Elise was speaking in a commanding voice. 'What my client is
asking for is completely reasonable and has the child's best interests
in mind.'

Lindy had been listening to Elise and Adrian volleying dismal
statements about the state of her life back and forth for nearly an
hour now. This was supposed to be a civil meeting by the end of
which they would have an agreement in place about Max and the
future of Maxxed Out. Apparently it was in everyone's best interest
to get this signed off among themselves and not involve a judge. So
far, not so good. Adam was being unbelievably stubborn. Knowing

she had evidence of his adultery hadn't remotely shamed him into going along with her wishes. He just didn't believe she would release it. Part of her wished she could be so selfish – as selfish as Adam! – but she would never. Obviously.

'Forcing a child to honour business obligations is not reasonable, it's ludicrous,' Elise was arguing. 'There is no precedent for it anywhere in any Irish commercial law or custody decisions. And if Mr Zelner decides to pursue this in family court, there is zero possibility of his winning. The judge will go with the well-being of the child, which, in this instance, doesn't involve trotting the child out for the internet.'

'A child's well-being is also supported by financial resources—'

'Resources your client depleted with flagrant investing.'

'My client was trying to generate more income for his family and was unlucky. If Mrs Zelner has her way, the family will most likely lose their home and may even end up in debt. All my client is asking for is eighteen months more. We will go to a judge if we must. And I am certain we will easily prove that Mrs Zelner's bid to block these contractual obligations is driven by a hurt ego and nothing to do with her son's well-being. Her husband told her he was in love with someone else and she is exacting revenge.'

'That is *not true!*' Lindy could no longer take the depressing commentary about her and her family.

'Lindy.' Elise placed a hand over hers to signal her to shut up; to Adam and his solicitor, she was scathing. 'You'll lose in family court.'

'Maybe we'll lose in family court but commercial court is a different matter.'

Lindy's eyes snapped up. Court of any description was to be avoided. They were public people; their lives going down in flames would be a bloody schadenfreude smorgasbord for the internet. 'Why would you put us through that, Adam? You know I want you in our lives still. Max's emotional well-being is more important than us having to work our way out of debt.' She resisted adding 'debt that is your fucking fault'.

'Commercial court is completely out of left field here.' Elise sounded brisk and bored. 'How do you propose proving that Lindy has done anything to deliberately damage Maxxed Out? Without any evidence of direct sabotage, revealing of trade secrets or fraud, good luck even getting to the initial directions hearing.'

Lindy arrived back to Ailbhe's house exhausted from all the legal bullshit. She'd asked Eileen and Roe to keep an eye on Max while she was gone. She knew she shouldn't be surprised but she couldn't believe Adam was prolonging this agony. The longer he refused to settle on an agreement, the more money they were spending on solicitors. They had just about managed to agree on one thing – Max would stay with Lindy and Maxxed Out would be on pause until things were sorted. This meant Max could get a breather from everything in Maxxed Out HQ, and she could show him how life could be without it all. In the hall, Lindy called for her son.

'In here,' he answered from the living room where, to Lindy's shock and immediate panic, she found Max playing with Tilly.

'What is happening? How is Tilly here?' *This cannot be good.*

Max shrugged as he pulled the hood of his green Maxxed Out jumper down over his face and then popped back out, to Tilly's gurgling amusement.

'Where's Ailbhe? They didn't leave? What the hell?'

'I dunno, Mom. They just came back. Ailbhe's out in the kitchen with her mom.'

'OK.' Lindy leaned down to kiss his temple.

'How did it go with Dad?' He gazed up at her, looking nervous.

'It's going fine, don't worry. We'll get it all sorted really soon.'

'And ... Maxxed Out? Is there nothing on the schedule? Do I not have to—?'

'Sweetheart, you don't have to do anything. I really want you to take a break. What do you think?'

He clicked his tongue at the baby and tugged playfully on her toes; she chortled happily. 'Yeah, a break sounds good. If it's OK with you and Dad.'

Lindy gathered him to her and breathed him in. 'My puppy.' He squirmed a little in her arms and she smiled. She was so grateful to have turned this corner with Max. Just a few more weeks of bureaucratic ball-ache with Adam and the solicitors and all would hopefully be fine. 'I have to go find out what's happened with Ailbhe and Tom, OK?'

She hurried through the hall, a twinge of unease at the sounds from the kitchen – glass tinkling and that loose laugh of Ailbhe's that always came with her drinking. Oh God. Lindy tensed. Was she about to find a shambolic Ailbhe with wine in hand? She'd been doing so well. *Maybe I can stop her.*

Lindy veered through the doorway. 'Ailbhe?'

'Lindy!' Ailbhe turned away from the video she was watching on her tablet and landed in Lindy's arms, winding her slightly.

On the other side of the kitchen, a miserable-looking Eileen was being soothed by Roe.

'I blame myself.' Eileen was shaking her head.

'No, no, you mustn't,' Roe protested, giving Lindy a desperate look.

'What's going on?' Lindy struggled to form the words, Ailbhe shuddering in her arms. Lindy's eyes drifted over her auburn curls to the video still playing. Ailbhe and Tom were laughing and cheersing on the screen. From Ailbhe's ivory tulle skirt and pale cashmere top, it looked to be their wedding party. Lindy had never seen the pictures – they looked happy. 'Please tell me what's happened,' Lindy repeated.

Ailbhe withdrew from Lindy's embrace, wiping her face with her palms. 'I told Tom,' she whispered, her eyes bleak. 'And Mam.'

'I wasn't a good role model for relationships. It's my fault.' Eileen shook her head again.

'It's not, Eilers!' Ailbhe cried. 'Stop that! It was me. I thought I had it all figured out and I wouldn't listen to sense.'

'What exactly happened? Where's Tom?' Lindy lowered her voice. 'Is he here?'

'I have no idea where he is,' Ailbhe wailed. 'He didn't say a single thing, Linds. Nothing. I've never seen anyone look so—' She welled up again. 'He was destroyed.' She shook her head.

Lindy chewed the inside of her cheek. Christ, there wasn't a relationship between them left intact. Her phone buzzed and Lindy gratefully turned away from the other three to take the call – which was from, of all people, Fitzy, Rachel's husband.

'Lindy?'

'Uhm, yeah, Fitzy?'

'Thank God, I got your number off the Snag List website. I'm desperate.'

'Uh-huh.' Lindy wasn't sure she liked the sound of this opener.

'I had no idea who to call,' he said.

'Are you positive it had to be me?'

He ignored this, breathlessly continuing, 'You have to get over here. Tom and Eddie are wrecking the buzz.'

'Where's "here"? What do you mean wrecking the buzz?'

'I'm down in Camp Happy and they are not fucking happy, man.'

On Fitzy's side of the call, music blared and a wall of shouting seemed to be competing with his words.

'What's Camp Happy?' Roe, Eileen and Ailbhe were all now watching her with interest.

She saw Roe mouth 'Camp Happy?' at Ailbhe, who shrugged, her eyes still damp but her curiosity piqued.

'Camp Happy's the alternate Monteray. You know, Lindy, the Marriage Pause place on the western side of the compound. A few of us have been down here for a couple of weeks, a break from the whole family grind. Just to get some … perspective.'

Lindy strained to make out what was being said on his end. It sounded like grinding machinery mixed with crying and punctuated by the odd high-pitched squeal of a pig.

'Fitzy. What perspective? It sounds feral over there.'

'All good clean fun.' Fitzy was defensive. 'Or it was until Tom showed up a couple of hours ago. He's got some guy with him. They're doing some screaming thing and it is freaking everyone out. Eddie Kelleher showed up yesterday saying he was too lonely in the gaff since Roe moved out. He's been crying in his room. These guys are having real marital problems and, like I said, it's killing our vibe. Can you come get them out of here? Please?'

'No! They're not my problem, Fitzy. I'm sorry they're spoiling your free gaff with their feelings—'

'Tom is not just having feelings, Lindy. It's gone way beyond that. He's been screaming for hours up on the top floor. It's fuckin' weird.'

'Hate that for you, Fitzy,' Lindy said bluntly and hung up. She turned back to the others. 'OK. Update: Tom is over in the alternate Monteray at some debauched party, screaming. Fitzy says he's been going for hours and there's some guy coaching him.'

'Oh God.' Ailbhe grimaced. 'I know there's no appropriate way to respond to … the … ugh … news earlier, but *why* does he have to make everything so weird?'

'We should go over there,' Roe announced firmly.

'Eddie's there too, Roe,' Lindy said.

'Oh, fuck that then.' Roe slumped back against the wall. 'Look,' she said evenly. 'We'll live here and they'll live there just as nature intended.'

'It's a really good sign that Tom's there,' Eileen announced. 'He left you at the airport. He could've gone anywhere in the world but he's back here to be close to you, pet.'

Ailbhe looked like she wanted to believe this. 'But Mam, we're in his house with his maybe baby – he's probably just trying to figure out how to get us out of here.' She pulled out her phone to check it and sighed. 'He hasn't messaged. He obviously doesn't want me going down there.' She started scouting around the room until she found her black studded ankle boots. 'I mean, he'd have come here if he wanted to talk.' She pulled on the boots and then her green silk bomber.

'Where are you going?' Roe's eyes narrowed.

'I'm going down there.' Ailbhe was nodding frantically. 'I know it's a bad idea but I can't not, know what I mean?'

'Oh. Right.' Roe looked freaked.

'You're coming too.'

'No.' Roe shook her head.

'Chop chop.' Ailbhe tossed Roe's trainers at her. 'We have to talk to them. Come on, Lindy, we need numbers! Safety in numbers. And if it's all going to shit, we need you to convince Eddie and Tom that you were the bad influence.'

Lindy grinned, leading them back through the hall. At the living-room door, she checked in on Max. 'I'll be back in an hour. Don't forget to charge for your babysitting,' she told him, and then they all marched out onto the deserted crescent. Mid-afternoon on a Thursday meant most people were working.

'So where is this place?' Roe was refreshing her email, as she had been every ten minutes since her Zoom meeting with the *Newsies* producers had gone so well the day before.

Lindy fired off a quick message to Pierce and turned back to the other two. 'So it's somewhere on the far side of the compound but we get to it by the underground tunnels. I've messaged my life curator, Pierce, to bring us there.'

Ailbhe, despite her agitation, burst out laughing. 'Amazing. Has Monteray Valley finally jumped the shark?'

Roe shook her head playfully. 'It's gone full Stepford! Lindy ... are you a robot wife about to stab us down in the tunnels?'

Lindy grinned. Speaking of robots, she could see Pierce's robotic little trot approaching. She waved and then frowned. He had someone with him.

'Oh, crap, it's Rachel,' Roe hissed.

Ailbhe craned to see. 'Oh, it is, I'd know those breasts anywhere.' Roe whipped around to glare at Ailbhe, who in turn spun round to Lindy. 'I'm sorry, Linds! I wish I didn't.'

'Monteranians! Hello!' Pierce, as ever, was approaching the interaction with all the ease of an AI machine trying to emulate human gestures. 'You all know each other, I presume.' He waved vaguely between them and Rachel. 'We're actually just coming back from the MMP compound ourselves. Rachel and her husband are just some of the many Monteranians benefiting from the service, so no need to feel any shame or sense of failure, gang.' He smiled kindly at each of them.

Rachel pursed her lips and gave a slight nod of her head. 'It's horrific over there.' She scowled. 'It's like spring break. Wall to wall peen – the smell.'

'I'm going down to try to get Tom,' Ailbhe spoke up.

'Yeah, I heard him,' Rachel said delicately. 'He's really letting it all out. And I saw Eddie.' She nodded at Roe. 'Everyone's totally messed up. It's like there's something in the water.'

Pierce snapped to attention. 'I can categorically state that there is absolutely nothing in the water except the very low dose of escitalopram, which every resident signed off on prior to moving here. Monteray cannot assume responsibility for any marital dissatisfaction incurred on the facility. The Harmony Gauge can only do so much.'

'Right.' Rachel rolled her eyes at Lindy. 'How's things with you, Lindy? I was sorry to get your note about The Snag List. You're not relocating over to the Pause, I hope. It's the pits. The Monteray helpers are down there round the clock but they're fighting fire. The amount of unsteeped cereal bowls ...' She shuddered.

Lindy toyed with putting on a good front for the sake of saving face in front of Rachel, but with everything she now knew about this woman, she wasn't sure she cared any more. Fitzy was a headwreck; Rachel was a troll. It was a sad existence. Lindy had been thinking about it for days and found that she really didn't bear ill will towards this woman any more. Lindy had never really understood the whole 'blaming the other woman' thing. Sure, it was a shit move, but Rachel hadn't made a vow. She didn't owe Lindy anything. She hadn't broken a trust: Adam had.

'Things with me are horrendous.' Lindy laughed maniacally. 'I'm trying to finish with Adam, which is proving extremely difficult because, while he doesn't give a shit about losing me and our family, he is hell-bent on keeping Maxxed Out for another year and a half. That is what the man cares about because he's been fucking our money out the airlock on goddam tech bro bullshit.'

'Oh my God!' Rachel's expression was hard to read. Of course, Lindy didn't know where Rachel and Adam were even at – still riding or awkward post-ride comedown? *She might be worried that I know and am going to do something kamikaze*, Lindy realised. *As if I'd wreck her family just because my own is a dumpster fire.*

'Look, it's really hard because I want Max out of this thing. And Adam is really digging in, threatening to take it before a judge in family court and in commercial court. Two courts, like! And every second we so much as breathe near our solicitors, it's costing us more and more money. It's really stressful …' To her mortification, Lindy could hear her words wobbling as she lost her grip on the facade of detached control.

'Lindy,' Rachel looked stricken, 'I am so sorry.'

Lindy shook her head, trying to shake off the tears. 'I just ...' Lindy looked up to hold Rachel's eye. She needed to subtly let her know that she wasn't going to pull the Fitzsimons down with her. Poor Fielding had enough to be dealing with. 'I wish there was a way to expose what a shitty person Adam is being but I would never do that to Max. Ever. I'll just have to do it the old-fashioned way – slogging it out with custody agreements and solicitors.'

Rachel appeared to receive the information – Lindy definitely felt like an understanding had passed between them.

Pierce gave a dry little cough to indicate his eagerness to stop airing life mess on the flawless hallowed ground of Monteray crescent 2b.

'We'd better push on, Rachel,' Ailbhe cut in. 'My own probs are even worse, if you can believe it.' She gave a cheery little wave and linked arms with Pierce. 'Let's go. If this jaunt doesn't involve crossing the River Styx, it's gonna be a major letdown, Pierce.'

'Rager! *Raaagerrr!*' A sweaty, purple-faced Sports Casual Dad bashed his way past Roe roaring into the living room just off the hall where a posse of Sports Casuals were frolicking in foam emitting from a large machine to the dulcet tones of Sean Paul's seminal work, 'Just Gimme the Light'.

'It's like Ayia Napa in 2003,' Ailbhe whimpered, trying to protect her bomber from the sweat that seemed to be pumping directly from the walls around them.

'It feels like a window's never been opened in here. Ever.' Lindy grimaced. 'This air has ... like, a texture to it.'

'Oh good Jesus, why do I feel like one of us is going to be masturbated at in here?' Roe started to clink her way through the hall carpeted in artisanal IPA bottles. 'Nobody ingest *anything.*'

The light throughout the ground floor was dingy. In the kitchen, so many filthy oven trays and barbecue racks were crowding every available countertop that someone had begun to stack them on the floor.

'We should've got a pre-emptive tetanus shot,' Ailbhe muttered just as Roe's phone started buzzing. Roe looked down and her heart stuttered: an English number.

'I have to get this – it's *Newsies!*' Lindy gave her a thumbs-up and Roe hurried through the kitchen to the back doors, instinctively keeping her head covered like a soldier in a war zone. 'Hello?' she answered as she slipped into the garden. The gently waning sunlight was a bizarre contrast to the wannabe rave inside, and the garden was surprisingly unscathed and tranquil. 'Colin?'

'Roe! So glad I caught you – I didn't want to email.'

'Oh. Right. I see …' The rush of adrenaline that had flooded through her seconds before reversed direction abruptly. The English were polite souls: he was definitely about to let her down gently. An Irish person would just lash it in an email.

'We had a chat, the director, the casting director and I, after our Zoom yesterday and we're in agreement that, no matter what, there's a role for Roe O'Neill in the Christmas 2022 West End revival of *Newsies.*'

'Shut up.' Roe clapped her hand over her mouth. To her relief, Colin started laughing raucously down the line.

'Love it, Roe, you are going to fit in *so well* with the company as it stands. There's a lot to put in place in a short space of time. As usual.

When you come over for your in-person audition we'll formalise the roles, but I know you are our Katherine.'

Roe looked into the kitchen to wave to Lindy and Ailbhe but they'd disappeared. Colin was now deep into logistics. Roe would need to be in London with a place to live by mid-September at the latest. *Voices of Glory*'s three-week run would be ending right around then, and she'd probably have to be on a flight the day after the final performance.

'Offers and opportunities tend to snowball for talent like yours.' *A West End producer is talking about ME!* Roe wanted to scream. 'I have a friend who's an agent with incredible pedigree. I should be trying to get you for cheap *buuut* I need to bank some good karma since casting Ant and Dec in *The Birthday Party* last year. Harrowing but not in the way Pinter intended. Anyway, when we hang up, ring Roberta Temperly – she's expecting you. I'll email all the details. She'll come back to me with some extortionate price for you, no doubt. It'll be well deserved. *Bisous.*'

'Bisooooh …?' Roe hung up and spotted Colin's email dropping in. She'd ring Roberta Temperly when she was in a better state to ring a person with a name like Roberta Temperly. She felt untethered by it all. A new road stretching before her. Rehearsals. A London flat. An agent. The dream that she'd assumed was too farfetched to even try for.

She pulled out her phone and opened WhatsApp. The top three chats were the Snag List, the SopranHoes and Eddie.

She typed: **I have news and you're the only person I care about telling.** It blue-ticked immediately, just like all the rest had in the last five days. She saw Eddie was typing but then seemed to stop and didn't resume.

She flicked over to the Snag List. There was a new message from Lindy.

We've found Tom on the very top floor – just follow the screaming. Gird your lady loins, Eddie's here too and they are messier than a couple of gals in the loos of a teen disco.

As Lindy said, the screaming started to dominate the thumping tunes as she hit the third-floor landing. A Monteray Mama was yelling into her phone. 'I don't give a shit, Esme, I need a transfer. It's like a frat house. I am the only woman here. I was promised a fucking marriage pause. As in a *break*. Not to be parachuted into a fucking dick stew.' She looked up and spotted Roe. 'Wait! Shut up, Esme.' She held the phone away from her ear. 'Are you new? I haven't seen you. We need to get out. I'm trying to organise an extraction.'

'No, no. I'm not staying, I'm looking for my husb—' A long, shrill squall from above surprised them both.

'Fucking Christ, I thought that was a bird of prey.' The Mama resumed shouting into the phone. 'Did you hear that, hun? That is what I am dealing with over here. Where's my airbrushed life now, Esme? I took a piss in the downstairs loo and there was a number two in there. What kind of psychopath doesn't know that it's number ones only in a downstairs toilet?'

Roe started up the final flight of stairs towards the caterwauling. She could now also make out a soothing voice intoning, 'That's it, that's it. So good, Tom. *So* good.'

On the top step she took in the scene. Tom knelt in the centre of the attic space surrounded by candles, cushions and fur throws. A tall man circled him, weaving his arms in and out as though he was conducting Tom's screams. Ailbhe and Lindy were standing over to her right looking baffled. Roe scanned the rest of the attic and at last her eye snagged on a lump that looked like Eddie, prone, under a pile of blankets under the eaves. A few upended bottles of vegan wine lolled nearby.

Oh God, I've driven him to this. She rushed over to him and knelt by his head. 'Eddie? Eddie?' She had to lean right in to be heard over Tom. She gazed at the auburn curls at the back of his neck and felt a stab of regret. He was the most familiar thing in the world to her but she felt like she no longer had the right to touch him. 'Eddie, please can we talk?'

He rolled over to look at her and she pulled back in shock. He looked like he'd been punched. *He's been crying*, she thought, feeling the sting of her own tears starting. 'Why are you here? Why did you leave the house?'

He didn't answer, just stared at her. She sensed if she started to cry, he'd lose it at her again.

'We have to talk ...' she tried again. She could hear Ailbhe shrieking a similar plea at Tom at the other end of the room. The bawling out of Tom was nerve-shredding, and Roe was relieved when the scream conductor made a complicated signal for Tom to stop. The signal involved him licking Tom's elbow. *No comment*, thought Roe. Tom collapsed to all fours, panting like a rabid animal. He didn't look at any of them.

'Let me introduce myself – I'm Soren, Tom's scream therapy advisor.' His features were angular and his eyes bulged perhaps from so many years of screaming. 'You must be Ailbhe.' He approached and gave a very formal nod. 'Tom is still feeling his feelings after today's events, Ailbhe. It's not appropriate for you to be here at this time. We are finalising a timeline of Tom's projected processing, but we've earmarked 1 September for a potential reconvene. How does that sound?'

'It sounds bananas, Soren. I want to talk to my husband. Tom,' Ailbhe shouted over the arm Soren had raised to block her. 'Tom! Please, I love you. Come home, please. We need to figure this out somehow. We need to talk.'

At this, Tom rose and turned towards Ailbhe. 'Talk? I'm not ready.' His voice was barely above a whisper.

'That's it, Tom,' Soren encouraged him. He turned back to Ailbhe and Lindy. 'Between screaming bouts, it's important to counter the soul's roar with the heart's burbling stream.'

Beside Roe, Eddie snorted, and she looked down with surprise and renewed hope. 'What does that even mean?' she whispered.

He smiled faintly but then his face fell serious again. 'Tom told me the whole Tilly thing,' he whispered.

'Yeah.' Roe sighed. 'It's so bleak.'

'I didn't think there were things much worse than our stuff.' He propped himself up on his elbow.

'Uh-huh.' Roe held herself in check. She didn't want to get her hopes up, though this sounded promising. Maybe Ailbhe's catastrophe could start her and Eddie down the road to forgiveness.

But what about the other road ...?

'So, what's the news you only wanted to share with me?' Eddie asked, reading her mind.

Roe drew in a long, measured breath, holding his gaze. 'I've been invited to take part in a West End musical.' She smiled sadly.

He nodded slowly. 'That's great, Roe. It really is.'

'Is it something you could see yourself doing ... with me?'

He sat all the way up now. 'Do you actually want that, Roe? Truly?'

'I ... I ... do. Of course I do.'

'I'm not sure you do, Roe. Maybe we've outgrown each other. It happens when people get together in college. Half the guys here got with their wives in their early twenties and now they've grown up to be completely different people. It's a mess.'

'But have you outgrown me?'

'You don't get to give me Sad Voice. You lied to me. For months.' He shook his head. 'Look, Soren wants us all to take some time. I need to get my head straight. So do you, to be frank. When's the opening night of *Voices of Glory*? It's the nineteenth?'

'It's been pushed to the twenty-third now.'

'Fine. Just ... let's just be apart. I can stay here if you want to go home, and we'll just give this all some room to breathe.'

'But with this musical, Eddie, I have to let them know. Would you come with me?'

'Roe, you're on your own. You need to make this decision for you, not me.' With that he stood. 'Soren? Tom? You guys cool if I go?' He moved to the centre of the room, taking the spot Tom had just vacated, and proceeded to wail.

Ailbhe, Lindy and Roe all started to move as one towards the stairs.

On the next floor down, they stopped to regroup, though with the screaming above and the drunken chanting coming up from below, it wasn't much of a reprieve. At least the Monteray Mama was gone.

'I have no words for how bizarre that was.' Lindy was shaking her head. 'In college, we covered some pretty out-there therapies. In a state-funded facility in Canada they had patients with psychopathy counselling each other. Naked. On acid. But that …? As mid-life-crisis behaviour goes, I'd nearly prefer Adam's stupid affair.'

Roe nodded. 'Tom's a bad influence. Where the hell did he find Soren at such short notice?'

'The night I met Tom he had a guy with him who'd just been on a screaming retreat in Donegal. I guess he got him down? Tom can be unstoppable when he wants something.' Ailbhe's gaze drifted up to the ceiling as more shrieking continued. 'Maybe there's something in it? The screaming, like.'

'Yeah, maybe.' Roe wasn't convinced.

'Remember when seeing a therapist was the most outlandish thing you could do in Ireland? And now everyone has them,' Lindy said, checking her phone. 'Oh God, what now?' She held her phone away from her as if it was infected by something. 'It's Adam. I can't cope with his shite. You read it, Roe.'

Roe accepted the phone and examined Adam's text.

I've just seen TubeDramZ. I have no words, Lindy.

Roe could see he was still typing.

'What's TubeDramZ?' She asked, trying her best to sound casual.

Lindy's eyes flashed with fear. 'TubeDramZ is a YouTube drama channel. It's all gossip and scandal about YouTubers and it's massive. Probably a million subscribers at least. Why are you asking?' Lindy started pulling on her lower lip nervously, her face suddenly ashen.

Roe glanced down to see a new message from Adam:

Your jealous little stunt has cost us the company and robbed Max of his innocence. You sicken me. This is deliberate corporate sabotage. I think we'll have no problem ruining you in commercial court now, Linds. My guy's already submitted the application and is petitioning for a fast track given the involvement of a minor. Thanks for making it all so easy.

'Eh ...' Roe kept the screen tilted away from Lindy. *How am I supposed to read this to her? Fuck, fuck.*

'Something's on TubeDramZ.' Lindy sounded resigned. 'I cannot believe it. If it's the—'

'Let's not freak out unnecessarily,' Ailbhe jumped in. 'Maybe it's a small thing. Maybe they're just talking about your hair or something.'

'What's wrong with my hair?' Lindy was indignant.

Roe ignored them, frantically inputting T-U-B-E-D-R-A-M-Z into the search bar. She flicked her thumb over the videos on their page. They had titles like 'MUA SPAT! These Rowdy Bitches are all Contour and Maximum SHADE!' and 'How Abbi Ganna DESTROYED Her Career' and 'Why the Internet HATES RaeRae's World'.

'What's RaeRae's World?' Roe asked.

Lindy shuddered. 'RaeRae's World started out as a kids toy channel very similar to Maxxed Out, though I'd say they were bringing in way more money. The channel bankrolled RaeRae's whole extended Texan family until ten-year-old RaeRae had a very public meltdown and fired everyone connected to her empire, her parents included. Then a series of bizarre confessional videos appeared on the channel revealing that she was addicted to Adderall medication after being overprescribed at her parents' insistence, that she hated old people and that she was actually twenty-three playing a ten-year-old.'

'What the hell even *is* the internet any more?' Ailbhe groaned.

'Yeah and they're hounds for the drama on there.' Lindy nodded. 'Tell me, Roe. What's up there? What's Adam saying?'

Roe scrolled back to the top of the feed and clicked the most recent video called 'Borderline Old People MATING but with a YouTube TWIST', the thumbnail of which was ominously blank.

The video opened on a still of Adam and Max, whose face was blurred, dressed as safari rangers. Roe recognised the chorus of 'F*ckboi' playing as a woman's gleeful voiceover began.

'Welcome back to my channel, guys! It's your gal, Emma Tea, aka @EmmaSpillsTea on Insta – follow me there, follow me here. Don't forget to hit like and hit subscribe and RING THAT BELL to get notifications whenever a new dramarama-filled show drops. Today's TubeDramZ vid is explicit with a capital X, so if you are a younger viewer … prepare to learn a little something about the birds and the bees and being a SCUMBAG!'

Roe only needed to skip a few minutes into the video to confirm what they already knew. It was Adam's video with this Emma one narrating it. Roe shuddered.

'This is not looking good.' Roe x-ed out of the channel. 'There's no need to watch it, Lindy. I am so sorry.'

Lindy slumped back against the wall and slid to the floor.

'No, no! Get up.' Roe gestured to Ailbhe to grab Lindy's other arm and together they heaved her to her feet. 'You don't know what's living in that carpet. We have to get you back to Max before he ...' Roe couldn't bring herself to finish the sentence. How do you tell a kid his dad has a sex tape on the internet? What does that do to a kid?

'How did this happen?' Lindy sounded desperate; she leaned on Roe helplessly.

'Show me Adam's messages.' Roe watched her face crumple as she read them. 'Shit,' Lindy muttered. 'Shit, shit, shit.' She pulled herself upright again. 'We've gotta go. Thank God it's not term time – this would blitz through school. Hopefully, with a few weeks to go before they go back, it'll have blown over?' Lindy's voice tipped up into a hopeful question mark and Roe didn't have the heart to do anything but lie.

'I'm sure it will.' She smiled weakly. A low moan and a high-pitched scream joined together in harmony from above, and Ailbhe and Roe exchanged a glance.

'It feels like every time we settle on whose life is the worst, some other shit happens to drag someone else down.' Roe was aiming to lighten the mood, but it was clear Lindy was barely registering what was being said.

Lindy peered down the stairs to the next storey. 'Can you hear that? Is that the music from the video?' In a flash, Lindy was bounding down the stairs.

Now that Roe was listening, tuning out the cacophony from the attic, she realised she could hear the girl from the YouTube channel prattling on in another part of the house. Roe swooped after Lindy with Ailbhe on her heels. On the landing two floors down, they started opening doors, eventually finding the channel blaring from a huge TV in the living room. A dozen Sports Casuals were lounging and providing an alternate running commentary.

'Oh-hooo, Zelner's caught a live one here.'

'Oh shit … whoever he's caught is HOT!'

They were all so engrossed they hadn't so much as glanced at the door when Roe and the others burst in.

On screen, Emma was chatting on, contextualising the video for her viewers as the dimly lit sex between Adam and Rachel raged on.

'Adam Zelner has been known as a fairly inoffensive quintessential YouTube dad for a few years now. He runs a channel, Maxxed Out, with his young son … you've guessed it … Max. A video like this will presumably kill a family-orientated brand. The Zelners could *maaaybe* have weathered this shitshow if it wasn't for the teensy-weensy problem that this is *not* Adam's wife he's maxing out there but, in fact, a civilian. Reports are circulating that the mystery woman is allegedly the mother of a Maxxed Out fan. Gross. Now I must stress that this is all unsubstantiated. Gotta be careful when you're a full-time internet gossipmonger.' She winked at the camera. '"Allegedly" is your best friend!' She laughed. Next a picture of Lindy, Adam and a younger Max, again with his face blurred out, replaced the depraved turn the video had taken.

'Get back to the boning,' one of the men screamed as Emma now zeroed her focus in on Lindy. 'This is Zelner's long-time wife and until recently the CEO of Maxxed Out. It's unclear whether this video surfacing at this crucial juncture is connected to her leaving her role, but we can all agree that the timing seems … interesting.' Emma gave the camera a meaningful look.

'What is she even trying to get at with that?' Lindy hissed beside Roe.

'She doesn't know what she's trying to get at.' Roe attempted to soothe her.

Emma had now brought up the article Lindy had been featured in the week before. 'Here in the *Irish Independent*, Lindy's new life-coaching business venture projected to roll out early next year is being hailed as a zeitgeisty antidote to post-pandemic malaise. The Snag List, as it's called, is supposedly going to help clients address their regrets. After this sex-tape leak, Lindy could well be her own neediest client.' Emma smiled savagely into the camera. 'Forgot to put "bang the husband" on your snag list, did you, Lindy?'

'Oh my God, this woman is horrendous.' Roe threw her arms around Lindy. A hug felt massively inadequate in the face of such scalding humiliation, but Roe had no idea what else she could do for her friend. Lindy remained rigid in her arms. She was still staring at the screen over Roe's shoulder.

'Well, TubeDramZers, until next week, when I'll be covering This Scandi Life and dishing on the scandal brewing over "all natural" Sigrid's allegedly DYED hair. In the meantime, if you are still thirsty, sign up to my Patreon to watch the full video of Adam Zelner *in flagrante*. Plus top-tier patrons get bonus clips of Zelner's full tail-wagging interlude. YIKES! Like, subscribe and remember: watch the drama, don't *be* the drama. Love you guys, thank you so much for supporting my work here at TubeDramZ.'

31

'SO, HOW'RE YOU FEELING ABOUT TODAY?' Fionnuala was barely in Ailbhe's front door before she'd cornered Lindy for a loving interrogation.

'Feeling rough.' Lindy accepted her sister's hug. The 'today' in question was the second day of her and Adam's hearing in commercial court. The speed at which they'd arrived at this juncture had been dizzying and would never have been possible in the normal course of things. The judge and solicitors had agreed that legal action relating to a family business centred around a child's life was a unique situation with no precedent whatsoever, and so it demanded quick resolution. Without an official ruling on the business, arrangements for separation and custody couldn't be resolved. So here they were now, at Adam's dogged insistence, picking through the downfall of Maxxed Out for a judge to attribute blame.

For the last two weeks, Lindy'd been in hiding. From Giuliana, she'd gathered that the internet's forensic dissection of the clip (now being referred to as TailGate) didn't look to be waning anytime soon. She said it had died off for a minute, but the second Adam and Lindy's date in commercial court leaked, the spotlight was back on them. Usually YouTube drama didn't make it to the mainstream media but their nightmare, according to one podcast host, was 'irresistible' and 'had it all' in terms of salacious box-ticking: extramarital sex, weird sex, creepy man-child of whom there was a hundred hours of footage in all manner of ridiculous outfits thanks to the Maxxed Out videos. The front pages of the papers had been adorned with Adam dressed as a fireman, a sailor, a pirate, Pikachu, a king, a clown, a bear and a puppy. Seemingly, all their birthdays had come at once for the headline-writers: 'Internet Dad's Depraved Dalliance'; 'Forget YouTube! Here's YouLube'; 'Cyber Sicko Sends Family YouTube Community into Tail-Spin'; and the worst one of all, 'CliMAXXED Out'.

For once, Monteray's creepiness was advantageous. With the 'keep the citizens in and the world out' policy, no media had been able to breach the compound. Max was mercifully still unaware of the disaster. Lindy had come home the day of the TubeDramZ leak and dropped Max's phone into the toilet 'by accident' so that it needed to be sent for repairs. She had then disabled Ailbhe's router and blamed Eileen any time Max complained, but she knew it was all only staving off the inevitable. She'd been able to get the video taken down from the YouTube drama channels and she'd also engaged Digital Reputation Rehab, a service that helped people to bury negative things online. Still, even if the DRR made it incredibly hard to find the actual clip – they did complicated things to manipulate the Google search results – people knew about it, the papers had reported it. The time left for protecting

Max was slipping through her fingers. School was starting in a matter of days – the day after Roe's opening night. Max needed to be told, the best she could hope is that he'd never have to see it.

No matter what happened before the judge today, they would survive and this chapter would end. That's what Ailbhe and Roe chanted practically round the clock. *This will pass, this will pass, this will pass.*

Everything eventually becomes old news.

'Are you listening, Lindy? Are these the bags I'm taking, Linds?' Finn waved a hand at the five stuffed bin-liners grouped in the hall. It was her and Max's winter clothes – the move to Finn's had begun.

'Yes, that'd be great, thank you.' Finn was also taking Max back to her house to show him his new room and distract him from Lindy's second day in court. He knew scraps of what was happening, and he also knew something far bigger was being kept from him.

'Where did you leave things during yesterday's session?' Finn was whispering as they passed the living room where Max was watching *Godzilla vs. Kong* for the twentieth time.

'Adam's solicitor asked me why I thought I was the right person to be fixing other people's regrets and I said, "Fucked if I know!"'

'Aw, Linds …'

Lindy gratefully allowed herself to be folded once more into Finn's arms. 'It's OK.' Lindy inhaled sharply. *It's not OK*, she silently railed. 'I just never realised that guilt could be such torture. I feel like I'm under an avalanche of it. Paralysed and suffocating. I need to tell Max and I have no idea how.'

'It's OK. This is why I'm here – we'll do this together.'

In the kitchen, Roe was pacing and muttering lines to herself – opening night was finally here. Ailbhe was slouched on the chaise feeding Tilly and scrolling on her phone. Eileen, meanwhile, was pouring coffees.

'This place is getting more like *The Golden Girls* by the day!' Finn said admiringly. 'I'd almost be jealous if it weren't for the whole shit-spectacularly-hitting-the-fan bit.'

'It's how we like it,' Ailbhe called. 'We keep it spicy. OK, Lindy, I've got a new one. Tonya Harding's kid, Gordon.'

'Okaaay.' Lindy perked up.

'I didn't know Tonya had a sex tape?' Roe paused in her mutterings.

'Yup.' Ailbhe scrolled on. 'Made on her wedding night in 1990 but the douchebag husband didn't give it to the papers till '94 when Tonya was knee deep, so to speak, in the whole Nancy debacle.'

'What are you on about?' Finn accepted a coffee from Eileen, who provided the answer.

'They're trying to find other people with sex tapes to see how their kids are doing now.' She drifted out of the kitchen to ferry a plate of toast in to Max.

'Ailbhe's been trying to gather intel for days but it's pretty niche.' Lindy sighed. 'What age is Gordon then?'

'Oh, hang on, never mind, he's only eleven. He wasn't even born when the tape leaked so maybe not such a great example. We're trying to see how to get the kids through it unscathed,' Ailbhe explained.

'Tommy and Pam have a kid, don't they?' Finn suggested brightly. Lindy was touched that she was entering into the spirit.

'Yep, Brandon Lee.'

'And how's he doing?'

'Reality star.' Lindy sighed.

'Oof.' Finn grimaced.

'Look, everything passes eventually. Max's dad is a laughing stock. Not Max and not you.' Roe was trying valiantly to put a decent spin on it and Lindy did appreciate the effort. Anything to distract from her spiralling thoughts.

Finn was nodding vigorously. 'Max will be OK.'

'I just don't get how the fact that Adam made this video in the first place isn't killing his whole case?' Roe flopped onto the couch beside Ailbhe.

'They have the judge and everyone else *convinced* that I gave it to TubeDramZ as revenge. *The Sun* called me "Monteray Medea" yesterday! Said I was willing to destroy my own son to get back at my cheating husband. GOD! I wish I was on the stupid screaming retreat.' She grabbed a throw pillow from beside Roe and roared feebly into it.

'OK, feck the papers,' Finn said. 'They'll be bored in a day or so. How are we going to prove that you didn't do this?'

'I asked Emma Tea to give testimony, but she says it just came in via a burner account, which doesn't help to rule me out.' Lindy fecked the throw pillow away. 'Maxxed Out is a disaster, so Adam is no longer pushing his whole keep-going agenda. But if the judge sides with Adam and says I deliberately sabotaged the business, they could bury me in damages to pay and I'm afraid this is really going to go against me in the custody agreement. Adam doesn't even want full custody, I know he doesn't. But he'll do it out of spite.'

'OK, first things first.' Finn rubbed Lindy's arm. 'It's time …'

'I know.' She picked up her coffee and tried to calm the clamour of anxiety in her chest as she made her way to the front room.

Max, Lindy and Finn sat cross-legged on the floor in a circle. Lindy had been trying to say something that made sense for fifteen minutes already.

'So,' she started over. 'Dad made this video. And it's not a nice thing but it's out there online. But you never have to see it. Just don't …' Lindy cast around for something better than 'don't ever look for it'. Despite the work that Digital Reputation Rehab had done, it didn't mean it would stay gone forever.

Finn, clearly sensing Lindy was stumped again, swooped in to pick up the thread. 'Look, Max, sweetheart, there's a lot of bad stuff online: pictures of crime scenes, animal porn—'

'Can you *not* give examples?' Lindy interrupted. 'Max, what aunty Finn is trying to say, however badly,' she shot her a look, 'is that we don't go looking for the horrible things online.'

Max looked uneasy. 'OK, Mom …' He looked to be grappling with his next words.

'Go on, Max, you can ask me anything.'

'Is Dad's thing embarrassing or, is it like, EVIL?'

And just like that her eleven-year-old had handed her a massive dose of perspective.

The video was embarrassing but so what? There were infinitely worse things.

'It's silly and embarrassing, but don't worry, it's not evil. At. All.' Lindy flashed him a grin – amazingly, articulating this helped her feel a bit lighter. She could dig into this and make it some huge tragedy or she could keep it to what it was: a bit mortifying, but all in all Adam's problem, not theirs.

'OK, phew.' Max laughed. 'Everyone's parents have embarrassing stuff on the internet. No offence, but your generation is super messy online.'

Lindy quaked a little. *Oh God, he's going to think it's nothing.* Before she could say any more Max carried on. 'Jenna Jace's parents are the worst – I feel so sorry for her. They scam their viewers out of money. And they're so gross, they had photos in that magazine. Ick. Jenna says she can't wait till she's sixteen and can get emancipated.'

Lindy startled at Max's knowing what emancipation was, though it stood to reason that just as there were hundreds of thousands of opinionated commenters on the internet, there was also a whole swathe of YouTube kids hitting maturity with their own thoughts and opinions about what their parents were doing. The Jace channel was an absolute hellscape of constantly unfolding scandals. Unlike Maxxed Out, it wasn't a toy channel but video diaries of the family's relentless high jinks. Outrage was perpetually mushrooming around the pranks they played on their kids, their steely focus on the bottom line and, of course, their nude shoots for *Playhouse* magazine. The outrage was absolutely warranted and made Adam's scandal seem amateurish by comparison.

'Ha, please don't emancipate me, OK?' Lindy knelt and pulled him close. 'We'll talk more about Dad's video later.' *Probably with the help of a child psychologist,* she added silently.

Finn shifted behind them. 'It's getting on time to go, Linds.'

Ugh, more public humiliation. Yay for me!

She gave Max another squeeze and then released him. 'How are you doing without the channel, sweetie?'

'Cool.' He shrugged. 'It's kinda nice not being so online.'

'Really?' Lindy held his bony little shoulders and searched his eyes.

'Yeah, Mom, I have *way* more free time. And I'm kind of excited about going back to my old school and just being able to be myself.'

Lindy's thoughts spun to the dark place where she often became trapped agonising over what long-term effect Maxxed Out would have on her son but she caught herself. *I can't undo the last few years but everything is going to be better now.*

'OK,' she pecked his forehead and stood, 'I am booking us in for climbing this weekend. I need to beat that white route I froze on last time! Plus, I was talking to Matt, the manager, and he says there's a club that meets on Saturday mornings, all kids around your age. They climb together and go on trips sometimes.'

'Sounds great, Mom. Break a leg in court today – have fun, LOL.'

His parting words rattled around Lindy's head as the taxi shuddered and stalled through the Thursday-morning traffic. Fun. When was the last time she had fun? The early days of The Snag List were fun. At a certain point it had felt like she really was on to something. Maybe she could write a book about the whole experience. People love a trainwreck – she'd probably make some money. *How to Win Friends and Then Ruin Their Lives. And Yours While You're At It!* would probably be a bestseller. She had decided she was still going to do the life-coaching course, it started in a week. Even if she never became a practitioner, she wanted to do it for herself. And thank God for Finn and Skin

Love. The second this legal nightmare was over she could get on with making some kind of ordinary life for herself and Max. Beside her, Elise was suddenly alert and rapidly tapping out something on her phone.

'Lindy, my assistant says something's going down with the other side,' Elise muttered at her. 'She's saying Adrian and Adam and the team were all sitting outside in the hall, and some woman showed up and Adam freaked out. They've all gone into one of the side rooms, and she says even through the door it sounds heated.'

Lindy automatically pulled out her phone to check her messages in case she had any updates. The Snag List group was bopping, with Ailbhe and Roe sending encouraging memes and chatting about the opening night of *Voices of Glory*, just ten hours away. Next she opened her emails but there was nothing new.

'Oh shit!' Elise exclaimed gleefully. 'They've just this SECOND emailed with a settlement proposal! They're running scared!'

'Seriously?' Lindy couldn't believe it.

'We have to figure out what's going on. We'll be there in five so I'll tell them to their faces that there's no way in hell we are going to pay them! You never did anything wrong.'

Unlikely we'll ever prove that, Lindy thought sadly. In theory, anyone could've shared that clip. The internet was a slippery place: no matter how careful you were, nothing was unhackable.

Minutes later, they pulled up in front of the commercial court building to see Adam and his team spilling onto the street. Adam looked furious and his solicitor was obviously trying to calm him down. She heard him say, 'It's over, Adam.'

'Do you want to stay here and I'll suss everything?' Elise asked.

'No way, I want a front-row seat.' Lindy scootched along the back seat to follow her out.

'Please wait for us,' Elise called back to the driver. 'I have a feeling this won't take long.'

'Ms Enyi-Amadi! Mrs Zelner! You got our email?'

'Yeah and you're obviously high or senile if you think we'll be settling with you when your whole case has *clearly* suddenly been derailed. Who or what is messing with your heads?' Elise was openly revelling in this new turn of events.

At that moment, Rachel Fitzsimon walked out of the building.

'Rachel!' Lindy was stunned. 'What are you doing here?'

'Lindy! I am so sorry.' Rachel rushed towards her but Lindy held her arms up to stop her.

'Rachel, please leave me alone. Look, I don't care, all right, but I don't want to see you. Why are you here?'

'Rachel says she leaked the tape, Lindy,' Adam spat, glaring at the ground.

'Meaning your whole charge of corporate sabotage against my client is in the toilet.' Elise was jubilant.

'Why would you do that?' Lindy was baffled. 'No one knew it was you in the tape. Now this will get out, Rachel. Fitzy will find out. And Fielding.'

'I couldn't live with it.' Rachel reached for Lindy again and this time Lindy tolerated her hand on her arm. 'I was so guilty about being with Adam. And then you told me how he was pushing you to keep Maxxed Out going, and I thought if the video got out he'd have to drop it and you'd be free.'

'Right.' Lindy frowned. 'I wouldn't say it's the most helpful thing anyone's ever done for me, to be honest. I get what you were trying to do but—'

'Then,' Rachel burst into tears, 'when I realised he was even going to use that against you, I was sick. I am so sorry, Lindy. You've really helped me these last couple of months and I just couldn't let him do this.' She wheeled around to Adam. 'You are a sick prick,' she screamed. 'What kind of person does this …?'

Lindy backed away wearily and slid into the car, closing the door behind her. Through the glass, Rachel's ranting at Adam was mercifully muted. A guy passing on his bike stopped to film the altercation. *And the circle of internet life is complete*, she thought wryly.

Elise jumped in beside her. 'Well, that was unexpected. I had blocked off my whole day so I'm afraid I'll still have to charge you my day rate. But when you counter sue, you'll be raking it in!'

Lindy laughed. 'I won't be doing anything except putting this behind me. Adam doesn't have any money, Elise.' She stared at her husband getting a dressing down from his mistress as they pulled away from the kerb. 'He has less than nothing.'

She sat back and texted the Snag List group.

Adam screwed Rachel and then Rachel screwed him. Heading to Finn's to celebrate. I'll see you both at the show and fill you in on everything.

32

'STAGE MANAGER SAYS FIFTY MINUTES TO *showtime!*' called Danny, traipsing through the backstage area of the Liberty Theatre, where the inaugural run of *Voices of Glory* was being staged. Everywhere stage hands and choir members were running to and fro, pulling last-minute bits together for opening night. It was pretty dark backstage except for the bulbs of each dressing table, which glowed like constellations in the gloom. Roe was getting started on her own make-up as earlier, before she'd left the house, Ailbhe had been freaking out about even coming to the show. Tom and Seb were about to be in the same building. Tom had been 'processing' with Soren the scream therapy advisor for the last couple of weeks and this would be the first time Ailbhe was seeing him since the afternoon in the Monteray Marriage Pause. Roe hadn't seen Eddie either. She'd texted him the details of the opening night but he'd been non-committal.

Danny paused by Roe's dressing table and leaned down to her ear.

'And fifty minutes to *no-show time* for you, missy!'

'Can you not make light of my relationship right now?' Roe was blending her make-up violently, fighting her nervy nausea. She couldn't decide which was making her feel more sick: the thought of curtains going up and her standing in front of a packed house; or the thought of curtains going up and her standing in front of a packed house that did not contain Eddie.

'Danny!' Róisín appeared out of the gloom beyond Roe's dressing-table lights. 'How dare you be so insensitive!' Roe felt a burst of affection for their domineering director. *She actually gives a crap.* 'If you psych out my star and this show flops like her relationship, I will maim you. Or at least be putting you on probation – no solos for a YEAR. I mean it.'

OK, so giving a crap is a reach ...

'I'm sorry, Róisín!' Danny protested. 'I was just joshing. Trying to lighten the mood. Roe knows we're all rooting for her.' Róisín disappeared and Danny's voice dropped to a whisper. 'What the Helena Bonham Carter! Does she just manifest anytime someone threatens her precious little production?!'

'Do you really think Eddie's not going to come?'

Danny turned towards her with the same look he gave her the first time she'd drunk Malibu and gotten sick on Junior Cert results night. It was a look of awkward pity and seemed to say 'I suppose I'll be the one cleaning up this mess, will I?'

'Do you definitely want him to come?' Danny fixed her with a look.

'Yes! Of course I do.' *Do I?*

'Do you?' Danny looked doubtful. 'Maybe you need to sow your slutty oats for a while. You could be free and easy in London.'

Roe dropped her foundation brush and started lining her eyes. 'I can't just break up with Eddie. We've been together forever.'

'Just because something's been that way forever doesn't mean it's a good relationship ...' He leaned in to her mirror to fluff his Flatley Mullet – or the Flullet as they now affectionately called it. 'I think if you were in a relationship that was good you wouldn't be having to hide your feelings or having to *lie* about ... well ... anything, Roe!'

She smudged the liner and scowled at him. 'Look what you made me do.'

His words were drawing out the doubts she had been trying to push down for the last couple of weeks. To her relief, he shrugged and stormed off.

Since things had fallen apart with her and Eddie, she'd noticed herself becoming more and more curious about what it might feel like to not fix them. The thought made her feel sad and vulnerable but also excited. Life in London on her own would be so hard but, on the other hand, it could be anything she made it.

'Roe, what have you done?' Ailbhe appeared and grabbed her face. 'This is a mess – why didn't you wait for me?' Ailbhe pulled up a nearby stool and began carefully removing the offending smudge.

'I didn't know you were here! When I left you earlier at the house, you were saying you might just flee the country.'

'Oh, I know! But that's just how everyone gets right before their two possible baby daddies are about to be in the same room together,' Ailbhe said airily. They looked at each other and laughed.

'Seriously, though. What's the plan?' Roe leaned in.

'What's *your* plan?' Ailbhe countered.

'I asked you first!' Roe cocked an eyebrow.

'My plan is to fix your face before this shine,' she indicated Roe's forehead, 'blinds any members of the audience. And, OK, my second plan is to tread extremely carefully with Tom. We agreed to meet after the show.'

'I can't believe you've spent all summer literally pretending you don't have a family in front of Seb Knox and now you're just casually walking in with a husband and child?'

'No child, just husband,' Ailbhe clarified.

As if that's better somehow! Roe thought.

'Look,' Ailbhe continued, 'Tom finally agreed to stop the screaming sessions in the sad dads pad and meet me, but only on condition that I told him who the other potench dad was. I literally couldn't risk another lie and I'm trying to show him that I've changed. So I told him it was Seb and then he announced he wanted to come down here and get a look at him.' Ailbhe winced extravagantly then carried on. 'So, yeah, it's a disaster in the making. All I can hope is that he's all screamed out and might, through some miracle, have decided to forgive me.'

'I'm sure it'll be OK …?' Roe tried to sound convincing, twisting her hands in her lap nervously. 'Looks like we both have a lot on our plates tonight.'

'Places, everyone,' Róisín called. 'Ten minutes to curtain.'

As if summoned by Satan himself, Gavin suddenly descended on Roe and Ailbhe, camera hoisted up on his right shoulder.

'Thoughts, Roe? Feelings? Any last words for the viewers?'

'If I open my mouth, I might be sick on your shoes,' Roe muttered through gritted teeth. It was true: her queasy nerves were hitting a crescendo.

Gavin barrelled on, unfazed. 'C'mon, Roe, we're gathering soundbites for the emotional climax. No inspirational messages for the kids at home?'

Roe just rolled her eyes as, with Ailbhe lining her lips, she couldn't speak.

'OK, Roe.' Gavin was obviously not giving up today. He fixed her in the camera's sights. 'If you could see anyone in the whole world right now, who would it be?'

Roe wasn't sure she liked where this was going … who had they dragged into this? Ailbhe finished her lips. 'What are you at?' Roe asked suspiciously.

'That's right!' He beamed, ignoring her. 'We have your boyfriend and your parents here to wish you luck and tell you how proud they are!'

Roe stood and whipped around, nearly taking out Gavin and the camera in the process. There was Eddie, hands hanging, looking wary, and beyond him Pat and Maura being shunted into position by Gavin's production assistant.

'Hi,' Eddie said.

'Hi,' Roe said. She leaned around to see her parents. 'Hi, Mum, hi, Dad.'

'He asked me to come back here,' Eddie clarified, nodding at Gavin.

'Yes, us too,' Maura supplied quickly, as if to dispel any notion Roe might get that they wanted to be there.

'Well, I appreciate you all coming.' Roe was measured but she wanted to scream at Gavin. How could he bring them here right before she had to walk out on stage and sing the first song of the show? 'I know none of you are that thrilled with me right now—'

'Ahem,' behind her Gavin cleared his throat, 'can you guys … ya know …' Gavin waved a hand encouragingly. 'We're looking for that big emotional payoff – a feelings orgasm, if you will. Remember, this will be the *Glee Me* finale.'

Roe pressed her lips together.

'Big moment,' Eddie said.

'Yeah.' Roe nodded.

'Was it worth it?' His eyes were dull, his tone lifeless.

For days, Roe had tried to picture this moment; she had tried to imagine what she might possibly say to him. Up until this second, she'd struggled to know how she felt, but now it was coming into focus.

Was it worth it?

'Yes, Eddie. It was worth it but I'm sorry it had to be this way.'

'It didn't have to be this way!' He exploded. 'You made it this way. I am not the asshole here.'

'I ... I know you're not ...' Roe struggled to remain composed. She hadn't meant for any of this to happen. For the last two months, she'd just been stumbling from decision to decision, dodging any thoughts of the future or the potential fallout.

'Hey! *Hey!*' Out of nowhere, Seb came in between them. 'Man, I don't know who you are but you have to calm down.'

'I'm going.' Eddie backed off immediately. 'He brought me into this.' He pointed at Gavin.

Roe checked her watch – she had less than five minutes. She couldn't let this be their end. She darted past her parents and after Eddie, who was already nearly at the door that led out into the back corridor.

'Eddie, wait, please. I am so sorry. Will you please stay? You came here to watch the show. Please do and we can talk after.'

'What'll you say then that's different to now?'

'I don't know! It's just that I'm about to walk out on stage,' Roe pleaded. 'I can't get my words right. I'm under pressure.'

'So going out there and doing this show is more important than us?'

'Eddie, I have to do this for me. And if you loved me and we were meant to be together then you'd think that too.'

He looked away from her towards the backstage area, where Maura and Pat were still standing awkwardly. He shook his head, incredulous. 'I suppose you think *they're* going to support you like I have all these years.'

'No,' Roe said. 'Of course not. You have supported me and taken care of me and done so much for me. But I need to take care of myself now and believe in myself. Look, this show has brought me so much – it's not some little amateur thing. You know I have this opportunity to go to London and perform in the West End. I'll be over there for four months. But it's not like I'm emigrating. We could still see each other. Obviously, we have stuff to work through, things do need to change, but I really hope you'll stay for the show and at least see *why* I have to do this, Eddie. Why I will never be happy if I don't try.'

'Niamh Kavanagh, three minutes to get to your mark!' Róisín's call from the wings cut Roe off and Eddie turned away.

'Break a leg, Roe,' he muttered as he walked away without a backward glance.

Regret flooded in as she watched him go. Suddenly her mother was beside her. *Oh God, what now?* Karma was kicking her while she was down.

'Mum, I need to get out there,' Roe whispered. 'Can you just postpone the berating for once?'

'Yes.' Maura sounded softer than usual and Roe looked over at her.

'Thanks for coming,' Roe added politely. 'I know you're not happy with me. Your last message was—'

'Unfair,' Maura cut in, and Roe wondered for a moment if she'd misheard her mother but Maura carried on, choosing her words with precision. 'My last message was unfair, Rose. I was very upset when Esther and Philip told me what had been going on with you. I was hurt that I was getting the information from them and not you. And I was very upset about what you'd done – the morning-after pill is not … well … I found that very hard to take. I don't agree with it, Rose, you know that. But since then I can't stop thinking about it, about how you didn't feel like you could speak up for yourself. You did a very extreme thing all because you were afraid to admit what you really wanted. And I realise I have to take some of the blame for that.'

'Mum—' Roe didn't know where to begin catching up with this sudden shift in her mother.

'Don't.' Maura held up a hand. 'You need to go to your … mark, was it? We'll talk after. I just wanted to say that …' She clasped Roe's arm. 'I don't want to be out of your life. I know I've found certain things hard to accept but I am going to try—'

'Roe, sixty seconds and you'd better have your head in the GAME!' Róisín was a woman on the edge.

Roe was grateful she didn't have to answer her mother right then and there. Maura was going to try? Roe didn't know what to do with that. The woman had annihilated Roe's confidence and been openly disdainful of her choices for years. But, Roe supposed, people had the capacity for change. *Just look at me.* She gave her mother a swift nod and jogged back into the buzz of backstage. As she made her way to the side of the stage, she was showered in quiet words of love and encouragement from her castmates. And Roe felt she was right where she should be, here with people who understood her, her theatre family. Right before she stepped onto the stage, Ailbhe threw her arms around her.

'We love you, Roe,' she whispered. 'We're so proud of you. Lindy's down in the audience with Max. I'll be back here. You're going to be amazing. Good luck.'

'Good luck to you too, darl. With Tom, I mean.' Roe blew her a kiss and stepped into the darkness behind the heavy velvet curtain.

The next few seconds stretched out before her. She felt like she was on a very high ledge. But it wasn't scary: it was exhilarating. The curtain began to rise and the country twang of the first number rose up from the orchestra pit. She readied her body, feeling every muscle from her feet to her shoulders engage. The curtain was rising but it felt like she was plunging – diving straight off and down into the first notes of the song. And as the words rose from her throat, she began to fly.

'I was an underdog kind of singer,
Relationships put me through the wringer,
I had passion yet I had no love.
But my songs helped me rise above.'

Even as the music took her higher, her eyes fell to the crowd. Her parents were there and Lindy and Max. But no Eddie. It didn't surprise her.

'I was an underdog kind of woman,
But I believe my day's a-comin'.
All I got was hate and derision,
But one day I'll get to Eurovision.'

★

As the show ended to roaring applause, Ailbhe finally spotted Tom lurking at the back of the hall and made her way down to him. The rest of the crowd were howling their approval at the cast, who were coming on and off stage to bow and bow again. Roe was right in the middle, accepting hugs and flowers with tears in her eyes, and the *Glee Me* crew were capturing the whole thing.

'She's incredible' were Tom's first words when Ailbhe reached him.

'She truly is,' Ailbhe agreed. 'The producer … eh … Seb …' She could barely meet Tom's eye at the mention of Seb's name. 'He … eh … recommended her to a producer friend of his. So she's on the cusp of big things.'

'THE Seb, eh?' Tom replied.

Oh, this is not going to be easy. 'Uh-huh.' Ailbhe tried to sound non-committal and stood beside him facing the rest of the hall and the stage.

'Which one is he, then?' He was scanning the various crew members dotted around the theatre.

'Are you sure you want to—?'

'Yes, Ailbhe, Soren recommended this. He said we'd never get past this if I didn't have all the information. And this is quite a crucial bit of information.'

Ailbhe nodded, shamefaced. 'So you do think that we might be able to … get past everything?'

'I don't know, Ailbhe. It depends if he's hotter than me or not.'

She looked up sharply. *Was that a joke?* She couldn't tell – he looked completely solemn. If it was a joke, then that seemed very promising. *Best not to hope,* she told herself.

'Can I just say something before I point him out?' She moved to stand directly in front of Tom, and she tentatively placed her hands on either side of his face. He made no move to shake her off. A good sign. 'I love you, Tom. I love our daughter. And she is *our* daughter. You're the only father she's ever known. I've put us in an impossible situation and I hate myself for it. I wish I had done the right thing at the very beginning of this mess. And I regret every day that I didn't. I was scared of ruining the best thing that's ever happened to me. I was scared of wrecking Tilly's life when it'd barely begun. I don't want to make excuses because there is no excuse that makes what I've done OK. But I want to say that I love you and I am sorrier than you'll ever know.'

Tom said nothing for several minutes and Ailbhe silently repeated an AA mantra she'd clung to in the uncertainty of the last couple of weeks while Tom had been doing his medicinal screaming. *Revealing is healing, revealing is healing, revealing is healing.*

I have done the right thing. Even if he can't love me again, even if he leaves us. This was the right thing to do.

'Ailbhe, have you ever screamed for a prolonged period of time?'

'What?' She took her hands back and pushed them through her hair. 'Screamed? No.'

Oh God, is he going to suggest couples screaming therapy or something? she wondered.

'So as you know, I've been screaming for a couple of weeks now and it's been … really fucking boring. And very strenuous.'

'Oh, yeah?' She didn't dare smile at this.

'Yeah, it was exhausting. By the end, I was like "screw this", if it's a choice between screaming or forgiving Ailbhe … well …' He ran his hand down the side of her face and neck.

Ailbhe felt a cautious joy bloom and spread inside her. 'Really? Are you serious?'

He leaned down and brushed his full soft lips against hers and

Ailbhe's heart leapt. The relief was overwhelming. She pulled him to her, her hands in his dark curls, breathing him in. It wasn't till they pulled apart that she realised she was crying.

'But, Tom, you know there are other options apart from just screaming or forgiving me? Like—'

'I know! I was kidding. I've thought about it every which way and I just keep coming back to the fact that I love you and I love Tilly. And it means something that you told me, Ailbhe. It couldn't have been easy, but you did. About a year late, but you did. And I keep thinking it happened this way because this was the way it was meant to happen. If you'd told me you'd slept with Seb back then, who knows what would've happened? We might not even have Tilly now. Or each other.' He pulled her close again. 'Don't cry, honey. I forgive you.'

'You're genuinely fucking amazing.' Ailbhe laughed through her tears. 'There's no one like you.'

'There isn't,' Tom agreed soberly. Then he broke into a smile. 'There's just one thing.'

She leaned back in his arms and raised a brow. 'Is it to do an IE-ANL? Cos if ever there was a time to ask I suppose it's now.'

He laughed. 'No, don't worry. Though, unfortunately, it's probably even more uncomfortable. I want you to tell me which one's Seb because I want us to tell him about the *situation*.'

Ailbhe blanched. 'You don't.'

'I do.'

'But … but … what would happen? He won't know what to do. It's … I just …' Ailbhe floundered. She had no idea what to say. *I should have seen this coming. Tom is not a normal person. Of course he'd have some batshit plan. Does he want us to throuple up to raise Tilly?*

'Ailbhe, calm down. I looked him up online. He's a single guy in his forties – he's not going to want anything to do with Tilly. But we have to give him the option. If it was me I would want to know. Also it's 2022 – Tilly will probably do a 23andMe kit before she's five! We'll have to face this info sometime. Look, we're together, I'm her dad, I will always be her dad. But he has to know there's a possibility he has a daughter. We have to have a paternity test.'

Ailbhe turned back to the auditorium. She scanned until she spotted Seb down by the stage off to the right. 'C'mon.' She took Tom's hand, resigned. 'We'd better do this.'

They edged through the crowd, waving to Roe who was standing in the centre of her folks and Lindy and Max, all relating their favourite bits of her performance, to Roe's obvious delight. Eddie, it seemed, had not stayed for the show, Ailbhe noted, but maybe it was for the best.

They reached the stage.

'Hi, Seb!' Ailbhe's mouth was dry.

'Hey!' He grinned, not registering Tom beside her. 'So will we try and get that drink—'

'Seb,' Ailbhe spoke over him. 'I want to introduce you to my husband.' She put her hand on Tom's shoulder.

Seb looked from Ailbhe to Tom.

'Your ... husband?' Seb spoke slowly, evidently stunned.

'Hi, Seb, I'm Tom. Listen, we need to have a bit of a chat ...'

'Do we?' Seb looked perplexed but unconcerned.

This is the last time Seb Knox is going to look this relaxed for quite some time, Ailbhe thought, smiling awkwardly.

Epilogue

10 weeks later

'WHHHAAA! LOOK, LOOK – THE DOOR SAYS "ROE O'Neill"!' Ailbhe grabbed Lindy in an overzealous hug, crushing her slightly in the tiny backstage corridor of the Carousel Theatre.

'Owww, please, my neck is still cranky from sleeping on the plane.'

'Who sleeps on a forty-five-minute plane journey?' Ailbhe rapped on Roe's dressing-room door.

'I'm very tired. I'm studying and working full-time and mothering and tolerating my ex! *And* living with my sister, which is very emotionally taxing.'

Ailbhe laughed. Despite her grumping, Lindy was doing amazingly since she and Adam had come to a détente. They'd packed up the house and Lindy had gotten straight into studying for her coaching certificate. Max, Ailbhe knew, was doing really well back in his old school and learning to live the civilian life.

All Lindy needed was to go on a date or two, which Ailbhe was insisting needed to go on Lindy's next snag list asap.

Just then Roe appeared in the doorway before them, interrupting Ailbhe's musing. 'If it isn't the Snag List bitches!'

'Roe!' Lindy squealed.

'Roe!' Ailbhe joined in the squealing. 'I cannot believe how huge this theatre is. It's massive. There's gotta be two thousand seats. And look at your dressing room!' She barged past Roe into the cramped room, dominated by a large pink sofa in the shape of lips, a mirror and a rail with Roe's clothes and a make-up station crowded with products and a bottle of champagne. Signed posters adorned the walls.

'How are you feeling?' Lindy gave Roe a squeeze. 'We've missed you! I suppose Roberta Temperly is doing all your life coaching these days – probably for the best.' She winked.

'Any pre-show nerves?' Ailbhe circled Roe.

'Yes,' Roe grinned, 'so distract me, please!' She turned to Lindy. 'What is with this one? She's extremely amped.' She gave Ailbhe an appraising look. 'You're not off the wagon are you?'

'No!' Ailbhe pretended to pout. 'How dare you! I am four months sober. Not a substance in sight … But I do have good news! Lindy doesn't even know. I didn't want to say until we were together.'

'Go on.' Roe poured two glasses of champagne and produced a white chocolate Magnum from the freezer of the mini fridge.

'So,' Ailbhe accepted the Magnum, 'you remember Seb was extremely weirded out by the whole Tom and Tilly and me situation. He was all iffy about taking the test. So we had told him to just think about it, that he didn't have to do *anything* even if he *was* Tilly's biological father. Well, he went quiet on us for a while but then three weeks ago he suddenly got in touch and said he'd do the test. *Aaaand* …' She grinned at Lindy and Roe who were frozen in anticipation. Ailbhe drew out another '*aaaand*' for a few more seconds until Lindy said, 'Ailbhe, I swear to God—'

'OK, I'm sorry, I'm sorry. Seb is … not Tilly's father!'

'Fuck, YES!' Roe hollered.

'That is fantastic!' Lindy jumped up and hugged her, and Ailbhe beamed. It was so good to be all together again. Ailbhe missed them. They still chatted on the WhatsApp, but Lindy had gone back to Drumcondra and Roe was in London; irony of ironies, Ailbhe had ended up the last one left in Monteray. She and Tom had decided to stay put for the foreseeable future. With everything that had happened over the summer, they needed a bit of downtime. Monteray had also calmed down considerably since the summer. The Marriage Pause compound had cleared out when school resumed with most of the couples apparently deciding it was easier for logistics to just stay together.

Ailbhe was happy she was staying close to her mum, especially while she continued to work on her recovery. Now that there was no need to run away to America any more, she was in no hurry anywhere. She was happy soaking up Tom and Tilly. If Seb had been the father, they would've made it work, but it was a helluva lot easier without the added complication. The relief had been enormous.

'So has Eddie been in touch?' Ailbhe asked with trepidation. Tom and Eddie still hung out in Monteray occasionally, and though Tom kept their conversations vague, she sensed Eddie was struggling without Roe.

Roe pointed to a beautiful orchid on the floor among some teddies and other good-luck gifts. 'He sent it yesterday.' Roe smiled, picking up a gold envelope. 'His card was sweet. He said it had taken him some time but now he understood what I did and he said I was,' she consulted the card, 'right where I belong. Shining, bright and beautiful.' She pulled a goofy face but then smiled. 'He said he's going to come over in January on the last week of the show's run. He needs more time. We both do, I think. But he's asked me out for dinner. Like a date.' She looked bemused. 'So who knows? It's not the main thing on my mind. Right now, I'm just trying to soak up every single golden drop of this experience. My West End début! I mean what the fuck, like? Plus off the back of *Glee Me* airing, I've had two amazing offers to do more TV back home, though I've told them the stage is the only place for me! And I owe it all to you gals.'

'I don't know about that, Roe!' Lindy laughed. 'Good of you to say but it was looking veerrrry ropey there for a bit. At one stage, I was, like, "How am I going to get out of this WhatsApp group where I've wrecked everyone's lives?" I was thinking I'd set an alarm for 2 a.m. and leave in the dead of night. 'Course ye'd still wake up in the morning and see *Lindy has left the group*!'

'I am so happy you didn't leave!' Roe grinned and they dove into a big group hug, holding each other tight until Lindy pulled away and raised her glass.

'To the Snag List! And ruining our lives for the better!'

Acknowledgements

WRITING THIS BOOK DURING 2020 AND 2021 WAS A singular experience, at times intensely challenging and at times sanity-saving – who didn't need an escape from reality during the pandemic! What's certain is it couldn't have happened without the incredible dedication of the people working on the front lines in this country. I'm especially grateful to the wonderful teachers and staff of St Matthew's school, everyone at Giraffe IFSC, and those working on St Paul's ward in St John of God's Hospital in the summer of 2020.

I am indebted to my editor, Ciara Doorley whose belief in my work and this story sustained me. Ciara is the most perceptive, creative and wise editor, I am beyond lucky to have her. I would also like to thank Joanna Smyth, Elaine Egan and all at Hachette Ireland. Also big huge thanks to my gorge agents, Tanera Simons and Sheila David and the team at Darley Anderson.

Thank you from the bottom of my creepy lil heart to my friends, many of whom I am so lucky to get to work with: Jen

O'Dwyer, Cassie Delaney, Louise McSharry, Emer McLysaght, Liadan Hynes, Lisa Coen, Sarah Davis-Goff, Louise O'Neill, Esther O'Moore-Donoghue, Sooby Lynch. Gemma Fullam, Jane Doran, Marian Keyes, Mary Kate O'Flanagan, Yvonne Hogan, Madeleine Keane, Leslie-Ann Horgan, Bill's pals, Aoife McElwain, Chiamaka Enyi-Amadi, Rebecca Murphy, Feargh Curtis, the Creeps and the Mother of Pod crew.

My family: Anne Harris, Constance Harris, Mungo Harris, Nancy Harris, Kwasi Agyei-Owusu, Vivianne White and the whole White family.

My nearest and absolute dearest: Mary O'Sullivan, Kevin Linehan, Sebastian White, and Rufus, Arlo and Sonny White.